# Scarecrow in the Graveyard
## -A Paranormal Romance-
## - P.Srigley -

Join the author's mailing list to win monthly give-aways
and receive author/artist updates –
**SrigleyArts.com**


WigglesWorth Press
SrigleyArts.com

## More titles by the Author

**The Storyteller's Curse (Book 1)**
**The Storyteller's Quest (Book 2)**

**Universe Idol**
**Fire-scape**
**All Planetary Shipping**

**The April-May June Series**
**Deeply**

ISBN – 978-0-9880081-1-3
Library and Archives Canada Cataloguing in Publication:
Please contact the publisher for this information at SrigleyArts.com
Published by: Wiggles Worth Press and SrigleyArts.com

# Contents

1. We Don't Call Them Zombies ................................................................ 1

2. The Boy Next Door to the Reaper ............................................................ 8

3. On-the-job Training........................................................................... 18

4. Cleaning Zombie .............................................................................. 25

5. Corpse with a Cold ........................................................................... 36

6. Night of the Evil Cannonball.............................................................. 44

7. The Reaper Commandments................................................................ 53

8. One Hump or Two? ........................................................................... 63

9. What Killed the Dead Man? ................................................................ 78

10. Jack the Biter .................................................................................. 88

11. A Reaper and a Zombie Walk Into a Bar…........................................... 98

12. The Long Puppet-walk Home.......................................................... 108

13. Party Like There's No Tomorrow ..................................................... 120

14. Three Heads are Better Than One ..................................................... 135

15. A Zombie's Best Friend ................................................................... 150

16. It's All Fun and Games Until Somebody Loses a Head ........................ 164

17. Kiss of Death ................................................................................. 176

18. Would You Like Ketchup With That?................................................ 188

19. In The End ..................................................................................... 201

# 1. We Don't Call Them Zombies

I was sound asleep when someone hammered on my bedroom door, loudly and urgently. "Have you seen a young man wandering about the house? Goes by the name of Warren?" my dad bellowed. As a matter of fact, I had seen Warren, but I wasn't about to admit that to my dad, not when Warren was sleeping shirtless beside me.

"You woke me up," I called, avoiding a direct lie.

"Well, I need to find him right away. He's a client."

My eyelids flew opened so fast and wide, I thought I might eject my eyeballs. "Warren is one of your clients?" I screeched, my pitch high enough to shatter glass. "You brought a zombie home?"

"We don't call them zombies, Baby. They only eat brains in the movies. Just get up and help me find him before he gives the neighbours the fright of their life." My dad tromped away, down the hall and then down the stairs.

What I really wanted to do was chase him down and strangle him with my bare hands. What I really did not want to do was look at the body beside me, because I now knew that's exactly what it was—a *body*. But my eyes had a mind of their own. They looked and I whimpered.

It wasn't the first time I'd slept with a boy. It was, however, the first time I'd slept with a dead boy, emphasis on the 'slept' part, thank heavens. Admittedly, there had been some kissing and cuddling, and a bit of childish romping around on my bed, but that's all.

Warren's unnatural pallor and absence of breath were blatantly obvious in the light of morning, in a way they hadn't been in the dark of night. No doubt about it, Warren was one hundred percent dead.

Dead or alive, sex or no sex, no way in hell was I about to tell my dad that a boy had spent the night in my bed. He would have a level ten meltdown.

I nudged Warren and he was as rigid as a tree trunk. His rigor mortis was full blown. It meant that he had been dead for about twelve hours. Nine hours ago, we had been having a great time, what with the kissing and cuddling and silliness.

In hindsight, I felt kind of stupid that I hadn't put two and two together. Chance meeting with a cute boy who's wandering rather aimlessly on the dark

1

street in front of my house, plus my dad is a reaper who's been falling down on the job lately. Two and two equals four. I was usually good at math. If I hadn't been so needy and messed up inside lately, I probably would have figured it out before I started hanging out with a zombie, and invited him to a sleepover so I wouldn't cry myself to sleep again.

I was so lucky that zombies didn't actually eat brains, or my head would be a bloody mess on my pillow right now, and I would be every bit as dead as Warren, instead of freaking out beside his corpse.

Warren's soul would be clamouring for freedom, but I couldn't sense it. When one of the recently deceased goes rogue and turns zombie, their soul disappears into an impenetrable hidden nook. It's a lot like a black hole in outer space, except this black hole is inside the body. It's born of the earthly evil every person accumulates over their lifetime, with every dark thought or sinful deed, no matter how small. That accumulated evil is still inside their soul when they die.

Everyone, no matter how good or young they are, has some ration of evil. If a person has no evil at all, or dies at birth, they are angelic, but that's another issue entirely.

Upon death, every bit of evil is evicted from the soul, leaving behind only the person's goodness and light. The evil, being evil, doesn't want that goodness and light to escape back into the world to make it a better place, so the evil tries to suck in the soul, leaving no trace of it for a reaper to sense. It's an odd quirk of death that makes a reaper's job that much harder.

The longer a soul is trapped in a body before it's reaped, the more chance that the evil will overwhelm it and suck it into the black hole, resulting in a zombie, so rapid reaping is crucial. Unfortunately, a small percentage of the dead, especially those who die young and/or violently, go zombie straight away for reasons known only to them.

And if a zombie is never tracked down, and its soul isn't reaped, a phantom ghost is the end result. There's nothing a reaper can do at that point. Phantoms are handled by a very hush-hush sister society, also under the auspices of my dad's boss.

Luring a soul out of the black hole and reaping it is how you stop a zombie in its tracks, at least in this civilized century. Warren's soul had to be reaped before he woke up and started staggering stiffly about my room.

I rolled out of bed, still mostly dressed from the night before. My shirt smelled of sweat. I yanked it off over my head and grabbed the nearest T-shirt off a pile of dirty clothes on the floor, hoping it was fresher. I pulled it on and grimaced. Definitely not fresher. It smelled funky.

I glanced down and Warren's black T-shirt, complete with rock band logo, stared back at me. The skull wore a mocking grin as if it had somehow managed to rearrange its cloth face into the sardonic expression. And of course Warren's shirt smelled funky—he'd been wearing it while he was dead! My room

2

probably smelled funky and I probably smelled funky. Summer heat and dead meat is never a winning combination. I would probably have to burn my mattress.

I tore off Warren's shirt and opened a drawer. I found a clean burgundy tank top and gray sweatpants in the very bottom of it. I was way overdue to do laundry. They were both blatantly wrinkled, but at least they were clean. I tugged them on.

Since I had to relocate Warren to a location other than my bed, I had to put Warren back in his shirt. But first I had to reap his soul, since stuffing him into clothes and dragging him across the floor was guaranteed to wake him up.

It probably sounds like I'm a reaper like my dad, but I'm not. I'm only a reaper-in-training, and releasing the soul of a client who has gone zombie is good practice for me.

I opened my door and listened hard. My dad was moving around downstairs, searching for Warren. Quick and quiet, I snuck down the hall to his room and helped myself to the supplies I would need to do the job.

I made it back to my room unseen and relocked the door behind me. "So far so good," I murmured and set the tools of the trade on my bedside table. I had watched my dad reap countless zombie souls over the years. I had even reaped a few myself while under his supervision, so I was familiar with the process. "Piece of cake," I breathed, trying to control the nerves I was feeling for what I was about to do, flying solo.

Reaping the soul of a person who has gone zombie is a slightly more complicated process than reaping the soul of someone who is simply dead. The first thing you have to do in a zombie reap is draw the soul out of the black hole, and the evil does not want to let it go. The more evil a person has inside them, the harder it is to free the soul from its clutches. Reapers use what I think of as a fishing lure. It isn't a worm, but a trace of *angelus spiritus*, or 'Angel's Breath' in English.

I picked up a small round capsule. It looked like a hollow glass bubble, and it looked empty. It wasn't. You just can't see divine breath, which is as invisible as clean air.

I carefully placed the pearl-sized capsule between my teeth. I plugged Warren's nose, sealed his lips with mine and bit down, breaking the capsule and releasing the *angelus spiritus*. I exhaled into Warren as if I was trying to revive him, which I was not.

My kiss was no kiss of life; it was a kiss of death. I blew the Angel's Breath into his corpse as deep as it could go, then removed my mouth from his to chant an incantation in an incredibly dangerous language from an ancient and forgotten time when spoken words held power in and of themselves. My dad calls it 'the tongue of the gods'. Reapers, and reapers-in-training, are one of the few beings sanctioned to speak the forbidden language.

3

A small collection of reaper incantations and assorted chants are all that remain of the most powerful dialect ever spoken, which is probably a good thing. In the wrong hands, or the wrong mouth, words in the unearthly language can cause as much damage as a massive asteroid smashing into the planet, or birth a deadly plague of biblical proportions.

Reapers have given the incantations Latin names so they can speak about them without causing accidental world chaos. The one I chanted to lure Warren's soul out of the darkness and into the light is called (in Latin) *Licentia Ex Obscurum*, which means (in English) 'freedom from darkness'.

I pronounced the words very carefully; there is no margin for error. As always, speaking the words in 'the tongue of the gods' made my mouth prickle hotly inside, as if it was electrified. It's a borderline painful sensation, like I'm sipping too-hot coffee with a bad case of pins and needles in my mouth.

I repeated the incantation twice, until I could sense Warren's soul, free of the black hole. There hadn't been much evil in him for it to be released so readily.

It was time for step two. I laid a hand on Warren's unbeating heart and spoke the simplest and shortest of the standard incantations to free his soul from the dead flesh where it was imprisoned. It's an incantation that I've known by heart since I was about eight, although I've only been allowed and able to speak the words for a year now. One year ago, I was ordained as an official reaper-in-training.

The incantation is called, in Latin, *Flat Lux ad Astra*. In plain old English, that means something like 'let there be light to the stars'.

Warren's soul rose out of its corpse coffin and burst like a mini firework, releasing its goodness back into the world. It illuminated my room like a camera's flash. It's a light that only reapers and reapers-in-training can see, under normal circumstances anyway.

As the wave of light passed through me, for just a fraction of a second, I felt Warren's essence intimately and shared his soul's pure joy at being free. I swallowed hard and whispered, "Bon voyage, Warren." He was truly at peace now.

After the soul is gone, the body still contains the evil remains. Evil doesn't depart with the soul. It's simply too weighty. Evil is of the earth, not the heavens. It lingers behind like a filthy waste product, and that malevolence is not something you ever want to escape a corpse, and it can once the soul is gone.

The soul is what anchors the evil in the body and now that I had reaped Warren's soul, I had to seal the evil in his bones so it couldn't escape to taint those who handled his corpse or hovered around the dearly departed or kissed his cold cheek in fond farewell. Once I had locked the evil into the bones, it would decompose over time and return to the earth as dirt, or in the case of cremated remains, return instantly to the earth as ash.

4

I opened a vial of black powder called 'Devil's Ash'. It's an essential tool of the reaper trade. I took a generous pinch of the heavy gritty substance, and dropped it into the back of Warren's throat. I dribbled natron salt on top of it, from an authentic and priceless Egyptian salt jar, then forced Warren's stiff jaw closed. I spoke a third incantation in the same language as the others. It's a sort of body lock, so the evil can't bleed out of the bones on its own or be drawn out by black magic. Reapers call the incantation, slangly, *Corpus Delecti*, which loosely translated means 'body of evil' or 'body of the crime'.

Warren's reap was finished. It had gone off without a hitch. Feeling rather proud of myself, I gathered up my dad's supplies and snuck them soundlessly back to his room. Our house might be old, but it's well built with thick beams and thick floorboards that don't squeak and creak.

Back in my room, I dressed Warren's shell of a body. It is no easy task to pull a shirt on a body in full rigor mortis. The shoes and socks were no piece of cake either. Human skin is not nearly as slippery as plastic Barbie doll skin. I was so glad he still had his pants on, and not just because it would have been really hard to put them back on him.

When Warren was finally restored to his clothes, I apologized to his remains for what I was about to do. I gripped his ankles, and pulled him off the bed. I made sure he landed on my heap of dirty clothes so there was no big thud. From there, I dragged him out the door. He really was as stiff as an ironing board, and heavier than he looked. I didn't want to move him any farther than was absolutely necessary. I glanced around for someplace that my dad might not have checked already. My bathroom was the nearest handy space.

"You really need a shower, Warren," I whispered and dragged him into the bathroom. I managed to slide him over the edge of the tub quietly enough, and reclosed the shower curtain. My dad had his own ensuite bathroom, so chances were he hadn't done more than peek through the doorway of mine in his search for Warren.

I stepped out into the hall and shouted, "Dad, Dad! Where are you? I found Warren."

When he didn't answer, I trotted down the stairs. The June day was already humid enough to make a crow sweat and I was sweating up a storm. For a whole lot of reasons, including the body I had cuddled beside all night, I needed a shower as badly as Warren, but it would have to wait until the coast was clear, and my tub was clear.

Through the stairwell window, the sun was bright and almost directly overhead. If it was still morning, it wouldn't be for much longer. The house was a mess. Sunlight made it look neglected and dusty. Heck, it was neglected and dusty since my mom died. The layer of dust on the floor was thick enough to show footprints.

I should have spent some time cleaning, but I had too much homework. And looking after my remaining parent was a fulltime job in itself. My dad had developed a bit of a problem lately—a drinking problem. Given his line of work, it could be and often was problematic, if not downright disastrous.

I found him sitting at the kitchen table, sipping from a glass of orange juice, or what appeared to be orange juice. "I found Warren. He's in the tub in my bathroom. I wanted to practice so I reaped his soul," I said. "I hope that's okay. I knew you were here if things went south."

"Any problems?"

I shook my head. "Nope, it was an easy reap. There was hardly any evil in him."

He nodded. "Good. I'm glad you found him. I thought he might have wandered away. He wouldn't stop moving long enough for me to convince him he was dead and reap him."

"Is that why you brought him home?" I had forbidden him to bring problem clients home, but clearly, he was going to ignore that rule just like he ignored all the other household rules I had tried to impose recently.

"Didn't know what else to do with him, short of hogtieing him, and that would have riled him up. Least he finally settled down."

Zombies usually did when they fell asleep, if they fell asleep. Since it is almost impossible to reap an irate zombie, because anger strengthens evil's hold, you need a calm zombie to get the job done. Unfortunately, zombies are restless by nature, as if they instinctively know they've reached their expiration date and only have a few short hours to tie up all the loose threads in their life. More often than not, getting them to calm down involves patience and waiting, not bondage.

My dad drained his glass and rose a bit unsteadily. "I'll take his body back where it belongs now. Poor kid. Seemed like a real nice boy."

"How did he die, Dad?" There hadn't been a mark on Warren's skin, not that I had seen anyway.

"Drug overdose. He tried out some of those new-age chemical drugs they're cooking up in meth labs these days. Wasn't even an addict. He was an athlete. One pill can kill. Don't you ever take drugs."

I rolled my eyes. "Not my style, Dad."

"It wasn't Warren's style either. Kids can be so shortsighted, and so damn foolish." He sighed deeply and headed upstairs to retrieve Warren's remains.

I sat down on the chair he had vacated. I felt so sad for Warren. He had been far too young to die. Besides being gorgeous, he had been sweet and considerate. Since a person's innate character remains intact after they go zombie, I knew he would have been the same in life.

The young are usually the ones that can't get it through their heads that they're dead, and they just keep walking around in a sort of dream state, believing they're still alive. They're the fodder behind zombie movies. My dad hates that label for them, but that's exactly what they are—zombies, the animate dead, minus the insatiable Hollywood hunger for human brains.

6

I absently noticed that the kitchen smelled like rum. I picked up my dad's glass and sniffed it. Yup, mostly rum with just enough orange juice to turn it orange. I sighed and surveyed the room. The bottle of rum was on the sticky counter surrounded by chip bags and assorted crumbs and flies. A few of the flies were stuck in the stickiness, trying to lick their way out, and probably getting plastered in the process.

There was a splash of rum left in the bottom of the bottle, so I helped myself, tilting the bottle upside-down to empty the dregs into my mouth. I swished the liquid around to rinse away the taste of mouth-to-mouth contact with a zombie. Alcohol is every bit as effective as mouthwash for killing germs. I spat the rum into the sink, ignoring the fact that it was full of crusty dishes. At least three or four days' worth. Maybe even five.

# 2. The Boy Next Door to the Reaper

A tentative knock on the side-door made me jump. I spun around and the cutest guy in the world was watching me through the screen. The boy next door. My lifelong crush. Insert heartfelt sigh here.

Now, when I say cutest guy in the world, that's only my personal opinion. Adrian isn't the classically hot kind of guy you would go out of your way to stalk, but most of the time I wanted to stalk him so badly, it hurt. Unless I was in a dark mood, then the specter of our tragic past reared its ugly head. Okay, maybe it wasn't tragic, except in my mind. Regardless, at those times, I wanted to punch him more than I wanted to strip his clothes off.

When it comes right down to it, I suppose I have a sort of love/hate relationship with Adrian. Most of the time I love him, but sometimes I hate him. The line between love and hate is reputed to be a thin one.

Back to Adrian—he isn't flashy looking. He's cutely quietly handsome, being not overly tall at about 5'10", and he's wiry rather than bulked up with muscle. He's kind of shy and has rebellious brown hair and soft brown eyes, and much of his cuteness is in his facial expressions and the cadence of his voice, and his smile, and the way his eyes crinkle at the corners when he laughs … I could go on and on, ad nauseam.

We were inseparable when we were younger, and then, out of the blue, he didn't want to be my friend anymore. He stopped talking to me and he wouldn't even tell me why. If he saw me coming, he would turn around and go the other way. If I called on him, he wouldn't come to the door. My feelings had been so hurt, I had stopped calling on him. Maybe I had loved him even back then, based on the number of times I had soaked my pillow with tears.

Seven years later, we talked to each other in a stilted polite way as if we had never been best friends at all. And now that we were basically grownup, I wanted to be his friend once more, but in a very different way from when we were kids. Although I wouldn't be opposed to playing doctor with him again.

In spite of his childhood dumping of me and all my conflicted emotions, I did not appreciate Adrian seeing me at my worst, with bed-head hair, wearing wrinkled clothes, and swigging from a bottle of rum when it was still morning, maybe.

"Hi Adrian." I put down the bottle of rum as nonchalantly as I could. I took a few steps toward the door, wondering if I dared to go any closer. Exactly how much of Warren's eau de corpse had rubbed off on me? Or was my morning breath even worse than that reek? No, my breath would smell like rum, which wasn't so good either. I didn't invite Adrian in.

"Elvis." He stood there kind of tongue-tied, glancing at me through the screen, but mostly avoiding direct eye contact.

Yes, Elvis is my name. And yes, I am a girl. My dad chose not to worry about that little detail when he christened me 'Elvis'. He was thrilled that I was born on January 8th, the same day as *the* Elvis. My dad was, and still is, the most obsessed Elvis Presley fan in the world. If he'd had a dozen kids instead of just one, he probably would have named us all Elvis—Elvis One through Twelve. At least he hadn't named me Priscilla, or Gladys, after Elvis's mom. That would have been worse, although the name Jesse would have been cool. He was Elvis's identical twin brother who died at birth.

My dad owns a collection of Elvis-style jumpsuits in all the classic colours, and he wears them. I'm not talking about in the house or on Halloween. He just about lives in them, and every last one has sequins and flamboyant embroidery and enough rhinestones to drown him if he ever happened to fall into a swimming pool wearing one.

He even got in touch with the reaper who reaped the real Elvis—yes, Elvis did go zombie for a couple of days, hence the rumours that he didn't really die. I don't know how my dad managed it, but he acquired a lock of Elvis's hair, complete with a few follicles. He has it framed under glass. It's his most prized possession. If scientists master human cloning in the near future, my dad will no doubt grow his very own Elvis, and I'll have a brother who craves peanut butter and sliced banana sandwiches, fried in bacon grease.

Adrian's bedroom window looks out over my yard and I know he's seen some crazy shit over the years. Heck, he probably could have sold tickets to the reality show called 'Elvis's Bizarre Home Life' and saved up enough to buy himself a Porsche.

I edged a little closer to the door and stepped on something roundish and kind of rubbery. I glanced down and sighed. No, not rubbery—fleshy. A severed fingertip was rolling around on the floor. I knew it wasn't Warren's because his hands had been completely intact. He also hadn't had long red fingernails. Given my dad's line of work, stray bits of bodies did turn up on occasion, but I didn't have to like it. I kicked the finger under the kitchen table as discreetly as I could.

"What's up?" I prompted, not quite pulling off the cool casual tone I'd been aiming for.

"Uh … I was wondering if you had a copy of Rushburn's final assignment. I forgot mine in my locker and the school server is down. I really want to work

9

on it this weekend." Adrian must have been desperate to work on it if he was willing to cross the white picket border into my territory and face me down.

He darted a glance at my floor, looking anywhere but at me. His eyes widened and stayed fixed there. I followed his gaze. The fingertip hadn't made it all the way under the table. It was lying right out in the open, looking grisly in a sticky puddle where somebody—my money was on my dad—had spilled rum or orange juice or some combination of the two.

"One of those fake fingertips leftover from last Halloween, I guess," I said lamely. It did look enough like a fake to pass for one, thank goodness, especially because of the garish red fingernail. "You didn't think it was real, did you?" I raised an eyebrow, hoping for one of Adrian's quirky grins.

He frowned and turned noticeably red. "Of course not."

Given my family's track record, I couldn't really blame him for thinking it might be as real as it was. I changed the subject. "Rushburn's paper? Ya, I brought it home. I was going to work on it this weekend, too." Or what was left of the weekend. I wasn't driven to get top grades even though I did okay when I made the effort. I wouldn't be going to university. My career path was carved in stone, or written in blood. Reapers beget reapers, and I was destined to be a reaper.

"Can I copy it down?" Adrian asked.

"Or I could just email it to you, or snap a pic and text it to you." I wasn't about to invite Adrian in to meet Warren or smell Warren.

"Sure, either would be great." He grimaced endearingly, at least it was endearing to me. "And my mom wanted to make sure you were doing okay, you know, since your mom ..." He trailed off.

"Since my mom died," I said for him. It's funny how most people have trouble saying the 'D' word. In my house, you couldn't have a conversation without spouting it about half a dozen times.

"Yes. She noticed a lot of your lights going on and off last night. She thought there might have been an emergency or ... or something." He trailed off again, looking decidedly uncomfortable. His flushed cheeks got even redder.

I closed my eyes for a moment. It felt like my brain was cramping. There was a distinct lack of privacy in the suburbs. Had my curtains not been fully closed when Warren and I had been romping around on my bed? Had our bit of play wrestling looked X-rated? Had Adrian's mom seen us? Misinterpreted the situation, and tattled on me?

"You know my dad and his weird nocturnal activities," I said, trying to shift the blame. "Maybe he was practicing his Elvis routines again."

Being an Elvis impersonator is part of my dad's cover, since being a reaper is a lot like being a spy. It's highly classified information and nobody is supposed to know. My dad used to play Elvis for my mom and she would play the part of his Priscilla. A few times I'd found panties in odd places, so she had probably been throwing them at him like a deranged groupie. Now he was Elvis

10

without an audience, unless he brought home one of his problem clients to enjoy the show until they stopped being animate.

"I didn't hear any loud music and it usually wakes me up," Adrian said, a bit evasively, "so I don't think it was an Elvis thing. A lot of stuff goes on here that I don't understand, Elvis." Our eyes met, and held. Time stood still, at least for me, until Adrian blinked and took a hasty step backwards. I think my house scared him, and maybe my life scared him—or I scared him. "Anyway, can I tell my mom you're okay? I mean, you look … okay."

I didn't like how Adrian hesitated before he said that, and if there had been a mirror handy, I would have glanced in it. "I'm okay," I said firmly. "Thank your mom for asking. And for the cookies she sent over last week. They were great. She doesn't skimp on the chocolate chips, does she?"

"No. Uh, she wants you and your dad to come over for dinner tomorrow, Sunday dinner, if you're not busy," Adrian blurted out, almost against his will. There was no gun at his back, but his mother was probably watching us through her kitchen window.

Have I mentioned yet that Adrian's mother is a saint? Most neighbours would have called the cops on my dad about a hundred times by now, and here she was inviting him over for supper. A few hours in Adrian's company would make my weekend, or my year.

"I have to check with my dad, but I'm sure it will be okay," I said. "Can I let your mom know later today?" I could hear two sets of feet tromping down the stairs. One of the bodies was stumbling and banging into walls. I was hoping that was Warren and not my tipsy dad.

Adrian glanced that way. He could hear the thumping as well as I could. And it sounded too much like what it was, a body bouncing off the walls. He opened his mouth, probably to ask questions. I didn't give him a chance. "I'll phone her. I have to go. And I'll email you the assignment. Bye, Adrian. See you tomorrow, I hope."

I shoved the solid interior door closed and leaned against the wood. Could I have sounded more pathetic? Ya, I could and I often did where Adrian was concerned. Unless I was in the mood to hate him, then I just sounded bitchy.

I picked up the fingertip and handed it to my dad when he puppet-walked Warren into the kitchen. He glanced at it and tucked it into his pocket. "Bad car accident last evening, I had to crawl into the crushed car to reap the lady. Guess I brought home a little souvenir."

"I guess you did." I didn't ask for more details. They would have been gruesome. I opened the connecting door into the garage and held it wide so my dad could steer Warren through it.

Warren staggered stiffly by me with my dad's hand on his back. In my opinion, puppet-walking is one of the creepiest sights to behold, especially when a body is in full rigor mortis, or worse, in the putrification stage. Enuf said. And reapers don't call it puppet-walking. That's what I call it. Reapers

11

refer to it as 'client mobility', as if they're some sort of cell phone network. A reaper has the ability to make a dead body walk, but it's not a natural gait. It's as spastic and lurching as a string-puppet in the hands of a toddler.

My attempts to make a body puppet-walk were more like puppet-stagger-and-fall. I was a complete novice and tended to lose control of the legs. The skill took practice and I didn't practice it since it creeped me out.

I avoided looking at Warren's stiff jerking limbs as he lurched toward my dad's work vehicle—a black van with tinted black windows. And yes, it does have an Elvis mural airbrushed onto the side. The van was parked in the nearest spot in the expansive two-car garage. My dad's recreational vehicle was parked in the other spot, on the far side.

I opened the rear door of the van and we lifted Warren inside. His stiff limbs couldn't bend enough for him to step up. My dad removed his hand, breaking contact. Warren dropped to the floor of the van, exactly like a puppet whose strings had been cut. I straightened his limbs so he looked less macabre. It somehow just made him look defenseless and vulnerable, and so damned lifeless—dead.

I bit my lip hard when a tidal wave of grief and sadness welled up, escaping from the tidy little box where I normally kept those emotions locked away and under control. Tears escaped too, and trickled down my nose to drip on Warren. And then more tears, until I thought I might drown in sorrow. I didn't want him to be dead. I wanted him to open his eyes and smile, and go home to his family. I hated that he was dead, I hated that people had to die. I hated that I had to see it on a daily basis. And most of all, I hated that death had visited my house and taken my mother from me—with my dad's help.

"Hey, it's okay," my dad said, putting an arm around me and moving me aside so he could close the door.

"No, it's not okay. It's not. I didn't get to say goodbye," I sobbed and jerked free. I had completely lost it.

"Baby, he's dead. He's at peace."

"I know, I know, but I can still say goodbye," I sputtered, my eyes and nose streaming. I hadn't gotten to say goodbye to my mom, but I could say goodbye to Warren, even though he was dead.

I wrenched open the door and looked down at his still face. He did look peaceful, and sad, and dead. "Goodbye, Warren," I whispered and brushed his hair off his forehead so I could kiss it.

"Did you know him?" my dad asked.

"No, not really." And I would never know him because he was dead. I stood there looking down at him as if I had been turned to stone, while tears kept trickling down my cheeks.

My dad gently moved me aside. He shut the door again, and I fought to gain control. I could usually block out the emotional aspect of death. I mean, you had to be able to control yourself to be a reaper. But sometimes I couldn't block it out. Sometimes the sadness escaped and came gushing out, like a backed-up sink, although that usually happened when I was in the privacy of my bedroom with no witnesses.

I raised the hem of my shirt and wiped my face. I took a few deep breaths, pushing the grief back down into the box, so I could lock it away again. I bit my lip hard and rocked against the van until I felt in control again. Until I was in control again.

My dad waited patiently, clearly at a loss over how to deal with his emotional teenage daughter, who was not acting at all like a proper reaper. Finally, I cleared my throat and sniffed and said, "I'm okay. Sorry about that, it's just … he's my age."

"I understand, Baby." He sighed and pulled me into a one-armed hug. "Don't feel bad about a few tears. Our job isn't an easy one."

That might have been the biggest understatement in the universe. I nodded and wiped my nose, and changed the subject. "Mrs. Lyon invited us over for dinner tomorrow night. Can I confirm we'll be there?"

My dad went still and didn't answer. I stepped back so I could see his face. He crossed his arms and leaned against the van, worrying his lip.

"What?" I said, since he was acting kind of weird.

"I won't be available. I have plans," he said in a clipped voice.

"Plans?" I inquired.

He sighed. "Okay. I'll just come right out and say it then. I've got a date."

I blinked like an owl. "A date?"

"That's what I said."

I blinked some more. "A date date, like with a woman?"

"Yes, Elvis. I haven't switched to the other team since your mother died."

"But … who are you seeing?" I was flabbergasted that my father was dating. My mom had only been dead four months, and my dad had been the one to reap her. I think doing it just about killed him. Or maybe it was what he had done before he reaped her that ate at his soul. At least she hadn't turned zombie. It was only since her death that my dad's drinking had gotten really out of control.

Lately, I had been thinking that my dad preferred the company of the dead more than the living, but if he was dating, I was wrong. Unless he was dating a zombie. "Dad, who are you dating?" I repeated when he hesitated to answer.

"A lovely woman. A bit like your mother."

It sounded like a hint, except I didn't get what he was hinting at. "Where did you meet her?" I asked.

"Through … my work."

I eyed him suspiciously. "She's not dead, is she?"

"No, no … not dead." His voice lacked conviction and he dodged around me to climb into the driver's seat. "We'll talk later. I have to deliver Warren back to his death site now that he'll stay put."

"Dad, you've been drinking. Why don't I drive? I need the practice." My learner's permit was only a couple of months old and I needed all the practice I could get. I was not a natural born driver and tended to hit things, things like my previous boyfriend, Blake.

That sounds worse than it is. I didn't kill him or anything, thank goodness. It was simply an accident, but I probably don't need to mention that our brief, ill-fated relationship ended right there, with the screech of tires on pavement. And I think it earned me a reputation as someone it was highly risky to date.

My dad leaned out the van window. "I only had one tiny drink, Elvis. A little hair of the dog. I'm fine to drive. It's safer than putting you behind the wheel."

He did have a valid point. Before I could suggest going along for the ride, he added, "And you might want to get dressed before you go out in public."

I frowned. "I am dressed."

"You might want to clean up a bit, then." He pressed the automatic garage door opener that he kept clipped to the van's visor and started the engine with a roar. The garage door was still cranking up when he floored the van, going backwards, almost running over my bare toes and scraping the garage door. It wouldn't be the first time he'd left a dent in the garage door, although he had yet to run me over. Maybe I took after my dad in lack of driving skills.

I watched the van until it was out of sight. It didn't sideswipe any of the big old trees that lined our dead end street. I closed the garage door and went back into the house, trying to decide what I should do first. Clean me or the house, or tackle Rushburn's paper? Before I did anything, I had to email Adrian the history assignment, which meant I had to enter my room.

I opened the door and took a cautious little sniff. The bouquet of death lingered strongly inside. I made a beeline for my window and opened it as far as it could open, then stripped the sheets off my bed. I was shaking the pillow out of the pillowcase when I caught a glimpse of myself in the dresser mirror. I froze—I didn't just need to clean up, I needed to be hosed off, or maybe burnt at the stake.

"Shit and double shit," I groaned. My eye makeup was black smeared smudges, like I had two black eyes, and my dark, red-streaked hair was sticking up as if I'd been electrically shocked. My bed-head was defying gravity. It was like my hair thought it was in an old western movie—it was reaching for the sky. My lips were kind of puffy, from kissing Warren. And was that a hickey? I peered closer. Yup, no doubt about it. Even dead, Warren had managed enough suction to mark me. I looked like a deranged clown. And my burgundy tank top, well, let's just say it could have used a bra under it. At least my boobs were small enough to go unnoticed, not that I usually thought of that as a good thing. And front and center on my top was a big damp snotty splotch—thanks to my emotional meltdown.

Adrian had seen me looking like this—well, without the snotty splotch and runny mascara. Then again, my mascara had probably been pretty darned smeared even before my crying jag, since I'd been wearing it all night. Adrian had seen me looking like a human train wreck, standing in my disgusting kitchen, surrounded by flies and swigging rum directly from a bottle before noon, like some sort of suburban pirate-girl.

I glared at myself. "You really need to get your shit together, Elvis." I missed my mom and I was having trouble coping. Not like my dad with his drinking and keeping company with zombies, but in my own way. Inside, my soul felt haunted by the ghost of my mother. I knew a big part of that was because of how she had died, and the role my dad had played.

I opened my laptop and emailed the assignment to Adrian. That done, I was strongly motivated to shower. Death's bouquet was lingering on my person as well as in my room.

One long and refreshing shower later, I looked and felt a hundred percent better. I dressed and primped with care before I crossed the lawn. It seemed silly to phone Adrian's mom when I lived right next door. And maybe I wanted Adrian to see me looking clean and shiny. Maybe I was hoping that my sleek hair and little silky skirt would somehow erase how I had looked earlier. The skirt was a bit dressy for Saturday around the house, but it had been hanging in my closet, and it was one of my few presentable items of clothing—until I did laundry. I had even put on makeup to walk next door, and I hoped I wasn't overdoing it.

Adrian's mom answered my knock. She has the kind of eyes that look into you, rather than at you. Adrian's eyes are so like hers, I almost have a crush on his mom, too. I'm pretty sure she knows I'm in love with her youngest son and have been forever. And I'm pretty sure that, as sweet as she is, she does not want him to love me back. Who would want a daughter-in-law named Elvis? Who would want to share my family's peculiar lifestyle? Not anyone normal, that's for sure, and Adrian's family is so normal, it's almost abnormal.

His mom and dad are still married. They keep their flower garden weeded and their lawn neatly mowed at all times. They have three kids. Jackson, the eldest, doesn't live at home anymore and I don't know him very well. Julia, the middle child, is a few years older than me and Adrian. She's going to university and only comes home on special occasions. She did come home for my mother's funeral, which was really sweet of her. If I'd had a big sister, I would have wanted her to be just like Julia. And then there's Adrian.

"Hello, Elvis." Mrs. Lyon stepped back and motioned for me to come in. The house smelled lemony fresh. I like the Lyon's house. It isn't cluttered with stuff. The walls and furniture are all light soft colours. It makes the rooms feel more spacious than they actually are. My house has the same basic layout in mirror-image, but its old-fashioned wooden paneling make the enclosed spaces feel darkly oppressive, especially lately.

"How are you?" Mrs. Lyon asked as if she really wanted to know, and really cared.

"I'm … okay." I couldn't say good or fine. That would have been a blatant lie. I was lonely and needy enough to invite a strange boy into my bed to keep me company so I wouldn't cry myself to sleep, which was one way of coping I suppose, except Warren had turned out to be every bit as dead as my mom. "I wanted to thank you for inviting me and my dad to dinner. My dad can't come, but I can, if you want me to come without him, or maybe you would rather wait until we can both come, but if not, I can come tomorrow." I was babbling.

"Of course we would like you to come for dinner tomorrow." Mrs. Lyon gripped my hands and squeezed. "Is your dad working on a case, or does he have a gig?"

My dad's complete cover story is that he's a private detective who moonlights as an Elvis impersonator. He really does do weddings and banquets, as Elvis. The unusual jobs account for his odd hours and all-night comings and goings.

"He's working a case." I didn't want to say that my dad was dating already. It would have raised eyebrows. And it felt so wrong to me.

"We'll have your father over for dinner another time." Mrs. Lyon patted my arm.

"Okay. Um … what time should I come over? Adrian didn't say."

"How about six o'clock? We never eat too late, especially on Sunday."

"Great. Can I bring anything?" I asked, although I had no idea what I could bring that they would want to eat. An image of sausage rolls with severed fingers inside flashed through my mind and I almost smiled.

"No, just bring yourself. And your dad, if his plans change. There's always plenty," she assured me.

"Okay. Thanks, and I'll see you tomorrow." There was no sign of Adrian so I headed out the door.

Back at home, I did laundry, lots of laundry, and I worked on Rushburn's paper. The state of the house simply overwhelmed me, but a homework assignment I could handle. It also kept my mind off my angst.

When my dad returned with the empty van, I suggested hiring a cleaning lady. He grimaced. "We can't have a stranger seeing what goes on in this house. Imagine the chaos if they dusted my vials and mixed up my powders. And some of the stuff I keep in my office would have them calling 911. Nope, far too risky." He sat down at the kitchen table and rested his chin in his hand. "We'll have to clean it ourselves, especially now that I have a lady friend." My dad was prone to using outdated expressions. He liked talking that way, but not as much as he liked talking like Elvis, complete with the drawl.

"I can barely keep up with my homework, Dad. And final exams are coming up. I don't have a lot of extra time for cleaning, and you never do any." I sat down across from him.

"I know. We'll figure something out." My dad was an experienced procrastinator.

16

He rose restlessly and took a box of Lucky Charms out of the cupboard. He poured two bowls without asking me if I wanted Lucky Charms for lunch or dinner or whatever this meal was. We ate the cereal with borderline sour milk and talked more than we had in awhile.

I got him to tell me a little bit about the new woman in his life. Her name was Kendra and she was an elementary school teacher, at least until recently. He said that she had been sick, so she was on extended sick leave.

"What was she sick with?" I asked.

His cell phone began blaring *All Shook Up*, one of Elvis's greatest hits. *All Shook Up* meant that my dad had a work-related text.

One of the many drawbacks of my dad's job is that he's always on call. His cell phone is always turned on. When he gets summoned, he has to drop everything and go take care of his client or clients. The dead wait for no man, or no reaper, and if they have to wait, the reaper is probably going to have to track down a rogue zombie. There can be a lot of damage control required in those cases. Luckily, a reaper has special abilities to deal with the fallout.

My dad read the text for a rather long time. "What is it, Dad?" I asked.

"Looks like a triple." He kept scrolling.

"Car accident?"

"Nope."

"Multiple homicide?"

"No."

"Fire?"

He cast me an exasperated glance. "Birthday party, if you can believe that. Two NC's and one MA."

"At the same birthday party?" I asked incredulously. NC means natural causes and MA is a minor accident.

"The text never lies. You can help me with this one, Elvis. Time for some on-the-job training."

"Can I drive?" I asked.

"Not a chance. Let me get changed." He headed upstairs.

I didn't bother to change, my laundry was still wet. I tossed a load in the dryer and started a second load washing before my dad came downstairs dressed in his reaper costume of choice—a black jumpsuit lavishly trimmed with gold. Black doesn't show bloodstains nearly as much as other colours, so he has two of the black jumpsuits, and a matching cape that he wears in the winter.

Reapers no longer don the outdated hooded black robes that were in fashion for eons. Modern reapers rarely feel the need to appear as ghostly apparitions, and when reapers are on the job releasing a soul, people simply don't see them. Reapers reside in their mental blind spot, as invisible to as fresh air.

We got in the van, my dad in the driver's seat. At least he hadn't been drinking so I could relax and enjoy the ride.

17

# 3. On-the-job Training

Reaping is in the blood, as my dad says. It's my destiny to become a reaper like him, and like his father and mother before him. They were both reapers. It's customary for reapers to marry reapers. They do have a whole lot in common.

My dad has introduced me to a few young reapers, sons of his counterparts, perhaps hoping Cupid's arrow would strike a bull's eye. Not one of the young reapers has made my heart go pitter-patter like a fleeting glimpse of Adrian is guaranteed to do. Whether I am loving Adrian or hating him, my heart goes into overdrive whenever I catch sight of him.

Most of my reaper on-the-job training has happened when my dad is too drunk to perform his duties. Most of it has taken place in the last four months. Not all of it has gone smoothly, and that is a colossal understatement.

In case I haven't mentioned it yet, I don't like being a reaper. It's gross and sad and often just flat-out heartbreaking. It can even be dangerous. I know somebody has to do it, but I don't necessarily want to be that somebody, even though the ability to channel souls is in my genetic material. The Black's—yes, that is our last name—have always been reapers. At the dawn of humanity, when cavemen were thumping each other on the head with their clubs and getting trampled by mammoths, we were probably right there in the thick of things, reaping their caveman souls.

It took ten minutes to reach the location of the reap. My dad slowed to a crawl and drove by a pretty standard two-story suburban house at the very northern edge of his territory. Every reaper has their own district. Unless a reaper is subbing for another reaper, or there is a major disaster requiring multiple reapers, they don't reap outside their own borders.

The front of the house was country-ish, with fieldstone walls and moss green trim. The garage door was painted a matching moss green. The double driveway was full of cars. There were more cars lining the road in front of the house.

My dad pulled up to the curb in an empty spot in front of a fire hydrant and turned off the engine. He checked his watch. Even though his phone keeps time, he still likes to wear an old school wristwatch with a clock face and hands. It's big and flashy and gold; it matches his reaper outfit perfectly.

"Whose souls are we releasing?" I asked.

18

"Katherine Glashan/Michaelson, she's eighty-nine, and Susan Glashan/Ingrams, eighty-nine, twins. And Gertrude Glashan/Cole, eighty-six. She's the birthday gal. They're having a big barbeque for family and friends."

I could smell the sizzling meat. I was suddenly hungry in spite of the Lucky Charms, which is a hollow unsatisfying kind of food. Being a reaper, you'd think I would have opted to become a vegetarian, but I haven't. I like sinking my teeth into a medium-rare steak as much as the next carnivore.

At least the souls we were about to reap were all past their prime. Reaping the old isn't nearly as emotionally wrenching as reaping the young. That's just flat-out shattering.

"Blood sisters?" I assumed.

"Blood sisters," my dad confirmed.

We cooled our heels for about fifteen minutes, listening to an Elvis CD. I was tapping my toe along to *You Ain't Nothing But a Hound Dog*, pondering what could kill off three tough old birds in one fell swoop, when I felt the pull of a trapped soul.

My dad straightened up on his seat. "That's one," he said. "Let's go."

We stepped out onto the road. Nobody would notice our van, or ticket it for being in a no-parking zone. It has a sort of charm on it, compliments of The-Powers-That-Be, as we refer to my dad's boss. When the van is on the job, it is as unseen as the reaper who drives it. That doesn't mean that other vehicles smash into it because it's invisible. It's more like it has a psychic forcefield around it and everyone simply avoids the space it occupies, without question or conscious thought.

The front door of the house wasn't locked, and even if it had been, it wouldn't have been a problem. There are no locked doors for reapers when they've been summoned. One touch of a reaper's hand and any door will open. My dad's boss is one omnipotent entity.

We walked through a house that had far too many fussy porcelain knickknacks everywhere. An army of miniature glass women in flowing Victorian skirts and classic ballerina costumes had invaded every available surface.

The guests were outside. It was a humid day for early summer and perfect weather for a barbeque. Through the kitchen window, we could see the happy crowd in the backyard, eating and drinking and chatting. Unseen, we walked by a woman carrying a tray of empty glasses to the sink. My dad turned left into a mud room. A closed door on the left looked like a closet door. And a heavier door on the right clearly connected to the garage.

"Where's the soul?" my dad asked, testing me.

I could feel it as clear as day, a fluttering bird trapped in a cage, beating its wings and trying to fly. I pointed to the door on the left. "In there. Eager to go. Is Katherine in a closet?"

19

My dad grinned. "I don't think that's a closet. Good sensing, Elvis." Sensing souls is one of my better reaper abilities. According to my dad, as far as reapers go, I have ESSP—Exceptional Soul Sensing Perception.

He opened the door and I slammed my eyes closed. It was not a closet. There are ways to die with dignity and falling off a toilet with your pants around your ankles is not one of them, especially if your butt is eighty-nine years old.

"Stop being so squeamish. You have to get over that. You do this one." My dad stood back.

"I'm not squeamish about reaping. It's … that." I motioned in the direction of the naked old butt, still not looking directly at it. It was definitely past its prime.

My dad nodded. "You're right. We can't leave Katherine so flagrantly exposed." He squeezed into the tiny powder room and struggled to lift the little old lady. "Upsy-daisy, Katherine. Pull her pants up, Elvis."

"Dad!"

"Hurry it up. The poor woman is catching her death, here."

I groaned and replaced her pants. My dad lowered her back to the floor and retreated out of the close quarters. There definitely wasn't room for three of us, especially with Katherine taking up all the floor space.

I crouched over her, a hand on her still heart. Since Katherine had died more or less peacefully, and really old, she required only the simplest of the standard chants. I spoke the short version of *Flat Lux ad Astra*. It was such a short chant, my mouth barely stung at all. 'Let there be light to the stars' was certainly fitting in Katherine's case. As soon as her soul was free of its flesh coffin, it burst in a blinding explosion of light that would have lit up the whole city if it hadn't been contained by the walls of powder room, not that anyone but reapers would have seen it. The essence of Katherine was scattered brilliantly back into the world as a phenomenal amount of goodness and light. It left me, as a channeler of souls, awestruck.

"Wow, quite a woman," my dad murmured reverently.

The amount of light had been remarkable, especially for one so old. Maybe it was even enough light to reach the stars in the heavens. The crime rate in the city would be way down for a week or so, and selfless good deeds and random acts of kindness would be way way up.

"A saint," I echoed. Even with my limited reaper experience, I knew that her soul had been astounding. Mind-boggling. A bit of the blowback of Katherine's goodness lit my soul with pure happiness and brought tears of joy to my eyes. I wanted to hold onto the feeling forever, but it wasn't mine to keep. It was Katherine's. The feeling faded. I felt bereft without it, as if I was once again alone in a rowboat without any oars, adrift in the bleak, gray, foggy sea that was my life.

My dad nudged me. "Get a move on. Here, you'll need this." He unclipped the fanny pack that he wore around his waist and handed it to me. He kept his reaper kit in it since his jumpsuit didn't have a pocket to speak of. Not being a sanctioned reaper, but only a deputized reaper-in-training, I didn't have my own kit yet.

I unzipped the little pouch and pulled out a vial of Devil's Ash. Katherine probably didn't have a trace of evil in her, except for the small ration that each man is born into the world with, but even that had to be anchored.

I added the ash and salt, spoke the *Corpus Delecti* incantation, and the job was done. Katherine had been an easy reap, and a virtual saint. The last act I performed was to close her eyes and smooth down her hair, which was simply a human courtesy, not a reaper rite.

My dad extended a hand and pulled me to my feet. He closed the door. He touched his finger to the doorknob to lock it, as it had been locked before he opened it, and said, "Let's see what the chef has to offer."

It was better than going back to the van and sitting there in the humidity waiting for Susan to die. We went out into the waning sunshine and moved unseen through the crowd. Bodies instinctively stepped aside, avoiding us. A buffet table was setup near the barbeque. It was loaded with enough food to challenge a pro hockey team.

"So much better than Lucky Charms," I said, and helped myself to a mini skewer with five cubes of marinated chicken impaled on it, along with a cheerful combination of green and red pepper wedges. It was so good, I had another. Since neither my dad nor I could cook, we had been living on takeout and packaged crap for four months. The real food tasted like ambrosia.

I was finishing the second skewer when I felt the tug of a soul. My dad stilled, too.

"That was quick," he said. "Wonder what happened to Susan." The exact time of death is not information that a reaper is privy to, except in those rare circumstances where timing is crucial to the reap. It's something of a safeguard to keep reapers from interfering in the natural order of life and death, in case they're tempted to save a soul rather than reap it. Reapers may not be as open to temptation as a regular person, but it has been known to happen.

We headed back to the mud room. The bathroom door was still shut, but the door into the garage was ajar. My dad said, "After you," and waved me forward.

I took a peek through the doorway. A little old lady, a twin to the one in the bathroom, was prone on the garage floor, three big cement stairs down. This would be the MA. It was pretty obvious that she had fallen hard. When you're eighty-nine, a fall like that can kill you, and it had killed Susan. There was no spreading pool of blood or anything gruesome. A broken wine bottle lay beside her and she had a small cut on her hand, that's all. Her soul was fluttering away with more urgency than her sister's. Since her death had been harsher, it was to be expected.

"You do this one, too." My dad handed over his fanny pack.

I knew he was having me reap these souls because they were such simple, straightforward reaps, and good practice for a beginner. I took the pack and descended the steps. At least Susan had her pants on. She was face down so I turned her over. A big bump marked the side of her forehead. "Hello Susan. I'm Elvis and I'll be your reaper today," I said, looking down into her wrinkled face.

"Elvis," my dad chided. He didn't like graveside humour during the actual reap, even though there was no grave. Out of respect for the deceased, it should be a solemn affair.

I repeated the ritualized process to release her soul. Its essence was nicely bright, but not nearly as dazzling as Katherine's. A decent woman, Susan had not been in the same league as her saintly sister. I anchored the evil in her body before I turned her back over and went to look for my dad, who had wandered. I found him near the makeshift bar that was setup on the kitchen table, sipping scotch on the rocks.

"Dad, there's still one more soul," I reminded him sharply.

"It's just one drink, Elvis, and it's an NC. Stop nagging and go have some birthday cake or something."

"I'm driving home," I threatened him, and went to find cake. I didn't get there. A soul stopped me. "Gertrude," I murmured. The birthday gal. She was in the backyard, bobbing in the pool in one of those floating recliner chairs. Everyone else was too busy eating to swim, and she looked to be catching a little shuteye on the water.

None of the party guests had perceived her quiet death yet, probably from a heart attack or stroke. In slack repose, Gertrude looked older than her sisters, and she was even shorter.

"She's in the pool, Dad. I didn't bring a bathing suit." And I didn't feel like getting wet. "Why don't you unzip your jumpsuit and do this one? Boxers are like a bathing suit."

"Who says I'm wearing boxers? Elvis used to go commando under his jumpsuits, you know."

I groaned. "TMI, Dad."

He chuckled, plunked down in the nearest empty patio chair and sipped his drink, looking for all the world like he was Elvis Presley on vacation in Hawaii.

I sighed. "I have to do this one too?"

"Good practice, nice easy reap."

I snorted. "Except for getting wet."

"You won't melt, Baby. Lovely day for a swim." He arched an eyebrow in the direction of the pool.

"But my mouth is getting sore." I was exaggerating. It was only stinging a bit from the three 'tongue of the gods' incantations I had spoken that day, or maybe the chicken had been spicier than I had realized.

My dad simply motioned for me to get on with it by flapping his hand as if shooing me away like a fly. I knew it wasn't a battle I was going to win. Plus,

22

there were far worse locations for performing a reap than a swimming pool on a summery day, and I had experienced a whole lot of them with my dad.

"Fine." I flounced toward the pool, dropped the fanny pack by the edge and waded in. The water was surprisingly warm; the heater must have been turned up pretty high. I swam over to Gertrude and guided her chair toward the fanny pack. A towel was within reach—probably Gertrude's. She wasn't going to be needing it. I dried my hands on it before I unzipped the pack and removed the necessary powders. What I was about to do would be as unseen as me and my dad and our van.

I put a hand on Gertrude's chest and chanted. Her soul practically leapt out of her body, indicating that she had suffered a lot in life, either physically or emotionally or mentally, maybe all three. There was a respectable amount of light when her soul dispersed, just a little less than Susan's. A couple of the more perceptive guests (women) paused and looked around, sensing something unusual in the air.

Without wasting any time, I placed the Devil's Ash and natron salt in Gertrude's mouth and spoke the *Corpus Delecti* incantation. I stuffed the tools of the trade back into the fanny pack and waded out, as soaked as a girl can get. I was pretty sure the pool water had ruined my silky skirt.

We didn't stay for birthday cake. The birthday girl was dead and it wouldn't be long before one or another of the sisters was discovered in their lifeless condition. We didn't want to witness that sadness. Plus, I had reaped three souls, four when you counted Warren's earlier that day. Even though the sisters had been the easiest reaps imaginable, channeling a soul requires an input of spiritual energy from the reaper that is quite draining. And then there was my tender mouth from speaking such powerful words. My mouth would toughen up as I became a more experienced reaper, or so my dad said, but it wasn't used to 'the tongue of the gods' yet.

My dad and I slipped out of the yard through a side gate. I wrung out my skirt as best I could before I climbed into the van. My seat still got soaked. I didn't fight my dad for the wheel. He'd only had one drink that I had seen, so he could still drive much better than me.

"I wish they were all like that. I wish all deaths were so peaceful," he murmured, coasting along the dusky road.

"Me, too," I said, blocking out any thoughts of my mother's death.

The sun had almost set and the sky was clouding over. It started to drizzle lightly, which seemed symbolic of all the tears that would be flowing in the house we had just left. Across the distance, I could almost feel the grieving for three sisters. It hadn't been a birthday at all, but a deathday.

Back at home, I ignored my homework. I took care of my laundry before I showered off chlorine, and donned the oversized pink t-shirt I often wore as my nightgown. It smelled as fresh as a daisy, thanks to the dryer sheet's perfume.

I so wanted to crawl into my bed, except I hadn't decontaminated it yet. And I couldn't really burn my mattress in the backyard, not without Adrian thinking I was a witch and/or calling the fire department. The best I could do was flip the mattress and put fresh sheets on it. As soon as it was fit for human habitation, I crawled under the covers.

Feeling swamped by loneliness as I so often did lately, I gazed through my window at Adrian's window with all the longing of a prisoner looking through iron bars at freedom. And Adrian was just as unattainable. True confession—I have an uninterrupted view of Adrian's bedroom window when I lay in my bed. It has a lot to do with how I've positioned my bed right beside the window, and the fact that I keep the branches of a certain tree pruned, secretly, at night. The tree looks like it has a bite out of the side, but no-one seems to have noticed. I admit, when I'm up in the tree sawing off new growth, I do feel like an honest-to-goodness stalker—and maybe I am.

Adrian's light was turned off. Well, it was Saturday night. He was probably out with his friends. I hoped he was out with male friends. At least he didn't have a girlfriend at the moment. At least he wasn't a player. I fell asleep listening to songs about heartbreak and unrequited love, and totally relating.

A persistent noise disturbed me at 3:13—a.m. not p.m. I might have buried my head under my pillow except that it sounded like a vacuum cleaner. The middle of the night is an odd time to vacuum, especially in my dirty house. The sound cut off and was replaced by the clinking of dishes. We were either being burgled by a neat freak or my dad was up to something.

# 4. Cleaning Zombie

I hauled my butt out of bed to investigate the noise. The hall light was on. In fact, most of the lights in the house seemed to be on, and someone was definitely rattling around in the kitchen.

I tiptoed down to the main floor and could hear my dad crooning the lyrics of *You've Lost That Loving Feeling*. He was sitting at the kitchen table in his black and gold reaper jumpsuit, drink in hand, serenading a grandmotherly woman who was at the sink. She was scrubbing dishes as if her life depended on it. The rest of the kitchen sparkled with cleanliness. The counters had been cleared of debris and scrubbed. The piled garbage and recycling had vanished. Even the flies had somehow been evicted, or swatted.

"Dad?" I said. He stopped serenading and peered up at me through bloodshot eyes. "Dad, who is that?" I flapped an arm at the mad scrubber.

"S'prise! I got us a clean lady - " He hiccupped loudly.

"A clean lady?" The woman didn't look that clean in her work clothes and soiled apron.

"No, a ... a cleaning lady," he said proudly, and tipsily. "Hannah, meet my kid, Elvis. Elvis, meet Hannah."

"Ees strange name for young lady," the woman said in a heavy accent, Russian maybe. She kept washing dishes without missing a beat. "Yesss, ees good I am com'ink here. Very dirty here. Very dirty house."

"Dad, is Hannah a zombie?" I hissed, not able to tell for sure. It's as impossible to sense the soul of a living breathing person as it is to sense a zombie's soul.

My dad winced. "Don't call her that."

"Is she a problem client then?"

"Hannah is dead," my dad admitted. "Had a stroke while cleaning an office building. She jus' hasn't 'cepted it yet, and she wouldn't stop cleaning, so's I thought to myself, Adam, why look a gift horsy in the mouth?" He motioned around the room with the hand holding his drink. Liquid sloshed over the rim and splashed onto the freshly mopped floor.

I planted my hands on my hips. "She's not a horsy—a horse, Dad!"

"You know what I mean."

Unfortunately, I did. "So you thought it would be a good idea to bring a dead woman back here? To clean our house? In the middle of the night?" My voice rose steadily in pitch, letting him know I was irked.

"I surely did. I let her drive," he whispered, as if it was a big secret.

"That's good," I whispered back. I didn't bother lecturing him about drinking and driving, and bringing his problem clients home. He was simply too drunk. My words would have flowed in one inebriated ear and right out the other.

"She's a fan ... fan ... fan'stastic cleaner, and as speedy as ol' Speedy Gonzales." My dad motioned again, splashing more liquid onto the floor.

Hannah must have had eyes in the back of her head. She hurried over with a rag and wiped up my dad's spills, grumbling under her breath even though she wasn't actually breathing.

"This doesn't seem right, Dad. How hard did you try to tell her she was dead?"

He shrugged expansively. "Hard enough."

It was time for some more on-the-job training. I gripped Hannah's hand and pulled her into a standing position. "Hannah, I have some bad news for you," I said gravely, squeezing her damp fingers. Even though they had just come out of warm soapy water, they were cold.

"No bad news." She jerked her hand free. "Ees not time to be dead. Too much working to do to be dead. House is piggy sty. Only fit for piggies, not peoples." Humming loudly, she picked up a towel and started drying dishes.

"Hannah, listen to me. You had a stroke. It was fatal." I edged beside her and tried to look deep into her eyes. "Do you remember? The pain? The darkness?"

She backed away. "I am remembering no such things." She shoved the towel into my hands, spun on her heel and went into the den. The vacuum started up again.

I tossed the towel on the counter. No way was I drying dishes at three in the morning. I turned to my dad. "Isn't it unusual to have two zombies—I mean, two problem clients in only two days?"

"Unusual, yes, but it happens sometimes. There was this one week my dear ol' daddy tol' me about, when none of the dead would give up their souls. He thought it had somethin' to do with a mash -" He hiccupped loudly.

"A mash? What's a mash?" I asked.

He shook his head like a cow being pestered by flies. "No. A mash ... a mass ... a massive solar flare that happened at the same time. There were power outages all over and the dead kept walkin' as if they hadn't died. All part of the mysteries of the universe, I s'pose." He waved an arm drunkenly around the room, as if the kitchen was the universe, adding, "That's when The-Powers-That-Be gave him the Dead Man's Breath an' that damned Dead Man's Shirt, to be used in 'mergencies."

His mention of the Dead Man's Shirt caught me completely off-guard. Since my mom's death, it was something we avoided talking about at all costs. My dad now kept it locked in his office safe and he was the only one who knew the combination. The alcohol may have loosened his tongue, but mine was as sober as a judge. It avoided the topic of the Dead Man's Shirt like the plague. "Dead Man's Breath?" I said instead. "That sounds familiar."

"Maybe 'cause it passed to me, jus' like that … damned shirt." He took a big swig, trying to drown his sorrows, and swiped at his suddenly watery eyes.

I wished he would shut up about the shirt. And I didn't want to see him cry. It hurt too much to see my big strong dad cry. If he cried, I would have another meltdown, and two meltdowns in one day were simply unacceptable. I swallowed hard and sat down beside him. I leaned against his shoulder and asked, "What is Dead Man's Breath for? To stop zombies?"

He cleared his throat roughly and put an arm around me, hugging me tight as if he needed something to hold on to. "It won't stop zombies, Baby. They don' breathe, do they?"

"No. But it can't be to stop the living. We don't kill, it says so in the Reaper Commandments."

He tilted his head one way, then the other, waffling, before he said, "There's still some things you don' know 'bout reaping."

I rested my head on his shoulder. "Such as?"

"Sometimes souls get stuck in limbo. It's happening more and more, 'cause of so-called modern medicine. The soul is dead, but the body is being kept alive by some damn machine." He snorted in disgust. "*Non mortuus, non victus, civitas inter*—not dead, not alive, but straddling the line. Soul is dead and evicts the evil, but the body keeps on breathing. The soul is trapped in torment. Dead Man's Breath is for that, when the soul is ready for release, but trapped in a body that's still breathing—being forced to breathe by a machine. *Non mortuus, non victus.*"

"So the breath finishes off the body so the soul can be released?" I assumed. My dad nodded once. "But I've never seen you use it." And I didn't think he would use the shirt ever again.

"I've never taken you on one of those cases, and I kind'a mislaid the breath." He frowned into his glass and swiveled the melting ice cubes around.

"I suppose it would be easy to misplace air, I mean, air is invisible." I yawned. I was tired and my dad's shoulder was very comfy and warm. Most of the human contact I experienced was of the deathly cold, or at best, rapidly cooling variety. Warm felt so much nicer. I yawned again. It was the middle of the night, after all. I idly wondered if Mrs. Lyon was awake, too, trying to figure out why our whole house was lit up like Christmas.

"The breath doesn't look like air, Babycakes," my dad mumbled.

"What does Dead Man's Breath look like then?"

"Believe it or not, it looks like a little ol' spray can."

I looked sideways at him. "You mean like spray paint?"

My yawns must have been contagious because he shook his head and yawned so wide, I could see his silver fillings. "No, littler, and it doesn't say paint on it. It doesn't say nothing. It's jus' a little ol' black spray can."

"How long ago did it go missing?"

He mulled that over. "Long time. Years."

"So what do you use instead, when you have to take care of one of these *non mortuus, non victus* souls?" I asked.

"I use the old-fashioned approach," my dad said with a wince.

"Which is?"

"A pillow or something. I don' take you on those cases, Baby," he repeated.

"Good. I don't want to go on those cases, ever. What are you going to do about Hannah?" I asked, changing the subject. There are some things that should not be discussed, or imagined, in the dead of night. My dad smothering his clients with a pillow definitely fell into that category.

"I'll let her clean for a few hours, get it out of her system, then I'll convince her she's dead. She might figure it out for herself when she gets sleepy. Soon as she'll sit still, I'll release her soul an' drive her body back to the office building. No rush since it's Sunday. She won't be found 'til Monday." He knew that for a fact. Time of discovery was information that was normally included in the texts from his boss.

I stood up, simply too weary to argue. And he was the expert. Plus, it would be nice to have a clean house. "Is she going to do upstairs? And does she do bathrooms?"

My dad winked. "You bet your blue suede shoes she does bathrooms."

"I'm going back to bed then. Don't let Hannah clean my room, and don't let her wander off, and don't you dare drive until you're sober. Maybe you should let Hannah drive and reap her when she's back where she belongs."

"Maybe I will." My dad leaned back in his chair and closed his eyes as if he was going to have a nap. At least he didn't pour himself another drink.

"Night, Dad." I kissed his cheek and returned to my bed with cotton balls stuffed in my ears. I slept undisturbed for the rest of the night and awoke to a lovely fresh house, and room. It smelled as lemony as the house next door. Hannah had cleaned around me while I was snoring. I could see my floor, all of it. There wasn't one scrap of dirty laundry left for me to trip over. Hannah must have finished washing my clothes. I went directly downstairs to make sure all was well.

All was not well. The kitchen smelled like fresh baking and my dad was nowhere in sight. Through the window over the sink, I spotted Hannah sweeping the porch—outside, for all the world to see. And she was starting to look rather dead. Rigor mortis had set in and her movements were as stiff and jerky as Frankenstein's monster.

I hurried out onto the porch. "Hannah, come inside. Now!"

She kept sweeping. I grabbed her arm and tugged her back into the house. She didn't put up much of a fight and mostly staggered, arms stiffly outstretched. I slammed the door and the timer on the oven buzzed.

Hannah jerked her arm free and lurched toward the oven. Before I could stop her, she opened the oven door and reached inside to remove a muffin pan with beautifully browned muffins. Only problem was, she didn't use potholders. At least she no longer felt pain. She plunked the muffins on the top of the stove and smiled gruesomely, her facial muscles too stiffened to work properly.

"You are having no boobies. Eat ... eat ... little round breads," she mumbled, sounding like her mouth had been completely frozen by a dentist, and she had lost enough brain cells to forget what muffins were called.

"They look great," I said, trying not to think about the burnt bits of skin that were clinging to the muffin pan. "Dad! Where the hell are you?" I hollered. I heard a groan from the living room and headed that way, towing Hannah.

My dad was sprawled on the couch in a tidy, dust-free, vacuumed living room. He was the messiest thing in the room. "Dad, Hannah was outside, sweeping! And she's looking pretty darn dead. I think you better take care of her sooner rather than later, like now!"

He rubbed his hands over his face and blinked up at me, eyeballs so bloodshot, they might have been marinating in tomato juice. "Hannah?"

"The zombie you brought home to clean our house. She's still here, still keeping busy."

"Oh, that Hannah." He didn't even call me on the 'Z' word.

"Just how many Hannahs did you bring home last night?"

He didn't bother answering my question, which was deeply rooted in sarcasm. He stood up, swayed alarmingly, and said, "I'll take care of her now. Just ... shush." I guess I was shouting a bit.

"You can't let zombies wander around, Dad. If you do that, you're going to get fired for sure. And what will the neighbours think if you let zombies tromp all over their lawns?" I demanded, since I didn't think he was taking my concerns seriously enough.

"It's only one zombie—problem client. Just one. Now shush. Hannah, where did you put the aspirin when you cleaned the kitchen?" he asked his problem client.

Hannah grunted something that sounded Chinese and staggered toward the kitchen. My dad followed her, staggering a bit himself.

I shook my head in frustration and stomped back upstairs. About an hour later, I heard the van drive away. Only then did I return to the kitchen and pour myself a glass of juice. I eyed the muffins. They looked good, and Hannah hadn't actually touched them with her cooked hands. She had only touched the pan.

I picked one up and broke it opened. It didn't appear to have any weird ingredients. Craving some home cooking, I sampled a tiny piece and gagged. If

I wasn't mistaken, Hannah had used salt in place of sugar. Well, she was a zombie and most zombies couldn't cook. Disappointed, I spat the bite out and dumped the muffins in the garbage. I had toast instead.

I spent the afternoon in my room, working on homework in case Adrian wanted to discuss Rushburn's paper over dinner. It would give us something to talk about other than the weather, and I wanted to sound smart. Finishing the paper took a huge chunk out of my Sunday, but I was glad to get it out of the way, even though it wasn't due until Thursday.

With a good hour left to get ready for dinner at Adrian's house, I showered, dressed with care, applied makeup, and fussed with my hair. Then I took inventory in my mirror, trying to decide if I had found the right balance. Did I look cool and attractive? Without looking desperate, lovesick and stalker-ish?

I struck a few model's poses, to help me decide. My hair was in a casual, slightly messy upswept bun/ponytail combo. It looked good from the front and back. "Hair, nice," I said.

My makeup was not overdone. I had mainly darkened and emphasized my eyes and lips. In my opinion, my eyes and lips are my better features. My nose isn't cute or small. It's too prominent for a girl. At least it has a nice enough shape, but I don't go out of my way to make my nose standout when I apply makeup. My nose does that all by itself. Some days, when I'm feeling particularly down on myself, I'm pretty sure my nose juts out more than my boobs.

"Makeup, acceptable," I said.

Deciding what to wear had been tough. Normally, I favoured understated Goth. Given my life, it's only natural I suppose. But Goth and Sunday night dinner at the Lyon's just didn't seem to go together. There was something wrong with that picture, so I had toned down my fashion stylings and was wearing one of my long summery tops, or short summer dresses. I could never decide which they were—top or dress? The one I was wearing was crimson, strapped and comfortable. It was the same colour that I had painted the longest wall of my bedroom. After black, crimson is my favourite colour.

My outfit showed a hint of cleavage, if you had a good imagination, but it wasn't low cut enough to be considered slutty. I was wearing the top/dress with black shorts. The outfit made my legs look long. Heck, they were long, since I was tall for a girl.

My dad says that all reapers are born tall and strong for when they need to haul the dead around or wrestle a zombie into submission. No such thing as a petite little reaper exists. At least I wasn't taller than Adrian. If I didn't wear heels, he was exactly one inch taller than me. Perfect for kissing or gazing deeply into each other's eyes.

I opted for flat sandals instead of my usual Goth boots, so my outfit wouldn't raise any parental eyebrows. And my feet would be a lot cooler. The worst thing about Goth boots in the summer is that they're like little saunas for your feet.

You have to wear thick cotton socks just to soak up all the foot sweat. On the other hand, Goth boots are perfect for wearing to reap sites where what you're stepping in and on is not something you want touching your skin.

"Clothes, approved." I smiled at my reflection. It was time to go next door.

Downstairs, my dad was looking pretty spiffy himself. He had slicked his lively dark hair back into its classic Elvis style, like a cresting wave flowing back from his forehead. It wasn't a full pompadour, but close. Instead of a jumpsuit, he was wearing tight pants and a black blazer over a silky patterned shirt. The buttons were undone almost to his navel.

"Ready for your date, Dad?" I asked, doing up three of the buttons.

He nodded and undid two. "I suppose, I suppose."

He looked unusually flustered. He looked like he wanted a drink, but I couldn't smell any alcohol. In case I haven't mentioned it yet, reapers can smell as acutely as bloodhounds, probably for when they have to track down renegade zombies.

"Is Kendra coming here for dinner?" I did up one button and smacked his hand away when he tried to undo it.

My dad pulled a face. "Not with my cooking. I don't want to scare her off, so I'm taking her out."

"Where?"

"The Old Mill Pub. It's only our fourth date, so I don't want to go anywhere too intimate. And I don't want to go anywhere too loud. I like talking to Kendra."

The fact that my dad had even thought about such things meant that this date was important to him. "It sounds like a good choice, Dad. I'm sure you'll have fun. Did you take the night off?"

"Booked it off. The reaper from Senville is covering for me." He looked at me—really looked at me. "You don't mind that I'm going on a date?"

"It feels weird, but … Mom's dead." We both knew, better than most, how final death truly was. "I'll get used to it, I suppose. Just don't rush into anything because you're lonely." Lonely was how I felt most of the time and I knew it could make you hook up with the wrong person—or wrong zombie. I made a grand sweeping gesture toward the door and said, "You have my blessing."

He patted his pockets to make sure he had what he needed, saluted a farewell and headed outside. Since he wouldn't be called to work, he was taking his recreational vehicle. He had already pulled it out of the garage and polished it up.

The white, pink-roofed, 1961 Cadillac Coupe de Ville was a twin to the one Elvis had bought for himself after he got home from military service in Germany. Unlike the van, my dad kept his Cadillac in mint condition. It was his second most prized possession, after Elvis's hair. I've never driven it, and I don't expect I ever will.

31

As soon as the car roared away, I locked the house and walked next door. I was as flustered as my dad even though I wasn't on a date with Adrian. It was more like I was on a date with his mom, since she had invited me to dinner, but Adrian would be there. I was trying not to smile like the world's biggest lovesick fool when I knocked on the front door, but I'm pretty sure I was doing just that.

Mrs. Lyon opened the door. "Elvis, come in. Don't you look pretty. I saw your father's car go by. Can't miss that fancy car, now can you?"

"No." I looked around for Adrian and only saw Mr. Lyon. We exchanged polite greetings and I said, "It smells great in here." It smelled like roasted chicken and potato salad and blueberry pie.

"Thank you, Elvis." She ushered me to the kitchen and I sat on a stool at the island counter. We didn't have an island in my kitchen because we had never updated our house.

"Would you like some iced tea?" Mrs. Lyon asked, already pouring.

"Sure. It looks delicious." The glass was in my hand before I finished answering. Mrs. Lyon was one organized woman. "Can I help with anything?" I asked when she began breaking up freshly washed lettuce.

"No. You sit and relax. I'm sure you have to do enough cooking at home, now that your mother is … gone." She smiled apologetically. Gone is a word people often use in place of 'dead', although it really isn't the same thing. If someone is simply gone, they can come back. If they're dead, they can't.

I did not volunteer the information that I really didn't cook and asked, "Is Adrian around?" The yearning in my heart would not be silenced.

"Adrian isn't home yet, Elvis. He's out with friends and must be running late. I hope you don't mind sharing dinner with just Mr. Lyon and yours truly."

What could I say to that except, "Of course not. I'm looking forward to it." Meanwhile, my heart got another little crack in it, or a big crack. It felt more like a big crack. Heartbreak Hotel. One of these days, my heart was going to shatter into as many jagged pieces as a sheet of ice trampled on by a herd of elephants wearing stiletto heels.

I managed small talk with Mrs. Lyon until she served dinner at 6:30 on the dot. The food alone made the meal worthwhile, and I would have enjoyed it if not for Adrian's blatant absence. I was pretty sure it meant that he was avoiding me and didn't want to spend any time with me at all. It hurt as badly as if he had run over my poor cracked heart with his mom's car, or tossed it under a herd of tap dancing elephants.

As much as I tried to hide it, I think Mrs. Lyon could tell I was upset. She was warmly attentive while she kept the conversation flowing. I heard all about what Jackson and Julia were up to. Mr. Lyon didn't help much in the small talk department. He's nice enough and has a kind look in his brown eyes, as well as a quirky sense of humour that rears its head when you least expect it, but he isn't talkative. He operates on a sort of 'need to speak' basis, at least when I'm around.

We were finishing up with pie and ice cream when the front door opened. I held my breath, ears on high alert.

"Adrian, is that you?" his mother called.

"Yes, Mom. Sorry I'm late." Adrian entered the room and looked sort of taken aback to see me sitting there. He had either forgotten I was coming to dinner or hoped I'd gone home by now. Either way, he wasn't thrilled to see me sitting at his table. I think I actually heard my heart break in two, with a sharp splintering crack.

"Oh, hi Elvis." He stood deer-in-the-headlights frozen for a moment before he approached the table. His cheeks were sun-kissed and his hair was windblown. It looked like he'd spent the day at the beach. I could smell the lake water and sand, and even the sunshine coming off his casual T-shirt and shorts.

"You're just in time for dessert," his mother said, breaking the strained silence.

"I haven't even had dinner yet." Adrian served himself a plate in the kitchen. He sat down and dove in with his fork. When he darted a glance my way, I realized that I was staring at him as hungrily as he was digging into his meal. At least I wasn't drooling over him.

"The dinner was really great," I said, only realizing how lame I sounded once the words were out there, hanging in the air. "My dad and I have been living on takeout and frozen dinners, and chips, and cereal, and cookies," I added, with no idea where I was heading. The list of food items was simply leaking out of my mouth. The ringing phone was a blessing as far as I was concerned, but not for long.

Mr. Lyon answered it and he began to frown. "Yes, of course, Adam. One moment." He offered me the phone and I just looked at it as if I had never seen a phone before. "It's your father," he said.

"Oh." I did know my dad's name. I was simply dismayed that he was calling me here and now. It could only mean one thing, that something was very very wrong. I accepted the phone. "Hello, Dad?"

"You didn't answer your cell phone," he said accusingly, with a distinct slur.

"It's at home." I had left it there on purpose.

He began slurring a mile a minute, something about an emergency in his territory, and he didn't think he could drive, and he'd left his work phone and fanny pack at home anyway, and could I take care of things for him. Considering that he didn't have his work phone on him, I knew The-Powers-That-Be must have contacted him in some alternate way, like phoning the restaurant. It meant that something big and bad was going down.

I smiled apologetically around the table. My dad finally stopped rambling and took a breath. I cut in. "Okay. Yes, I'll take care of it. The van is here, so I'll take care of it. I'll check the location on your phone. I can pick you up before or after if … if you can't drive." I said the last part quietly, but I was still heard by everyone at the table. "Anyway, I'll figure it out, Dad. You're at the Old Mill Pub, right?"

He confirmed his location and hung up, although it sounded more like he dropped the phone. I turned the Lyon's phone off and put it down on the table. Three pairs of brown eyes were watching me. "Sorry about that. Uh, my dad has a bit of an emergency with the case he's working on and I have to help him out." I stood up. "I have to go. Thank you for dinner, it was so good."

Before I could make a run for it, Mrs. Lyon said, "But you only have your learner's permit, Elvis. You can't drive alone, and you can't drive at night."

"I'll have to, just this once. I'll drive really carefully and slowly." I backed away from the table.

Mr. Lyon looked at Adrian. "Adrian, why don't you drive Elvis to meet her father. It would be safer."

Adrian hesitated to agree, as if he was trying to think up some excuse as to why he couldn't drive me. His reaction wounded me, and I bit my lip and took another step backwards. "That's okay," I said. "I'll be fine. Thanks again for dinner. Bye." I was out the door before anyone could stop me.

Tears stinging my eyes, I crossed the lawn, stubbing my toe on a patio stone. Served me right for wearing sandals. My toes never got hurt inside Goth boots, which were like foot armour. I needed a pair of Goth boots for my heart, or at least one Goth boot.

I had forgotten to leave the porch light on and had a terrible time finding the lock and fitting the key into it. My watery eyes made it that much harder. When I finally succeeded in unlocking the door, I wasn't alone.

"Come on, Elvis, let me drive you. I don't mind," Adrian said.

I wanted to pick him up and heave him off my porch like a pro-wrestler. "Don't mind?" I said as coldly as any grim reaper of old. Frost probably coated the porch around us. And then I didn't know what to say. Shouting something along the lines of, 'I want you to be thrilled that you can spend time with me!' would have just scared him and shamed me. I shoved the door wide and stepped into the kitchen, flicking on the light.

Adrian followed. At least my house was a hundred times less disgusting than the last time he had seen it. I kept my back to him and blinked rapidly, trying to clear my eyes.

My dad's phone was in plain sight on the counter. The text message button was flashing red, brightly and urgently. Only The-Powers-That-Be text messages flashed red like that. I picked it up and blotted my eyes so I could read it. "Shit," I muttered.

"Problem?" Adrian asked.

"Nothing I can't handle." Maybe. I glanced at Adrian. He was watching me rather anxiously, or he was worried about being alone with me in my house. Adrian could never be accused of having a poker face. "It's okay, Adrian. You don't need to drive me to my dad. I'm not going to pick him up after all." It was the truth, and at the same time, it was a lie of omission.

"You're sure?"

"Positive. But thanks for the offer, and thank your mom for dinner."

"You already did that, a few times." He offered a tentative smile. He was acting kind of nice so maybe he was feeling sorry for me.

"Well, I still feel bad about running out like that. I didn't help her clean up or - "

"She wouldn't have let you," Adrian interjected.

"You're probably right, anyway, I have to deal with this." I waved the phone I was still holding and as if I had shaken the song out of it, *All Shook Up* began to play. A second text was coming in. I glanced at the message and felt the blood drain from my face.

"Elvis? Is it bad news?" Adrian was still standing there, hands shoved into his pockets.

I repeated, "Nothing I can't handle."

"Maybe you shouldn't have to handle it."

"Maybe I don't have a choice. You should go home and finish your dinner." I opened the door, showing Adrian the door. Time was of the essence, otherwise there's no way in the universe that I would have been trying to get rid of Adrian. I would have been locking him in my house with me. Just the two of us. Alone. Two warm bodies. I've had that fantasy a few hundred times.

"Well ... okay. Later, Elvis."

He left and I ran to get my dad's fanny pack.

# 5. Corpse with a Cold

Reapers see a lot of gross and bizarre crap. I suppose that goes without saying. My dad started taking me to work with him when I was about five, so I've got years' worth of disturbing memories crammed into my brain— memories of people who have died in industrial accidents and fires and car crashes, and worse. But what I had to deal with as a substitute reaper on that night, when someone must have forgotten to lock the gates of hell, was completely off the map. And not just for me, as an inexperienced reaper-in-training. It would have been unchartered territory for any reaper, even my dad.

The two reaps were at the same location. Both clients were flagged as ASAP's and AWC's. In reaper lingo, AWC means 'approach with caution'. Carl Waring, the first client, had been listed as clients normally are, by name, age and location. He was tragically young to be dead, almost as young as Warren. Cause of death was cited as unnatural, which usually means some sort of fluky happenstance that often boils down to someone being in the wrong place at the wrong time. The second client had not been listed normally. He had merely been recorded as *Male R* with his age and location. No information about cause of death was included.

I had never seen a text message from The-Powers-That-Be that did not identify a person by name, although cause of death was not always included, especially if it wasn't relevant to the reap being successfully carried out.

Unfortunately, the location was nowhere near the Old Mill Pub. It was in the opposite direction, and since it was a double ASAP reap, I couldn't detour and get my dad. I couldn't even call him for advice since I had his phone. I had to go directly to the reap location—do not pass go, do not collect two hundred dollars.

I got behind the wheel and started driving as fast as I dared, trying to keep the van in the middle of the lane. Our enhanced GPS, another perk of my dad's job, told me exactly when and where to turn in a sexy British baritone, and the GPS was never wrong. I had christened it, or him, 'James' and often talked to him even though he never talked back, except to give directional information. James the GPS made finding the site of my double reap pretty straightforward even though it was way off the beaten track, where the city encroaches on nature.

I pulled up beside an overgrown field with an impressive skid on loose gravel, and turned off the engine. The crickets were a loud chorus in the night, and the only sound I could hear. I stumbled out of the van, then leaned back in to get the fanny pack I had almost forgotten. Since it was too dark to see the ground underfoot, I groped in the glove-box for a flashlight. With its beam leading the way, I hurried into the field until I could sense one of the souls.

It was somewhere in the middle of the long grass and weeds, and this soul was no fluttering bird. It was clawing to get out, and no wonder. Evil wrapped the poor thing like a straightjacket. I normally wouldn't have sensed the evil, but this malevolence was so intense, it tainted the humid evening air like a toxic gas. My skin prickled sharply and painfully, as if I was standing in an acid wind. This man's evil was not going to release his soul without one hell of a battle.

I couldn't sense the second soul at all, which was odd. I was pretty sure both my clients were already deceased based on the ASAP status, but maybe the evil haze was camouflaging the second soul—unless the client had already turned zombie, just to spice things up.

My heart began to pound in fear. I was already sweating in the heavy evening air, but I began to sweat even more, until my top/dress stuck damply to my skin. The writing was on the wall in big spray-painted graffiti letters. This wasn't a reap I should be attempting alone. A reaper isn't immortal or indestructible, and the rituals aren't foolproof. There are always risks involved when performing a challenging reap, and that's what I was facing—a desperate soul, oodles of evil, an aura of madness and a possible zombie. Add to that, an inexperienced reaper and the peculiar text message—well, the whole scenario stank like an overly used outhouse.

I couldn't see either body because of the night darkness and long grass, but the soul I could sense drew me to the location as if it had a fishhook through my lip. It kept reeling me in and if I balked, I felt a ripping pain, so I kept stumbling along in the weak beam of the flashlight, which was getting weaker by the second. The batteries were running out of juice and there was no spare set in my dad's fanny pack. I switched off the feeble light to conserve it for when I really needed it.

Without the flashlight's beam compromising my night vision, I spotted a little patch of embers glowing just up ahead. I was downwind of it, which explained why I hadn't smelled any trace of smoke. The soul was near the coals. I hurried forward, tripped, and went sprawling into a patch of prickly weeds. What I had tripped over felt too soft to be a log or a rock.

I had found one of my clients.

"Ouch, ouch, ouch," I cried, trying to disengage myself from the prickles without losing too much skin. I stood up and turned the flashlight on, aiming it in the general direction of the body. With a very unreaper-like and girlish shriek,

I dropped the flashlight. Regardless, what I had glimpsed was imprinted on my brain like a cell phone snapshot.

Unnatural death was an understatement. This client hadn't just died. He had been killed, sickly and brutally, and he wasn't much older than me. He was also smoking, and I'm not talking about cigarettes. His bare arm was in the coals as if it was a log, and I could smell that. I swallowed hard, willing the contents of my stomach to stay put. I could sense no soul in the body even though it wasn't animate.

As much as I didn't want to examine details, my role as reaper required that I do just that. I groped around for the flashlight, found it, and aimed it directly at his face. It looked like a butcher had been practicing his trade. Strips of flesh had been removed with what appeared to be a razor-sharp blade and a confident stroke. I swallowed hard and shifted the beam, then wished I hadn't. Perhaps even more disturbing than the sliced face was the fact that his arm seemed to have been gnawed on.

"What the hell?" I leaned closer. Yup, he had bites out of his charred arm, which was still rare on the inside, and they didn't look like animal bites. They looked exactly like human bites, the same shape and size as that first bite you take out of an apple.

Even so close, I could not sense a trace of the young man's soul. Based on the age info in the text, I knew this was my named client—Carl Waring. And someone had violated his remains in the worst imaginable way.

The dying embers cast virtually no light to speak of, so I turned the flashlight in the direction of the soul I could sense. I spotted a running shoe with a foot inside it—my second client, the mysterious Male R. My two clients were laid out practically side-by-side, with the coals between them.

I took a step closer and ran the beam over the second body, hoping to find it in better condition than the first. The light revealed a man who was about my dad's age. Male R's mouth was coated in blood, but it didn't appear to be his own blood. His mouth was undamaged, as was his face. Was the blood Carl Waring's? Male R could well be the murderer, and the biter, since he was the only other person in the vicinity.

I swallowed hard and looked up at the stars, trying to slow the panicky beating of my heart, before I dropped dead of a heart attack and added to the body count.

As far as I knew, my dad had never reaped a murderous cannibal, and I didn't have a clue if it required a customized incantation. I could feel the polluted evil of the deed tainting Male R's remains, and maybe even his soul. It was clawing madly to be free. There was such a vulgar amount of evil, I couldn't be sure that some of the darkness hadn't tainted the light of the man's soul, which was probably a feeble light indeed if he was the murderous cannibal that the evidence suggested he was. I suppose it was even possible that there wasn't enough light in his shriveled soul to keep the darkness out, after it had been evicted by death. His was a rare soul in the very worst way. After death, only serial killers and murderous psychopaths had earthly darkness inside their actual souls where there should be nothing but goodness and light.

My dad knew the reaper who had reaped the soul of an infamous serial killer of young boys in the early 1970's. The reaper had claimed that the man's soul had been so overrun by black evil, it was barely a soul anymore. He had described it as an oily rag with little more than a sputtering candle's worth of light. The dead man had been virtually soulless. And so much evil had been polluting his earthly remains that the corpse had been considered toxic waste. The reaper had had to perform a series of archaic rituals to bind the evil together and lock it into the bones of the body. I wondered if I would have to do that tonight, even though I didn't know how. That was Reaper Doctoral Studies, not Reaper 101.

"First things first," I said. I had to take care of poor Carl even though I couldn't sense his soul. I knelt beside him. A cursory examination proved that he was completely inanimate. He was young and had died horrifically and his reap had been delayed, so why hadn't he gone zombie? And why couldn't I sense his soul?

It was a mystery to me, but I opted to proceed as normal. I didn't know what else to do. I propped my flashlight in the grass so only an edge of the weak light touched him. I really didn't want to see more than I already had.

With a hand on what was left of his bloody charred shirt, over his heart, I spoke the longest version of the *Flat Lux ad Astra* incantation, adding a *Per Aspera* clause to recognize his suffering. I wasn't sure I'd used the right words because no soul rocketed out of the mutilated body. Curious and curiouser. I tried a few other all-purpose incantations. Nothing happened, except that my mouth started to sting rather badly. Finally, I tried to reap him as if he was a zombie, without actually placing my lips on his mutilated face.

My dad keeps a little device in the fanny pack for just such circumstances, when a client's face is so messed up, lip-to-lip contact is guaranteed to make you lose your lunch. It's a flat plastic barrier, normally used for mouth-to-mouth resuscitation, to protect the rescuer from catching nasty germs. It fits over the injured party's mouth and nose, and there is a hole in the middle with a one-way valve for the rescuer to blow through. I wasn't your normal type of rescuer, but I was here to rescue the soul from torment and being overwhelmed by evil.

I unfolded the barrier and laid it over Carl's lower face. Ready to proceed, I took the capsule of Angel's Breath between my teeth, sealed my mouth over the barrier, broke the capsule and exhaled a full breath deep into Carl's body.

Nothing happened. I still couldn't sense his soul. It was as if Carl had no soul, and I couldn't even sense any evil in him. I would have scratched my head if my hands hadn't been sticky with blood. It was as if he had already been reaped, or maybe his murder had been so unbearable, his soul had found its own release. I recalled my dad saying that such a thing could happen under extreme

39

circumstances. He had referred to it as a sort of divine intervention. Maybe that's what had happened here.

"It's not true that only the good die young, but I'm so sorry you did," I whispered to Carl, closing his eyes with a hand that shook. I felt like I had failed him by not releasing his soul. And he was so young. It was hard to see because, for the second time that night, my eyes were leaking tears.

I blinked them away. "This is your job, act professionally," I told myself. "Stop blubbering like a baby and get on with it."

So I did. I carried on as if it was a perfectly normal reap. I put the Devil's Ash into his mouth, then the natron salt. I spoke the standard *Corpus Delecti* incantation to anchor whatever earthly evil remained inside Carl, although it seemed as AWOL as his soul, unless Male R's plethora of evil was simply masking it. And then the reap was complete, in theory anyway.

Carl taken care of to the best of my limited reaper abilities, it was time to tackle my second client, the mysterious Male R. "One down, one to go. Ya, the worst one," I muttered. I really had to stop talking to myself.

My dad kept a travel pack of baby wipes in the fanny pack. I used one to clean the congealing blood off my hands before I turned my attention to Male R. In the feeble light of my dying flashlight, his body looked almost picturesque. It was lying spread eagle, staring up at the stars as if in wonder. The blood on his mouth could have been mistaken for cherry sauce or ketchup. In death, he didn't look like a monster. He probably hadn't in life either. There is no hard and fast rule that says the evil inside has to show on the outside. Evil is clever enough to wear a mask.

I studied Male R's face and frowned. He seemed vaguely familiar to me. I stood over him, gazing down. The bloody mouth and blank staring eyes didn't help me to identify him, although I was pretty sure I had seen his face before.

With a mental shrug, I ran the flashlight beam slowly over the rest of him, trying to spot what had killed him. There wasn't a visible mark on his body. A different brand of divine intervention perhaps? It had been known to happen. Except if he had been struck down, wouldn't his soul have been reaped by the Big Boss, and the massive amount of evil inside him nullified? It was anything but nullified. It was churning around inside his earthly remains like it was in a cement mixer, and who could blame it? It would not be travelling to the stars. It would be locked into a bone coffin where it would decompose gradually over the eons and do no measurable harm, unless the body was cremated, then the evil would be instantly nullified as it turned to ash.

Wishing I had taken the time to switch into my Goth boots, I used my foot to flip Male R over. There were no obvious marks on his backside either, although it was hard to be sure with all the dirt on his clothes, and the increasingly feeble rays of light I had at my disposal.

For just a second, I was tempted to go and find my dad, but from the way the evil was roiling around inside the body, if it wasn't reaped now, Male R would probably go zombie. A homicidal cannibal zombie was not something I wanted terrorizing the streets of my city. Clearly, it would be too risky to leave this body alone for even a minute. I had to reap Male R now, ASAP, as the text had instructed.

"Here goes nothing," I said and shifted my supplies closer to my second client. I made sure the flickering flashlight was shining right on him, in case the evil in his corpse tried to pull some underhanded trickery. I thought hard about what incantations to use to release his meager soul. I'd never had to reap a truly malevolent client before, but the longest version of the *Flat Lux ad Astra* chant should still draw the soul from his body, no matter how dimly lit it was, while leaving the depraved evil behind. Anchoring the colossal amount of evil in the earthly remains would require a more powerful binding chant than *Corpus Delecti*, however.

From the fanny pack, I removed my dad's little notebook of chants etc. I flipped through the section that listed binding incantations. There was one for murderers that I thought would do nicely. I practiced reading it silently so I wouldn't mess up the words. At the end of the incantation, in brackets, my dad had noted that the quantity of Devil's Ash must be increased tenfold. It was to be sprinkled over the body and placed in all bodily orifices, and he had underlined the *all*.

"You've got to be freaking kidding me," I cried, thoroughly disgusted. "That's the last straw. I am definitely not going to be a reaper when I grow up."

I held the vial of Devil's Ash in front of the fading flashlight's beam and groaned. My dad hadn't refilled the vial. There wasn't much of the black powder left. Certainly not tenfold the usual amount. Maybe three if I was lucky, which I didn't seem to be tonight. Three pinches of the powder wouldn't be enough to complete the advanced binding ritual, but it might be enough to hold the evil at bay while I ran home for more powder. And maybe I could fetch my dad at the same time.

"Stop procrastinating," I told myself. I laid a hand over Male R's heart even though I really did not want to touch the corpse that was simply oozing with evil. It even felt like the noxious nastiness was seeping up my arm, but I knew that was impossible. Evil cannot escape a body until after the soul has been reaped. The soul, by its very nature, is the most powerful anchor for evil in existence.

I shuddered and spoke the *Repello Malum* incantation to strengthen the soul and help it repel the evil surrounding it, and then the *Altivolus Supremus Malum*, to help the soul rise above the festering quagmire of evil that filled the body. And then the long version of *Flat Lux ad Astra*.

Nothing happened.

I repeated the incantations again in my most forceful voice, and thought I sensed something rising up, yet I couldn't swear that it was the soul. The evil aura was overwhelming me and making it hard to sense the shriveled thing, even though my client's soul must be struggling like mad to escape.

I spoke the chants yet again, adding several powerful summoning phrases, including a *Viribus Alas*, or 'Wings of Strength'. At that point, my mouth was stinging so bad, my tongue felt like it had been burnt. And in spite of all my efforts, the darkness still seemed to be clinging to the soul that I could only sense in sputtering flashes now, yet the evil shouldn't be able to get out of the body along with the light. The two are like oil and water.

And then Male R began to retch. Very odd behaviour for a corpse. I had never seen a dead body do that before and I had watched my dad reap more than a thousand souls. Never once had one of them retched. I didn't think it was a good sign. In fact, I was pretty sure it meant that something was going disastrously wrong with my reap.

I removed my hand quickly. For a second, it looked like a dark shadow clung to it. It had to be an illusion created by the dying flashlight. Clueless about what to do, I sat frozen in place.

The body retched harder and then it sneezed. Black smoke spewed out of the nose and hung in the air like super dense fog, connected to the nostrils by spaghetti-like tendrils of inky blackness.

I was gaping at the cloud, the likes of which I had never seen or even heard about, when it began to churn as if a nest of snakes writhed inside it, or as if it was alive somehow. Even more alarming, as if things weren't already plenty alarming enough, the body began to shake with a wracking cough. Tendrils of slimy blackness spewed out of the mouth. They rose as if magnetically drawn toward the squirmy black cloud. Somehow, the evil was escaping even though I hadn't managed to reap the soul. I knew such a thing was impossible, yet it was happening right in front of me.

In a panic, I did the only thing I could think of. I opened the vial of Devil's Ash and threw the contents over the black cloud and Male R's face, shouting the *Corpus Delecti* chant to anchor the evil in the body.

If I'd had more Devil's Ash, it might have sent the evil cloud back into the body, but I didn't, so it didn't. At least the ash stopped the rising black tendrils. They snapped back into Male R's mouth as if he was sucking up spaghetti noodles. The black cloud, however, did not go back into the body. It floated toward me, roiling madly inside. A rank odor filled the air, as if the cloud was farting rotten eggs. Black tendrils reached out for me, rather like elongated skeleton's fingers, if the bones were blacker than the night.

I didn't want the noxious thing anywhere near me. I flung a handful of salt into the center of the cloud while shouting the chant to repel evil. At least I knew that one by heart. My dad had made sure of that.

The dark cloud backed off, but it still didn't go back into the body, and I didn't know what to do. I honestly didn't have a clue. I had somehow freed a virtual monster and I had no net to capture it. When it came at me again, I grabbed up the fanny pack and hurtled across the field, aiming directly for the van. Maybe I could lure it to follow me all the way back to my dad. He would know what to do, if he had sobered up by now. I prayed that he had. The way things were going lately, his drinking was going to be the death of me.

At the edge of the field, I tripped over what was probably the remnant of an old fieldstone wall. It was as hard as one would expect rock to be. I landed on something equally hard and kind of sharp. For a heartbeat in time, the world transformed into a black swirling void of nothingness. Then even that was faded away.

# 6. Night of the Evil Cannonball

Reality came roaring back in a blast of pain that surged through my body like a tsunami. After a bit of screaming and writhing, I staggered to my feet. I dropped back to my knees when I couldn't even stand up. I tried to inhale through the pain and caught a whiff of rotten egg farts. It was motivation enough for me to find my feet and stumble forward. There was no time to check if my injury was life threatening, which it didn't seem to be. It just hurt like hell.

I limped as fast as I could toward the van with no idea how close the cloud of evil was in the darkness. I climbed in and shouted, "Home, James!" at the voice-activated GPS. I screeched away with the speed of a drag-racer. The van was on two wheels when it rounded the corner of the first left turn James told me to make, in his sedate British voice.

"You wouldn't be so calm if you were being chased by escaped evil," I snapped at him. He told me to turn left again, onto Oakley Road. Oakley Road had streetlights. As soon as I was on the lit street, I slowed down and took a good look in the rearview mirror. I didn't see a slimy black cloud chasing me, but I kind of hoped it was. I needed to lure it to my dad.

Blood was trickling down my leg, wetting the gas pedal and dripping onto the carpet. I could smell the coppery tang and for some reason, my mouth watered. I felt disoriented and struggled to stay alert and on the road as I automatically followed James' directions until I knew how to get home on my own.

The Elvis-mobile was parked in the driveway. I was so relieved to know my dad was home that I skidded to a stop behind it with a loud screech of tires, almost crashing into the Cadillac.

Scanning for evil black clouds, I practically fell out of the van. I should have been scanning for people instead. There was a small crowd on the lawn between my house and Adrian's house. They were standing in the shadowy border area marked by the white picket fence where little light from either house reached.

"Elvis, there you are." My dad hurried toward me. He was followed by Adrian, Adrian's parents, and one stranger, a woman who could only be Kendra. She looked like an elementary school teacher, a nice one.

"What happened?" Mrs. Lyon gasped.

"Huh?" My adrenaline rush was wearing off and I felt so faint, I staggered.

"Your leg is bleeding, a lot," my dad said, reaching me first. He looked at my face. "And your nose."

I hadn't hit my nose, I didn't think, so I didn't know why it would be bleeding. I licked my upper lip and tasted warm salty blood. Before I could lick more blood, my dad pulled a hankie out of his pocket and pressed it over my nose, saying, "Hold that."

I did and leaned against him for support. He smelled strongly of booze, but at least he seemed to have sobered up enough to be capable of dealing with a crisis. "Big, big problem," I whispered while his ear was close. "Black cloud of murderous canni ... canni'bal evil 'scaped ... may have followed me home." My mouth wasn't working as well as usual and I was slurring as if I had been the one imbibing too freely, rather than my dad.

"An evil cannonball followed you home?" he murmured.

"No, a ... a - " I had no chance to say more.

Mrs. Lyon put a hand on my shoulder and gave it a comforting squeeze. "You need to sit down, Elvis. Let's get you inside and have a look at that leg."

"Yes, inside is a very good idea," my dad agreed. "Linda, do you have a first aid kit? I'm a bit short on medical supplies."

Mrs. Lyon nodded. "I'll fetch it." Mr. Lyon went with her. Adrian made to follow them until my dad said, "Adrian, want to give me a hand getting Elvis inside? I don't think she should be putting any pressure on that leg."

"Uh, sure." Adrian moved to my other side. Together, they helped me up the porch stairs, supporting most of my weight. Kendra held the door into the kitchen ajar. She hadn't said a word yet. I wondered if my dad had spilled the beans about our unusual family business, when his tongue had been loosened by alcohol.

Being so close to Adrian almost made me forget my painfully throbbing leg, and the massive pressure headache that was blossoming behind my eyes. Touching his skin awoke a craving inside me that was almost more than I could bear. I leaned in his direction rather than my dad's and felt bizarrely hungry for Adrian. My heart had always been hungry for him, but this was more like a physical starvation. I wanted to taste him. Devour him. Eat him up. Sink my teeth deep into his sweet flesh.

"Oh no," gasped the part of me that hadn't yet been smothered by black evil. "Dad, something is very wrong. It's ... it's here."

"I thought I smelled sulfur. Adrian, put her in the chair, I have to get something." My dad ran, literally ran, in the direction of his office.

45

Adrian assisted me toward a chair and I was mortified when the part of me that had succumbed to black evil nuzzled his neck and licked him. My teeth nibbled hungrily, biting into his skin. It must have hurt him, because he jerked away, looking shocked. We had reached the chair anyway and while he didn't shove me into it, he did sit me down with force.

"Ouch," I cried when his leg banged into mine.

"Sorry." He backed away quickly and from the way he was eyeing me, I might have been a two-headed alien monster.

I hadn't sprouted another head or alien antennae, but I was a monster. I was possessed by inhuman, perverted evil. It was spreading like poison now that it wasn't hunkering down inside me. It was trying to take me over completely, and it was winning. "You better go, Adrian," I said, truly afraid of what I might do. He was the last person I wanted in range if my head started spinning in circles, complete with projectile vomiting.

"Okay, uh, feel better." He left so quickly, I would have been insulted if I wasn't so relieved. I was starting to sweat in terror. My sweat smelled like rotten eggs. The saliva in my mouth tasted like rancid raw meat.

"Dad!" I screamed. "Where are you?"

He shouted back, something garbled about searching for a pail or a grail, or maybe a nail. I really hoped it wasn't a nail.

Kendra stayed near the wall, well back. I had forgotten she was even there. She looked terrified. I sniffed, sure I could smell some trace of my mother in the air. "You're Kendra?" I drawled in a voice that wasn't quite my own.

"Yes. And you're Elvis. I had hoped to meet you under better circumstances," she said politely.

I laughed, and not in any good way. "Do you know what my dad does?" I asked, feeling the twisted smirk that reshaped my mouth, yet unable to control my own muscles now.

"I do. He told me tonight when this … emergency arose and he needed a drive home. Although, I have to admit, I didn't realize that being a … a reaper was such a risky affair."

I rose and the pain in my leg felt good. I liked it. I stepped closer to Kendra, sniffing. "Why do I smell my mother on you?"

She edged toward the door. "I'll let your father explain. Adam, hurry please!" she shouted at the same moment that someone rapped on the door. They opened it themselves, as if they were expected, and I suppose they were.

Mrs. Lyon entered with the first aid kit and frowned at me. "Elvis, I don't think you should be walking around on that leg. It's still bleeding quite a bit. It's going to need stitches."

Kendra proved that she was a cool-headed customer when she took the first aid kit, saying, "Thank you so much, Linda. Elvis isn't quite herself at the moment. I think she hit her head and knocked herself senseless. We're going to take her to the hospital, but I'll put a pressure bandage on her leg first, so she

46

doesn't lose too much blood." While she talked, she ushered Mrs. Lyon out the door. They shared a few quiet words before Kendra closed it. I used that moment to open a drawer and remove something beautifully and wickedly sharp.

Kendra faced me down, eyes fixed on the long carving knife I held in my hand. It felt so right. It belonged there. I took a step toward her, quite unable to stop myself. My body and most of my brain had been hijacked. Worse yet, my mouth was trying to speak a phrase in 'the tongue of the gods' It was a phrase I wasn't familiar with, but, given the level of twisted anticipation my possessor was feeling, I was pretty sure it would cause something grandly catastrophic to occur.

It was pushing hard, trying to force the words out of my mouth. Something was blocking that from happening. And it wasn't the tiny fraction of me that was still hanging on—I was putty in the evil's hands. No, something else was stopping my tongue from shaping the words. It was as if my tongue was paralyzed.

The two forces warred inside me. The battle took its toll on my body. My heart began to pound so hard, each beat felt like a hammer hitting my chest, shaking my ribcage until I thought bones might crack. My nose began to bleed again and my knees turned so weak, I staggered and almost fell.

Abruptly, the evil stopped trying to force the words out, as if it had admitted defeat. It refocused fully on Kendra while my body panted for air, trying to recover. She pressed against the door with the first aid kit held in front of her chest like a shield. "Stay back, Elvis. Please."

Evil doesn't listen to anyone but itself, no matter how polite they are. I stepped closer, anticipating, drooling, and yet pissed that the words I wanted to speak wouldn't come out.

My dad charged into the room and interrupted me. I swung around and raised the knife in one smooth motion. Before I could slash my dad's throat out, something hit me on the back of the head with enough force to rattle my brain. I'm pretty sure it was the first aid kit. The world turned into an inky whirlpool. It sucked me in and pulled me under.

I woke up strapped to one of our dining room chairs, the one with arms. It had been dragged into the kitchen. The evil was still ruling me. I wanted to carve up my dad and his slutty girlfriend. They were busy at the kitchen table, preparing something that smelled sickly sweet and putrid at the same time. My dad had his most antiquated potion book propped opened. I read the heading—*Eradico Malum.* Latin was almost my second language and I knew my dad was about to perform an exorcism on me. The evil squatting inside me didn't want that to happen.

I rotated my wrists, trying to free them. My bonds didn't budge. "Duct tape?" I snarled, making Kendra jump. "Really, Dad?"

"Very effective when dealing with an Evil Elvis," he said. If he was trying to lighten the mood, it wasn't possible. "So, Elvis, what have you gotten yourself into, or what have you gotten into yourself? I think that's the better question."

The evil had invasively read every thought in my brain and absorbed every emotion that lurked inside me, including my repressed resentment over how my mom had died. "Are you going to kill me, just like you killed Mom?" I screeched. And then I said much worse to my father, a vile stream of things that I would be ashamed of for the rest of my life.

When I finally shut up, he must have counted to ten, because about ten seconds passed before he said, "I found my phone in the van and checked the text, so you must be Carl Waring."

I managed to gasp, "Not Carl, other one. Male R," before the evil got control of my tongue again.

"I doubt that very much," my dad said, which made no sense to me at that moment. "Elvis is going to tell me all about you once I get your taint out of her."

"Can't be done without killing me," my mouth said, and the evil believed it was the truth.

"Wrong. Very very wrong." My dad ground some powder in an ancient mortar with a charmed pestle. It crunched sharply, like glass. He added it to a larger stone bowl and stirred, speaking an incantation I had never heard. Next, he ground up a small bone. It went into the bowl, too, with a different incantation to grant it power.

"What are you making?" I demanded, squirming uselessly. There was no escaping the duct tape.

"I'll teach you this little ritual once you are yourself again, Elvis. It's one hundred percent effective for eradicating evil that is in possession of a living soul. Separates the good and evil, forces the evil to rise like oil on water." He struck a match and tossed it into the mortar. The ingredients caught fire with a hot whoosh. While they burned, he propped another old tome opened beside me, so he could see the chant on the page.

I scanned the first line. It read '*Adepto de tenebris macula, revertaris in terram de qua venisti*'. Translated into English, it said something like, 'get out dark stain, return to the earth from whence you have come'.

Another brand new chant. There was so much I didn't know.

The fire in the mortar bowl died, leaving only ash behind.

"Gravy baster," my dad said, holding out a hand. Kendra slapped it into his palm like a surgical nurse. He squeezed the bulb and stuck the nose end into the ash in the stone bowl. When he released the bulb, a whole lot of the fine powder was sucked up into the basting tube.

"This will be the messy part," he warned Kendra, approaching me with the gravy baster.

I spat in my dad's face and the tiny bit of me that was still me cringed. He wiped his face with a paper towel. "I raised Elvis better than that. Say goodbye to my daughter, you revolting leech."

I clamped my lips and teeth together and glared at him in challenge. He sighed. "Kendra, I'm going to need a third hand, I'm afraid."

She moved closer with obvious reluctance. I spat on her, too.

After she cleaned up, my dad circled behind me and wrapped his arm around my neck in a headlock. "Plug her nose," he said through gritted teeth.

Kendra tried to latch onto my nose. I tried to bite her. My dad tightened the headlock and I began to feel faint from lack of air. Kendra got a hold of my nose and plugged it. It didn't take more than a few seconds before I was completely out of air. I cracked my lips to drag in a breath, keeping my teeth clamped together.

My dad cursed and tightened his arm, until I was half-strangled and the world began to fade away. In the throes of passing out, I must have relaxed my clenched teeth. He was quick to jam the turkey baster down my throat and squeeze the bulb.

Desperate for air, I inhaled the awful ash deep into my lungs. If I had inhaled molten lava, it would have hurt less. I screamed and choked, convinced I was dying, especially when I gagged on something rising up in my throat— something that was too big to fit.

"Hold the book up so I can see it," my dad said.

Kendra did. He began chanting the incantation and refilled the turkey baster. I shook my head wildly, gasping, "No, no." I was already suffocating, I didn't need more ash clogging up my tortured lungs. My dad was merciless and dosed me again, chanting the entire time. I screamed with abandon. I coughed up blood and savoured the taste.

The thing inside me ascended with agonizing sloth. It felt like a big fat boa constrictor was wriggling up my throat, taking its time about it. I wretched and dry heaved in the grossest way until my mouth filled with something that wasn't solid or liquid or gas. It was some abominable combination of all three, topped with a generous portion of foamy slime.

The revolting substance finally percolated high enough to start bubbling out of my mouth and nose. My dad picked up a veil that was yellow with age, blood-stained and liberally coated with Devil's Ash. At least it wasn't a nail. He dropped it over my head and wrapped it tight around my face. The evil that was flowing out of me had no choice but to pass through the veil, which transformed it. It rained down as harmless dirt, returning to the earth from whence it had come.

I kept spewing the gross stuff and there was a vulgar amount of it. My eyes stung and my ears rang and I knew I was dying because I could barely breathe, yet still it kept bubbling out of me.

Mercifully, I must have passed out. When I woke up, my dad was pulling duct tape off my wrists. My little arm hairs were going with it, but I was too weak to protest. I felt like a skinned pelt, scraped raw and empty inside. On the bright side, I didn't want to stab or bite anyone, so I wasn't Evil Elvis anymore.

"It's all gone?" I whispered. My throat was so raw, it felt sandpapered. I could taste blood, which no longer tasted delicious to me. Quite the opposite. Every breath was agony, as if I was locked into one of those archaic torture coffins lined with spikes, and every inhalation caused them to puncture through my chest.

"It's gone, Baby. Sorry about the process, but it was the only way." My dad smoothed sweat dampened hair off my face and scrutinized me. Kendra handed him a wet facecloth and he washed blood off my face and asked, "Are you okay?"

I shook my head and started to cry for the third time that night, or maybe it was the fourth. Crying was a very bad idea given the condition of my throat, but I couldn't stop.

"You'll feel better soon," he said gruffly. I didn't believe him for a second. "Let's get you to bed now." He picked me up, and I was no small burden. I tried to remember the last time he had carried me around. I think it was when I was about ten, when I couldn't stop crying because Adrian had stopped being my friend.

My dad made it up the stairs and lowered me onto my bed. "Sleep," he said, tucking a blanket over me when I started shaking.

"Daddy, the second body … still has evil in it, not anchored yet. In field. Ran out of Devil's Ash." I felt I should say more, because there was so much more to explain.

He shook his head and said, "Hush. I'll take care of it. I have the information on my phone. You just sleep now." He kissed my forehead. "We'll talk when you're feeling better."

I clutched his shirt and held on, wanting him close. "Sorry I called you names and spit on you." I was still leaking tears.

"That wasn't you, Elvis."

"I don't really think you killed Mom," I blubbered.

His face tightened. "We'll talk when you're feeling better."

"But - "

Kendra tiptoed in carrying a glass of water. I released my dad's shirt. I apologized for spitting on her, too. I drained the glass that my dad had to hold for me and I must have passed out again.

I prefer not to remember the next couple of days. Let's just say I got better, but I'll never be able to look at a gravy baster again. And I no longer like duct tape, no matter how handy it is. At least my dad had stitched up my leg while I was unconscious. He's pretty handy with a needle and I ended up with a neatly sutured white line that would probably leave only a little scar.

After I had missed three days of school, I had a most unexpected visitor. I was still bedridden, propped up on pillows, watching a sappy movie on my laptop computer, when my dad shouted up the stairs that I was about to have company. Adrian appeared in my doorway and he looked as wonderful as he always did to me. The humidity had made his hair curl and he'd been catching some sun. I felt as pale as a vampire in comparison.

"Hi, Elvis. How are you feeling?" He didn't move past the threshold.

"Okay. You can come in, Adrian." My voice was still husky, maybe it even sounded sexy. I wanted to add 'I don't bite', except it wasn't strictly true. He entered carrying a manila envelope. "Homework?" I guessed.

"Homework and a couple of corrected assignments. With exams coming up, you'll need them. I told Rushburn I would make sure you got them."

It explained why he had braved the trip next door. "That was thoughtful of you. Thanks," I said politely, even though I did not feel up to tackling homework yet. "Take a seat." I waved a hand in the direction of the desk and closed my laptop.

He perched on the edge of my desk chair and rolled close enough to hand me the envelope. "You look like hell," he blurted, as if he couldn't stop the words.

"Concussion," I said, which was more or less true, and accounted for why I was still swooning in bed like the heroine of a historic romance novel.

His eyebrows lowered anxiously. "How did you get hurt?"

"I don't remember," I lied. "I don't remember what happened or how I got home. All I remember is waking up here, in bed." The best part of my lie was that I didn't have to apologize for licking and biting him. "My dad said I was knocked senseless, and I guess I was."

"You're lucky you made it home."

"Yes." I was luckier than he knew.

"How's the leg?" He glanced at where my leg was hidden beneath the covers.

"All stitched back together," I said.

"You told me you weren't going to drive anywhere that night." He shifted on the chair, less perched and more sitting.

I shrugged, a bit shamefaced. "I said I didn't have to pick up my dad. I had to go somewhere else, to do with the case he was working on, so I didn't *really* lie. What's been happening at school?"

He accepted the change of subject. "Carrie said she would call you. And Mark and Bianca broke up today." Mark was a friend of Adrian's, and Bianca was a friend of mine.

"Again? That's like the tenth time this year."

"At least. Do you think they'll get back together again?" He grinned.

I grinned back. "They're probably already back together."

"Ya." Adrian relaxed enough to lean back in the chair, and we chatted for a few minutes. It was nice to have company, especially Adrian's company. And he seemed more at ease around me than he usually did. Maybe he felt safe because I was bedridden, and I think he was relieved that my inappropriate advances toward him weren't even a memory, except to him.

Before he left, he asked when I would be returning to school.

"I'll try to make it tomorrow, if I can. I have another assignment due, and with exams coming up, I don't want to miss more days." I was still prone to exhaustion and closed my eyes for a moment when my eyelids felt too heavy to hold up. When I opened them, Adrian was studying my face rather intently, as if it was a jigsaw puzzle that was missing a few key pieces.

"What? I'm not drooling, am I?" I asked.

"I'm sure you never drool, Elvis." He gave a funny little half smile and said, "I'm driving my mom's car to school tomorrow. If you want a ride, I can take you." He must have been feeling really sorry for me. He'd never offered me a ride before, not that he usually drove.

"Sure. Thanks," I said.

He rose. "I'll pick you up at eight."

Eight was a lot earlier than I usually went to school, but Adrian was a more academic type than me. "I'll just walk next door," I said.

"Okay, see you then." With a little wave, he left.

I fell asleep as soon as I was alone and slept right through to the morning. I probably had a dreamy smile stuck on my face for the whole fourteen hours.

# 7. The Reaper Commandments

I limped into the kitchen the next morning and my dad was already there, reading the newspaper and cutting up the newspaper. His hobby is scrapbooking and he's made a decorative album that showcases his collection of obituaries. In it, he's pasted a scanned and printed copy of an obituary for every soul he's reaped, since he took up scrapbooking. And for those souls who did not get an obituary in the newspaper, my dad wrote one himself.

When I showed no interest in sharing his hobby, he started an album for me, of my reaps. Now he works on two reaper albums, as well as my mother's memorial scrapbook and his Elvis scrapbook. I think the scrapbooking is good for my dad in a therapeutic sort of way. He gets so into it, he forgets to drink.

Coffee was brewed and I really needed one. I poured half a cup and added an equal amount of milk. A couple of sugars sweetened it and I gulped it down.

He arched an eyebrow and asked, "Where do you think you're going?"

"School. I can't miss another day."

My dad raised his empty cup in my direction and I refilled it.

"Adrian is going to drive today and he offered me a ride," I added.

"Ah," he said, the one tiny word filled with significance. I'm almost one hundred percent positive that my dad knows I'm in love with Adrian, even though I've never told him so.

"Look at this, Elvis. It's for your book." He handed me a lengthy obituary that he had already cut out, adding, "I think I'll reprint it on lavender paper and make a flowery border. Old ladies always like lavender." My dad has a good eye for colour, and he makes the obituaries as decorative as he can.

"The three sisters," I said with a smile. Each of their photographs had been taken when they were much younger. They had all been attractive before time and gravity ravaged their bodies. I skimmed through the lengthy text. All three were predeceased by their husbands. "It's a very nice tribute, Dad. Was there one for Carl? Or the … the other man?" Even referring to Male R left a foul taste in my mouth.

I was on a first name basis with death, yet the condition of Carl's body had really upset me. I was doing my best to forget what I had seen, yet I hadn't been successful. I guess I had been traumatized by the botched reap, and the being possessed. The exorcism had been no bed of rose petals, either. Maybe I needed therapy, if such a thing as a reaper therapist exists.

"No obits yet," my dad said. "The police are still investigating. They haven't released the bodies."

"How come the murderer wasn't named in the text you got from your boss?"

He didn't answer my question directly. He said, "We have some things we need to discuss when you're feeling up to it. How about this weekend?"

I hadn't yet been debriefed for my botched reap. I also had a few pressing questions of my own. And my comments about my dad killing my mom lay between us like a line drawn in the sand. "This weekend works for me." I handed my dad the obituary.

He laid it down on the table. "Don't overdo it today, Elvis."

I pulled a face. "School is almost as boring as lounging in bed, so I won't be overdoing anything."

"If you need a ride home, phone me. As long as I'm not working, I'll come get you." He did the finger/gun pointing thing he liked to do, aiming at me.

"Thanks, Dad." I picked up my pack and went out the door. Adrian was waiting beside his mom's car even though I was punctual to the minute. Being a reaper, I have the utmost respect for the almighty clock.

He held the car door for me as if I was an invalid, or maybe he was simply being a gentleman. I settled into the comfy seat and allowed myself an indulgent little daydream in which Adrian was my boyfriend, driving me to school.

"Seatbelt," he reminded me when I was too busy fantasizing to remember to strap myself in.

I clicked the belt in place and wished the drive to school was a five day roadtrip, not a five minute hop. In no time, we were pulling into the parking lot. Adrian was early enough to get a decent parking spot so we didn't have far to walk to the front door, which was a good thing. My legs lacked any sort of stamina and walking pulled on my stitches. I was already having some serious doubts that I would last through the day.

Adrian held the front door for me and said, "Meet me at the car after school and I'll take you home."

"Okay." Then and there, I vowed that I would survive the whole day.

We went our separate ways. I found Carrie and Bianca at their lockers. They were BFF's and I was included in their small circle of friends. I think they found me interesting, like an oddity. It was hard for me to have a BFF and always had been. I had learned early on that inviting little girls over to my house to play resulted in them never wanting to come back and/or crying hysterically. The early teen years had been no better. Nothing about me fit the teenage mold, so I was teased and gossiped about. I was too tall, and being called Elvis and having an Elvis-style dad had resulted in a whole lot of ridicule. Not by choice, I could be something of a loner.

54

Having a boyfriend had proved to be even more problematic than having a BFF, and that was even before I ran over Blake. The few short relationships I'd shared had been tricky to manage. It's hard to be close with someone when you can't talk about most of your life, and you have to lie all the time and cover things up—things like reaping souls and touching more dead bodies than an overworked mortician. I couldn't even talk about my future hopes and dreams. I would be a reaper. Death was a major part of my life and always would be. I just had to keep it a secret.

Carrie and Bianca fussed over me, which was nice. After I told them I was fine and didn't remember my accident, Bianca wanted to talk about her breakup, which was still in effect. Carrie had probably heard the story too many times to count, and looked thoroughly bored. Bianca claimed to be truly heartbroken, but I don't think she was. She was wearing eye makeup, proving she wasn't crying all over the place. Maybe I'd even shed more tears than her lately.

It felt good to be back in my usual routine. I was content to be surrounded by the soap opera that was high school. It helped me to distance myself from the nightmare of being possessed.

The day was a bit of a blur, but I caught up on all that I needed to. And I picked up my exam schedule. It was both good and bad. Most of my exams were at the beginning of exam week, which meant my summer holidays would start a few days earlier than expected. On the down side, I wouldn't have enough time to study. I wouldn't have time to do anything but study madly if I wanted to graduate. And I did, even though I wouldn't be going on to a higher education, not in the traditional sense anyway.

I was scowling at my exam schedule when Adrian found me leaning against the trunk of his mom's car, soaking up some sunshine while waiting for him. "Is it that bad?" he asked, recognizing the page for what it was.

I handed it to him.

He scanned it. "At least you'll finish early since all your exams are on the first three days. Not much time to study, though." He handed it back.

"How's your exam schedule?" I asked.

"A lot better than yours." He pulled it out of his pack and I took a look. His exams were nicely spread out, although he did have one on the very last day. I memorized his schedule in case I wanted to accidentally bump into him at school.

"Trade you," I said.

"Not a chance." He returned his schedule to his pack and we got in the car.

I leaned my head back against the seat, ready for a nap. Adrian glanced my way and actually smiled at me before he started the engine. I wanted to lean over and nibble on his neck again, not because I was evil, but because I was in love.

"Are you still planning to work with your dad as soon as school is finished?" he asked, pulling out of the lot with the exodus of student cars.

"Ya, he's always wanted me to work with him. You know he's been taking me on cases since I was little. I've been on more stakeouts than I can remember, and now that I'm going to graduate, he's getting serious about me following in his footsteps." I'm pretty sure the entire Lyon clan has bought into my dad's cover story, that he's a private detective who moonlights as an Elvis impersonator.

Adrian glanced over again and our eyes met for a charged moment, at least it felt electrically charged to me, before he focused on the road again. "Is that what you want to do? Follow in your dad's footsteps?"

I could have said yes, but I wanted to tell him at least one thing that was true. I hated lying to Adrian more than I hated lying to anyone else. I gave a little shrug. "Not really, but he's been going through a rough patch since my mom died. A really rough patch. I don't want to upset him, so I'll let him train me."

"That's really considerate of you, Elvis, but maybe you should put yourself first. I mean, I don't think it's right that he calls you for help when he's too drunk to drive, or do his job."

I kept my eyes on the road. "He's my dad, Adrian. I'm sure he'll get his drinking under control soon. He's only been really bad since my mom died." It was time to change the subject. I asked Adrian about his future plans, even though I already knew what they were.

For the last couple of minutes of the drive, Adrian talked about how much he was looking forward to starting university. He was going into environmental engineering, and I have to admit that I was envious. Listening to him talk, I wished that I was starting university, too. At least Adrian wasn't going away to school. I'm pretty sure if he had moved away, it would have shattered my heart into so many jagged little pieces, like Humpty Dumpty, nobody could ever put them back together again. Lucky for me and my heart, the local university had a great program, and it was a lot more affordable for him to live at home while he was going to school. His parents did okay, but they weren't rich, and he was their third kid to attend university.

He dropped me off in front of my house and drove away, so I knew he had made a special trip just to bring me home. It made me feel all warm and fuzzy inside, and hopeful that maybe we could be friends again, or maybe we could be so much more than that.

\*\*\*

Friday night, my dad and I had our talk over takeout Chinese. He ordered all my favourite dishes, so I think he was still feeling bad about the exorcism. It was such a beautiful night, we ate on the porch. He brought out his reaper manual, a notebook and a pen, so I figured our dinner fell under the heading of Official Reaper Business. Or ORB, as I called it. Maybe he would even claim the special meal as a business expense.

56

In-between savoury bites of shrimp and pork, I described every detail of my botched reap. My dad didn't comment about Carl's missing soul. In fact, none of what I reported seemed to unsettle him, not until I mentioned that the evil had escaped from Male R before I had reaped his soul, and that I had never actually completed the reaping of his soul.

He put down his chopsticks. "No, you must be mistaken, Elvis. There was no soul in … the second body. All I could do was complete the ritual to anchor whatever evil remained inside it, although there wasn't any to speak of. It must have all come out in the black cloud that possessed you."

"No, it didn't. I saw some of it go back in the body when I threw Devil's Ash over it. The whole body was still shaking so there was definitely evil inside it, and not just a little." I swallowed a bite of eggroll that suddenly felt too big to go down my tight throat. "It's weird that you couldn't sense the evil or the soul, but I didn't reap it. You know I'm really good at sensing souls. It was still in there when I had to … leave." I was feeling distinctly queasy to think of a soul being trapped that long in a body. Yet, if that was the case, Male R should be roaming the countryside as a flesh-eating zombie, just like in the movies.

My father shook his head decisively. "After what happened to you, I checked … the body out thoroughly. There was no soul inside. I'm one hundred percent certain."

My dad kept faltering before he mentioned the body and I recalled that Male R had looked familiar to me. And he was from my dad's generation, not mine. "Did you know him?" I asked, following a hunch.

He topped up his glass of red wine and took a slow sip before he said, "Yes, I knew him." The bleakness of his tone chilled me to the bone.

"Who was he, Dad?"

"I didn't want to tell you this, Baby, but I suppose you have to know. He was my replacement that night, the reaper from Senville. Scott Frost."

The staggering news hit me like a boxer's knockout punch. Of course I recognized the name. He and my dad were always talking on the phone, consulting each other about unusual cases. I had even met him in passing a few years back, when I was shopping with my dad. "Scott?" I gasped. "That's what Male R means? Male reaper?"

He nodded once.

I couldn't help but think that if my dad hadn't taken the night off, he might be the deceased Male R. It was my turn to put down my chopsticks, so unsettled inside, my hand felt numb. "It could have been you," I said.

"Scott was capable and experienced, so yes, whatever happened to him probably would have happened to me," he said gravely.

I got up and hugged him, and kept holding onto him, scared to let go. "It was almost you."

"Hey, it wasn't me. I'm still here, Baby." He patted my arm. "I'm still here." I didn't hear his sigh, but I felt it when his chest deflated.

I sat down again, even my legs were feeling shaky. And another detail clicked into place. "That's why I couldn't sense or release Carl's soul. It had already been reaped by Scott."

"I believe so." He tapped his pen on his notebook.

"But he must not have completed the reap, and that's why we got the text about Carl Waring."

"Looks that way."

"But … Scott wasn't evil, was he?" I tried to read his expression.

"No, he was one heck of a nice guy. Salt of the earth. I'm going to miss him." He swallowed hard.

"I'm so sorry, Dad."

He nodded, a tight jerk of his head, keeping all his emotions bottled up. That's what reapers did. That's what reapers had to do.

"But … so where did all that evil come from?" I asked.

"My guess would be the body he reaped, Carl Waring's body. Carl must have been a very bad man, and something must have happened after Scott released the soul, before he could anchor the evil, and it got into him. Unfortunately, that's not the worst of it," he said in a warning tone.

"Then what is?" I asked.

"I haven't wanted to worry you, Elvis - "

"Well, I'm worried now. Spill it, Dad." I leaned forward, to better read his face in the subdued light.

He cleared his throat roughly. "Scott called me last week. He was concerned about some mysterious deaths in his territory. No discernable cause of death, no evil in the bodies. Very weird stuff."

I shivered. "Were the souls still present and accounted for?"

"Ya, they were still in the bodies." Dad tapped his pen harder, in frustration.

"How many deaths?" I bit my lip.

"Two that he'd noticed. He was calling other reapers to see if the same sort of thing was happening in their territories."

"And have any mysterious deaths happened in your territory?" I demanded, in case my dad was still thinking of keeping me in the dark.

He shook his head. "Not until Scott's own death."

"And you didn't figure out any cause of death for Scott? Because it wasn't listed in the text." Even though we weren't police detectives, we always liked to know cause of death. Maybe it was even a factor in this highly disturbing case. I recalled my own lack of light at the scene and made a mental note to put extra batteries in the van, and maybe a second flashlight.

"There were no signs of trauma on his body, and after getting that phone call from him, I did look." My dad stared off into space and a frown line as deep as a knife wound appeared between his eyebrows. "There were big boot prints around the bodies. Not Carl's, and not Scott's of course." A reaper leaves no trace of their presence when they're on the job. My sandal prints wouldn't have shown up either.

I frowned, too. "Maybe Scott's killer? Or Carl's killer? Or maybe the guy in boots killed them both."

"If Scott was killed by a man, then yes, maybe the guy in boots was his killer. I don't know who else would have been lurking around the bodies. Size thirteen feet, deep impression so he wasn't a lightweight, and wearing work boots or hiking boots, judging by the tread."

I wondered how close the owner of those boots had been to me when I had been trying to reap the souls. I hadn't noticed anyone in the vicinity, but I had been kind of distracted by the tragedy I was dealing with. Plus, I would have been invisible to prying eyes, since I was on the job.

I mulled things over, trying to imagine how the nightmare scene could have played out. "So Carl Waring dies in a field. Scott is summoned to reap the soul. Something goes wrong before he can anchor the evil. It manages to infect Scott and take him over like it took me over. That would explain why he was snacking on his client."

My dad winced at my blunt phrasing. "It could have played out another way. Maybe Bigfoot kills Carl, mutilates him, and … worse. Scott is summoned to reap Carl, and finds the young man's body already in that condition. Maybe Bigfoot is still there, still … partaking. Perhaps the sight is more than Scott can bear and he tries to stop Bigfoot. Trying to stop Bigfoot could have made him visible, and vulnerable. He ends up getting killed."

"And the blood on his mouth?" I asked

Dad shrugged. "Maybe he got punched by Bigfoot."

I suppose it was possible. A cut lip could bleed quite profusely. "But how does Bigfoot kill Scott without leaving a mark on his body?" I asked, with skepticism.

"Aye, there's the rub, isn't it? I don't know." He dashed a hand through the crested wave of his hair.

I nibbled on my lip. "Do you think the evil was able to get out and infect me, because it wasn't Scott's evil, so his soul couldn't hold it at bay? Or maybe because the evil was so strong, it kind of overpowered his soul?"

My dad shrugged. "I don't know, Elvis. A lot of things simply don't add up. Maybe Bigfoot didn't even play a part."

"Maybe he didn't," I agreed. Of the hundred questions in my head, one begged asking more than all the rest. "So, where did Scott's soul go?"

He rubbed his temple as if he was getting a headache. "You said the evil came out of his mouth, and that Scott's corpse was animate?"

"Nose and mouth. And it wasn't animate exactly, not like he'd turned into a zombie—I mean problem client—or anything. It was more like the evil was strong enough to force its way out, making the body cough and sneeze in the process. Like the corpse had a bad cold."

My dad frowned, making his face look old before its time. "I've never even heard about anything remotely like this. The good news is that you did nothing wrong, nothing that could have or should have let the evil escape." He knew that from my debriefing. "Where is the soul? That's the million dollar question, Elvis. I'm going to research this and see if there are any similar cases in the family journals." He closed his book as if we were done.

"Dad, there's more."

"More?"

"Not about the reap, but about … when I was possessed." I hated even mentioning the subject. I was so deeply ashamed of the things I had said and done.

My dad simply waited for me to continue.

"When the evil was controlling me, it tried to make me speak a phrase in the forbidden language, in 'the tongue of the gods'."

His eyes widened in shock. "Which phrase?"

I shrugged. "That's the odd thing. It was a phrase I didn't know. So how could the evil know it?"

"From Scott," my dad said, without missing a beat.

"Oh, right." The evil had known all my thoughts, so of course it would have known Scott's, and he knew so much more than I did about the reaper trade.

"Do you remember any of the words?"

I thought hard, recalling the battle that had waged between me and my possessor. "I don't, since I never spoke them. But the evil was trying so hard to make me say the words, and I couldn't, really couldn't. The evil could force me to do anything else, even … even kill you. But it couldn't force me to speak those words. Something was blocking them from coming out. And not speaking them, it felt like it almost killed me."

My dad reached out and squeezed my hand too tight. "That was one hell of a night, wasn't it?"

I snorted. "Hell being the operative word."

"I wonder if the evil tried too hard to make Scott speak those same words, and that's what killed him," Dad said.

"Oh. Yes, maybe." It was a terrifying possibility.

"If you remember any of the words, let me know." He opened his book back up and jotted down a short note. "I think I'll take a little trip down to the morgue to have another look at Scott's remains. In the meantime, when a reap goes really wrong, there are a few standard damage control strategies you can employ to buy yourself some time."

I informed my dad that I had to study all weekend for my exams and that I didn't have time to study the reaper manual too, not until my exams were over. He left it at that for the time being. I knew that after I had graduated from high school, my reaper training would begin in earnest. I just hoped that I would be up to the task, and that I would get paid. I wasn't sure if my dad's boss dealt in

60

hard cash, and I doubted that any bank would cash a cheque signed by The-Powers-That-Be.

My dad went on to apologize for the shortage of Devil's Ash, which had been one of the factors in my reap going so dangerously wrong. He said he would keep two vials in his fanny pack from now on, and make sure they were refilled after every single reap. I agreed that it was a wise precaution.

He continued apologizing, sort of. "I deeply regret that you had to suffer through that possession. I'm just glad I knew how to deal with it. I'm going to teach you everything I know once you've taken the Reaper's Oath and been sworn in as a Reaper. For the time being, you won't do any more reaps without me."

I didn't argue. After my intimate contact with Carl's slimy evil, I wasn't in any hurry to reap without my dad guarding my back. I wasn't in any hurry to reap, period.

My dad glanced at his watch. He tossed back the rest of his wine. Before he could make a run for it, I blurted out, "Are you still dating Kendra?"

"Yes, although she's a bit skittish after the other night, and I can't really blame her. She saw the darkest side of reaping. And she feels bad about knocking you unconscious, although I keep telling her she didn't have a choice. She's worried that you're mad at her. You're not, are you?"

I pulled a face. "Of course not. I was going to slice and dice her and I spit on her. If anything, she should be mad at me."

Before I could bring up the topic we had avoided quite successfully so far—my appalling accusation that he had killed my mom, *All Shook Up* interrupted us. The other pressing question, about why Kendra smelled intrinsically like my mom, would also have to wait.

My dad glanced at the text. "I've got to go. It's a single reap. I'll see Kendra after. I won't be home until late. Good luck with the studying."

He hurried into the house and came out five minutes later wearing his trademark black and gold reaper jumpsuit. He was carrying an overnight bag, suggesting that he wouldn't be home at all that night. The fanny pack clipped around his waist looked fuller than usual, so he had probably already added the second vial of Devil's Ash, and maybe a few more supplies, just to be on the safe side.

"Later, Elvis." He ruffled my hair in passing as if I was five years old again. I didn't mind.

"Be careful, Dad." I had never worried about him when he was on the job before, but that had all changed.

He drove off in the van, the sound of the engine drowned out by *Don't Be Cruel* playing on full volume, my dad singing along, also on full volume.

After the music faded into the distance, the night seemed too quiet in a disquiet sort of way. The missing soul was really bothering me. If my dad was wrong and the soul was still inside Scott's body, it would feel like it was buried alive in hell. But my dad was rarely wrong about such things, although he had been drinking heavily that night, which certainly could have impaired his judgment.

The mystery of the missing evil was bothering me almost as much as the missing soul. If it had escaped Scott's body, it could be roaming around the city, helter-skelter, maybe in possession of some other hapless victim. The very possibility made the hair on the back of my neck stand up and shiver.

On the other side of the picket fence, Adrian's bedroom light was on. I guessed he was studying, as I should be. "Now, Elvis," I told myself. I cleared the table. While I was in the kitchen, I made an extra-strong instant coffee to take upstairs where my books were waiting.

# 8. One Hump or Two?

My dad didn't come home until Sunday afternoon, and then he barely had time to take a shower before his phone played *All Shook Up*.

I ate cereal for dinner. There was no time to waste on cooking, not that I could cook. I had two exams the next day and I studied late into the night. My dad came home around two. Even if I hadn't been awake, I would have heard him.

From the crashing and banging, it sounded like he knocked over a kitchen chair and fell down. I wasn't sure he would be able to get up again. I headed downstairs. The smell of liquor was overpowering and my dad was sprawled on the kitchen tiles. He wasn't even trying to stand. Two chairs had been toppled.

I righted them before I crouched beside him. "Hey, Dad."

"Elvis?" He blinked at me, red-eyed and bleary. His breath almost made me fall down, too.

"Yes, it's me. The daughter you named Elvis. Why are you in this condition?"

He sniffed. "Problems with Kendra. She broke up with me."

I didn't like talking to my dad when he was plastered, so I didn't ask for any details about the breakup, or how he had gotten home. Sometimes I was convinced that James the GPS drove him home, courtesy of my dad's omnipotent boss. "Want some help getting to bed?"

"I'm tired," he said.

"Do you want to sleep on the kitchen floor?"

He tried to shake his head and banged it into a chair leg. "Too hard, s'not comfy."

"Okay. Let's get you to bed then." I stood up and pulled on his arm.

Even with my help, he could barely find his feet. And when he did find them, he couldn't balance on them. I propped him against the counter and insisted he drink a big glass of water, before I draped his arm over my shoulder and escorted him upstairs. He fell on the top of his bed and started snoring before I could even stuff a pillow under his head or pull off his shoes. I did those things anyway, and removed his fanny pack. Nothing disturbed him. I added a blanket and said, "Sleep in, Dad. You're going to feel like hell's bitch tomorrow."

63

Back in my room, I turned off my computer and closed my books. I needed sleep more than I needed to cram any more useless historical dates into my brain. I was drifting off nicely when *All Shook Up* began to play. I waited for my dad to answer even though he was in no condition to do so, and all the wishful thinking in the world wasn't going to magically sober him up. *All Shook Up* just kept playing.

"Not now, not tonight!" I rolled out of bed and stomped down the hall. The phone was in the fanny pack. I wrestled it out and read the text.

I blinked, rubbed my eyes and read it again, convinced that I was having a nightmare. I mean, I had just been cozily falling asleep in my bed, right? So maybe I was still sleeping. It was silly, but I pinched myself hard. It hurt so I knew I was awake, yet I was still in the middle of a nightmare.

The soul to be reaped was Adrian Lyon's. The address of the reap was as familiar as my own, because it was right next door. "This can't be happening," I said to the phone, except it was. I was about to force my dad awake when I thought better of it.

Adrian wasn't dead yet and his death was listed as ROV, which means 'result of violence'. I have a pretty good imagination and I couldn't imagine what violence would be happening next door in my quiet neighbourhood, but I knew it could be prevented. I also knew the Reaper Commandments by heart. Rules for reapers to live by, like number three: Thou shall not reap a soul from the living. And number five: Thou shall not refuse a soul release. And number nine: Thou shall not steal from the dead.

And then there was Commandment Numero Uno: Thou shall not interfere in the natural course of death. But surely that first commandment didn't apply to Adrian's death.

Clutching the fanny pack and praying I wouldn't need it, I raced downstairs and dashed across the lawn toward the Lyon's house. I didn't even open the gate in the little white picket fence—I hurtled it like an Olympic track and field star.

Adrian's bedroom light was still on, as was the outside porch light. I ran up the steps and touched the side door that led into his kitchen. It unlocked for me, since I was a reaper on the job.

I stepped into the kitchen and paused. Thank heavens, I could sense no soul seeking release. I closed and locked the door behind me before I dashed upstairs, making no effort to be quiet. Since I was on official reaper business, I wouldn't be seen or heard.

I opened Adrian's door a couple of inches and peered into his room. The bedside lamp was on and he was asleep, blanket at half mast, covering him from the waist down. He had a book on his bare chest. It was rising and falling, so I knew he was breathing.

I wilted against the doorjamb, wondering if there had been some sort of soul mix-up, although I had never heard of such a thing happening. The-Powers-That-Be didn't make those kinds of mistakes.

I was still trying to calm down when I heard glass breaking on the main floor. A window pane maybe. It wasn't a loud noise, but Adrian turned over. The textbook slipped off his chest and landed on the floor with a thud. He sat up. Something creaked on the ground floor. Adrian cocked his head and shoved the blanket aside. He stood up, still drowsy with sleep, yet awake enough to investigate. He was only wearing boxers, but I was too afraid for his life to be distracted by so much smooth beautiful skin. Okay, I was distracted, and maybe a little disappointed that he wasn't wearing even less than that.

He reached for a pair of sweatpants. I eased his door shut and rushed headlong down the stairs ahead of him to investigate the situation. A scraping noise in the kitchen alerted me to the intruder's location. I veered that way and stopped dead just inside the room.

A very big man had broken in by shattering the glass window in the door. The light coming in from the porch illuminated his silhouette, moving stealthily across the room. He stopped and sniffed the air as if he was a dog. He swallowed wetly. I could sense the evil in him, and maybe even a whisper of a soul, which was odd because I'd never sensed the soul of a living breathing person before, or their evil. Only in death can a reaper sense such things. And I knew this man lived because I could hear his raspy breathing. Even though it was so dark that I couldn't see his face, something about him was disturbingly familiar to me in some intangible way.

A board creaked from the direction of the stairs. Adrian was tiptoeing downstairs to his death—if I did nothing, except I couldn't do nothing. I couldn't watch Adrian die any more than I could fly to the moon by flapping my arms and holding my breath. It simply wasn't possible. Fully aware that there would be serious repercussions, or reaper-cussions as my dad called them, I prepared to break the first of the Reaper Commandments and stop Adrian from dying violently before he had even started college.

My best advantage was that I was as invisible as the air. I scanned for something to stop the intruder, simply glad that there was enough light for me to see.

Mr. Lyon's bag of golf clubs was just inside the mud room, as if he had come in from a late game. I reached over and groped for the heaviest club. I slid it out, got a good grip and when the would-be murderer skulked by me, I swung it like a baseball bat. The big wooden club smashed him in the nose. I heard the crack of bone and he staggered back, but didn't go down. I swung again, catching him in the middle. He cursed under his breath and dropped to one knee.

"Who's there?" Adrian called, turning on the hall light. The intruder lurched to his feet and ran. I caught a fleeting glimpse of a tall muscular man in a black T-shirt, fleeing out through the door. He had a hand over his nose, and tucked into his belt, something metallic. I knew it wasn't a gun. I somehow sensed that it was a razor-sharp hunting knife, the kind my hand had itched to wield when I'd been Evil Elvis.

I froze, struck by an alarming thought—or revelation. I was still standing there like a slack-jawed statue when Adrian turned on the kitchen light. "Elvis?" he said, gaping at me.

I gasped. "You ... you can see me?"

"Of course I can see you. You're standing right there."

"Oh, I guess I am." I didn't know what else to say. Clearly, since there was no longer a soul to reap, I was no longer on official reaper business. I was fully visible. If I hadn't been dumbstruck by my revelation, I would have anticipated this and fled, just like Adrian's would-be killer.

Adrian stayed well back, as if he thought I was going to whack him over the head with his dad's golf club or something. The backdoor was swinging wide opened with its broken pane. Shards of glass littered the floor.

"It wasn't me," I said and hurriedly stuck the golf club back where it belonged.

"Then who broke in?" Adrian countered, very accusingly.

"A big man. I heard the breaking glass and ... and I followed him in. I hit him with the golf club and he ran away." It was the lamest story I had ever heard, and the best I could come up with on the spur of the moment. It was also more truth than lies, but Adrian didn't believe me for a second.

"Elvis, are you on drugs?" he asked pointblank.

"What? Of course not."

"Well, your eyes were pretty red when you came home all banged up the other night. And you were acting kind of crazy. And now you're breaking into my house in the middle of the night. Look, if you need help, if you need someone to talk to, there are counselors at school. I know it's been hard for you since your mom ... left."

"She didn't leave. She died. It's not the same thing at all." I had just saved Adrian's life and he was accusing me of breaking into his place and taking drugs. It made me furious. It wasn't the time or place to argue with him, but I couldn't help it. At least his parents were proving to be sound sleepers. They were sleeping through a whole lot of noise, and they would have slept through their son's murder. Except Adrian wasn't dead. He was alive.

In a heartbeat, I wasn't mad anymore. I was so filled with joy, Katherine's soul might have been revisiting me. Adrian was alive! I said, "Adrian, I didn't break in. It was a very evil man, not me. You should get an alarm for your house, so you'll be safe. I'm going home now, I have two exams tomorrow, I mean today. In a few hours. Just don't tell anyone I was here, please, but call the police, and make sure you have an alarm installed tomorrow. And put some more lights on until the police arrive." I clicked on all the lights in sight, brightening the kitchen.

66

I smiled happily at Adrian, before I navigated through the field of glass and out onto the porch. I hadn't taken the time to put on shoes before I left home.

I was still smiling when I spotted some boot prints in the garden beside the porch. The intruder had left his tracks behind. They were big, size thirteen or maybe fourteen, deep and treaded. The evidence supported the revelation I'd had. I would rather have been wrong.

"One and one equals two," I murmured, doing the math. The big man had felt evil to me, and familiar, but it was the evil that was familiar and not the actual man. If he was Scott and/or Carl's murderer, or if he had simply been near the bodies—wrong place, wrong time—some of the escaped evil could have possessed him, too. It could be controlling him even now. I mean, he didn't have a reaper dad. He had no-one to exorcise the evil from inside him. My theory explained why I could sense the evil in a living man, and maybe even a whisper of his soul.

I crouched down and had a closer look at one of the boot prints, memorizing the tread. There was a nick out of the back of the right heel. "You were at the crime scene and now you're possessed by evil," I murmured to the boot prints, since the man was long gone. Unless he was lurking in the shadows and planning to stab me with his big knife. It was a terrifying thought.

Even though I couldn't sense the evil nearby, I wasn't taking any chances. I ran across the yard and leapt over the picket fence for a second time. I locked myself in my house, shoving all the deadbolts into place before I went upstairs to my bedroom. I locked my door, too. Without turning on my light, I stood vigil at the window, watching Adrian's house. A lot of lights came on upstairs so I knew he had woken his parents, but had he told them I'd broken in, as he believed? When nobody came knocking, I dared to hope he hadn't.

And I had a more pressing thought buzzing in my brain like an irate bee. Why had the man targeted next door? Why Adrian? I flashed back to the awful sensation of being polluted by evil, and how it had twisted my longing for Adrian into a perverted obsessive hunger that knew no bounds. Perhaps the measure of evil that hadn't possessed me and had escaped into Bigfoot was now sharing that unholy desire for Adrian. If that was the case, maybe he had almost died tonight because of me.

I kept watch until a police car pulled up in front of the Lyon's house. Only then did I fall into bed. I was so keyed up, I didn't expect to sleep. On top of everything else, I knew that there was going to be hell to pay in the morning for breaking the number one reaper commandment. But I did fall right to sleep, due to sheer exhaustion no doubt. I managed four solid hours before I was rudely awakened when something smashed into my window.

I bolted to my feet and squinted at the pane of glass beside me. A gory splat of blood decorated what had been a sparkling clean window a few hours ago—Hannah had even done windows. I looked outside, and down. Directly below, a big black crow was sprawled on the grass with a twisted neck. It was an ill-omen if ever there was one.

"Exams first, deal with the dead bird later," I muttered, and went to splash water on my face. I dressed in shorts and a T-shirt. Fashion was not a priority during exams. Every high school senior knew that and it wasn't held against them. I drank orange juice and ate a banana before I stuck my books in my pack.

I wondered if I should wake my dad before I left, and bring him up to speed. I rejected the thought as soon as I had it. My dad was going to have a killer hangover, and I was in no hurry to come clean about my flagrant rule breaking. Once he found out that I'd made mincemeat of the first commandment, my dad might just kill me and reap me himself.

I rolled my bike out of the garage. It was the fastest way to get to school, short of driving. It was highly unlikely that Adrian would be offering me any more rides now that he believed I was into drugs, and breaking and entering. At least he hadn't sent the police over to arrest me in the middle of the night.

My first exam went well, all things considered. I met up with Carrie afterward. We ate lunch outside while we reviewed for our afternoon exam. We were getting a lot of sunshine for June and I was soaking it up. Adrian walked by and our eyes met. He kept walking for about ten paces before he turned around and detoured back. "Hi, Elvis. Carrie." He didn't sit down, but looked down, frowning.

"Hi, Adrian," I replied, that's all. So much for witty repartee. I didn't know what to say to him after last night's fiasco.

"Um, can we talk later?" He shifted his weight from one foot to the other, distinctly uncomfortable.

"Sure, we can talk." Maybe he had come to his senses and wanted to apologize.

We arranged to meet after our respective exams and Adrian departed. I watched him walk away, appreciating the sight. His jeans hugged his gorgeous rear. He had never adopted the fashion of wearing baggy pants that hung almost off, if not under, his butt, and I was really glad about that. Fitted pants were so much sexier, as least on Adrian.

Carrie grinned at me, her dark eyes gleaming. "Something finally happened between you two, didn't it?" She knew I was head-over-heels for Adrian, because in a moment of weakness, I had confessed all. I had needed to talk to someone, and Carrie was a really good listener. She could also keep a secret, which you couldn't say about most teenagers.

"Nothing happened, exactly. We just had a stupid misunderstanding that we still have to straighten out," I said vaguely. I couldn't tell her what had really happened. She didn't know I was a reaper-in-training, and that was one secret I couldn't share. Reapers and even reapers-in-training are bound by a strict confidentiality clause.

"Misunderstanding?" Carrie drawled, with undertones and overtones. "Come on, Elvis. Share!"

"It's nothing, Carrie. Really. I wish there was something to tell you, but there isn't, so I'm not going to bore you, and," I checked my cell phone, "it's time."

"Crap. I'm not ready for this English exam." Carrie hoisted her pack onto her shoulder and we trudged into the stale school, leaving the beautiful summer day behind.

I aced the English exam, it was one of my best subjects. And then I waited for Adrian on the grass in front of the school, already cramming for the next morning's exam. I was so immersed in math formulas that I didn't notice Adrian until he was standing over me.

I jumped to my feet. "How did your exam go?"

"Fine. Uh, do you want to walk home, while we talk? I don't have the car."

"Sure. Let me get my bike." I unlocked it and Adrian took it automatically. He pushed it along and we started home. Neither of us said anything for the first block. The silence wasn't a comfortable one.

Finally, I broke it. "You called the police last night?"

"I woke up my parents and they called the police. I didn't say it was you who smashed the door in. I guess you figured that out already."

I stopped walking. "Adrian, I did not smash the door or break into your house. I already told you that last night - "

He cut me off. "Ya, a big scary dude broke in and you chased him off with my dad's golf club." The sarcasm was overdone, and Adrian sounded intensely mad even though his voice was quiet. He hadn't been mad at me since we were about ten years old. I think I'd broken one of his transformers or something. I couldn't quite remember. It was right after that incident that he had stopped being my friend.

But I was equally mad, that he had so little faith in me—me! The girl who was so pathetically in love with him that she had broken the most important reaper commandment to save his life.

"I didn't just chase him off, I broke his nose with the golf club and probably cracked a few ribs. That's why he ran off," I snapped.

Adrian sighed and gestured at nothing with one hand. "Elvis, don't lie. You made a mistake. I know you've had a hard time since your mom died, and we both know that you've never had a ... a normal home life. I understand why you might do something reckless and stupid. You're having a hard time dealing, I get it, so I didn't tell the police it was you, but stay out of my house from now on, and ... and stay away from me."

My heart got the biggest crack yet, right down the middle. I was sad and mad and humiliated and my mouth ran away with me. "I'm not lying! And if you had a clue what I've risked to save your life, you wouldn't be standing here insulting me. You would be thanking me because you're still alive, not ... not dead." My voice faltered.

The anger faded from Adrian's face. He looked sad, too, and sighed. "Elvis -"

I jerked my bike away from him before I started to cry. I felt like I might. "Just make sure your parents install an alarm, because I'm not going to sit up nights guarding your house." I got on my bike. I rode away, head held high, stiff upper lip in place.

It might have been a dignified departure except that a squirrel, of all things, fell off an overhead branch and dropped into my path, as dead as a doornail. I swerved to avoid it and almost crashed into a tree. I did skid and fall off my bike, which was simply mortifying. Without glancing in Adrian's direction, I remounted and started pedaling.

When I passed his house, a home security truck was parked in the driveway. The glass in the door had already been repaired. It should have been one less thing for me to worry about, except I couldn't help but worry. If my half-formed theory was right, the escaped evil would continue to be drawn to Adrian, and crave him as much as I did. One little alarm couldn't stop pure evil.

At home, my father was waiting for me. I had never seen him look so grim. He actually looked like a grim reaper of old, in spite of the royal blue jumpsuit he was wearing. He didn't say a word, he simply watched me cross the kitchen. He had also been drinking rum. He hadn't bothered with the orange juice or a glass, he was swigging straight out of the bottle.

I plunked down at the kitchen table across from him, also without a word. His eyes were red and bleary. I couldn't tell if he was drunk or hungover, or I suppose he could have been both at the same time.

"Elvis, this is very bad. What you've done ..." He trailed off shaking his head.

"What I've done? You were so drunk, you couldn't even do your job. I can't believe your boss hasn't fired you yet," I cried, going on the offensive. My anger was still simmering below the surface, thanks to Adrian, so it didn't take much to spark it back to life.

His eyes dropped in shame and I felt so mean, but I was too pissed to stop there. "Yes, I saved Adrian's life and if I had it to do over, I would save it again." I didn't plan to say what came out next, I just did, as if it had been contained too long. "If you could have saved Mom, if she wasn't going to die from an inoperable brain tumour, but an accident, you would have stopped it from happening, instead of putting the dead man's shirt on her so she could die right ... right in front of me." That awful scene had replayed so many times in my head, sometimes I thought it would drive me mad.

"You weren't supposed to be home," he said, his voice husky.

"Well, I was ... I saw ... and you helped her die ... she didn't even say goodbye to me. I didn't get to say goodbye to her." My voice trailed off into a pitiful whisper.

70

"It was too hard for her, Baby. How could she say goodbye to the daughter she loved more than life itself? She was in terrible pain, and she wanted the pain to end. She asked for the shirt, she begged me to put it on her - " his voice faltered badly.

"You didn't have to do it! She could have stayed longer … with us." Hot tears burned my eyes. The emotions I had kept buried inside for months—the sorrow, the resentment, the yearning to have my mom back—they were finally escaping from the tidy box where I had stored them away, under lock and key.

"Baby, she was hurting too much, in her heart and in her head. She didn't want you and me to see her suffer. She didn't want the indignity of us having to feed her and change her diapers. She didn't want to put us through that. In her mind, the shirt was a kindness for all of us, and yes, giving it to her was breaking the rules, but I didn't care." He wiped his eyes on his sleeve. "You're right, you know. If I could have saved your mother, I would have done it. The rules wouldn't have stopped me." He took a shuddering breath. "She had forgotten my name that day. Married twenty-two years and she couldn't remember my name." He dropped his head into his hands and let out a ragged sob.

It just about killed me to see him cry. I think his pain was even worse than mine. He had loved my mother so much. They had been so good and right together. They had expected to grow old together and then it was all ripped apart.

"Don't cry, Daddy, please. I'm sorry."

He looked up, his eyes so filled with suffering, it hurt just to look at him. "The shirt was a blessing, Elvis. Your mom simply left without any more pain, on her terms."

"She didn't leave," I whispered.

"I know, Baby. She's not coming back, but she's at peace. Her soul's light was beautiful, wasn't it?"

I nodded and stood up. I rounded the table and hugged my dad hard, and cried silently, tears soaking his shoulder. He held me and rocked back and forth, soothing me as I tried to comfort him.

"I'm sorry, Dad. I'm so so sorry. I shouldn't have been so mean. I know you miss Mom, too. I know it's hard for you to not have her. I just forget that sometimes, when I get all twisted up in my own grief. I think maybe grief can make you selfish, so you only think of what you're feeling and forget that other people are sad, too."

He nodded and stroked my hair. "Drinking numbs the pain, Elvis. It's the only thing that does." He took another shuddering breath and sniffed hard.

I didn't say that drinking wasn't the answer. It was the wrong time for that. Instead, I went and got a roll of toilet paper since we were out of tissues. I unrolled some for me and handed my dad the rest of the roll. We mopped up and settled down, and I felt a little better inside, as if the burden I had been carrying around in my chest was lighter. I hoped my dad felt a little better, too. But there was still some talking to do—about Adrian. There was stuff that my dad needed to know.

I plugged in the kettle, leaned against the counter and said, "Dad, Adrian was almost killed last night because of me. It was my fault, so I had to intervene"

His eyes narrowed in bewilderment. "I don't see how it could be your fault."

"Bigfoot came here to kill Adrian. He was the intruder in the Lyon's house," I said.

He shook his head. "We don't know what happened in that field, Elvis. We don't know that there is a murderer, or that it is the fellow with the big boots."

I waved that off. "The guy who broke into Adrian's house last night, he was the one at the crime scene. The same boot prints were outside the Lyon's house last night. Whether or not this guy killed Carl or Scott, or just happened to be in the wrong place at the wrong time, he is now possessed by the evil that escaped—the evil that was left in the body when I fled. The evil that didn't go into me went into him."

"You can't know that," my dad said weakly.

"I do know, Dad. I could sense Carl's evil inside him last night even though the guy isn't even dead. I know the feel of that evil better than anyone." I took two cups out of the cupboard before I went on to make a full confession. "When I was being ruled by all that evil, it made me … hungry for Adrian in the worst way. Well, you saw Carl's body … maybe Scott was eating his flesh because of the evil that was ruling him. It craves human meat."

My dad swallowed hard, as if he might puke, but he didn't interrupt me. I took that as a positive sign. "Anyway, you might have noticed that I have a bit of a crush on Adrian." I'm sure my dad rolled his eyes, but I didn't see it. I kept my gaze fixed on the coffee cups. "And the evil warped that desire into something sick and perverted, and now I think, I'm pretty sure, that the evil possessing Bigfoot is sharing my desire for Adrian, I mean, it's all the same evil, isn't it? So it all has to be psychically connected. Why else would this guy break in next door and target Adrian?" I looked up. "He can't die because of me, Dad. He can't die because we screwed up. That would be wrong. I was right to stop his murder."

He stared into his bottle with such intensity, it might have been a fortune teller's crystal ball with all the answers swirling, or sloshing around, within. "Still, it was not your call to make," he said eventually, without his earlier conviction.

I shrugged. "I already made it, Dad. Adrian is alive."

"And you have no idea what the fallout will be, and there will be fallout because the scales of life and death are now unbalanced," he warned ominously. "Until those scales are in balance again, there's going to be trouble in my territory."

"I'm sorry, Dad, but I did the right thing." I unplugged the boiling kettle.

"Maybe you did." He sighed. "Well, right or wrong, it can't be undone. We have to take some precautions. I have to find a way to balance the scales. Never had to do that before. Tell me exactly what happened next door, and don't leave anything out."

While I prepared a couple of instant coffees, I described the events of the previous night in detail. I told my dad everything, well, everything except for how beautiful Adrian looked when he was almost naked. By the time I was finished, the coffee was ready. I brought the cups to the table and sat down. I slid one toward my dad and said, "Any questions?"

He shook his head. "I think you covered everything. I'm going to have to do a little research now. And you have some studying to do."

I nodded. "Ya."

"Get to it. And I'll be in my office, researching." He stood up and headed that way, his coffee in one hand and the bottle of rum in the other. I didn't expect much research was going to get done.

I felt bad that my actions were driving my dad to drink even more than usual and I simply sat there for a couple of minutes with my head buried in my hands, wishing I could turn into a turtle so I could hide in my protective shell. When I didn't turn into a turtle, I headed upstairs with my coffee. Studying would take my mind off my so-called life.

In my room, I crammed until the wee hours. Adrian's light turned off around one. I watched his house for awhile to make sure no-one was skulking around it. I didn't sense any evil and began to feel really sleepy. When I couldn't keep my eyes opened any longer, I crawled into bed.

The next morning, I was late leaving for my exam and took my bike again. A bloated dead raccoon was stinking up the driveway. I gave it a wide berth and phoned my dad to tell him about it. He didn't answer, so he was probably still sleeping. I left a message.

Two exams later, I rode my bike home. The raccoon was gone and so was my dad. The van wasn't in the driveway, so he was probably working. I remembered the dead crow and walked along the side of the house until I found it. Something had been gnawing into it. Another girl might have found it disgusting, but after all the dead people I had seen and handled, a feathery bird didn't even register on my personal Gross-O-Meter.

I picked it up by the tail feathers and was carrying it toward the garage, and the garbage can, when I almost stepped on a dead cat. I froze, staring down at the gray matted fur. The cat was a skinny tom with chunks out of both ears and bald patches on its scraggily tail. It had probably been a stray. Now it was just dead, like the raven and the squirrel and the raccoon.

Clearly, I should have clued into the abnormally high number of creatures dropping dead around me a lot sooner, but I hadn't, not until I laid eyes on that cat and had a eureka moment. In my defense, I had been rather preoccupied with exams and the looming threat of renegade evil.

"Shit," I breathed and put the bird down. I crouched, trying to spot cause of death, not to reap the poor kitty's soul. Animal souls aren't like human souls. They don't need to be reaped, because animals have no evil in them, not like humans. The animal version of a soul simply disperses back into the universe naturally, leaving no evil behind, but not contributing any goodness back to the world either.

The cat's battered body revealed a hard life, but no obvious cause of death. Maybe it had simply died because the scales of life and death really were way out of balance around me, and because of me.

I picked up the bird again, and the cat by its tail. I headed toward the garage to dispose of them. That's when I had the sixth sense that I was being watched. I stopped moving and concentrated. I was vastly relieved to sense no evil whatsoever. I glanced around, then I glanced up.

Adrian was framed by his window, gazing down, watching me cart around dead things. I realized my mistake. Most girls, heck, most people, wouldn't pick up dead things with their hands. They would use a shovel, or at least don gloves. Oh well, it was too late for a shovel or gloves, and I didn't care. I was still so furious with Adrian that I didn't care what he thought of me. The love-hate line might have been crossed. Okay, I could never really hate Adrian. I might resent him and be angry with him, but that wasn't hate. I was too in love with him to ever hate him, even though hate would have protected my heart from all the wounds that resulted from loving him.

I continued toward the garage with the bodies, adding a bit of a swagger for Adrian's benefit. After the animals were bagged and stowed in the garbage can, I toured my yard, this time with a garbage bag and a shovel. I was prepared in case I found another raccoon or something. All I found was a squirrel in the hedge, along with a couple of mice that were so small they didn't really need to be shoveled up. I shoveled them up anyway. I also found a large dead fish beside a shrub, which simply defied logic. I didn't even try to come up with an explanation for its presence in my yard. I shovelled the fish in with the rest of the critters, glad of the shovel at that point. Fish decompose quickly. They don't smell great when they're alive, and they smell even worse when they're dead.

Since they weren't likely to be the last of the dead, I left the shovel propped against the side of the house. The bag, I tied tight and hauled toward the garage.

I couldn't resist a peek at Adrian's window out of the corner of my eye. He was still standing there like a voyeur, gawking at the goings-on next door. I couldn't really blame him. He must be curious, and disturbed, by all the dead beasties in my yard. Maybe he thought I'd poisoned them, since he tended to believe the worst of me.

Inside the garage. I stuffed the bag into a garbage can and made sure to seal the lid tight. Under normal circumstances, animals did not go zombie, but these weren't normal circumstances.

After a thorough hand scrubbing, I cooked a frozen pizza for dinner, then got back to studying. Tomorrow was my last exam. At least it was in the afternoon so I could sleep in a bit.

I retired at eleven and my dad still hadn't come back. I slept like a baby until a repetitive chiming noise woke me up. Phone? No, doorbell, I realized hazily. I fought to open my eyelids. According to the bedside clock, it was 8:05. It wasn't alarmingly early for someone to come calling, although the persistence of the ringing was worrisome. If my dad wasn't answering, he wasn't home, or he was too hungover to fall out of bed. Either way, it left me to play doorman—or doorgirl.

"Hold onto your panties," I grumbled and yanked on my crimson kimono-style robe.

I opened the front door and a cop was standing there. "What?" I snapped rudely, because I was pretty sure Adrian had ratted on me for breaking into his house. Was I about to get hauled off to jail?

The officer was a good five inches taller than me with spacious shoulders. He was around forty and handsome in a mature way. With his big dark moustache, he resembled Tom Selleck in his younger, hotter days.

"Good morning. Sorry about the early call, but we've had a report of a body in your yard, at the side of the house." His head tilted to the left, indicating a direction. The direction was toward Adrian's house.

My heart went thumpety-thump. "A body?"

"A large animal."

Humans are technically large animals, so I was not reassured. "Could you be more specific?"

"A camel, it seems."

I blinked. "A what?"

"A camel," he annunciated.

"A camel?" I was sure I had misheard.

"Yes, a camel. C-A-M-E-L." He spelled it out, literally.

"Really?"

"I'll go have a closer look," he said reassuringly, as if I needed reassuring. "Any parents at home?"

"No. I better come along," I said in a much friendlier tone, trying to make up for my previous hostility.

We walked around to the side of the house, and sure enough, a big camel-shaped animal was sprawled limply on the grass. It wasn't just camel-shaped, it was an honest-to-goodness camel. The hairy brown hump on its back proved it.

It certainly hadn't been there when I'd done my yard patrol the previous afternoon. I mean, it wasn't something you could overlook. Flies were already

75

having a picnic, clustering around the eyes and crusty nostrils, and the gaping mouth.

The cop frowned at the deceased camel. I glanced up. I'm sure you can guess where. Adrian wasn't at his window, but I spotted him with his mom on their porch, observing. There were more neighbours on the sidewalk, gawking. I felt self-conscious as I circled the body, looking for cause of death. Nothing obvious.

Lying down, the camel seemed a much bigger creature than when it was standing up. I laid a hand on its shoulder and pushed a bit. The camel wasn't even cool. Its muscles hadn't started to stiffen. The ship of the desert hadn't been dead all that long, maybe only a couple of hours, although camels probably took longer to go into rigor mortis than humans, because they're so much bigger.

The cop said, "Have you ever seen this camel before?"

It was a dumb question. I answered in kind. "Not that I can recall. I don't think it lives in the neighbourhood."

"You've got a smart mouth," he remarked.

"You woke me up, and I'm in the middle of writing exams."

"Hey, life's tough. You should try being a cop." He flashed a grin that I could barely see because of his moustache. He seemed nice for a cop, and I think he even had a sense of humour.

We both gazed down at the camel again. "I wonder what killed it," he said.

The larger question was why it was there, on my lawn, at all. He didn't ask that. And he answered his own question before I could hazard a guess. "Could be a prank, I suppose, although it wouldn't be easy to haul the weight of a dead camel onto your lawn. Don't see any tire tracks, either, only hoof prints. Maybe it was lured onto your lawn and killed. Do you know anyone who would want to prank you?"

I brushed my hair out of my eyes. "Not like this. Can you get rid of it?"

"I could leave it here to fertilize the lawn." He winked to let me know he was joking.

I replied with, "I need a coffee. I'm going to make coffee. Want one?"

"Sure. I never refuse a coffee. Milk and sugar," he volunteered before I could ask.

"One hump or two?" I was punchy from lack of sleep.

He chuckled. "Two."

Before I could move, the phone clipped to his belt vibrated. A brief conversation later, he ended the call and said, "No time for coffee. I have to respond to a more urgent call."

"But what about - " I motioned at the camel.

"Apparently the zoo is missing a camel. They'll pick it up and examine the body to see what killed it. You'll be informed if there is anything you need to be concerned about. I'll come back if I have more questions, or need to talk to your parents." He pulled out a little black notebook. "I'm Officer Tommick, and you are?"

"Black, Elvis Black," I said, in my best James Bond impression. I definitely needed more sleep, and a little less hysteria simmering below the surface.

He didn't write. "Your real name is …?"

"Elvis Aron Black, really. Blame my dad." I had even shared my middle name, which was, no surprise, the same as *the* Elvis's.

The cop wrote. "And your parents' names?"

"My dad is Adam Black."

"Mother?"

"Deceased," I said, my voice catching.

He made eye contact. "I'm sorry. When do you expect your father home?"

I shrugged. "He works odd hours. I expect him when I see him."

Officer Tommick wrote down my phone number, handed me a card with his name on it, and drove off.

The crowd on the sidewalk wasn't dispersing, but growing all out of control as if my lawn was a free freak show. In my short red kimono, I felt as conspicuous as a dead camel on a suburban lawn. I hightailed it back into the house.

In a few short hours, I would write my very last high school exam. Camel or no dead camel, I had some major reviewing to do.

I showered quickly, gulped down an instant coffee drowning in milk, and fled my house. For obvious reasons, I was going to do my cramming at school.

# 9. What Killed the Dead Man?

For the last time, I walked away from my high school as a student. There was no party to look forward to, and nobody to celebrate with, since I was the only one of my friends who had finished their exams. Everyone else had another day or two left. Someone would have a party on the weekend, but it was only Wednesday, and I had a lawn to inspect.

I biked home and was delighted to see that my yard looked as it should, aside from some tire tracks in the grass. I did a perimeter patrol and only found a few little dead critters, although one of them was a skunk. They may be small, but they sure make up for their lack of stature with a mega-dose of stink. I definitely used the shovel to pick it up, and triple-bagged the body before I added it to the garbage can, holding my breath as much as I could.

Inside the house, I found a note from my dad on the kitchen table. It said, 'Gone scavenging. We will talk when I get home. Read this and start building, ASAP!!!' The three exclamation marks were his. Under his note was a page that was yellowing with age. It was sealed in a protective plastic sleeve.

"Build what? I'm on holiday," I informed his scribbled note before I tossed it in the trash. I didn't dare to toss the other paper away. It looked as old as a page from the original bible. The ink was so faded, it was like trying to read the shadows cast by letters, rather than the letters themselves.

I squinted at the heading on the page and groaned. "A scaredeath? What the hell is a scaredeath?" I kept reading. "More like a scarecrow—a scarecrow for the dead." I was talking to myself again. I did that way too much these days.

The items I would need to build my scarecrow, or scaredeath, were very specific. And some of them were downright gory. I didn't even know what a couple of them were. Most of them weren't hanging around the house, nor did I want them to be. I now understood why my dad was out scavenging, as he had scribbled.

I reread the list and muttered, "Start with the things that are handy, aren't gross, and don't have a shelf life." I headed for the garage.

In the space where the van was usually parked, I laid out a tarp. It was the best place to build the monstrosity. Even through three garbage bags and a sealed container, I could smell skunk. I opened the garage door to let in fresh air, and more light than the overhead bulb could provide. I looked around for something that could support my creation. In the corner of the garage was a long metal pole leftover from my mom's old standing clothesline.

"Perfect," I said, and skirted around the Elvis-mobile to reach it. I carried it back to the tarp, finding some scrap lengths of rope and a few bungee cords along the way. Next I needed some old clothing.

There was a bag of ruined clothes in the mud room, which also served as our laundry room. Reapers go through a lot of clothes. Blood and gore is tough to wash out, and there isn't always time to change into black. My dad didn't even try to wash his Elvis jumpsuits. Those went straight to his favourite drycleaners.

Without wasting time, I selected a nondescript pair of worn jeans and a man's cotton shirt that buttoned up the front and had long sleeves. Both had bloodstains, but that would just make the scaredeath look scarier.

I took the clothes into the garage to add to my growing pile of build-it-yourself scaredeath parts. Before I could decide what to hunt for next, the van pulled into the driveway. I waved to my dad before he could run me over. He waved back, pulled out of the driveway, then reversed in until the rear end of the van was encroaching on my space. The engine shut off before the garage could fill up with toxic fumes.

He hopped out and I was surprised to see him wearing regular summer shorts and a T-shirt. He hardly ever wore normal clothes. Except for the Elvis hair and sideburns, he looked like a regular dad. He was even holding a grocery bag.

"What have you got there?" I asked.

"Some entrails for your scaredeath."

"Entrails?" I cried. "That wasn't on the list."

"Just pulling your leg, Elvis. That's our dinner."

"Entrails?" I cried.

"Nope, frozen lasagna. Nothing to do with a scaredeath. I see you've started. Excellent! I don't want a repeat of the camel incident, so the sooner we get this done, the better."

"You heard about the camel, did you?" I said.

My dad gave me his look, the one that said I couldn't pull the wool over my old man's eyes. "I saw the thing being carted away. Made quite a show for the neighbours. We're supposed to keep a low profile, Elvis."

I laughed. I couldn't help it. "Low profile, Dad? Is that what you're doing with the jumpsuits and the Elvis-mobile and the midnight concerts?"

"Hey, I still gotta be me." He swiveled his pelvis and said, "At least it wasn't a dead elephant on the lawn."

"Ya." An elephant would have been much much worse. An elephant was so big, it could probably only be carted away in pieces. "All these animals are dying because of me, aren't they? Because I've upset the natural balance?"

"Not exactly. They were due to die anyway, just not here. They're instinctively drawn here to die because the scales of life and death are

79

unbalanced, because a death is owed here. And they're drawn to you because you are the one who upset the balance." He leaned through the connecting door and put the bag of groceries inside the house.

"And the scaredeath will fix things?" I asked.

"Nope. I'm afraid it's not that easy to fix this. The scaredeath will simply repel the dying so they won't be drawn to die here. And we need two. They work in pairs."

"Two? You didn't say we need two."

He retrieved the scaredeath recipe from the tarp where I had laid it and turned it over. On the backside, there was a second set of instructions. I squinted at the same faded curly lettering.

My dad tapped the page and said, "The scaredeath is to repel, that will go on our property. Its counterpart, the death-lure, will attract the dying to it, kind of like a magnet. We'll put that one in the graveyard."

I don't think I've mentioned yet that our backyard borders a graveyard. That would probably bother some people, especially since our address is on a dead end street, but it doesn't bother me. Once the soul is gone, a body is simply an empty vessel.

"Dad, if building these things won't restore the balance, how do we do that?"

"I'm still working on it, Elvis. A sacrifice would solve the problem, but it would have to be human, and that's an archaic solution. I'm trying to come up with something better." He laid the instructions on his work table.

I wasn't sure if he was joking or not, about the human sacrifice. Before I could ask, he opened the backdoor of the van. "This here is one of the essential ingredients for your scaredeath." He hauled out a bale of hay and a couple of lidded buckets.

"The hay?" I said.

"No, that's just good stuffing. I'm talking about what's in here." He pried the lid off one of the buckets and revealed what looked like watery muck.

"Muck? That wasn't on the list."

"It's special mud, and on the list it's called *Beata Vita* or good life. It's sort of a cocktail of life."

I had seen *Beata Vita* on the list. I just hadn't known what it was. "It looks like regular old muck to me." I leaned closer and noticed it had a distinctly funky odor. "How is it special?"

"It's full of the fluids of life. And seeds of the lily, to keep away unwanted visitors, and ground hyssop to ward away evil, and crushed acorn and sage, to extend life."

"Of course," I said, as if I had known it all along. "And what exactly are the fluids of life?" I made an educated guess. "Blood?"

"Blood and birth fluids, things like that," my dad said matter-of-factly, carrying both buckets toward my workspace.

"Where … how …?" Sometimes, my dad left me speechless. This was one of those times.

"I have my sources. Close your mouth, Elvis, unless you're aiming to catch flies. We have a lot of work to do, ASAP. Put these on and let's get started." He tossed me a pair of industrial rubber gloves that went up to my elbows. He donned an identical pair and we got to work.

With my dad's supervision and help, building the scaredeath and its counterpart only took a couple of hours. We ended up with what looked like two very creepy scarecrows, one male and one female. My dad had insisted on naming them Elvis and Priscilla, in spite of my most vehement protests.

They looked like a well-matched couple, but their essential ingredients were as different as their purpose. Based on their physical appearance, the scaredeath was the male and the death-lure was the female. The grossest components were hidden inside the stuffed clothes. And there were some pretty rank things inside Priscilla's party dress, including some of the rotting dead from the garbage can, and those critters were far from fresh.

Priscilla wore a long gauzy white gown that I had outgrown a couple of years ago. My mom and I had shopped for it together, for a special occasion. She had liked it a lot more than I ever did. She had always liked pretty girly dresses, while I had preferred comfy boys' wear or Goth fashions, and lately, Steampunk accessories. We'd had fun that day, shopping together, and looking at the dress on the death-lure, I wished I had more such memories. If I had known my mom was going to die so young, I would have made sure we'd had a lot more good times together, but I hadn't known. How could I? I was a reaper, not a clairvoyant.

My dad had vetoed my choice of jeans and shirt for the scaredeath. He had insisted on dressing Elvis in a jumpsuit, and had unearthed an ugly old mustard-yellow one that had gotten too scandalously tight for him to wear. At least there were no rotting dead inside Elvis's jumpsuit. He was crowned with a stovepipe top hat that my dad had worn a few Halloweens ago, when he had dressed up as a formal Elvis in a tuxedo jumpsuit. Elvis's head was a stuffed pillowcase smeared with *Beata Vita*. Overtop that was a Halloween Elvis mask, the thin rubbery kind that a person pulls on over their whole head. The scaredeath really did resemble the iconic singer, at least from a distance.

The stovepipe top hat was the most important component of the scaredeath. We had cut a big hole in the top and lined the hat's interior with multiple layers of tinfoil. Dad had added a metal pie plate, filled with a mixture of dry ingredients that he had blended in the house, complete with incantations. He lit the stuff in the garage and the smell was worse than skunk, if that was possible.

"Put the hat outside," I choked as soon as I got a whiff.

Instead, he plugged the hole in the top of the hat, extinguishing the fire. He waved away smoke and said, "Once we've got the scaredeath in place, this mixture will have to be kept smoldering at all times, if it's going to repel the dead."

"It's going to repel the living, too," I said.

"You'll have to keep replenishing the mixture, Elvis. Don't forget. It should smolder like incense inside the hat."

"If I forget to replenish it, I'm sure some dead visitor will remind me." I tightened the belt that held the scaredeath to the laundry pole. It was a fancy rhinestone one that had lost too many rhinestones to look anything but shoddy.

My dad circled our creations. "Looking good," he said, giving them his seal of approval. Priscilla was tied to an old tent pole and topped with a musty black wig that he had unearthed from the basement. I had never seen it before, and it made me wonder if he had tried his hand at being a female Priscilla impersonator at some point in his shady past. Or maybe my mom had played at being Priscilla.

Priscilla's head was another straw-stuffed pillowcase, this one wearing a black carnival mask. Dad had used a black marker to draw exotic eyes with long lashes, and a full-lipped mouth. He had coloured the lips in with a bright red lipstick that had belonged to my mom.

In spite of how grave the situation was, we'd had fun together making our death sentries.

My dad patted Priscilla's cheek and said, "We'll plant Mr. Presley first. We can secure the hat after he's in place."

"We don't have to put him in the front yard, do we?" We had already given the neighbourhood enough to gossip about, what with the camel.

"No, the backyard will be better because the sun sets in that direction. And Elvis will be closer to Priscilla. We'll plant him right in the backyard, facing west. Bring the hat and the pickaxe, I'll bring Elvis." My dad tucked the scaredeath under his arm and carted him out of the garage. I followed with the hat, trying not to inhale the residual wisps of putrid fumes coming out of the top, as if it was a real stovepipe, not a hat at all.

In the middle of the backyard, Dad started a hole with the pickaxe, then hammered the pole into the ground until it went deep enough to support the scaredeath securely. I set the hat firmly on Elvis's head and tied it in place. My dad added more of his potpourri mixture to the hat and lit it, blowing into the top. Smoke hazed the air around us.

I suddenly remembered Adrian asking me if I was into drugs. Anyone watching me and my dad would probably think we were smoking up with a scarecrow, using its stovepipe top hat as some sort of oversized pipe for pot.

I peeked over my shoulder and it didn't look like we were being watched from next door, although the kitchen curtain did twitch rather suspiciously. My dad circled the scaredeath three times, chanting an incantation I had never heard before, and dribbling a mysterious rust-coloured liquid from a small flask he pulled out of his pocket. He backed out of the smoke and said, "That should do it."

"What's in the flask?" I asked.

He capped it and stuck it back in his pocket. "Another type of repellant. I'll teach you about it when we get into potions and such. Now let's plant Priscilla."

"Shouldn't we wait until dark before we go erecting a scarecrow in the graveyard? I mean, the neighbours might think we're witches or into Satanism or voodoo or something." The scaredeath in our backyard was bad enough, but putting one up in the graveyard was another matter entirely. People tended to be highly superstitious about what happened in graveyards.

My dad considered the matter for a moment. "I guess we should wait for darkness. The sun is already setting so it won't be long. We can have dinner in the meantime. Lasagna should be ready, I put it in about an hour ago."

I was pretty sure it was more like two hours ago, and I hoped our dinner wasn't burnt to a crisp. My stomach was so empty, it couldn't even growl. "Dinner sounds good to me," I said and we headed inside, leaving Elvis the Scaredeath to do his job.

As soon as we stepped into the kitchen, my dad's phone began to play *All Shook Up*. He read the text while munching on a handful of salted almonds.

"Do you have to go to work?" I asked.

He nodded. "One soul to reap. I won't take you with me. You stay here and make sure the scaredeath's fire keeps burning. And you have to spread the *Beata Vita* around the perimeter of our property. The dying won't want to cross that line. It will be like a wall to them."

I had wondered why he had brought home so much *Beata Vita* when we'd only needed a cup of the stuff to smear on the scaredeath's head. "Spread it how? It's muck," I said.

"Rake it into the grass. Oh, and you better do the perimeter of the Lyon's property, too. If the dead can't die near you, they might end up next door. It's ground zero for the imbalance." My dad headed up the stairs to change.

"What about Priscilla?" I called.

He trotted back down the stairs. While I removed the overcooked lasagna from the oven, he scribbled on an unopened envelope that had come in the day's mail. Our dinner looked as hard and dry as layers of shale. It was probably still edible though, but it wouldn't be good.

My dad handed me the envelope saying, "When it's dark, plant Priscilla in the graveyard to attract the dead who have been repelled by Elvis. I would recommend the northeast corner, in the thicket of trees where she won't be seen."

I glanced at the envelope. "She doesn't have to smoke?"

"Priscilla is a healthy girl. She doesn't smoke. Once she's planted, circle her three times, clockwise, and recite this chant, three times." He took the envelope back, wrote a big 'three' on it, and handed it to me.

I opened my mouth to protest, to say that I would wait for him to get home. I snapped it shut when I realized there was no point. He might not come home for hours and hours, and this mess was my fault. Planting Priscilla wasn't hard labour, and a little gardening was nothing to freak out about, even if I was spreading a gross bloody potion instead of fertilizer, which, when it came right down to it, could be just as gross and a whole lot stinkier.

"Are you going to see Kendra after the reap?" I asked.

The stark sadness that washed over his face gave me my answer. I wished I hadn't asked the question, but I couldn't take back the words, so I said, "What happened between you two?"

He pulled a face. "She doesn't like how much I drink."

"Neither do I. Why does she smell like mom?" I blurted, without intending to.

He turned his back so I couldn't see his face. His shoulders hunched like a broken old man's. "This isn't the time to discuss it, Elvis. I have to go to work and you have a lot of damage control to take care of." Back he went up the stairs, dragging his feet as if they were anvils, and too heavy for his legs.

I felt like I had trespassed where I shouldn't, and rather depressed, which was nothing new. It was how I felt too much of the time lately.

I served the lasagna from the middle, where it was less overdone. I put one square onto a plate and a second bigger square into a Tupperware container. Crunching a handful of almonds, I went outside and set the Tupperware container, complete with knife and fork, onto the passenger seat of the van. While outside, I checked to make sure the stovepipe hat was still smoking. It was, so I fetched the buckets of *Beata Vita*, a rake and shovel, and the industrial rubber gloves.

My dad waved goodbye in passing. As soon as the van's taillights were out of sight, I started spreading the *Beata Vita* along the front edge of our property, scooping small amounts of bloody muck and raking it into the grass, making sure I didn't leave any gaps. I finished the perimeter of my yard and eyed the Lyon's property. It had gotten pretty dark, so maybe I could protect their perimeter without them being any the wiser.

Carting the remaining bucket of *Beata Vita*, I passed through the connecting gate in the picket fence and started raking my way along the back edge of their property, doing my best to stay in the shadows. I did the same along the far side of their yard. By the time I reached the final and front section, it was getting really late. Moving fast, I raked my way along the front. I was trailing a line of thick red muck across their driveway when a very familiar voice demanded, "What are you doing?"

I started and swung around, almost spilling the last of the *Beata Vita*. I hadn't heard Adrian come out of his house, but there he was, scowling suspiciously at me with his arms crossed. I was caught red-handed, or red-gloved as it were.

84

"I'm gardening," I said, brazening it out. I reached the grass on the other side of his driveway and scooped muck. I switched the shovel for the rake and kept raking.

"Why are you gardening in my yard? In the dark?" He crouched down to take a closer look at the line of red mud smeared across his driveway. He frowned all the deeper, making his forehead wrinkle.

"It's so the weeds won't spread from one yard to the next. And it's a lot cooler to garden when the sun's not out." It was all I could come up with on the spur of the moment.

"Uh-huh. And what is this stuff? It kind of looks ... bloody." Adrian peered into the bucket, but didn't touch. "And it reeks."

"It's organic fertilizer. My dad made it. He knows how your parents like a nice lawn." I kept scooping and raking, retreating back to my own territory as fast as I possibly could.

"Why are you wearing protective gloves? Is this stuff toxic?" Adrian followed me. He probably wanted to make sure I went home.

I shrugged. "Less toxic than a chemical fertilizer."

"And my parents were wondering about the scarecrow," he added, ever-so-casually. "And why it seems to be smoking."

"Is that why you're talking to me now?" I demanded. "Because your parents are scared the scarecrow will go up in flames and set the neighbourhood on fire?"

"They're not that worried, they've already gone to bed. And I was always talking to you." He stepped back when I sloshed *Beata Vita* near his sandal-clad foot. "Elvis, you can't blame me for being upset that you broke into my house." His overly reasonable tone made me want to smack him in the worst way.

"I did not break into your house," I said as slowly and clearly as if I was speaking to someone with an I.Q. in the single digits.

"There wasn't anyone else there, except you."

Adrian was never going to believe me, so there was no point in wasting my breath. Maybe it was time to stop loving him, if I could. Pining over him had caused me nothing but years of heartache and grief. I raked angrily and said, "The scarecrow is there because that camel and a ... a few other animals died on our property. My dad has suddenly gotten superstitious and he thinks his special scarecrow will purify our yard's chakra or something like that. The incense is another chakra cleanser. He found the recipe on the internet." I figured the added details would make the nonsense sound plausible.

I reached the edge of my property. Mission accomplished, I picked up the bucket. I was about to walk away when I caught the faintest whiff of evil tainting the air. Familiar evil—evil that would not be stopped by a measly little line of *Beata Vita*.

The evil I had freed was back. It was stalking Adrian and my dad wasn't even home to protect him. Only I was home.

I squinted around the dark street. I could spot nothing alarming. The neighbourhood was as deserted as a graveyard at midnight in January, and I didn't like that at all. I closed my eyes and strained my sixth sense. The evil felt stronger, as if it was edging closer. The epicenter seemed to be coming from a thick hedge across the street. "You should go inside now, and stay there. Make sure your alarm is on," I told Adrian.

"Is that a threat?" he asked incredulously.

"What? No, of course not. I … I spotted someone big and dark in the hedge across the street. Maybe the intruder has come back. You should go inside—now!" I dropped everything and ripped off my gloves so I could get a firm grip on the pointy shovel. It was a weapon of sorts. It was certainly better than nothing. I raised it.

Adrian backed away as if I was the threat. The evil kept drawing closer until I could taste its foulness in my mouth. I walked backwards, guarding Adrian's back even though he thought I was the one threatening him. He reached the steps leading up to his front porch and I breathed a sigh of relief.

I stood there like a bouncer, feet planted, facing the street. Adrian ascended the steps and stopped. I glanced over my shoulder. "That's not in the house, Adrian."

He wasn't looking at me. He was focused on a big dark silhouette standing immobile just outside the reach of the streetlight's glow. The threat to Adrian had broken cover. He was watching us intently. I had known the man was big, and he was. Six foot three, maybe more, and all of it was muscle, as if he lived at the gym when he wasn't busy stalking victims. Evil roiled off him. I could tangibly feel his twisted perversion. He was a starving man, and a starving man will do anything to satisfy his hunger.

He began moving toward us, skirting around the light rather than crossing through it directly. All of the sudden, my shovel didn't seem like much of a weapon.

"Elvis, you better come inside too," Adrian called urgently.

"I think you're right." I abandoned my post with cowardly haste. We both dashed inside. I set my shovel on a newspaper inside the door, not wanting to drip gross stuff in the Lyon's house.

Adrian shut and locked the door. He activated the alarm, while I went to the front window and pushed the curtain aside. The house was quiet and dark. Adrian's parents really had gone to bed. I didn't put on a light, to better see outside and remain unseen. The man had halted at the perimeter, but I don't think it had a thing to do with the line of *Beata Vita*.

Adrian came to stand beside me. "Is that him? The man that you said broke into my house?"

"That's him. See the bandage on his nose. I hit it with the golf club." I wasn't petty enough to say 'I told you so', but I did sound rather smug.

"I see it. He really is big. But … what's he doing back here?"

86

"Long story." And it was a story Adrian needed to be told if he was going to stay alive. I had already broken the first reaper commandment—a little old reaper confidentiality clause was nothing by comparison. Heck, my dad had already broken it with Kendra, so he couldn't get upset if I did the same with Adrian.

Before I confessed all, headlights appeared, lighting up the street. I recognized the shape of the headlights, and not many cars drove down our dead-end road unless they belonged on it. My dad was home.

The evil man melted into the darkness and disappeared from sight. By the time my dad parked the van and got out, I couldn't sense the evil anymore.

"Elvis, what's going on?" Adrian shifted restlessly from one foot to the other, so close I could feel the warmth of his body on my skin, as if he was the sun.

I turned to face him. "Come next door with me. We need to tell my dad that the intruder has returned. He'll know what to do."

Adrian hesitated before he said, "Let me get a house key." He reset the alarm so we could exit, me with my shovel. He locked the door after us. "Will my parents be safe?" he asked before we left the porch.

"Yes, it's you he's after." I held the shovel at the ready, just in case.

"Me? How do you know that?"

"We'll talk at my place. We really shouldn't stand out in the open any longer than we have to. Come on." We raced across the lawn to reach my house.

# 10. Jack the Biter

Adrian and I tumbled into my kitchen, breathless. My dad was standing by the counter, a drink in one hand, a fork in the other. He was digging into my stone-cold piece of lasagna, which I hadn't gotten around to eating.

I took the glass out of his hand. "This is not the time to drink. There's trouble brewing."

My dad looked between Adrian and me. He took his drink back and swigged it. "Trouble?"

"Trouble of an evil nature," I hinted broadly. "The intruder who broke into the Lyon's house is back. He's very bold."

"Is he now?" My dad was giving nothing away.

"It isn't safe for Adrian next door, Dad. He needs to know what's going on," I stressed.

My dad and I faced off. Adrian looked back and forth between us. "What is going on? How do you know that man is after *me*? And why would he be after me? None of this makes sense."

"This is a real can of worms you've opened, Elvis." My dad downed the rest of his drink and poured another, food forgotten. He carried the glass to the kitchen table and dropped into a chair.

"Well, that's helpful, Dad. And drinking, that's really going to fix this," I cried, so overwrought I tossed my arms melodramatically in the air. Just watching him drink now, when I needed him, made me so furious I had to vent. I guess I had hoped that after our cathartic talk, things would be a little better—that maybe he would feel a little better. But I wasn't seeing that, and I found it very upsetting. "And ... and it's not just my can of worms, Dad. I'm not going to take all the blame. It was because you were drunk that I had to deal with Jack the Biter the other night. And now he's after Adrian!"

"Jack the Biter?" Adrian said in the pregnant silence that followed my outburst.

"A case I'm working on," my dad said, assuming the role of private detective. He ran a hand through the cresting wave of his hair and avoided eye contact with me. He was thinking so hard, I'm sure I could smell smoke, or it was the scaredeath's, wafting in from outside. "Elvis had to step up for me the other night. That's why she got hurt," he finally said in a low voice.

"That man outside, he's the one who hurt you?" Adrian asked me, putting two and two together. Even though he didn't have all the true facts, he came up with an essentially accurate four.

"Yes, that was compliments of Jack." I had christened the evil, it seemed. Although I wasn't sure Jack the Biter was a better moniker than Bigfoot.

"But that's messed up. And how has this case put me at risk?" Adrian asked, focusing on my dad.

Even with a few drinks in him, my dad was quick on the uptake. He said, "I've been hired to gather evidence against ... Jack. He's a very dangerous man. When Elvis got involved in the case, he tried to stop her. He followed her back here after he attacked her, and he must have gotten the houses mixed up, must have seen your mom going back and forth with the first aid kit. Anyway, he probably intended to silence me or Elvis, except he broke into your house by mistake the other night, thinking it was my house. Now he must believe that you got a good look at him. He probably thinks that you can identify him, and he wants to eliminate you. It was dark, he didn't see who hit him with the golf club, likely assumes it was you. He is the type to seek revenge and stop you from identifying him."

He was laying it on a bit thick, but the cover story was a hundred times more plausible than anything I could have come up with on the spur of the moment. I had been ready to spill the beans and flagrantly disregard the reaper's oath of confidentiality. Not so my dad.

He motioned for Adrian to sit and Adrian did, heavily. He looked shocked to the core, and who could blame him? He had lived a perfectly normal life until his life overlapped with mine.

My dad was on a roll. He kept embellishing. "It was sheer luck that Elvis spotted him breaking in, and hit him with the golf club. He was injured enough to flee, so you weren't harmed. I didn't think he would dare to come back, but as Elvis said, he is proving bold. We're going to have to protect you twenty-four seven until I can gather enough evidence to have Jack arrested or catch him myself."

Adrian must have had a thousand questions. All he said was, "Shouldn't we call the police?"

"They won't provide personal protection. And I can't talk to them about Jack. I have to respect my client's confidentiality, plus, I don't have enough evidence to put him away—yet."

Adrian seemed to accept his reasoning, at least for the moment. He said, "But I have my last exam, first thing tomorrow morning."

"I'll drive you. Elvis can hang around the school with you. She knows what Jack looks like. She'll be able to spot him if he tries to get close to either of you."

"This is crazy," Adrian said, shaking his head. "I've never been stalked before."

Except by me, I thought, and on a related topic asked, "Where should Adrian sleep tonight, Dad?" I knew exactly where I wanted him to sleep, although I didn't think that was likely to happen.

"At his house, but we'll watch it overnight. We'll take it in shifts." My dad capped his bottle and stuck it back in the cupboard. I breathed a silent sigh of relief. "Now let's get you home, Adrian." He clapped the young man on the shoulder and Adrian stood up.

We both escorted him to his door. We waited until we heard the lock click before we left the porch. I collected the rest of my gardening equipment, and put it back where it belonged, then we walked the perimeter of the Lyon's property, making sure it was safe. It was a good opportunity to discuss all that had happened. "Sorry I got mad," I said, straight off.

He put an arm around my shoulders and kept walking. "Tough times, Baby, tough times," was all he said to that. "Now tell me everything that happened tonight."

It was true that there was a lot I hadn't been able to reveal in Adrian's hearing, so I told my dad all the details now, the most important one being that I could sense the evil before it got too close.

He nodded. "That's good, that's important. He won't be able to sneak up on you."

"Nope, he won't." A related thought struck me and I asked, "Can the evil come back out of its new host and move into someone else's body?"

"I don't believe so, but this seems to be a different brand of evil from any I've ever dealt with. It acts almost alive, except evil can't be alive since it has no soul." He angled toward our house. "I think Jack would need to die before the evil could escape his body, and then it could only escape if it wasn't anchored in the body. But I'm going to do some reading, to make sure. I don't know what to do about Jack the Biter. Was he a good man before the evil possessed him?" he posited.

"He could have killed Carl and Scott," I pointed out.

"We don't know that for sure, Elvis. There's been a lot of guesswork based on the crime scene, but we don't *know*." My dad paused at the picket fence. "We also don't know for a fact that Scott was murdered, since we don't even know the cause of death. That's another assumption. But let's say that our Jack happened upon a crime in progress, and witnessed Scott's mutilation of Carl."

"Because Scott was possessed by the evil," I interjected.

My dad nodded. "And Scott wouldn't have been invisible if he was harming his client rather than reaping him. Maybe he simply tried to stop a man who he thought was a murderer. That wouldn't make him an evil man by any stretch of the imagination, would it?"

I shook my head. "It would make him a good Samaritan."

"Exactly."

90

"Except if that happened, there should be some physical evidence, some marks on Scott's body."

"Right, and there are no marks, so we're missing part of the puzzle, and we're short on hard facts. I'm also not ready to rule out the possibility that it was the evil possession that killed Scott, by trying to force him to speak 'the tongue of the gods' " My dad gazed up at the stars that showed through the city lights. "Best case scenario, we catch Jack and I drive the evil from him, as I did with you."

I almost felt sorry for Jack. "And hopefully he's not an evil murderer in his own right."

"Ya, because that would be a problem." He sighed heavily. "I've never had to capture a living man before."

"It's not that different from catching a rogue zombie," I said.

"Oh, it's different, Elvis. Very very different." My dad opened the gate and motioned me through ahead of him.

"And if we catch Jack and you get the evil out of him, neutralize it, Adrian will be safe."

"My whole territory will be a safer place. I hate the thought of all that evil roaming around freely. It has to be stopped and nullified, or a whole lot of people might die."

I couldn't help but feel guilty about that, since I was responsible for the escaped evil, or at least partly responsible. I veered toward Elvis the Scaredeath. He was barely smoking so we replenished the stovepipe hat and relit the potpourri. It seemed to be doing its job. We hadn't tripped over any furry bodies.

"I didn't have a chance to plant Priscilla yet," I mentioned.

"Well, it's not going to get any darker. Let's plant her now, as long as you're not sensing any evil."

I closed my eyes and double-checked. "I'm not."

We went into the garage to get Priscilla. The smell of rot was so strong, I could barely breathe. I opted to carry the pickaxe, leaving Priscilla for my dad. He donned the industrial rubber gloves before he gingerly picked her up.

After I closed and secured the garage door, so Jack the Biter couldn't sneak in while we were gone, we crossed the backyard like shadows. My eyes were drawn to Adrian's window. It was dark, so if he was watching us, I couldn't see him. And if he was watching us, he must be wondering what the heck we were up to now. I had brought along a flashlight, but I didn't click it on while we were still in our yard.

At the back of the property, a wire fence and a high hedge appeared to block our way, except they didn't. Four months ago, my dad had cut a flap in the wire so it opened and closed almost like a swinging gate. And the hedge had been pruned near the base to allow us to worm through. My dad visited the graveyard a lot now that my mom's physical remains resided there, beneath a big beautiful statue of a winged angel that my dad had commissioned. He had spared no expense, which still seemed odd to me. We both knew, better than anyone, that human remains were nothing but an empty shell once the soul's goodness and light had been released back into the world.

He shouldered his way through the branches and pulled Priscilla after him. I followed with the pickaxe. On the far side of the hedge, it was a lot darker. I clicked on the flashlight.

Surrounding us were crumbling gravestones. The ones closest to the hedge were the very oldest in the cemetery. They were so old that the names and dates had been worn away by years of wind and rain and snow. A few small statues of angels and saints were missing their hands, and even their features. Over time, those had been erased by the elements, just like the names of the souls they had been entrusted to watch over. There were a number of little lamb statues, also well worn, from a time before modern medicine when too many children died from pneumonia and influenza and other common ailments.

The longer we walked, the newer and more legible the gravestones became. The statuary got bigger, too. My dad veered right, toward the corner of the graveyard that was overgrown with vegetation. It had been left that way and people seemed to enjoy communing with nature when they visited their dearly departed. There's nothing quite like chirping birds and a gentle breeze rustling through leafy branches to provide solace.

At the edge of the tangled greenery, we stopped. My dad said, "We'll put Priscilla in here. I doubt anybody will spot her, and hopefully we can retrieve her before anyone does."

"Maybe we should have dressed her in army camouflage, not a gauzy white gown. She might look like a ghost in the greenery." I aimed the beam of the flashlight into the thicket, searching for the easiest pathway in.

"There." My dad pointed out a bit of a trail. He waded in with Priscilla tucked under his arm.

I followed with the pickaxe over my shoulder. From a distance, it had to look like we were burying a body illicitly in the graveyard. I paused and closed my eyes for a moment to verify there was no evil in the vicinity. "Still all clear," I said.

As quickly as we could, we planted Priscilla, deep enough in the thicket that she wouldn't be seen. My dad did the circling and chanting since he knew the words off by heart, which was lucky. I had forgotten the envelope on the counter. And then we got the heck out of there.

"Who's going to take the first shift watching Adrian's house?" I asked as soon as we were back in our kitchen.

"You better do it. Wake me up in about four hours. And call me if you sense Jack." Dad didn't pull out his bottle. He kissed me on the top of the head and said, "Stay alert, Baby." He looked tired. All his drinking was aging him prematurely. His stressful job wasn't doing him any favours either.

It was a beautiful night and after my dad went upstairs, I settled on the porch with a piece of cold lasagna. I could guard Adrian all the better from the nearer vantage point, and Jack couldn't sneak up on me. I could sense his evil aura long before he arrived.

Adrian's light was on now, and it stayed on. The night remained quiet and peaceful. I stretched my legs every hour or so, walking the fence line and making sure the scaredeath was still smoking. At about the four hour mark, I spotted Adrian peering out his window. I flashed him the thumbs-up sign and he waved back.

Before I could wake my dad to take the next shift, *All Shook Up* did it for me. He didn't want to leave me alone, but he had a soul that needed reaping, so he didn't have a choice. He did make me promise to stay in the house and phone him if I sensed Jack.

I deadbolted the door and made a pot of perked coffee. I had to pace to stay awake for the rest of the night and did some kitchen cleaning while I was at it. By the time the sun rose, it looked like Hannah had paid us another visit, at least in the kitchen.

My dad got home in time to drive Adrian to school in the Elvis-mobile, and I went with him. We were early and the building was almost deserted. We settled in a corner of the empty cafeteria. I'd brought along a travel mug of coffee, and a couple of bananas from home. I offered a banana to Adrian and he shook his head. "I already had breakfast."

"Did you study all night?" I asked when he didn't say more.

"Ya, I figured I might as well since I couldn't sleep. You were up all night, too."

"I was, but I don't have an exam."

He stopped frowning at the cover of his textbook and looked into my eyes. Deep into my eyes. "I'm really sorry, Elvis, for accusing you of breaking into my house. I feel like such a jerk, I mean, that guy was huge and you took him on to keep me safe. And you stayed up last night like some sort of bodyguard, outside and alone. I can't believe your father let you do that. I mean, do you carry a gun?"

I smiled at the very idea. "No, and I don't want to. Stakeouts are part of the job, a job he's been training me for." I leaned closer. "We're going to catch Jack and then you'll be safe, but until then, you can't be alone. He's really dangerous."

"He looked really dangerous, not to mention huge. And he hurt you." Adrian took my hand in his, without me holding the gun I didn't own to his head. Hot tingles sizzled through me as if I'd stuck a wet finger into an electrical outlet. "I'm sorry about the drug comments, Elvis. And for not believing you."

"Apology accepted." I wasn't one to hold a grudge, especially against Adrian.

He smiled and squeezed my hand before he released it. My hand was bereft without his. I sipped my coffee and offered him the cup.

"Thanks. I don't normally drink coffee, but I think I need some caffeine today." He drank and then I drank so I could put my mouth where his had been. I had it so bad for Adrian, it was pathetic. I was pathetic.

While Adrian wrote his exam, I hung out with assorted casual friends and acquaintances. Ramona invited me to her party on Friday night. Most of my friends would be going so I said I would be there, and I would be there if I could. It would depend on how events unfolded with Jack the Biter.

When Adrian exited the classroom where he had written his final, I was waiting in the hallway like a lovesick girlfriend, except I was a lovesick bodyguard. Curious glances were cast our way. I knew there would be some texts and tweets about us hooking up.

"How did it go?" I asked.

"Aced it. All the extra studying helped." He flashed a tired grin.

Ted, one of Adrian's lesser friends, walked with us. I had never liked Ted, because he wasn't very nice. He could be really funny, but it was usually at somebody else's expense.

The guys discussed the exam all the way to the front door of the school. The Elvis-mobile was parked front and center. My dad was in his crimson jumpsuit with his dark hair combed back and gleaming, pompadour style. It looked like he'd had time for a shower, complete with hair products. *Are You Lonesome Tonight* was blaring out of the CD player he had installed in the classic car— the only upgrade he had allowed. He was singing along.

Ted smirked. "I thought Elvis was dead."

He didn't mean me. When I was younger, I had been embarrassed by my Elvis-style dad. Now that I was more mature, I respected his individuality, and except for his drinking, I was proud that he was my dad. I said, "Elvis is alive and well, and very cool."

Adrian grinned. "Do you think he'll drive us by a sub shop? I'm starving."

"I'm pretty sure we can talk him into it." I waved to my dad. He saluted back.

"Are you going with them?" Ted asked Adrian. There was nothing flattering about the way he said *them*, as if we were lowlife mobsters or something equally unsavory.

"Ya, I'm going to ride in the caddie. I'll catch you later," Adrian said easily. I'm not sure he had picked up on Ted's tone, or maybe he was simply ignoring it.

We climbed into the classic Cadillac. I even let Adrian ride shotgun, something I wouldn't do for anyone else in the world. My dad was happy to detour by the fastfood shop. We all got takeout and drove our lunch home. Eating any food in the vintage car was forbidden.

We were pulling up to the house when *All Shook Up* summoned my dad. He parked in the driveway and scanned the text. "Elvis, stay with Adrian, and stay inside. Make sure the doors are kept locked."

"I will, and I'll put your sub in the fridge," I said, as we disembarked with the food.

"No, I'll take it with me, in case I have to kill some time." He winked at me and took his sub out of the bag. "I'll be back as quick as I can." He got straight into the van. His fanny pack must have already been inside it, and he didn't even take the time to change into black. Maybe the reap was an NC, which rarely involved blood. Or maybe it was an ASAP. At least crimson was pretty forgiving when it came to blood—not as forgiving as black, but a close second.

Adrian turned to me. "We can eat at my place. It has the alarm."

I nodded. "Definitely safer. I think it's time for us to get an alarm, too." With Jack the Biter on the loose, I was going to put that on the top of my to-do list. Then again, I could foresee my dad setting it off every time he came home after a few too many, which would drastically cut into my sleep time. Maybe an alarm was not such a good idea.

We crossed the lawn and locked ourselves in Adrian's house. There were no cars parked in the driveway and his house was quiet. "My mom's doing her volunteer work at the hospital," Adrian said, setting two plates on the table. I wouldn't have bothered with dishes. We shared out the subs and dug in.

After everything was eaten, we went into the den. Adrian turned on the TV. Since we were housebound, it would pass the time. We got comfy on the couch and Adrian said, "What do you want to watch? I've got a lot of movies saved. Or I've got some video games."

"How about a movie? I am pretty tired. Pick something, as long as it's not horror or gore." My life contained enough of that without me watching it as so-called entertainment.

The Lyon's couch was one comfy piece of furniture. I felt myself unwinding for the first time in days. "I might get a bit of shuteye," Adrian said, relaxing beside me.

True confession—I've daydreamed about sleeping with Adrian, and it wasn't innocent napping on the couch. It wasn't innocent at all. Suddenly, I wasn't in the least bit sleepy. I was hot and tingly all over.

Adrian clicked on a movie with vampires and werewolves in it. At least there were no zombies. He kept the volume low and relaxed his head back against the couch. In two minutes, his eyes were closed and he was deep breathing. He hadn't slept a wink the night before, but still, it was insulting. I hadn't slept either and I wasn't nodding off. We were alone in his house, banded together against evil and living life on the edge. He should have been making some serious moves on me, and it's not like I was about to refuse him.

I shifted a bit closer. He didn't notice. I leaned in until my shoulder just touched his. Still nothing. I thought about being more proactive and kissing him, softly on the lips. I mean, guys weren't the only ones who should be allowed to initiate a kiss. Girls had rights, too, and desires. Except I wasn't that brave. If I kissed him and he ran screaming from the room, it would be really awkward. I was still his bodyguard, after all, and had to stick by his side. If he blatantly rejected my advances, I couldn't storm home and lick my wounds in the privacy of my room. No, kissing Adrian here and now was a very bad idea. Sadly, it didn't stop me from craving to do just that.

Before I gave into temptation, I got up and went to the bathroom. I spent some time washing my hands with a fancy scented soap and brushing my hair. The room was a lot more stylish than my outdated bathroom, and better lit.

I examined my reflection critically, trying to figure out why I had zero sex-appeal as far as Adrian was concerned. I wasn't fat or anorexic. I was fit rather than curvy, but I didn't think of that as a bad thing. Maybe Adrian did, or maybe it was my breasts, or lack of breasts, that left him cold. After all, guys were reputed to like big breasts more than just about anything in the world. My face was pretty enough, at least I thought so. I had a smooth complexion and my lips were full, kissable. Maybe Adrian didn't want to kiss me, because he thought my nose would get in the way.

I was looking at my face from different angles when the alarm went off. I had been so preoccupied with my nose that I hadn't been paying any attention to sensing evil.

Heart pounding, I flung open the bathroom door and raced into the den. Adrian was on his feet. I scanned for a weapon. A fire poker seemed ideal. I snapped it up and said, "Get behind me."

He didn't move and I shoved him back. He said, "Wait, Elvis, it could be - "

I clapped a hand over his mouth when he wouldn't shut up and kept shouting over the alarm. "Quiet," I hissed in his ear.

He nodded and I removed my hand from his surprisingly soft lips. Trying not to think about his lips, I edged toward the door of the den, poker leading the way as if it was a worthy weapon. The earsplitting alarm finally cut out. I wasn't taking any chances and stayed hidden behind the den door, poker raised over my head. When Mrs. Lyon stepped into the room, I almost crowned her.

She screamed bloody murder and I managed to stagger back, taking the poker with me. I would have concealed it behind my back, except that we had all seen it.

"I'm sorry, I'm so sorry. When the alarm went off, I thought it was another intruder." I placed the poker back where it belonged and looked to Adrian for help.

"Sorry, Mom. I guess we're all a little nervous after the other night." Adrian gave his mom a hug and picked up the bag she had dropped.

"But … what is Elvis doing here? I thought you had an exam."

"I did, last one. I wrote it this morning. Elvis is … keeping me company. She's finished exams, too. We're just hanging out." Adrian was overdoing the good friends' shtick.

"Well, I don't appreciate being threatened in my own home. I know I haven't mastered the alarm yet, but still, that's no reason to overreact, and no reason for violence." Mrs. Lyon's face was unnaturally pale, except for her cheeks, which were stained with two red spots, almost like a clown's makeup. I had given her a real fright.

"I'm sorry," I repeated rather desperately. "I really am. I was scared. I thought someone was breaking in again."

"You've always had quite an imagination, Elvis," Mrs. Lyon said, unbending. "Even as a little girl, you would tell the wildest tales, and you were quite fixated on death and bodies."

"Was I?" I attempted a smile. "I guess I do still have that imagination."

Adrian carried the bag into the kitchen for his mother. I didn't know where to go or what to do. After a bit of standing awkwardly in the den, I sat down on the couch and pretended to watch the movie that was still playing. In a few minutes, Adrian joined me.

"You didn't tell your mom the truth, did you? That you're the one in danger?" I whispered.

"No, it would only upset her. She worries even when there's nothing to worry about." Eyes on the TV screen, he murmured, "Now she thinks we're dating."

"That might not be a bad cover story for the time being." I was thinking aloud. "Since you can't be alone until we catch Jack, it would explain why we're suddenly inseparable."

"And I would have a reason to hang out at your place, where your dad can keep an eye on me. He must have a gun, right? Since he's a P.I.?" Adrian angled toward me.

"He has quite a few weapons at his disposal," I confirmed, without mentioning that they mostly worked on zombies.

"Good. Ya, I think this could work." This time, he shifted closer on the couch until our shoulders were touching. If I had been shorter, I would have rested my head on his shoulder. I was too tall for that. I would have gotten a crick in my neck.

I couldn't quite contain a smile. For the next few days, I was going to live my fantasy. Perhaps there was still a bit of evil lingering deep inside me, because I secretly hoped that Jack never got caught. And I was going to play the part of Adrian's girlfriend like an Oscar-winning actor. There would have to be some kissing, if we were supposed to be dating. Maybe lots of kissing, and maybe it would lead to a lot more than kissing, like getting naked. A girl could hope.

# 11. A Reaper and a Zombie Walk Into a Bar...

My dad texted me when he got home. It was almost dinnertime and he said he had food cooking, and news. I showed the text to Adrian.

"Let's hope it's good news," Adrian said, and stood up. "I'll tell my mom that we're going to eat at your place."

"Break the news gently." I grinned, in a buoyant mood, living in my fantasy world where I was Adrian's girlfriend.

I couldn't overhear their conversation, but there was no shouting. I called goodbye to Mrs. Lyon, and Adrian and I crossed the lawn to my house. Even the weather was in sync with my mood. The sunshine was soft and warm as the day came to a close. The grass smelled as green as summer. A lawnmower engine droned in the distance.

My dad was in the kitchen, drink in hand, making some misguided attempt to cook. I peered over his shoulder at two burnt lumps that had probably started out as steak. Two cuts of steak meant he hadn't expected me to bring Adrian home for dinner. Oh well, I was willing to share my steak, if Adrian wanted to share. I had my doubts, looking at that charcoaled meat.

"Why didn't you just barbeque?" I said. "You're better at that."

"Tank is empty. Forgot to fill it. Speaking of which, have you checked our friend in the backyard to make sure he's still smoking?"

I had forgotten all about Elvis the Scaredeath. He had ceased to exist in my fantasy world. I ran outside and the hat was cold. I replenished and relit it. When it was smoldering nicely, I gave the yard a cursory sweep. Nothing big and dead was blatantly stinking up the lawn, so I returned to the house. Dinner was served. We each had some cut up chunks of crispy dry steak teamed with undercooked fries and no vegetables. The meal looked sad and kind of forlorn. My dad had a refilled drink in front of him. Adrian and I had nothing. I opened the fridge and asked, "Juice or milk?"

"Milk, please."

I made sure the milk wasn't sour before I poured two glasses. I sat down and clinked them together saying, "To no more exams."

"To no more high school," Adrian replied.

We drank to that and tried to eat. The steak was as tough and chewy as a rubber tire. "Maybe we'll eat at your place tomorrow night," I quipped to Adrian, who simply looked embarrassed. "It's okay, Adrian. My dad knows he can't cook. You're not going to hurt his feelings by speaking the truth." I glanced at my dad. "But it was really sweet of you to try. So, what is this news you texted me about?"

He hesitated to answer and, too late, I realized he must have wanted to talk to me alone. His news was probably not fit for Adrian's ears. He gnawed on a bite of steak for awhile before he said, "On the way home, I stopped by the police station and had a word with my friend, Colin. I asked him how *the* investigation was going."

Colin Thornton is 'in the know' about my dad's true occupation. He is an official part of our reaper team, as a support system for my dad when he needs one, and he's a handy source of inside information.

"And?" I prompted.

"Turns out the coroner hasn't been able to determine a cause of death for Scott. He can't even find one. It remains a mystery, a very big mystery."

"So we still don't know if Jack killed him?" I picked up a fry.

"We don't know, but it doesn't really change things, does it?"

"I guess not." We would still have to catch Jack and exorcise the evil that possessed him, but that went unsaid since Adrian was gracing our kitchen table. "And Carl?"

"How he died is very odd. The coroner says he killed himself, stabbed himself to death. Not many people kill themselves that way."

The text I had received about Carl hadn't said that he'd killed himself, and that is normally information a reaper is privy to. Instead, the text had said 'unnatural', which could mean just about anything.

"The ... mutilation happened after he was dead," my dad added.

That was good news. Far better to be dead before that violation occurred. "The coroner could be wrong," I said, and nibbled on the fry. It was still cold in the middle.

"He certainly could be wrong about Carl's cause of death, but I think we can be sure that Scott didn't kill him." Until the evil possessed him, Scott had just been a dedicated reaper doing his job. In spite of the coroner's findings, we were still short on facts and long on supposition.

"Do the police have any leads as to Jack's real identity?" I asked

He shook his head. "They know he was there because of the boot prints, but they don't know who he is."

"We only know him by his alias," I told Adrian, adding ketchup to my plate, hoping it would make the fries palatable. Adrian extended a hand and I passed him the ketchup.

My dad leaned back in his chair. "So we'll have to wait for Jack to come to us, and we'll have to be ready for him. I'm going to set a little trap." He smiled quite nastily.

"What kind of trap?" I asked.

He winked. "A tricky kind. Can't reveal trade secrets." He raised his glass as if in toast and tossed back the contents. My dad couldn't speak freely until Adrian was out of earshot, but that didn't stop me from being curious. Zombie traps would work on a living man, so maybe that's what my dad had up his sleeve.

My curiosity was destined to remain unsatisfied. I was starting to hate *All Shook Up* with a vengeance. My dad checked his text, shoved a fry into his mouth and stood up. "We'll talk when I get back. Stay in, lock the door." He staggered and bumped into the counter when he cleared his plate. His utensils clattered loudly to the floor. He tried to pick them up and whacked his head on the counter when he bent over.

I rose and picked up his utensils. I wasn't sure how much he'd had to drink, but if he couldn't control his feet or dishes, it seemed like too much for him to be behind the wheel. "I'll drive you, Dad," I said.

"You can't leave Adrian alone." My dad clipped on his fanny pack, which had been draped over the back of his chair.

"Adrian can come with us. We'll wait in the van while you take care of business, then I'll drive you home." It sounded like a good plan to me. "I mean, we have to stay locked in the house anyway, a drive might be nice, and probably safer than staying here alone where Jack can find us." I glanced at Adrian, hoping he would clue in and support me.

"Uh, ya, a drive would be nice," he said.

My dad opened the door and motioned us out, saying, "If you're coming, let's get trucking."

I groaned. "Did we just travel back in time to the seventies?"

We exited the house. I took the keys out of my dad's hand and locked the door. Adrian headed for the Elvis-mobile. "The van," I corrected him. It wasn't locked.

The driver's seat was mine. My dad rode shotgun and Adrian got in the back. "Where are we going?" I asked, starting the engine.

The GPS activated automatically. It was wirelessly linked to my dad's phone and already knew the address. James' sexy voice told me to turn left at the first intersection.

With Adrian as a passenger, I was extra self-conscious about my less than smooth driving skills. At least I got us to the address without putting any new dents in the van. I stopped, one wheel half on the curb, in front of a low-rise apartment building. "Here we are. Is it one client, Dad?"

"One client." He showed me his text. I read it and wanted to shake him until he was all shook up.

"FS, Dad? You didn't tell me Stella was an FS!" I cried. FS is reaper lingo for suicide, or *Felc de Se*. It's what should have appeared in Carl's text if he really had killed himself, but it hadn't, indicating that the coroner was wrong.

It's an odd quirk of death that souls who are dead by their own hand rarely go quietly, even though they wanted to end their own lives badly enough to do the deed themselves. Accomplishing it leaves behind a very restless soul, and more often than not, an instant zombie.

"FS or not, the job still has to be done. You can circle the block a few times and then pick me up. Smooth as silk," my dad drawled.

"I doubt that very much." I wanted to bang my head against the dashboard. I restrained myself admirably.

My dad departed with a carefree wave and a tipsy stagger. Adrian climbed into the front seat and asked, "What does 'FS' mean?"

"Problem client." I pulled away from the curb, forgetting to check my blind spot. A blue pickup truck almost hit the van. It didn't honk, which surprised me. I deserved to be honked at, but the vehicle simply swerved around the van and sped away.

"Sorry," I said to Adrian. "I'm supposed to be keeping you safe, not getting you into a car accident. I haven't had a lot of time to practice my driving."

"Don't worry about it." He clicked on his seatbelt and tightened the strap.

I circled the block. It wasn't a pretty neighbourhood. It was a new development, one boxy low-rise apartment building after another in a barren human wasteland of concrete and pavement, where someone had thought it a good idea to cut down all the trees. All the buildings looked identical with their gray brick facades and wrought iron balconies. On the corner, we passed a gas station with an adjoining convenience store. Adrian motioned to it. "Do we have time to stop? I could do with something to eat."

We hadn't finished the awful dinner. I was kind of hungry, too. I pulled up beside the front door. "Can you get me an ice cream bar or something like that?" I reached into the ashtray where my dad kept spare change. There were lots of loonies and toonies in it.

"Sure." Adrian refused the coins I tried to hand him. It was almost like we were on a dinner date. He returned with ice cream bars, chips and pop.

"Very healthy," I commented.

Adrian flashed a grin. He opened the pop and chips while I drove. The ice cream bars were dessert. We had time to finish everything and circle the block about twenty times before James said, "Stop here," ever so politely. I couldn't spot my dad, but I knew to trust the all-knowing GPS, which was in communication with my dad's cell phone. I pulled over.

"Why did the GPS tell you to stop?" Adrian asked.

Before I could attempt an answer, the sliding door of the van opened on the passenger side. My dad appeared out of thin air. He had been standing invisibly in the mental blind spot where even I couldn't see him if I wasn't on the job with him—and he wasn't alone. It's just lucky that Adrian didn't have eyes in the back of his head or he would have seen my dad and an elegant woman materialize as if they had been beamed down from the Starship Enterprise.

Both of them climbed in. Adrian swung around and blinked. "Hey, where did you come from? I didn't see you at the curb."

"Start driving, Elvis, and don't say a bloody word," my dad ordered, slamming the door

I started driving, without a bloody word. My dad's companion, Stella, was beautiful and as pale as the string of pearls she wore around her graceful neck. She was also very dead. My dad didn't introduce her to us. Adrian must have sensed the tension in the van, because he didn't ask any more questions.

"Where to, Dad?" I asked.

"Home for now."

I had figured as much. I pulled into the outer lane, got honked at, and started driving fast enough to make Adrian clutch the armrests with such white knuckles, he might have been an astronaut blasting off the earth.

I was zooming along a main thoroughfare when Stella said, "I need to get out."

"Sorry," my dad said. "We haven't reached our final destination yet." Stella had her own side door. She gripped the handle to open it. "Oh no you don't." My dad leaned across the seat and grabbed her. She slapped him hard across the face.

"No need for violence." He tried to catch her hand so she couldn't do it again. They ended up wrestling in the back and sliding off their seats. I guess they hadn't bothered with seatbelts. Well, Stella couldn't get any deader and my dad was kind of tipsy. The wrestling continued on the floor of the van. I wanted to check out who was winning, but I had to keep my eyes on the road.

Adrian gasped, "Is your father ... are we kidnapping someone?"

"Of course not," I said, trying to sound reassuring.

The woman screamed. She must have kneed my dad. He screamed, too, his pitch almost as high as Stella's soprano. I heard the side door begin to slide opened. I screeched into the nearest parking lot before things got really messy. A zombie leaping out of a fast moving vehicle is as gruesome as it gets, especially if they're stubborn enough to get up again after they hit the pavement.

The woman jumped out with surprising agility given that she was wearing three inch heels. My dad staggered out after her, trying to catch up. I sat there for a moment in stunned silence, regrouping.

"Elvis, do you know what's going on?" Adrian asked.

"Uh ... sort of," I admitted.

"What kind of answer is that?"

"The only one I've got." I parked the van rather crookedly. "I think my dad might need some help. Come on." I wasn't leaving Adrian alone in the dark parking lot.

"Are you sure he's not kidnapping that woman?"

"Positive. Hurry, Adrian."

He came with me, but he didn't look happy about it. We followed my dad, who was tailing the woman. She turned left through the door of a rundown bar, cleverly named *Shaky Ground*. It was clearly the local watering hole. I groaned, as well I might. A bar was the last place I wanted to be with my drunken reaper dad and a rogue zombie—and Adrian.

The reaper and the zombie had been quick to make themselves at home. They were on stools at the bar, sitting side-by-side with drinks in hand, when Adrian and I caught up. The bar was unexpectedly full. More than half the tables were occupied, and, no surprise, everybody was checking out my dad in his flashy crimson jumpsuit. Stella was worth a second look all on her own, and she was getting a lot of those. Together, they made an eye-catching couple.

"Dad, this isn't the time to be drinking," I said through gritted teeth.

"Did you just get kneed in the rhinestones?" he snarled, tossing his drink back and motioning to the bartender for another. The older man was pouring before I could cancel the order.

"I don't have rhinestones." I claimed the stool beside him. He wasn't going to leave yet, and I couldn't make him. At least Stella the zombie seemed content to be exactly where she was. She motioned for another drink, too.

I was glad to see her drinking. Alcohol is a surprisingly effective way to sedate a zombie so you can reap its soul. I'm not sure why it works. A zombie's heart no longer beats to circulate the blood, yet somehow the alcohol soaks in anyway. Or maybe it's a placebo effect. My dad has plied his fair share of zombies with alcohol, and he never lets them drink alone.

Adrian slid onto the stool beside me. "What'll you have?" the bartender asked us. Apparently I.D. and being of legal drinking age were not priorities when you were standing in or on 'Shaky Ground'.

"Water, please. I'm driving," I said.

Adrian ordered a beer. I told the bartender to put it on my dad's tab. We sipped and my dad and his problem client imbibed.

Adrian leaned closer and said, "What happens now?"

I tilted my head toward the troublesome twosome. "As soon as they're amenable, I'll load them in the van and drive them home."

"But what about the woman? Who is she?"

"That's Stella, the problem client—not a kidnap victim. See, she's not trying to run away."

The woman was, in fact, getting quite chummy with my dad, chatting as if they were BFF's. It wasn't long before he was on his feet in front of a karaoke machine that no-one had been paying any attention to. A few thrown switches and pressed buttons later, and my dad was belting out *Shake, Rattle and Roll*, complete with wildly swiveling hips. The patrons loved it. More songs followed.

The far end of the bar turned into a dance floor. Too many Elvis fans bought drinks for my dad. Stella helped him to drink them. Adrian had another beer, but I wasn't worried. He took his time drinking, making his beer last. And he wasn't the designated driver.

When the clock struck twelve, Stella kicked off her shoes and danced like there was no tomorrow, which there wasn't for her. It made me depressed to watch her living it up when she was dead. Why had she killed herself? You only got one life, as far as I knew, and to toss it away was so tragic and wasteful. No matter how bad things were, a person never knew what happiness was waiting around the corner, if they could just hang in there.

Stella was vibrant and pretty. Except for being dead, she looked to be in good health. She wasn't old or infirm, and she had nice clothes and a home. So why had she done it? I wanted to ask her, but it wasn't the right time or place. I probably wouldn't get another chance, either. The longer a zombie is dead, the slower and hazier their brain gets.

Adrian seemed to enjoy the impromptu party. He watched the show with a tapping toe. "Your dad is really good," he said.

"Ya, he's a great Elvis."

"Why are you looking so sad?" Adrian asked.

I had been thinking about Stella the zombie, but I couldn't say that. "Just tired, I guess. Not much sleep lately."

Adrian smiled ruefully. "Ain't that the truth. Do you want to dance?" He tilted his head at the dance floor.

I almost said, 'Is water wet?' and stood up so eagerly, I banged my knee on the bar hard enough to make my eyes water. A broken leg wouldn't have stopped me from dancing with Adrian. We moved to the edge of the gyrating bodies and started swiveling.

I've been dancing to rock and roll since I could walk, so I'm pretty good. Heck, I'm really good. Clearly, Adrian wasn't used to dancing. He was kind of stiff, but he tried. The song ended and my dad segued into *Suspicious Minds*. He crooned the slow ballad in his deep rich voice as if he was singing to a lover. All the couples on the dance floor moved into each other's arms. I idly wondered if my dad had chosen the romantic waltz for my benefit. If he had, I owed him one. Maybe I would even buy him another drink.

Before Adrian could run, I stepped close, very close. "We're dating, remember?" I said, attempting to flirt. I had never been brave enough to flirt with Adrian and probably sucked at it. Or maybe not.

"How could I forget?" he said and put his arms around me. My heart almost burst with longing. I wrapped my arms around his waist and moved as close as I could without stepping inside his chest. We turned in a slow circle in time with the ballad. I never ever wanted the dance to end.

I closed my eyes, savouring the feel of Adrian right down to the molecular level—his arms around me, the warmth of his breath on my cheek, the taut muscles of his back beneath my hands, his subtle scent. And maybe I'm a fool, but I think his arms liked holding me too, because they tightened. Things were definitely getting very interesting.

If I had been a cat, I would have been purring up a storm. I might have purred anyway. I leaned in a bit more, swaying in time with the music. Adrian's hands stroked down to the curve of my waist. I think he was about to kiss me, or I was indulging in a whole lot of wishful thinking, when the song ended. Before my dad could launch into another song, the bartender shouted, "Last call." I have to admit, I did want to commit manslaughter at that point. There was a rush for the bar and the show was over.

After a lot of fond farewells to the Shaky Ground patrons, Adrian and I herded my dad and Stella into the van. They needed a lot of assistance. It was impossible to tell which one was drunker. At least they were well behaved in the back this time.

Adrian had a quirky little grin on his face when I pulled onto the road. "Why are you smiling?" I asked.

He glanced my way. "Is this a normal evening for you?"

"It's not completely abnormal, although I don't usually have company." I risked all and said, "It's nice to have company."

"Glad I could help out, and I had a fun time tonight. This is not a normal evening for me, by the way."

"I know. I live next door to you, Adrian." Our eyes caught and held for an endless moment, before I remembered that I had to watch the road. Luckily there was no oncoming traffic, because I had veered into the wrong lane.

We reached home without incident. I opened the sliding door on Stella's side to unload her, while Adrian took care of my dad. Stella was passed out cold. It was the opportune time for her soul to be reaped, except my dad was in no condition to do the job. I considered relocating her dead body to the house to release her soul, but I couldn't do that with Adrian as witness. Plus, she would have to be driven back to her apartment after she'd been reaped. It would be simpler to just leave her in the van, reap her there or when she was back at her apartment.

My dad was snoring in sputtering bursts, like an old engine trying to catch. Adrian was attempting to rouse him with polite little shoulder shakes. Clearly, he wasn't used to waking up drunks. I was and it takes a bucket of ice cold water, or a hose.

"Adrian, don't bother," I said.

He glanced at me questioningly across both slack figures.

I shook my head. "He's useless right now. He can't guard you or look after Stella, his client. I'm going to have to take care of her. You should go in your house and set the alarm, while I drive Stella back to her apartment. Don't hesitate to call the police if you think you're in danger while I'm gone."

I reached across Stella and pulled my dad's phone out of his fanny pack to read the details of Stella's case. Her body wouldn't be discovered for a couple of days, but it would be a lot easier to move her while the majority of the world was sleeping, and before she stiffened with rigor mortis, especially since my puppet-walking skills were worse than my driving skills.

Adrian frowned, gazing at her. "Stella doesn't look so good."

She didn't. Her pasty white face was slack and still, and there wasn't a trace of breath passing between her blue-tinged lips. At rest, she looked as dead as she was.

"She's just passed out." I slid my door closed, hoping it would motivate Adrian to do the same on his side of the van.

It did. He shut the door and walked around the vehicle to join me. The world was dark and still around us. We could have been the only two people on the planet. I really didn't like how alone and exposed we were with Jack's evil on the prowl.

"I'll come with you," Adrian said. "You might need help with Stella. It doesn't look like she's going to wake up anytime soon."

A truer statement had never been spoken—Stella was never going to wake up again. I would have appreciated Adrian's help, except he couldn't see what I was about to do. "I don't think that's a good idea, Adrian. You'll be safer in your house than outside in the middle of the night now that my dad is comatose. We don't want to offer you up to Jack on a silver platter, do we?"

Adrian bit his lip. "No, but Jack must be after you, too."

"He thinks you hit him with the golf club, not me. He's after you more," I said, aiming for a light tone.

"I don't want you going alone, Elvis. You said so yourself, your dad is useless now. I'm going with you." He wasn't asking.

And I couldn't let him. "No, Adrian, you're not. My job is to keep you safe, so I am not taking you with me, not when you've got a target on your back. Go and lock yourself in your house, set the alarm and put on the downstairs lights so it looks like someone is awake. Leave them on all night." Before he could argue, I hopped in the van and locked all the doors. He couldn't come with me if he couldn't get in the van.

He frowned and knocked on my door. I cracked the window. "Yes, Adrian."

"Let me in, Elvis."

"Not by the hair on my chinny-chin-chin." I think I was getting punchy from lack of sleep.

He jiggled the handle, to no avail. "I'm not the big bad wolf, Elvis. Let me in."

"No. And there is a big bad wolf after you, so go in your house and I'll be back as quick as I can." I rolled up the window and reversed out of the driveway, then idled on the road.

Adrian stood there for a long moment, gazing at me, frustration plain on his face. I pointed at his house, waiting for him to move. Finally, he started walking. He wasn't happy about the situation, but he wasn't mad either. He wasn't one of those guys with a hot temper and anger management issues. Even as a little boy, Adrian had been very reasonable, and that was one of the many things I loved about him.

As soon as his door shut and the downstairs lights went on, I put pedal to the medal.

# 12. The Long Puppet-walk Home

The roads were empty and I reached Stella's apartment quickly and easily. I parked right in front of the building in a no-parking zone. The van should be invisible. I was on ORB after all, even though I was taking over in mid-job.

My dad didn't notice when I climbed into the back and removed his fanny pack. He was as dead to the world as Stella.

Stella was a zombie as well as a suicide, so I had to use Angel's Breath first, to lure her soul toward the light. She was in pristine condition so I simply placed the capsule between my teeth, sealed our lips together and bit down, exhaling into her. Her lips were softer than a man's and her breath smelled not unpleasantly of rum sweetened with coke, probably the last drink she'd had.

I removed my mouth from hers and spoke the *Licentia Ex Obscurum* chant, followed by the incantation for a suicide. It's called *Felo de Se*, which simply means 'suicide' in Latin. As soon as I spoke it once, Stella's soul was lured up from the hidden recesses where it had been hunkered down since she went zombie. I had to speak it twice more before her soul was released from its flesh coffin. There was an average amount of light. Suicide is not an evil deed. A lot of religious types think otherwise, but they're wrong. Suicide isn't sinful, it's simply the last tragic act of a very desperate person.

After the long version of the *Flat Lux ad Astra*, I anchored the evil in the body in the normal way. I breathed a sigh of release that this reap had gone as planned. My mouth was barely stinging at all.

I put everything back in the fanny pack, opened the van door and climbed out. I stood on the dark empty road and swayed, almost falling over with dizziness. It was my second night without sleep and I really needed my bed. But first, I had to put Stella back where she belonged.

Getting her out of the van was the hardest part of moving her. She was tall for a woman, and sturdy. She outweighed me by a*t least twenty-five pounds. I couldn't lift her and had to sort of drag her out. She ended up in an ungainly heap on the road.

"Time for a walk, Stella." I crouched down to place a hand on her back and spoke the incantation that granted me control over her body's movements by twinning them to my own. I stood up, keeping my hand on her back. She rose with a jerk. One of her arms swung around and smacked me in the face, hard. "I'm sure I deserved that," I said, and started me walking, and Stella walking. I stepped straight, but Stella didn't. She zigzagged and banged into things, like the van. I think her corpse was drunk.

I concentrated to strengthen the body connection between us. That's where I always have trouble with puppet-walking. My link is weak for some reason. I focused on the walkway that led to the front door of her building and deliberately stepped toward it, steering Stella. She stumbled onto the grass and I had to follow since I had to keep my hand on her. I tried to angle her back to the level path, and somehow made her walk into a hedge.

"Shit!" I reversed out of the hedge. Stella walked backwards with me. Since the walking backwards seemed to be working, I kept doing it, drawing her along with me, all the way to the glass door of her building. The door opened when I touched it, as did the inner set of security doors. We rode the elevator to the fourth floor. As soon as we stepped out, she walked straight into a wall. I checked apartment numbers. Stella's was the first door near the elevator.

I walked her backwards into her apartment. It was immaculate. The carpets and couches were white. Except for a few wishy-washy pastel pillows and vases, everything was a white glare. Unblemished.

In my opinion, owning white upholstery is just plain nuts. How can a person ever relax in their own home if everything is white? I would be scared to eat, and scared to sit down, and scared to walk in case I left a trail of dirt in my wake. White is utterly unforgiving and utterly revealing. Life is simply too messy for white furniture and white carpets—especially my life.

Once I had her inside, I steered her across white shag to a little hallway. Her bedroom door was the second door down the hall. Everything was white in there, too. The bed had a puffy white comforter, although it was in disarray. Stella had died tucked in her bed, but there was no pool of blood. She had died neatly of an overdose washed down with a whole lot of alcohol. A few orange pills lay scattered on the carpet where they had been dropped.

I didn't see any obvious note, so maybe she hadn't left one. Most suicides did, but there are exceptions to every rule. Stella could be an exception. There was something very lonely about her apartment, so maybe there was no-one she wanted to share her last words with.

There were no family photos in the bedroom, only a modern flowery painting over the bed. It was mostly white, too, white lilies in the white rain against a white-gray background. In spite of the flowers, it was a truly depressing scene.

I got her to the edge of the bed and removed my hand. She flopped like a ragdoll carelessly dropped by a child. After I removed her shoes, I repositioned her until she looked like she was already in her coffin. I stroked her hair into place. She looked a lot more peaceful laid out like that, and she was at peace now that her soul had been released.

I eyed the comfy queen-sized bed. It tempted me to lie down beside the beautiful Stella, to keep her company so she wouldn't be so alone, except she was already gone. I kissed her cheek and said, "I hope you are happy in heaven." And I had to return to Adrian and guard Adrian, if I could stay awake.

Back at the van, my dad was snoring so loudly, I could hear him before I even opened the door. I slid into the driver's seat and turned on the radio, trying to drown him out. It didn't help. "Home, James," I said to the GPS. I knew how to get home, but his voice giving me directions would help me to stay awake behind the wheel.

I was about to turn onto my street when my dad's phone began playing *All Shook Up*. I groaned loudly. I had just been dreaming about my bed. I pulled over and read the text. At least it was only a single reap at a nursing home. A straightforward job.

"James, we aren't going home yet," I said, and he automatically provided me with directions to the nursing home.

My client was so ancient and bedridden, he should have been covered in cobwebs and dust. It was an easy reap, and when his soul was at peace, I aimed for home. I was within two blocks when I got another text. "No frigging way," I groaned, except I didn't say 'frigging'. I didn't usually swear, but these were extenuating circumstances, and there was no-one around to hear me. My dad was still snoring as loud as a blender full of chicken bones.

Unfortunately, it wasn't the last text I got that night, or I suppose morning would have been more accurate, so there was a good deal more cursing—and reaping—before I saw my house. I parked in my driveway as the sun was rising and my dad hadn't stirred once.

It was a relief to find a quiet neighbourhood. No police cars or ambulances. I did a quick check of the Lyons' house by walking all around it. The downstairs lights were still on. No windows were smashed in and no doors were broken down. I couldn't sense a trace of evil in the air, so I concluded all was well.

I got back into the van because it was warm and the air fell chilly to me, probably because I was exhausted. I wasn't looking forward to trying to get my dad into the house. He was too heavy for me to carry and I couldn't puppet-walk him since he wasn't dead. I also couldn't leave him in the van to sleep it off, not with Jack on the loose.

While I was considering my options, I rested my head back and closed my eyelids, which had gotten too heavy to hold up. When I opened them again, the sun was high in the sky, beating down on the van, making the interior of the vehicle as toasty as a warming oven.

Yawning and groggy, I straightened up and stretched my stiff back. I almost screamed when someone tapped on the window. Adrian was standing there, a coffee in hand.

I eyed it covetously and rolled down the window. "Is that for me?"

He held it just out of reach. "I'm not sure I should give it to you. You ditched me last night."

"It was for your own good." I held out a hand.

"You still ditched me."

"I'm sorry. Please," I begged.

He handed the cup through the window, saying, "It's hot."

"Good." I sipped. "Perfect. Thanks." I took a gulp. "Everything was okay last night?"

Adrian leaned against the door. "All good. You?"

"Yup, all good—except for the lack of sleep."

"I just woke up and spotted you sitting here." He opened the door for me and I slid out. In the back, my dad was still sleeping off his latest drinking binge. And I had been reaping one body after another, all night long. A wave of resentment and anger washed over me. I rolled the window back up, leaned into the van and turned on his CD, full blast. *Mean Woman Blues* started blaring. I shut the door and walked away.

"That wasn't very nice," Adrian said.

"I know. I know it was mean, I'm a mean woman," I said, like the song. I took another hit of coffee. "I know he's suffering and I try to be understanding, but his drinking just makes me so mad. And lack of sleep makes me grumpy." I kept walking to check on Elvis the Scaredeath. Even though the stovepipe hat was cold, I didn't spot any dead animals. I handed Adrian the coffee so I could pour in some of my dad's mixture and light it. Better safe than sorry.

Adrian watched me and sipped some of my coffee, or maybe it was his coffee. Or maybe he wanted to place his lips where mine had just been. Dream on, Elvis. I took the coffee when he handed it back.

"So, what's the plan for today?" he asked.

"I don't know yet. I need some sleep, proper sleep in a bed. And I have to talk to my dad about how he intends to catch Jack." And I had to guard Adrian until Jack was caught.

"Don't forget there's a party tonight at Ramona's," he said.

I had forgotten. "It should be okay for us to go, since we'll be surrounded by friends. We'll probably be safer at the party than here."

"Uh, can we talk about the party for a sec - "

"How about when I wake up," I said, cutting him off. "I'm honestly too tired to think straight."

Adrian hesitated for a beat before he said, "Okay, sure."

"You'll stay home, doors locked?"

He nodded. "I promise."

"Good. I'll call on you when I'm awake, when I wake up." I stifled a yawn. I drained the coffee and handed the empty cup back. "Thanks, that was really good."

"My mom made it," he admitted. "Sleep well, Elvis."

"You, too," I said, which didn't really make a whole lot of sense.

As soon as Adrian was inside his house, I went inside mine. My dad was in the kitchen, drinking juice straight from the carton. "Morning, Dad," I shouted, very very loudly.

He started and spilled juice down the front of his jumpsuit. "Cripes, Elvis, are you trying to give your old man a heart attack?" He sank gently down onto a kitchen chair. "Where's Stella?" His voice was so hoarse, he croaked.

"Back home in bed and reaped." I crossed my arms. "Just like half a dozen other clients. It was a busy night."

"But everything went well?" he asked sheepishly.

"Yes, it did, but it might not have." I sat down, too.

"I know, I know. Things got a little out of hand at the bar. I'm sorry. It won't happen again."

He had said that too many times to count, so I didn't have any faith, but I did have something even more important that I needed to talk to him about. And we could talk freely now that Adrian wasn't there. "Dad, we have to catch Jack before something really bad happens."

He propped his head up on his hand. "I know."

"You said you have an idea?" I wanted to know what it was before I passed out in my bed.

"Sort of. Jack is strongly drawn to Adrian, and he isn't going to give up. You can sense his approach. I doubt he knows that. That's our biggest advantage. We'll know he's coming, so we'll be able to catch him before he gets to Adrian. We'll provide a tempting opportunity that Jack won't be able to resist. We'll trap him and I'll drive the evil out of him. Easy-peasy." He leaned back and attempted a smile. It looked more like a wince.

"So you want to use Adrian as bait," I summarized.

He sighed. "I wouldn't put it quite like that."

I got up and poured myself a glass of orange juice. It didn't sound like much of a plan to me. And we weren't even sure of Jack's own character once the evil was evicted from him. Maybe we would still have a murderer on our hands— and it would be an angry murderer after we'd abducted and tortured him—and I knew better than anyone that an exorcism is akin to torture. "I don't like it," I said.

"You got a better idea?" my dad countered.

"Well, no. Not yet. I'm going to think about it though, while I nap. I'm too tired to think straight. Can you keep an eye on Adrian's house? He promised he'd stay locked inside."

"I'll keep an eye on the house, unless I have to go to work," he said.

"If you have to go to work, wake me up."

"I don't think that will be necessary in the middle of the day with Adrian's parents at home." My dad opened the cupboard. "Want some breakfast first?"

"No." I was too exhausted to chew. "Wake me up anyway, if you go out."

I hauled my butt upstairs and fell on my bed fully dressed. I slept until late afternoon, undisturbed, and woke up feeling almost human again. I showered until there was no hot water left.

I was going to be attending a party with Adrian, so I wanted to look as hot as I possibly could. I dressed with care, and fussed over my hair and makeup. It was dinnertime before I was ready, and I felt sexy in my hip-hugging belted shorts and black bustier-style top that was short enough to show a couple of inches of midriff, and my pierced bellybutton.

When I walked downstairs, my dad was in his office. His reaper's office is a bit like a mad scientist's lair. It's full of the tools of the trade: specimens, herbs, powders, bones, and lots of antiquated gadgets. There's also a wall of books, most of them so old that they're yellow and crumbling, and shelves of faded journals written by my reaper ancestors.

My dad's ongoing project is to scan every page of the books and journals into his computer, before all the valuable information has crumbled to dust and been lost to us. He hasn't even made it through one shelf yet. I'm pretty sure part of my reaper training will involve the boring scanning of a million book pages.

He keeps his scrapbooking supplies in his office, too, and that's what he was working on when I walked in. "All quiet?" I asked, pleased that water was the only drink in sight.

"Only one reap all afternoon." He pasted a yellow star to the corner of a pastel blue obituary.

He hadn't woken me up, but I didn't call him on it. "That's because everyone died last night," I said and peered over his shoulder. I didn't recognize the name at the top of the obit so it wasn't a reap I had been involved in. "Adrian and I are going to a party tonight. I figure we'll be safe surrounded by a crowd."

"So that's why you're dressed like that." He leaned back in his chair and motioned up and down at my getup, paternal frown in place.

I guess I was showing a bit too much skin for my dad's liking. "It's a party, Dad. And there will be girls there showing a lot more skin than me."

"That doesn't mean I have to like it."

I changed the subject before he could tell me to go upstairs and put more clothes on. "Can you drive us and pick us up?"

His phone answered for him with *All Shook Up*. He read the text and capped his glue before he stood up. "Party? Are you sure that's a good idea?"

"I don't think it's a bad idea." I was really looking forward to going to the party with Adrian. In my mind, I was thinking of it as our first real date. Hopefully our first of many dates.

"Well, stay alert, Elvis. And you'll have to drive yourselves. If this reap takes a long time, I won't be available to play chauffeur. And once you're at the party, you know I can't guarantee a pickup time." Facts were facts.

"I know. Does that mean I can take the Elvis-mobile?" I smiled as big as I could.

He chuckled. "Over my dead body."

"Not funny, Dad."

"See if Adrian can use his mom's car," he said over his shoulder, hurrying away to get changed for his reap.

I headed for Adrian's house, with a detour to check on the scaredeath. Its hat needed refilling. I also walked the property and didn't see one dead critter, proving the combination of scaredeath and *Beata Vita* was still working. Unfortunately, the *Beata Vita* was doing something else. The grass border all around the two yards was turning distinctly yellowish-brown. The *Beata Vita* was killing the grass. There was going to be some explaining to do next door.

Adrian answered my knock and he actually looked happy to see me, or maybe he was simply happy to be released from house arrest.

"Hi, Elvis. Come on in. You got some sleep?" He stepped back and I followed him inside.

"I did. You?"

"I had a nap." He raised his eyebrows. "You look really ... wow." I almost fell over with shock. Adrian had complimented me. Me! Before I could say something completely lame in response, he added, "My dad is barbecuing if you want to eat here."

"Sounds great." I had missed breakfast and lunch so I was ready for some food, especially food that was good. "My dad had to go to work. Do you think you'll be able to borrow your mom's car tonight, to drive to the party? I don't think we should risk public transportation."

"I already asked her about her car. I was planning to drive," Adrian said, then looked a bit guilty. Maybe he wanted to drive so he could get me alone. A wave of excitement gripped me. "About tonight," he started to say when his cell phone interrupted us. He answered a call and his mom summoned us to dinner.

We sat down at a table that had been set with placemats and folded napkins, things that had become extinct in my house since my mom died. After a perfectly cooked, marinated chicken breast, potato salad and garden salad, we finished up with a creamy cheesecake topped with cherries. I ate like a starving girl.

There was lots of polite conversation, although Mr. Lyon did mention that the grass at the edge of their lawn and ours was mysteriously turning brown. Adrian didn't volunteer a word about my father's so-called organic fertilizer.

I could tell from the glances Mrs. Lyon darted our way that she was puzzled that Adrian and I appeared to be on such good terms after avoiding each other for years. Over the dessert, she finally came right out and said, "It's nice to see that you two are friends again. I remember how upset you both were when you had that fight when you were younger."

"Fight?" I didn't remember any fight. All I remembered was Adrian dumping me as a best friend.

"We always thought it was just a squabble that would blow over, but it never did. And Adrian began having all those terrible nightmares. That's when he started sleeping with his light on. We had to buy him a nightlight, and Jackson kept teasing him that he was much too old for a nightlight."

"Mom!" Adrian scowled at her.

"I don't remember a fight. What was it about?" I asked Adrian's mother, hoping she would be more forthcoming than her son.

"It was about his hamster, wasn't it, Adrian? It died and you thought Elvis killed it. You were so adamant."

As if her words had unlocked a repressed memory, I suddenly did recall the hamster—Adrian's hamster. He had named it Optimus after one of his favourite transformer toys. We used to take the hamster outside on a little halter leash for walks, and give it rides in Adrian's red wagon, which it never seemed to enjoy. I tried to remember the death of the hamster and drew a complete blank.

"How did it die?" I asked.

Mrs. Lyon glanced at her husband, who grinned at Adrian. "Do you remember the story you told us? Talk about kids having an imagination," he said.

Adrian was not amused. "It's ancient history," he muttered.

"But I want to know," I said. "I can't remember what happened to Optimus."

Adrian turned to glare at me. "How can you not remember? You killed him."

"What? I did not!" I might not remember Optimus's death, but I knew I was no killer of furry little critters.

"You did. You spray-painted him."

I shook my head. "What are you talking about?"

"You spray-painted him and he dropped dead, just like that."

I suppose spray paint could be toxic, especially to something teeny tiny, but I really couldn't imagine myself doing something so mean to a living thing. Plus, I couldn't remember doing it. "I didn't, Adrian. You must be mistaken."

"I'm not. I saw you kill Optimus. He didn't stand a chance." Adrian's cheeks had flushed in anger.

Mr. Lyon interjected at that point, which was good because Adrian really was getting irate, and I was getting defensive. "That's the story Adrian told us, but I examined Optimus myself, and there was no paint on him. Not a speck. He hadn't been spray-painted. He probably just died of old age. He wasn't a young hamster." Mr. Lyon dipped his spoon into his dessert. "We tried to explain that to Adrian, but he wouldn't believe us."

I strained my brain, and still drew a blank. "I really can't remember Optimus dying. I liked him. He was so cute. I wouldn't have killed him."

Adrian snorted angrily.

"I wouldn't have. So that's why you stopped being my friend? Because you thought I killed your hamster?" I said.

"You did kill him." Adrian sounded so certain, and so accusing, that a tingle of alarm ran down my spine.

"What colour was the paint?" I asked.

Adrian frowned at his plate and muttered, "It was invisible spray paint."

"It made Optimus invisible?" I said stupidly.

"No. It had no colour, that's why my dad couldn't see it."

"Oh. What colour was the can?" I was following a hunch about my dad's missing can of Dead Man's Breath.

"Black, I guess, or silver. Some normal paint can colour."

I bit my lip. "What happened to the can?"

"You hid it."

Mr. Lyon couldn't contain a smile. "Adrian was such a serious little boy. He said that you had hidden the murder weapon so you wouldn't go to jail for killing his hamster. He wanted the police to arrest you."

It was my turn to glare at Adrian. "You wanted me to go to jail, because your hamster died?"

"No, I wanted you to go to jail because you killed Optimus."

We were back to square one. "Did you tell my dad about it?" I asked Mr. Lyon.

He shook his head. "It was a child's fantasy and we thought it would resolve itself. There was no need to involve your parents." And facts were facts, my parents and Adrian's parents had never been more than polite with each other when my mother was alive. They'd never had enough in common to be friends. The Lyon's certainly hadn't been Elvis groupies at my dad's spontaneous backyard concerts.

"More cheesecake anyone?" Mrs. Lyon asked.

Both Adrian and I refused. He stood up and said, "We should get going. I said I would pick up Ted, and buy some chips for the party."

I thanked the Lyon's for the great dinner and Adrian and I left, after his mother nagged him a bit about not drinking and driving. Walking to the car, we were both silent until Adrian said rather accusingly, "What did you put on the lawn?" He motioned at the dead grass which looked even browner and crispier than when I had walked into the house.

"I guess my dad's organic fertilizer didn't work," I said.

"No kidding," he muttered.

I think all the talk about Optimus the hamster had reawakened the resentment and anger that Adrian had held inside for years. I wanted to talk about his pet's death and clear the air, but I didn't know what to say. Maybe I had killed Optimus as thoroughly as I had killed the grass. If I had gotten my hands on the Dead Man's Breath, I might have killed anything in breathing range. And if I had been spraying Dead Man's Breath around willy-nilly, what had I done with the can all those years ago? And why did I have complete amnesia about the event?

We got in the car and Adrian started driving, still without a word. "I'm sorry about Optimus," I blurted out. "I wish I could remember what happened, but I really don't, Adrian."

He kept his eyes on the road. "You did seem kind of woozy after you spray-painted Optimus. You even fell down a few times. I think you breathed some of the spray."

That was a terrifying thought if it was Dead Man's Breath that I'd been spraying and inhaling. "Do you know where I got the can?"

He shrugged. "Your house, I guess."

"I always wondered why you dumped me," I said, aiming for a light tone and not pulling it off at all.

Adrian merged onto a busier street. "After that, I was scared of you. I thought you might spray me with the invisible paint and kill me, too. I suppose that's why I started having nightmares, and you were in all of them, chasing me with the spray paint."

Clearly, death had encroached on my life even back then. I had traumatized Adrian, and he had been too afraid of me to be my friend anymore. I just wished some glimmer of the memory would return. Adrian veered onto a suburban street, turned again, and stopped in front of a two-story brick house.

"Ted's?" I said, assuming.

"No." He hesitated and tapped the steering wheel before he darted a glance my way, his brow furrowed.

"So, who are we picking up?"

"Look, I'm taking Meghan to the party," he said kind of defensively. "I asked her last week, before all this crap happened, before you and I started hanging out because of Jack. I didn't think it would be polite to cancel at the last minute, especially since I'm going to the party anyway."

Except he was going with me. I clenched my hands into fists so I wouldn't wrap them around his neck and squeeze until his head popped like a ripe zit.

"I mean, we're only together because of Jack," he added.

"Right, and you think I murdered your hamster, and I was the monster in your childhood nightmares." I could hear the bitterness in my own voice. I clamped my lips together before I said something I was sure to regret, or worse, burst into tears.

Adrian sighed. "I tried to talk to you about this before - "

"All you had to do was tell me you had a date. There's nothing to talk about," I bit out.

He opened his mouth to say something. He shut it when Meghan stepped out of her house. "We'll talk later," he said.

"Nothing to talk about," I repeated breezily as he exited the car to greet her.

He was clueless. He was as brain-dead as a week old zombie. And if I'd had a couple of handy zombies, I would have happily sic'ed them on him. My heart hemorrhaging so badly it needed a tourniquet, I relocated myself to the backseat. It would have been simply mortifying if Adrian had to ask me to switch seats.

He opened the door for Meghan. She got in with a sweet and breathless, "Hi, Elvis."

"Hi, Meghan." I think she was as happy to see me as I was to see her, which was not happy at all. Meghan and I were not friends. She's all the things I'm not—popular and social and perfect, and involved in all sorts of school activities. She probably wouldn't be caught dead carrying animal carcasses around in her bare hands. At least on the surface, her life is as normal as Adrian's, so they probably have a lot more in common than he and I do.

Meghan is pretty in a cute, petite way, except for her boobs. They are not small. In fact, they're kind of big. Meghan is the opposite of me, and if she's the type of girl Adrian is attracted to, I didn't stand a chance. I'm pretty sure she thinks I'm weird, and maybe I am. Frankly, I've always been a little jealous of her happy, well-adjusted life. And now she had Adrian. It was the icing on my cake of misery.

Meghan's perfume was so overpowering, it made me want to gag. I rolled the window down so I could breathe.

Ted lived a few blocks away and Adrian picked him up next. Ted got into the back beside me and it was like we were on a surprise blind date that neither of us was expecting, or welcomed. I wasn't enough of a cheerleader type for Ted, and I was taller than him. He was too much of a bully for me.

He had brought along a rather full backpack and I didn't need to be Sherlock Holmes to guess what was clinking around inside it.

Adrian stopped for snacks next. I opted to wait in the car while the others went to buy junk food. I figured Adrian would be safe enough in the brightly lit grocery store, accompanied by his date and Ted.

They took their time and I was glad. I needed more than a moment to recover from the latest blow to my heart. I sat still, my eyes shut tight to dam any tears that might leak out. I was so engrossed in my angst that it took a moment to notice that something seemed off. Was I sensing a faint essence of evil? Or was it my own resentment and jealousy that I was feeling? I opened my eyes and surveyed the parking lot. I didn't spot anything alarming and got out of the car to keep watch on the front door of the grocery store, wishing I had eyes in the back of my head like so many of my teachers.

It was another ten long minutes before Adrian and company reappeared with bags of chips and pop. I concentrated hard and the whiff of evil remained elusive. Then again, it had been so faint that I might have imagined it. I got back in the car with the others.

118

Ted opened a bottle of coke and poured half of it out the door, which seemed strange until he produced a bottle of rum from his pack. He emptied most of it into the coke bottle. "Cheers," he said and guzzled the mixed drink before he offered some to me.

I shook my head. "No thanks." Alcohol has zero appeal for me, probably because it has too much appeal for my dad. And I've witnessed too much of its dark side, standing beside my dad as he reaped the souls of kids who got behind the wheel and crashed and burned after having a few too many.

Meghan didn't refuse a drink. Adrian did and I was glad because he was our driver. I could have offered to be designated driver, except I didn't want to be responsible for his mom's car. It was pretty new and I had already ruined the Lyon's lawn, and apparently killed Adrian's beloved hamster, and traumatized him. I didn't want to cause any more damage than I already had.

# 13. Party Like There's No Tomorrow

Even though it was early, the party was underway when we got there. Everyone was eager to celebrate the end of exams and high school, and the start of summer holidays. Ramona's parents weren't home, which was no surprise. If they had been home, the party would have been elsewhere. She also had a big in-ground pool, and it was being used. I had tucked my bathing suit in my purse, just in case. My leg was healed enough to swim, and most of my bruises and scratches from that ill-fated night had faded away.

I pulled Adrian aside before he could disappear with Meghan. "Adrian, remember to stay here, surrounded by people. Don't take off with Meghan. I have to be able to find you."

He scoffed at that. "Elvis, I'm perfectly safe here. Relax and enjoy the party. I plan to."

I gripped his arm when he tried to leave, and cast Meghan a 'back the hell off' glance when it was clear she intended to join our private confab. "You're not perfectly safe anywhere. I thought I ... glimpsed someone really big outside the grocery store." I had almost said 'sensed', which would have simply confused Adrian. "It could have been Jack following us, so make sure you stay here, and make sure I can find you."

"Okay, I will."

I released his arm and he rejoined Meghan. She was giving me all kinds of dirty looks, as if I was trying to steal her date, not keep him alive. I spotted Carrie sitting by the pool with some other girls from school. Bianca and Mark were swimming together and kissing wetly. It looked like they had made up again, or never broken up at all. I joined Carrie on her lounger.

It was nice to recline in the warm evening air and relax. I kept one eye on Adrian. Unfortunately, that soon became galling, if not torturous. Meghan was getting up close and personal, and Adrian didn't seem to mind. Of course he didn't, he's a guy and there's nothing wrong with the way she's put together. He was drinking beer, but moderately. Not so Meghan, and the more she drank, the handsier she got.

Many of the kids at the party were drinking or smoking stuff, but nobody was losing control, except for Ted. He was getting steadily louder and more obnoxious, so I hoped someone else would be driving him home. I didn't want him puking on me in the backseat of Mrs. Lyon's car. I'm sure she would appreciate it even less.

Carrie nudged me and said, "Stop glaring daggers, Elvis. Let's have a swim."

I realized I was scowling darkly at Adrian and Meghan. I did need to cool off in a big way. We changed and jumped into the pool. The water was heated and it felt heavenly. There was a floating basketball net and we ended up playing water basketball with a rubbery beachball. Bianca and Mark and some other kids joined in, and soon we had two teams playing against each other. It turned into an energetic match. Someone cranked the music way up and a lot of kids started dancing beside the pool and falling into the pool fully clothed, which put an end to the game.

I got out and joined the dancing. Adrian and Meghan were dancing much too close together for my liking, almost as close as when he and I had danced. To protect my heart, I stopped watching them and jumped back into the pool. I didn't leave the water until I was pruney, and then I couldn't spot the pair in the yard. I couldn't spot them anywhere.

The night felt chilly all of the sudden. I dried off with one of the pool towels, then wrapped it over my damp bathing suit before I entered the house. I helped myself to a can of pop and walked around on the main floor, patrolling for Adrian. I disturbed more than one couple who did not want to be interrupted. When I couldn't spot Adrian, I started to get really worried, even though I wasn't sensing any evil. And surely he wouldn't have been foolish enough to take Meghan to the car to make out, parked as it was on a dark street. Then again, guys were reputed to be as dumb as a rocks when they were thinking with parts other than their brains.

Instead of patrolling upstairs, where there were beds, which was the last thing in the world I wanted to do, I opened the front door to scan the lawn for Adrian. Two police officers were standing there, about to knock, or maybe they had been knocking and ringing for awhile and nobody had heard them over the music.

"Officer Tommick, fancy meeting you here," I said with a smile.

It only took him a moment. "Elvis Black, isn't it? Case of the dead camel."

I knew my name was memorable and he was proving it. The camel had also been the stuff of urban legends. I said, "That's right. Have you solved the camel caper yet?"

"I'm still working on it. This is my partner, Officer Jemp." Officer Jemp was a busty woman with shoulders that rivaled her partner's, even though she was a head shorter. She also lacked his sense of humour.

She got right down to business, saying crisply, "We've had several complaints about the noise. Any parents at home?"

"Not a one."

"Any underage drinking going on?" she asked.

I wasn't sure how to answer that, and opted for evasion. "I'm only a guest at this party. Let me get Ramona, she lives here." I moved to close the door.

Officer Tommick stuck out a big foot in a heavy shoe, stopping the door in its tracks. "Leave it opened. We'll wait here."

I hurried back to the pool, turning the stereo off in passing. Ramona had been dancing to the loud music. She said, "Why did you do that?"

"Cops are at the door. They want to talk to you." In a much louder voice, I broadcast, "Cops are here. Take evasive action." There was a flurry of people butting out or pouring out stuff they could be arrested for. Some guests left straight away, directly over the back fence. I saw Ted trying to climb it. Someone boosted him over and tossed his backpack after him.

Ramona was groaning as she headed for the front door. I didn't follow her. I had to find Adrian. He still wasn't around the pool or on the main level of the house. If he had snuck over the back fence without his trusty bodyguard, I was going to kill him myself.

I changed into my dry clothes quickly. The party was over, one way or another. A glance at my phone informed me it was much later than I'd realized. I had thought it was around eleven-thirty. It was closer to one. No wonder there had been complaints about the noise.

When I came out of the bathroom, the number of partiers had shrunk even further. Those guests who were sober were departing by the front door. The police were checking their condition, making sure they were okay to drive. One of the cops should have attended the rear. The kids sneaking out that way were the ones who shouldn't be driving. I really hoped I wouldn't have to reap any of them tonight.

I still didn't see Adrian anywhere. I risked a trip upstairs into bedroom territory. I peeked into all the rooms and they were blessedly empty. I didn't embarrass anyone, especially myself. Downstairs again, I returned to the front door to see if Adrian was waiting for me.

The cops were seeing off the last of the stragglers. Tommick smiled at me. "And how are you tonight, Elvis?"

"As sober as a judge. I'm looking for the friend who drove me here, but I can't seem to find him." Ramona was standing beside the cops, almost bug-eyed. She was completely freaked out and smelled like both booze and pot. "Ramona, have you seen Adrian and Meghan?" I asked her.

"No. Yes. I think they left." She sniffed and her eyes darted wildly toward the cops, like a trapped animal that is thinking of making a desperate run for it.

I leaned in and gave her a hug, whispering, "Everything will be fine, Ramona. A loud party with some drinking is no big deal." It certainly wasn't in my life, which was all deathly drama. Most things seemed minor by comparison. I gestured down the road and said, "I'm going to see if Adrian's car is still here. I might be right back, so don't lock me out, okay?"

Ramona nodded and I set off. The cops left almost on my heels, mission accomplished. The party was over and they were going easy on Ramona.

Hours ago, when Adrian had driven up to Ramona's house, the road in front had been so full of cars, he'd had to park around the curve. I couldn't tell if his car was still there, not without walking around that curve. The road was empty of cars now, and far too dark and deserted for my liking.

My footsteps barely made a sound when I walked in the middle of the road. Most of the surrounding houses were unlit. Around the bend, it was even darker. The overhead streetlight was out. "Figures," I muttered.

I kept walking until I could make out the silhouette of Mrs. Lyon's car, still parked where Adrian had left it, proving he hadn't abandoned me after all. So where was he? Maybe he was making out with Meghan in the car, and maybe I hated him. I had no choice but to check the car.

I moved closer and like a frigid wave, a deluge of evil washed over me. Jack was close—terrifyingly close. I half-expected a cold blade to slice through my flesh.

Too scared to take another step, I froze in place. My eyes darted around wildly, scanning for movement. As my vision adjusted to the darkness, I made out a black shape sprawled on the grass beside the car. It was as still and limp as a corpse.

"Adrian," I gasped out, fearing that I was already too late. And if I wasn't too late, I didn't even have a handy golf club to use as a weapon. I had never liked guns, having seen a few too many shot up corpses, but I would have traded my heart for a gun at that moment. It was broken anyway.

Before Jack could attack me, too, I screamed bloody murder. I have an impressive scream when I let it rip. I was hoping the cops were still close enough to hear me and rush in like the cavalry. I didn't approach Adrian, simply too sick with fear over what I might find. If his face had been mutilated in the worst way, I couldn't bear to look upon it.

An engine started up from somewhere behind Mrs. Lyon's car. High beams turned on, blinding me. The vehicle burned rubber straight toward me and I knew I should run. I did try to run, my feet simply didn't seem to get the urgent message my brain was sending them. Or I had stepped in a puddle of crazy glue.

Over the revving engine, I heard someone shout, "Elvis, move!" It sounded enough like Adrian for me to throw myself toward the curb. The bumper missed hitting me by inches. I landed hard on pavement and left some skin behind. For a moment, I lay there staring at the road under my nose, too stunned to move, then Adrian was crouching beside me.

He laid a warm hand on my back. "Elvis, are you okay?"

I rolled over and stared up at his shadowy figure in the darkness. "You're not dead," I said, stating the obvious.

"And you're not either, but it was a really close call." He gripped my hand too tight and helped me to my feet.

123

"That was Jack," I said. "He's been following us."

"No shit." He looked down the road, in the direction of the truck.

I did, too, and couldn't even spot taillights. "Did you see what he was driving?" I asked.

"Blue pickup truck, but I didn't get the plate number. Are you sure you're not hurt." He sounded worried about me.

My shoulder, elbow and knee were stinging, but none of the injuries felt deep. I would need a flashlight to know for sure. "I'm fine," I said as Meghan stumbled over. The body was still beside Adrian's car, except it wasn't a body. Ted staggered to his feet and promptly puked in the grass.

"Too gross," Meghan said.

I nudged Adrian. "Turn the headlights on so we can see." I didn't want Jack to revisit us.

While he unlocked the car, Meghan asked, "Why were you screaming?"

I pointed at Ted. "I thought he was dead, and a truck almost ran me over."

"Oh." She giggled for some reason, probably because she was pretty wasted, or maybe the thought of me getting crushed by a truck made her super happy.

The car headlights turned on and she blinked owlishly. I led her to the car and held the front passenger door for her. She had the right to the seat. She was Adrian's real date, after all. "Get in, Meghan. Adrian, we should leave, now," I stressed. "Are you okay to drive? You didn't have too much to drink?"

"Just a couple of beer, I'm fine. Let me get Ted." He went over to help his friend walk and loaded Ted into the backseat.

I got in beside him with great reluctance, and said, "Don't you dare barf on me. If you have to barf, do it out the window." Adrian rolled Ted's window down, just in case, and the air did need freshening.

Adrian started driving. I kept my head in the breeze by my window. Wisely, Adrian took Ted home first. I think we all heaved a sigh of relief when he made it out of the car without messing it up in the worst way.

When the car was moving again, Meghan said, "Are you going to take Elvis home now?" It was a broad hint.

"No, I'm going to have to drop you off first. I have to be up early and Elvis lives right beside me." Adrian sounded more apologetic than regretful, or I was deluding myself. Since he couldn't ditch his bodyguard, he couldn't get rid of me. He really hadn't thought this date thing through.

Meghan didn't say a word. The air turned rather frosty in the car, and it wasn't because Adrian had activated the air-conditioning. Luckily, Meghan lived really close to Ted. I didn't have to endure the uncomfortable silence for long. In about a minute, Adrian pulled up in front of her house. She got out and said, "Don't bother walking me to the door."

"Bye, Meghan," I said.

The car door slammed a lot harder than was necessary. Adrian got out anyway and walked her to the door. They had a brief conversation and she went inside. There was no goodnight kiss.

Adrian returned and slid behind the wheel. "Are you going to get in the front?"

"I don't think so," I said.

"What's wrong, Elvis?"

"Nothing." Even I didn't believe me.

He started driving slowly. "Are you mad at me because I said you killed my hamster?" he asked when I held my silence. Oh ya, there was that, too. In the wake of Jack's latest attack, I'd forgotten all about murdering Optimus with Dead Man's Breath.

"No," I said.

He adjusted his rearview mirror so he could see me instead of the road. "I didn't really think it was the hamster. That was a stupid thing to say. It's Meghan, isn't it?"

I met his eyes in the mirror. "No, it's not Meghan. It's you."

He shifted his gaze back to the road. "I should have called her and cancelled. Tonight was ... messed up, stupid. I'm sorry. All this has just snuck up on me, and I'm not even sure what this is."

"This?" I said. Adrian wasn't being very clear.

"You and me." Our gazes met and held, via the rearview mirror.

"Oh." Headlights flared behind us and I swung around in alarm. "Drive faster, Adrian. Jack might be following us." I pulled out my phone. "I have to call my dad."

He answered on the fourth ring and didn't give me a chance to say a thing. "I'm in the middle of something, Elvis," he gasped over the sound of someone crying hysterically. He must have been in mid-reap, with witnesses, and it didn't sound like it was going well.

"Call me back," I shouted as he hung up on me. I'm not sure he heard me.

While I had the phone in hand, I checked the time. Almost two. The headlights behind us turned off on a side street and there were no more cars in sight, to the front or rear. I breathed a sigh of relief. We were safe for the time being, except Adrian was automatically heading for home. Jack knew where we lived. He could be lying in wait and my dad wasn't there.

"Adrian, don't go home yet," I said.

He took his foot off the gas. "Why not?"

"Because my dad's not home and Jack could be waiting for us. He knows where we live, doesn't he?"

"Okay. Where to?" he asked.

"Somewhere well lit, somewhere with people. The more the better."

"Tim Hortons?" he suggested.

"Sounds good. They have coffee." I was feeling so drained and beaten, I needed something to perk me up. And the place was opened twenty-four/seven. No matter what time of day or night, there were always caffeine addicts hanging around getting their fix. A coffee and a doughnut sounded good to me. So did a bathroom. I had some stinging scrapes to take care of. I was trying my best to keep my blood off of Mrs. Lyon's upholstery, but I wasn't sure I was managing it.

Adrian pulled into the Tim Hortons lot. He parked close to the building, right under a light. I couldn't sense any evil so I slid out. The smell of coffee was strong in the air, at least to me. Senses on high alert for evil, I paused outside the glass entrance door and surveyed the interior. About a dozen patrons were slurping coffee. One girl was behind the counter aligning doughnuts into tidy rows, and a young man was starting a fresh pot. I was satisfied that it was enough of a crowd to keep Jack at bay, if he had managed to track us to the Tim Hortons.

"We should be safe enough here. I'm going to clean up in the washroom," I said quietly.

"You're bleeding, Elvis. You did get hurt," Adrian said, looking at me in the light. He lifted my arm and frowned at the scrapes. "I'm sorry."

"It wasn't your fault," I said automatically, then I thought better of it. "Actually, it kind of was. You disappeared when I asked you to stay in sight. I had to search for you outside in the dark. Jack could have killed you, and me. Where were you? Or do I want to know?"

"In the house for awhile." He left it at that. "And I did look for you, I couldn't find you either."

I suppose that was possible, I had dressed in the bathroom and patrolled upstairs. We could have missed each other in passing. "Whatever," I said and entered the doughnut shop. I was not in a good mood thinking about Adrian and Meghan swapping spit and maybe a lot more than that.

"Do you want a coffee?" Adrian asked, before I headed for the washroom.

"Sure. I'll have one with lots of milk and sugar. And a doughnut, chocolate. Double chocolate." I reached into my pocket for some cash.

"I've got it," Adrian said. "Go take care of your wounds."

I hauled out a five dollar bill and stuffed it into his hand. "I'm not your date. I'll pay for my own food." I spun around and headed for the washroom.

It was a single person facility, and it was empty. I entered and locked the door, so glad to be alone if only for a moment. I slumped against the wall and took deep calming breaths. I was painfully disappointed in how the evening had turned out.

I'd had such high hopes of a dreamy date with Adrian. And then between them, Meghan and Jack had spoiled it. Or maybe Adrian had spoiled it by bringing a date along on our date, which he hadn't realized was a date. The date was probably only in my imagination. In his mind, I was likely just his bodyguard, so he was willing to put up with me. Beyond that, I was persona non grata, because he thought I'd killed his hamster, or I truly had. I was beginning to believe it was the latter.

"Stop slacking on the job, Elvis," I said and shoved away from the wall. In the mirror, my reflection was not looking its best, so I knew I wasn't either. The swim had washed off all my makeup and not wearing makeup made my nose look bigger than it truly was. The pool water and humidity had also made a mess of my hair. If left untamed, it tended to get curly bordering on frizzy. It had taken full advantage of its freedom.

In the too-bright light, my scrapes were raw and angry red. The ones on my elbow and knee were the worst. I rinsed off blood and picked little stones out of my knee, then washed my hands and attempted to brush my hair. I soon gave up on that losing battle. I hurried back to Adrian, who shouldn't be left alone, because I was indulging in vanity. It was blatantly obvious that he didn't care how I looked.

He was sitting at a table near the serving counter with two coffees and a couple of doughnuts. I dropped into the seat opposite him and took a healthy swig.

"What now?" Adrian asked.

"Now I'm going to enjoy my coffee and doughnut, and then I'm going to phone my dad again. Hopefully he'll be finished the job he's working on. I don't want to go home until he's there." I took an appreciative bite of sweet chocolaty goodness.

"Ya. I can't believe Jack is following us around. Maybe it's time to call the police in." Adrian toyed with his cup.

I shook my head. "They won't be able to help. They don't have the resources to assign officers to guard you. It's not like on TV, Adrian. And my dad does know what he's doing, in spite of the drinking. He's your best bet."

Adrian didn't look convinced. The frown line stayed fixed in place between his dark eyebrows. Have I mentioned yet how much I like Adrian's eyebrows? They're thick, dark and straight, and he has a habit of raising them when he's feeling inquisitive, and lowering them when he's worried. They were so lowered now, they were almost in his eyes. Even though I was mad at him, I still liked his eyebrows.

"I don't know, Elvis. This has gotten really out of hand. I mean, a dangerous criminal is trying to kill me and he almost killed you tonight." Adrian leaned closer and lowered his voice. "I'm going to have to talk to my parents about this and see what they think. They'll probably want to call the police, and … and I would feel safer if the police were involved. It's not that I don't trust your dad, but if he gets drunk again …" Adrian shrugged apologetically.

I got what he was saying, but if he spoke to the police, my dad would be questioned about the case of Jack the Biter, that he was supposedly working on as a private detective. And Jack the Biter led straight to a brutal murder and mysterious death. Colin had covered for him on occasion in the past, when necessary, but this was simply too big for Colin to sweep under the proverbial carpet.

While I mulled over what I could possibly tell Adrian to make him change his mind, I finished my coffee and doughnut. My phone rang when I was thinking about ordering a box of doughnuts to take home as comfort food. I checked the caller I.D. My dad had perfect timing. "Hey, Dad. Everything under control?"

"Finally. It was a ... difficult reap, a baby. God, I hate those reaps. So, what's up?"

"Jack attacked tonight, he followed us to the party." I spoke quietly, not wanting to be overheard by the whole doughnut shop.

"Are you okay?" His voice was clear and steady, and so sad. Reaping a baby's soul is the very worst sort of reap. My dad has never taken me on one of those.

"I'm okay." A few scrapes didn't count when Jack was intent on murder and worse, feasting on human flesh.

"Where are you?"

I cupped my hand around the phone for added privacy. "Adrian and I are at Tim Hortons. I didn't want to risk going home with a killer on the loose, not until you were there."

"Smart thinking. I'm heading home now, be there in ten. I'll wait in the driveway with the headlights on, okay?"

"Okay. Be careful, Dad. I'll bring you a box of doughnuts." I, too, felt the need for a bit more comfort food.

"Much appreciated. And don't you worry about your old man. I already picked up a few supplies to help us capture Jack, without doing permanent damage to his body. I'm prepared. If we're lucky, we'll catch him tonight, then this will all be over." He even sounded optimistic.

"Great." I ended the call and glanced at Adrian. "He's meeting us at home, and he's perfectly sober. He thinks there's a good chance he'll catch Jack tonight, so there might not be any need to call the police."

"Let's hope." Adrian stood up and headed for the doughnut counter.

I followed and we picked out a nice assortment. Adrian paid. I lacked the energy to argue.

Before we left the bright safety of the doughnut shop, I concentrated on sensing evil. I didn't detect any. As soon as we were in the car, we both locked our doors. I sat in the front this time; I would have felt silly getting in the back.

Adrian drove home on dark empty streets. We pulled onto our dead end road without incident. Adrian's house was dark, except for the one porch light that was on. At my house, the van was in the driveway, headlights off.

"That's odd," I murmured.

Adrian glanced sideways. "What is?"

"My dad said he would leave the headlights on as a signal." I was hoping they would turn on when he spotted our headlights, but they didn't. "Keep going." I squinted into the darkness. And then it hit me like an icy stinging wind. Evil, stronger than I had ever felt it, as if Jack was reveling in some appalling activity—like killing my dad. I must have cried out, because Adrian slammed on the brakes.

"No, keep going! Don't stop, and turn the headlights off," I gasped.

Adrian did and we drove by my house. I didn't spot any movement, but evil was pulsating in the air all around.

"Elvis, what's - "

"Just keep driving," I hissed, "and turn around at the end of the street. Try not to slow down and whatever you do, don't stop."

The end of the road was a circle of pavement that was just wide enough for a car to maneuver in a tight turn, if the person behind the wheel was a good driver. I couldn't have managed it, but Adrian looped around without any stopping and reversing.

"Adrian, I'm going to hop out. You'll have to slow down, but don't stop. Then get the hell out of here. Maybe you should drive to the police station." I was sick with fear that my dad was already dead. My voice shook badly.

"I'm not letting you out and driving away, Elvis. Your dad probably just forgot to leave the van's headlights on. The lights are on in your house, so he probably went inside to have a drink."

Given my dad's track record, it was an easy thing to assume. I might have assumed the same if not for what I could sense. "No, no. Jack is here." Tears stung my eyes, blinding me. I dashed them away. "My dad is in trouble, if he's not dead already. I'm going to try and help him while you get backup." I put a hand on the door handle. Adrian gripped my arm. I yanked free and shoved the door opened. He slammed the brakes on. I staggered out of the car in too much of a panic to think about a plan. I was simply reacting. Time was of the essence.

"Get out of here," I shouted over my shoulder and took off running. I reached the van and peeked into the driver's side. The van appeared to be empty. The two front seats certainly were. Nausea gripped me when I smelled fresh blood.

"Dad," I sobbed and stumbled toward the house, cutting through what felt like a fogbank of evil. I heard footsteps behind me and knew who it was without even looking. "Adrian, if Jack doesn't kill you, I'm going to do it myself," I bit out.

We rounded the corner of the porch and I stopped dead. Adrian bumped into me. I spun to face him. "At least go to your house and wake up your parents, and call the police. We're going to need help."

Adrian shook his head. "I'm not going to wake them up if there's nothing wrong."

"You think I'm imagining things?"

129

"I didn't say that. Let's just check if your dad is in trouble first," Adrian whispered.

"He is in trouble, or worse!" I bit my lip hard, to keep from screaming.

Adrian shook his head. "How can you know that?"

"I just can, I just do." I started moving again, tiptoeing up the porch steps toward the door that led into the kitchen. At least the outside porch light wasn't on to spotlight us. Only the outer screen door was closed. The inner wooden door was ajar. An open invitation for any serial killer to wander on in. It was another sign that all was not well—that all was very very wrong. I needed a weapon of some sort before I stormed in. I recalled leaving the pointy spade leaning against the house, to the right of the porch.

Before I could backtrack to fetch the shovel, Adrian stepped forward and peered through the screen door. He straightened up and gripped the handle, saying, "Your dad is fine. He's sitting at the table having a drink." Before I could stop him, he opened the door.

The evil haze was so thick in the air, I could taste the foulness, so I was dumbfounded when I heard my dad say calmly, "There you are. You took your sweet time getting back here."

I was so relieved to see him alive, not dead, that I stepped into the kitchen. He was sitting at the table with a drink in hand, smiling expansively.

"Dad? What's going on? You didn't leave the headlights on. I thought Jack had hurt you. He's here," I said ominously.

"I know he's here. He's in the garage. I already took care of him." He raised his glass as if in toast.

"Really?"

"You bet your blue suede shoes." He stood up and his jumpsuit was torn. No, it was cut—slashed, and his chest was bleeding.

"Dad, you're hurt!"

"Nothing to worry about." He plucked at his jumpsuit. "It's only a little nick. Doesn't even need stitches." He seemed to be smiling too widely, but maybe that was from the drinking, or his victory over Jack. "Come have a look at my prisoner."

Adrian and I shared an uneasy glance. Something didn't feel quite right to me. It looked like Adrian shared my disquiet. I shut the door we had just entered through, including the heavy wooden door. I slid the locking bolt into place, because I still felt endangered.

"Wait here, I'll go have a look," I murmured to Adrian.

Again, he didn't heed my words. He came along when I followed my father through the connecting door into the garage. My dad flicked the light on and I blinked.

A big cage held a limp figure. The cage hadn't been in the garage the last time I looked. If I wasn't mistaken, it was a kennel for a really big dog, or maybe a bear. Chicken wire had been wrapped around the sides as an added security measure. An impressive padlock made sure the door couldn't be opened by human fingers, not that Jack was going to be trying to escape anytime soon— or ever again.

"Is he dead?" Adrian gasped. Death was not a part of his life. He sounded shocked to his core.

Jack couldn't have looked deader, short of missing his head. His eyes were opened and staring. And most telling of all, his neck had a sagging wound. Even though his T-shirt was black, it was sticking to him wetly due to all the blood loss. His skin was as white as Stella's apartment. His nose was crooked and still swollen, but I knew that was my doing.

I closed my eyes, trying to sense a soul even though my dad should have already reaped it. I couldn't sense anything except smothering evil. It was all around me, yet it didn't seem to be emanating from the cage. Had it escaped the body once the soul had been released? Yet again? And if so, where had it gone?

When my dad didn't say a word, I gasped, "Dad, you killed him."

"Self-defense," he said too cheerfully. In fact, my dad was sounding less and less like himself. The Elvis drawl had disappeared completely, and was he acquiring a British accent? I stood up and moved away from the cage. My dad's gaze stayed fixed on Adrian, hungrily, avidly.

In that instant, I knew beyond a shadow of a doubt that he wasn't really my dad anymore. The evil had escaped Jack's body and found a new host and a new home. Somehow, the evil had beaten my dad at his own game.

The nightmare of a night wasn't over after all—it was just beginning. And the unfolding events were so unexpected and twisty that I was having a hard time wrapping my head around them. For very different reasons, both my dad and I were now craving Adrian. And I had to find a way to save Adrian without killing my dad. Exorcising the evil was the obvious solution, except I had never performed an exorcism, only been on the receiving end of one. And my dad wasn't strapped to a chair with duct tape. He was roaming free.

Adrian hadn't moved. He was still gawking at the dead body as if he had never seen one, which he probably hadn't, not in real life anyway. "Have you called the police?" he asked my dad.

"Not yet. I was waiting for Elvis to get you back here, safe and sound." The diabolical intent in his voice was barely masked. I had to wonder if my dad had guessed that I had figured out his rotten inner identity. I risked another glance at his face. His eyes were too wide and almost bulging. They were looking crazier by the minute.

If he believed I was falling for his charade, now was the time for me to act and stop the evil in its tracks. I didn't have a shovel to whack him over the head with, but the garage was full of a wide assortment of items that could be used to temporarily disable a man. I scanned what was in reach. The pickaxe was really close, but it was too dangerous to use on my dad, same for the chainsaw.

I didn't want to kill him, merely render him senseless for as long as it took to restrain him.

There was a baseball bat propped near the door into the house. If I didn't hit him too hard, maybe I could use it. My dad who was no longer my dad said, "Let's go back into the house and call the police."

I pretended to be clueless and said, "Okay."

As much as I wanted to place myself between my dad and Adrian, I hung back so I could snap up the bat. My dad had his own conniving plans and waited for me, keeping a close bloodshot eye on me. Our eyes met and in the frankness of the gaze, we both knew that we weren't fooled. We both knew exactly what the hell was going on. Only Adrian was somewhat oblivious.

"Come along, Elvis. We don't want to keep Adrian waiting, now do we?" My dad smirked. I recognized the same nasty sneer that had ruled my face when Carl's evil had been riding roughshod over me, digging its spurs into my brain.

Adrian paused on the threshold between the garage and the kitchen, and looked back with a frown. "Keep me waiting for what?"

"Death," my dad said, savouring the word in a way he never had before. The gloves were off.

"Death?" Adrian looked baffled, but not unduly alarmed yet.

"Run!" I screamed, lunging for the baseball bat.

Evil Dad lunged, too. I got to the bat a fraction of a second before he did. I swung it up into the air in his direction. He dodged back and the end of the bat whistled by his ear. I swung it again, toward the side of his head. Clearly, I was no baseball player. I missed his head entirely—strike two, or maybe I simply couldn't bear to hit him.

Before I could swing the bat a third time, he crouched low and pounced. He caught the bat in two hands and ripped it out of my grip. When he hoisted it over his shoulder into the position to swing, I knew he would have no reservations about bashing my brains in. When I had been possessed, I'd certainly had no qualms about slashing his throat.

I fell back and spotted Adrian still standing there, trying to make sense of the bizarre scene. "Run or you're dead meat," I screamed. "Adam isn't my dad, he's possessed." Ya, like that explained things really well.

Evil Dad chuckled and swung the bat viciously at my head. I fell back and ducked behind the big cage. The bat smashed into it with such force, the bars bent inward. If the blow had made contact with me, my brains would have been decorating the walls.

I kept the cage between us and scanned wildly for anything that I could use to defend myself. Adrian wasn't fleeing for his life as he should be. He was looking around too, although I'm not sure he knew what he was looking for. This insane fight scene between father and daughter was totally outside his realm of reality.

An old milk carton almost tripped me. I picked it up and flung it at my dad. He hit it out of the way with the bat, splintering it. I grabbed a length of chain off the pegboard on the wall. It was heavy, but desperation gave me the strength to swing it around over my head. When my dad swung the bat again, trying to connect with my face, the chain made contact with it and the bat went flying. It almost crowned Adrian, who ducked out of the way at the last second.

Unfortunately, the chain was redirected into the top of the cage. I tried to yank it out, but it got stuck. Before I could free it, my dad bent down and lifted his side of the cage. It toppled over and I couldn't get out of the way fast enough. It fell against me with the weight of Jack's big body inside and my dad leaning on it. I was pinned against the Elvis-mobile. The corner of the kennel left a big dent in the vintage car.

My dad laughed, uncaring, sounding completely unhinged. He turned his head to check on Adrian, who had retrieved the bat. He held it out in front of him and said, "Stay back. I don't know what's going on here, but stay away from me."

"I have no intention of staying away from you, Adrian." Evil Dad shoved hard away from the cage and moved toward him with menace in every step.

"Run, Adrian. Get help," I screamed, trying to shift the cage and squirm to freedom. It was heavy and too many ends of chicken wire had snagged on my top, and skin.

Evil Dad kept stalking him, not taking the threat of the bat seriously in Adrian's hands. "I'm not going to leave you. Should I hit him?" Adrian shouted.

"Yes! He's going to kill us. I don't want you to die, and I don't want to die." It seemed like the right moment to tell him I loved him. We were likely doomed, so it was probably my last chance. But I didn't. I'd kept that secret too long to just spill it, willy-nilly, in the middle of the mayhem.

Evil Dad lunged at Adrian. Adrian swung the bat. A glancing blow clipped the top of my dad's head, but it didn't even slow him down. He wrenched the bat away from Adrian and shoved him into the wall so hard, Adrian's head cracked against the wood with a terrible hollow thud. He didn't drop where he was standing, instead he balanced against the wall for a moment before he slid down it, as if sitting for a much-needed rest. He stopped sliding in a slumped position, eyes closed and face deathly still. I would have thought he was dead except that I couldn't sense his soul.

"Thanks, thanks a lot. Now he'll never want to go out with me," I shrieked, on the verge of hysteria.

"That's the least of your worries, Elvis. And quite immaterial since neither of you has any future to speak of." He closed in on me where I was trapped and halted, on the opposite side of the cage. He studied me as impassively as if I was an interesting amoeba specimen under a microscope.

I glared at him in return. The physical body was that of my father, yet the face was somehow that of a deranged stranger. The degree to which the evil inside him had altered the character of his face was actually quite remarkable. Clearly, a face wasn't just a mask that a person wore. It did reflect their inner essence, for want of a better word.

I tried to look deep into his eyes, to find my father. "Dad, I know you're in there. You have to fight Carl's evil. I know I couldn't, but you can. You're stronger than me, and you have years of experience in dealing with these things. Please don't kill Adrian, and please don't kill me. We're too young to die." It wasn't the most original thing to say, but it was true.

Evil Dad reached out and stroked my cheek. His touch made my skin crawl. "Oh, Elvis, I am looking forward to tasting your tender young flesh almost as much as I am craving Adrian's skin. I'll save him for last. Dessert," he drawled.

It felt like my heart broke into a hundred pieces. It did have a lot of cracks weakening its structure. I tried to breathe and couldn't quite manage it. My chest and ribs were causing me agony, and not just because there was a weighty edge of metal digging into them. It went so far beyond that.

When my dad leaned his full weight hard against the cage and reached toward me, pressing the metal edge and pointy chicken wires deeper into me, I was almost sick with the pain. His avid gaze stayed fixed on my face, drinking in my suffering as his hands closed around my neck. His grip tightened and he kept watching me as I suffocated from lack of oxygen. Carl's evil was truly sadistic in its nature.

I wanted to fight, but my limbs had lost all feeling. Everything got hazy and distant. My life didn't flash before my eyes, maybe because it hadn't been much of a life, and it was over before it had truly begun. I had never even kissed Adrian, not once. And my poor dad would be left all alone, eternally tormented by the memory of murdering his daughter, if he survived.

I whispered, "I love you, Daddy. I'll try not to turn into a zombie," right before my world ended.

# 14. Three Heads are Better than One

I didn't expect to wake up ever again. People simply don't wake up from death, and I could recall my death with vivid clarity. My dad strangling the life out of me wasn't something I could forget, no matter how many brain cells I had lost due to oxygen deprivation.

The awful memory of my demise was looming large as I revived. Returning to my body with its throbbing head, raw throat and screaming ribs was not a pleasant experience. My dad had also found the roll of duct tape I had hidden. Or maybe he had bought more. And he had added tie-wraps to his repertoire of restraints.

I was taped face down on the top of the dog kennel, by my neck. My arms were tight against my sides, tie-wraps strapping them to the thin bars. My legs were simply taped together at the ankle and knee. They jutted off the end of the kennel since I was longer than it was. My dad had really gone to town with the tape and I felt like a duct-taped mummy.

My cheek was pressed against the cage bars and it took a hazy moment to notice that the dead body inside the kennel was moving. Had Jack gone zombie below me? No, my dad had reaped his soul, allowing the evil to escape, so Jack couldn't be animate. So how could he be moving? And what about me? Here I was thinking I was alive when I could remember dying. Maybe I was a zombie now, too. I fit all the criteria. I was young, and my death at the hands of my own father had been both traumatic and tragic. There was no-one around to reap my soul. And zombies didn't realize they were dead, did they?

All the evidence supported my conclusion. I was a zombie. I had awakened in some sort of zombie hell, if such a place existed. Upsetting the balance of life and death was probably a major crime against the underworld, so maybe zombie hell was where I belonged.

I think I was slipping into a full-fledged panic attack when a hand gripped my fingers. Its touch was surprisingly gentle. My fingers tingled and I knew at once that it was Adrian's hand. He was inside the kennel and I was taped to the top. And I was pretty sure I was a zombie.

I blinked to clear the fogginess from my eyes. My eyeballs felt swollen. All I could see was the top of Adrian's head. His arm was reaching up to hold my fingers through the bars. "I think I'm dead," I said. My voice came out as a hoarse rasp.

Adrian looked up with red-rimmed eyes. "You're not dead, Elvis. I thought you were, so I checked your pulse."

"I have one?"

"Yes, you have one, and you're talking to me." He squeezed my fingers too hard. I didn't mind.

I drew in a ragged breath and realized I was breathing. Proof of life. "That's good. I thought I was dead, until I woke up, and even then I wasn't sure." I almost spoke the 'Z' word before I remembered that Adrian didn't know about the animate dead, except for the movie version. "Are you okay?" I said. Stupid question. Of course he wasn't okay.

"For now," he replied, showing a brave face.

"How's the head?"

"It's still there."

"And Evil Dad?" I asked.

"He went into the house, to get a … a knife. He said he's coming back to kill me. Slowly. He was very clear about that." The catch in his voice revealed the terror he was controlling, and brought tears to my eyes.

"I'm so sorry, Adrian." A hot tear dripped down my nose, followed by another and another. My tears were raining on Adrian.

He squeezed my fingers again. "And he almost killed you, his own daughter. What's wrong with him? Is he schizophrenic or something?"

"No. It's … he's been possessed by evil."

Adrian shook his head once. "That's not possible."

"Yes, it is. It's all too possible. Welcome to my world," I quipped.

"You live in a different world from me?"

"In a lot of ways, I do. Long story. I'll tell you about it sometime." And if we survived, I would, and to hell with the confidentiality clause.

"How about you tell me now?" he said.

"I think we should try to escape first. Do you know why he didn't finish me off?" I couldn't figure that part out.

Adrian thought for a moment. "I'm not sure, I was unconscious. I woke up in here, with you up there, although he did say something about … about preferring to use a knife. And his victim being awake so they could scream."

No real surprise there. I swallowed hard. "What happened to Jack?"

He pointed toward the Elvis-mobile. "He's in there."

I turned my neck as much as I could, which was only a fraction of an inch, and strained my eyeballs. Out of the corner of my eye, I could make out Jack. He was slumped in the backseat of the Elvis-mobile, bloodying up the leather. If I had needed further proof that the evil was ruling my dad absolutely, which I really didn't, that would have been it.

"I don't suppose you have your cell phone handy?" I said.

136

"Your dad confiscated it. He took yours, too."

"How about a pocket knife or anything sharp that could cut through a tie-wrap?" Hope springs eternal.

"Nothing." Adrian must have had one hell of a headache after being concussed, because he shifted around to lie flat in the bottom of the kennel with his knees bent. I looked down at him from overhead. It was like we were in bunk-beds, except there were no soft pillows or blankets, or even mattresses. Adrian couldn't have been very comfortable down there in the bottom of the cage, because I knew I wasn't, draped on top of it.

"I don't think there's a way out of this," he said, "so tell me about your world. Tell me what's going on here. I mean, it's like a bad drug trip."

A good story might distract him, and he needed distracting badly. Then again, there were better ways to distract him, and me. Shouldn't every condemned soul get one last request? I said, "Okay, I will, if you grant me a final wish."

"I'm not a genie, Elvis." Did he almost smile, just a bit?

"Oh, this wish is entirely in your power to grant," I assured him.

"Okay. What is your final wish?"

"A kiss," I blurted, before I chickened out.

He looked surprised by my request. "A kiss? On the lips?"

"Of course. With tongue," I added.

He blinked. I think he even flushed. It was hard to tell in the garage's dim light. "With tongue. Okay, I think I can manage that. I have a tongue."

"There's one prerequisite to this kiss, Adrian," I said.

"And that is?"

"You have to want to kiss me." I sounded serious all of the sudden, because I was.

He struggled to sit up in the confines of the kennel, then he had to reposition his body directly under me, angle his head and stretch upward. I couldn't turn my head much at all, and then there was my nose to consider, getting in the way of the bars. Our lips couldn't quite connect.

I sighed. "Oh well, it was worth a try."

"I wish I could grant your last request." He leaned back against the door of the cage. Maybe he was in the mood for some true confessions, or he was aware that it was the last chance we would ever have to talk, because he said, "When I thought you were dead, it was awful. I had all these regrets for the years we didn't get to be friends, because I was scared of you, because of a misunderstanding. I've learned a lot about you in the last few days, Elvis, and you're not scary. I mean, your life is scary, but you're really brave."

I wasn't brave at all. I was sick with terror for what was to come. I didn't tell Adrian that. I said, "Death isn't normally scary, it's usually just sad. The evil that was in Jack is a one-of-a-kind phenomenon. My dad said he's never encountered anything like it. And somehow, even though he knew what he was dealing with, it still managed to escape Jack's body and possess him—turn my dad into a monster." And that monster would be back any second to finish them off.

"Death and evil—that's not your normal P.I. stuff, is it?" Adrian said questioningly.

My head was still foggy and I wasn't explaining things very well. "No, my dad kind of specializes in weird cases—supernatural and paranormal stuff. It does exist." I left it at that, not quite up to enlightening Adrian on all things reaper. Before he could ask more questions, I said, "I don't suppose you have a final wish that I could grant? Like a blindfold and a cigarette."

"I don't smoke, and I don't want to start now."

"Good, because I don't have a cigarette. The scarecrow in the backyard is the only smoker around here." And I had forgotten to replenish the stovepipe hat. It would be stone cold by now, not that it mattered. Elvis the Scaredeath might well be redundant now that Jack had been killed in the garage, kind of like a human sacrifice.

Thinking about the smoking scaredeath, I remembered something I had in my pocket, something that my dad had not confiscated. I could feel it pressing into my upper thigh. "Adrian, can you reach my pocket? I have a lighter in there from lighting the scarecrow's potpourri. The right pocket. My right."

"How will a lighter help?" he asked, reaching up to grope in my pocket with two fingers.

"Tie-wraps should melt. It's worth a try. It's not as good as a knife, but - "

"Desperate times," he agreed. Adrian had to really wiggle his fingers to get them deep into the front pocket of my tight shorts, and I had to squirm around, trying to make the pocket more accessible. He had a lot of intimate contact with the zone below my belt buckle while exploring the depths of my pocket. It wasn't as romantic as a kiss, but it was still a pleasure to feel his touch. I would have enjoyed it a lot more if I wasn't about to die.

"I feel something," Adrian said.

"So do I, so whatever you're doing, don't stop," I drawled like Mae West, trying to keep our morale up.

He worked the lighter out of my pocket by degrees, until it dropped into the cage. He caught it and held it up. "Success."

"Start burning through the tie-wrap on my right wrist," I said. "Once I have one free arm, I should be able to get the rest of me free."

He hesitated. "It's going to hurt you, Elvis. The tie-wrap is pretty tight around your skin."

"It's not going to hurt as much as dying slowly. Hurry, Adrian."

Adrian did his best to burn the tie-wrap and not skin. I bit my lip and didn't make a sound, even when he was burning skin. I could feel the tie-wrap weakening. I tugged. It stretched a bit, because it was melting.

"Keep burning," I said through clenched teeth.

"I'm not enjoying this, Elvis."

"I know. I'm sorry. It's okay, I can handle it." I bit my lip so I wouldn't scream from the pain, which might bring my dad running. The reek of burnt flesh was strong to me, and sickening, especially since it was my own.

A few more seconds of hellish heat, a couple of good tugs, and my arm came free. I unwound the tape from my neck first, yanking out a lot of hair.

Unfortunately, releasing my second arm also required some burning, since I couldn't reach anything to cut through the remaining tie-wrap. Finally, I had two useable arms. I rolled off the cage to liberate my legs. Freeing one leg from the other was a piece of cake.

I turned back to the kennel. The industrial strength padlock needed a key to open it. I didn't have a key. I glared at it. Adrian said, "I already tried to open it. It's impossible without the key. Go without me, Elvis. Go get help."

"Like that's going to happen." I reached a hand toward the lock, daring to hope that freeing Adrian could be considered ORB. I was trying to save both my dad and Adrian from evil that had escaped during a botched reap. My hand was shaking when I touched the lock and pulled. The padlock clicked opened.

Adrian's jaw dropped. "How did you do that?"

"All part of my world." I swung wide the door of his prison.

"Which you are going to tell me all about, once we get out of here." Adrian exited the cage and stood upright. He swayed and I steadied him. He looked deep into my eyes for a long moment before he leaned in and kissed me.

I wasn't expecting the kiss. My lips weren't in the least prepared. Regardless, the kiss was fantastic, perfect. It was hot and sweet and Adrian didn't forget to use his tongue. His hands stroked down my back and settled on my waist, warmly gripping the exposed skin, pressing us intimately together. The kiss lived up to all my greatest expectations. I never wanted it to end, but of course it had to. We were risking our lives to hang around kissing, yet in my mind, it was so worth it. Then again, I wanted to live for a whole lot of reasons, not the least of which was the possibility of more such kisses.

When Adrian ended the world's best kiss, it did seem to be reluctantly. "We need to get out of here," he whispered, nicely breathless.

"Ya. I'm going to open the garage door." I pointed to the big rollup door, normally used for cars. "Stand beside it and get ready to run. I'll be right behind you."

Adrian moved into position. I eyed the keypad that would automatically open the door. It was going to make enough noise to alert my dad that we were escaping, but no way was I going to risk cutting through the house. Priority number one was staying alive.

The keypad was on the wall right beside the connecting door into the house. I moved quietly toward it, straining my ears to hear any sound. I couldn't help but wonder why my dad hadn't come back to kill us yet. As hungry as he was for Adrian, I wouldn't have expected him to delay the proceedings, unless he was sharpening up a knife.

I pressed in the first three numbers and then hesitated. I leaned my ear closer to the door when I thought I heard the murmur of voices. Yes, my dad was talking to someone. A woman. Her voice was soft and harder to hear than his rumbling. Kendra maybe? Or Mrs. Lyon, trying to track down her missing son? If she had phoned him and he hadn't answered, maybe she had been worried enough to come calling in the middle of the night, or was it morning? I didn't know how long I had been unconscious, and the garage didn't have windows.

Regardless of who it was, they were in mortal danger. I couldn't decide if I should open the garage door or not. That could make my dad strike his visitor down on the spot, so he could chase after us. Or it could give the woman a chance to escape, if she knew she needed to escape. I was in a real quandary about what to do.

Adrian motioned to me questioningly. I made an impetuous decision to open the garage door so he could get away. I would lie in wait for my dad when he rushed through the door. Best case scenario, the woman in the kitchen with him would be fine. Maybe he even had her taped to a chair, so he wouldn't be in a hurry to kill her.

I picked up the baseball bat and pressed in the final two numbers of the code. Nothing happened. I waited ten seconds and pressed the entire code in again, carefully. Still, nothing happened. A third time confirmed it—Evil Dad had changed the code. The only way out was through the house.

I beckoned to Adrian and we met in the middle of the garage. "He's changed the code. I can't open the door," I said, straight off. Before he could interject, I delivered the rest of the bad news. "Adrian, my dad is talking to a woman. He's probably going to kill her, too. It could be your mom."

"Ya, she might have come looking for me. It would be just like her. She still thinks I'm ten years old. So we have to go through the house and ... and incapacitate your dad. We have to save her," he said with a desperate resolution.

Was it wrong that I wanted to kiss him again, in the middle of a crisis? "We will, Adrian," I promised.

We armed ourselves. I tucked a heavy wrench into my waistband and kept the baseball bat. Adrian chose the pickaxe. I cringed. "Please don't kill him. I can exorcise the evil and he'll be my dad again."

Adrian didn't ask questions about that. There was no time for questions. He simply nodded and we moved toward the door. I turned the handle as quietly as possible and eased it opened a crack. At least it wasn't locked. The voices became clearer and louder. I knew at once that it wasn't Mrs. Lyon in the kitchen. Kendra had come to call, or my dad had phoned her, to lure her over to add to his menu of victims. If the evil had turned my dad's affection for her into a perverted hunger, he might be craving Kendra as much as he was craving Adrian.

I leaned toward Adrian's ear and whispered, "Not your mom. Kendra."

"Thank god," he mouthed, an expression of profound relief on his face.

I pushed the door a bit wider and peeked in. Luck was on my side, at least for the moment. Evil Dad had his back to the door. He was looming over Kendra, who was facing my way. He'd been busy with the duct tape again and Kendra wasn't going anywhere. She had some bruises blooming on her face and a bloody neck, but not bloody enough to indicate a fatal wound. He had also unbuttoned her blouse, exposing her white bra. He was in the process of tracing red lines on her chest, with a finger he had dipped in her own blood. He was saying, "I'll cut here, and here, and here. I'll cut it out and it will be mine." It did look like Kendra had some surgical scars exactly where he was tracing.

She spotted me and her eyes widened. I shook my head. She immediately shifted her gaze back to my dad without giving me away. She was even helpful. Definitely cool-headed. She started talking louder and faster, begging for him not to kill her. She told him she loved him and was sorry for breaking up with him. It kept his attention focused on her, and her voice covered up any noise we made, slipping into the kitchen.

Unfortunately, it didn't cover the sound of my dad's phone playing *All Shook Up*, which was on the counter behind him and beside me. He swung around. In his left hand, he was holding something that had been hidden until he turned. I didn't recognize the big sharp knife, so maybe Jack had brought it with him. Maybe it was the weapon that had cut my dad's chest while they wrestled for it—the knife that had slashed Jack's throat. My dad did look surprised to see us, and really pissed.

"Two against one," I muttered, to give myself confidence. I raised the bat higher into a swinging position. Adrian stepped up beside me, gripping the pickaxe in two hands. And the phone kept playing *All Shook Up* as if it was the musical soundtrack for our bizarre standoff.

Maybe the evil didn't like Elvis music. My dad grabbed up the phone and clicked off the sound. He even read the text. "Perhaps I'll have a tasty treat," he said revoltingly, slipping the phone under his rhinestone belt.

"You're not going anywhere. Put the knife down," I ordered.

In answer, my dad flicked the knife at me, in a movement faster than my eye could track. I reacted instinctively and managed to bat it out of the way. It clattered against the cabinet door and bounced a few times. Luckily, it didn't hit anyone because it was one weighty knife. I moved between the weapon and my dad, bat at the ready.

He was thinking about rushing me. I could see it in his mad eyes and the slight crouch of his knees. Adrian stepped closer and said, "Don't even think about it."

Our unified front must have been daunting enough to make him reconsider going on the offensive. Instead of fight, he opted for flight. He lunged toward the door into the garage. He was through it faster than I would have believed possible. The evil had made my dad a lot quicker on his feet than he usually was.

I couldn't let him get away. If he escaped, he might go on a killing spree that would see my real dad in jail for the rest of his life. I shared a glance with Adrian. "I have to go after him."

"I'll be right behind you." And he was when I rushed headlong into the garage.

Evil Dad had gotten his hands on the chainsaw. It was a newer model that started with the press of a button. He pressed the button and the high-pitched whine it produced made the hair stand up on the back of my neck. There are few sounds more chilling than a chainsaw in the hands of a madman. My bat and Adrian's pickaxe were paltry weapons by comparison.

I changed my mind about confronting my dad and screamed, "Back! Go back!"

There was only one place we could retreat to—the house. We fell through the door. I slammed it shut, locked the handle and slid the deadbolt into place. Kendra watched us, wide-eyed, from her prison of a chair.

"Chainsaw," I gasped unnecessarily. Its whine was loud, even through the heavy door. The saw turned off and I was deeply relieved—until the garage door started cranking up.

"He's making a run for it," Adrian said.

"Or planning to come through another door or window. Lock the kitchen door." I was already moving. I locked and deadbolted the front door and rushed back to the kitchen. The garage door was cranking down again, probably so we couldn't slip out after him, if he was intent on escaping. Adrian had almost finished freeing Kendra. She was wincing when the duct tape peeled off her arms.

"Are you okay?" I asked her.

"I've been better. Your father is not himself today." She tried to button her blouse with shaking fingers.

"No. The rest of the escaped evil is inside him." I shifted a curtain to peer through the window above the sink. The sun was over the horizon, but I couldn't see my dad anywhere. An engine fired up, started with a heavy foot and way too much gas. I winced when Mrs. Lyon's car careened down the road as if it was in a drag race, not on a quiet suburban street in the early morning hours.

"Damn," I groaned.

"What?" Adrian asked.

"My dad got away … in your mom's car." I expected Adrian to be upset, but he wasn't. He actually smiled.

"He did take the keys when he confiscated my cell phone. After almost killing us, the car doesn't seem like such a big deal, does it?"

"I guess not," I agreed.

"And at least we're safe," Kendra said, managing the last button.

142

I handed her a roll of paper towel to mop up the blood still welling out of the cut on her neck. "Safe for now, but the rest of the world isn't. I have to track him down somehow." I just didn't know how I was going to pull off that miracle yet.

When my legs threatened to give out, I collapsed into a chair. Adrian sat, too, gently, as if his head was a cracked egg with the shell barely holding in the goo.

"I would like to help," Kendra said. The elusive smell of my mother hung around her like perfume, even now, distracting me. I was tempted to ask her about it again, except she was injured and I had more than enough pressing disasters to deal with.

"Thanks, Kendra. I'm probably going to need help."

Adrian said, "There's a body in the garage. Shouldn't we be calling the police?"

"No," I said.

His beautiful eyebrows lowered. "You don't call the police in your world?"

"Only as a last resort, then we call one particular cop. He helps my dad out when things get messy."

"Colin?" Adrian remembered the name from our earlier dinnertime conversation.

"Yes, Colin," I confirmed.

"Shouldn't we be calling Colin now? I mean, things have gotten pretty messy." He gestured toward the door into the garage.

There was no denying that. "I know, but first I have to find my dad and get the evil out of him. Once my dad is himself again, he'll decide if we should call Colin about the body in the garage." I sounded much more confident than I felt about restoring my dad to his normal self. And collapsed legs or not, there was no time to lounge about.

Before I could summon the strength to stand, Adrian got up and ran the tap. He wet a couple of paper towels. I thought they were for his head until he approached the table and wrapped them gently around my wrists where burn blisters were popping up.

"Thanks." The coolness felt great. It felt so good, I found the strength to stand. I put one wrist, then the other, under a cool stream of water at the sink. At the same time, I drank a couple of glasses of water. It helped to steady me. Caffeine would have been a better pick-me-up, but there wasn't time to brew coffee or even boil the kettle.

I handed out water to Adrian and Kendra, then picked up the fanny pack that was draped over the chair. My dad had forgotten to take it along. I suppose it didn't matter. He wasn't going to be doing any actual reaping in his present condition. That meant that I was going to have a collection of zombies to corral in the very near future.

I slung the fanny pack over my shoulder like a purse and said, "Adrian, lock yourself in your house, alarm on, and I think you should take Kendra with you."

He shook his head immediately. "I'll stick with you. You owe me an explanation, and I can help you with your dad. Strength in numbers and all that."

"Three heads are better than one. We should stay together," Kendra added, with a tremulous smile. She stood up, turned even whiter, and sat down again rather quickly.

I was impressed that she was willing to help, but she wasn't in any condition to chase down a madman and battle him into submission. She was probably in mild shock and her neck was still welling blood. It did need stitches. "Thanks, Kendra, but I think you should get your neck taken care of first. Tracking down my dad will take some time. I can phone you once I've made some progress."

"Okay, but make sure you call me. I do care about him and ... I know this isn't his fault."

She certainly had a forgiving nature. "No, it's not," I agreed. I spotted a couple of cell phones behind some dishes on the counter and picked them up. Mine and Adrian's. They were both turned off. I handed Adrian his and keyed Kendra's phone number into mine. As if on cue, the house phone rang.

I grabbed it up quickly, in case it was my dad, in case he had come to his senses. "Hello," I gasped.

"Elvis, I'm glad I reached you," Mrs. Lyon said.

I winced and said, "Good morning, Mrs. Lyon."

She said, "I was wondering if you knew where Adrian went. I saw my car go by. It was speeding, and he's not answering his phone."

"Uh ..." I shot a 'help me' glance at Adrian. I didn't have a clue what to tell his mom.

He took the phone out of my hand and said, "Hi Mom ... no, I'm fine ... your car? Mr. Black had to borrow it for the case he's working on. He needed a nondescript vehicle." Adrian shrugged at me, pulling a face. "No, I'm not saying your car is boring ... he'll bring it back as soon as he can ... no, I'll be home later... I'm taking Elvis out for breakfast ... I'm not ten years old, Mom." Whatever she said made him turn remarkably red. "That's not what happened last night. I have to go. Bye." He ended the call fast, before she could get another word in.

"She thinks we spent the night together, doesn't she?" I said. It was pretty obvious.

"Yup. Well, we did, didn't we?" His lips quirked unexpectedly.

I smiled. "True, but not in the way she's thinking." If only that were the case.

"Maybe we should hit the road." Clearly, Adrian did not want to discuss the details of what his mother had said.

"Roadtrip," I agreed. "Kendra, I can drop you at the hospital. You'll be safe surrounded by lots of people. And I'll call you when I've found my dad. Okay?"

144

"Yes." She rose unsteadily. Adrian tucked a hand under her arm. The knock on the door made us all jump about a foot, especially because it came from the door that connected to the garage.

"I thought your dad drove off," Adrian whispered.

"He did." I frowned at the door when the knock came again, a polite little tap, tap, tap, three times. It certainly didn't sound like my dad trying to break in. He would have used the chainsaw.

Heart in my throat, I edged closer to the door and said, "Hello?"

"Hello. I'm not quite sure how I got here, or where I am," a male voice called through the door. It wasn't my dad's voice, and there was only one other person, or body, in the garage. Apparently my dad had not reaped Jack's soul, so how had the evil escaped to possess him? Such a thing should have been impossible—one hundred percent impossible.

Some weeks, it just doesn't pay to get out of bed. I picked up the pickax that was leaning against the cupboard, just in case. "This is going to seem odd to you," I warned, before I unlocked and opened the door.

Jack walked in. He hadn't been dead long enough to stiffen. His gait was quite normal. Except for the gaping neck wound, the blood-soaked shirt, his extreme pallor and cloudy eyes, he might have been alive. In the confines of the kitchen, he seemed bigger and broader than ever.

Adrian fell back and Kendra sat down very quickly. Luckily, she landed on her chair. Jack gazed around the kitchen dazedly and smiled at us. "Good morning. Sorry to disturb you folks so early, but I'm not sure where I am or how I got here."

Jack had gone zombie, and it was as plain as the nose on my face that he wasn't at all murderous now that the evil was gone from him. In fact, he seemed downright mild-mannered, especially for someone so big and strong. Since a person's inner nature remains intact when they go zombie, he would have been the same in life.

"What's your name?" I asked.

"Jerry Lavinsky." He extended a hand politely.

I shook it, ignoring the tacky blood that covered his palm and made our hands stick together. "I'm Elvis. It's nice to meet you, Jerry. And how you got here is … complicated. What's the last thing you remember?"

He considered that with a faraway look in his eyes. "I was walking my dog. It was a lovely evening. My dog is usually very well behaved, but she took off after something. I had to chase her into a field." He frowned. "She found … she found something bad in the field. A body."

"Just one body?" I asked.

Jerry had to think hard about that. "I only remember one body. It was very dark though. I hadn't brought a flashlight. I tripped over something. Maybe it was another body.'

"Then what happened?"

"Then … I don't know. I can't remember anything else, except being here. Did I get hit on the head? I think there's blood on my shirt. It's damp." Zombies are not known for their high I.Q.'s. Too many brain cells have died for them to be anything but the dullest tool in the shed. It's a kindness, really, because their emotions become equally dulled, leading to hazy acceptance rather than despair. And I had been gifted one very important answer—Jerry/Jack had not murdered anyone. Who or what had killed Carl and my dad's colleague remained a mystery.

I gripped Jerry's hand in mine and looked up, making direct contact with his cloudy eyes. "Jerry, I have some very bad news. You don't remember what happened, because you died. You're dead and not at peace yet." I didn't even mention the being possessed. There was no point.

"Is my dog okay?" he asked.

"I'm sure your dog is fine, Jerry, but you're dead. You need to realize that, so I can take care of you."

"I don't feel dead," he said. "I think you're wrong. I have to go find my dog." He released my hand and headed for the door.

Adrian and Kendra hadn't said a word. They both looked completely freaked out, although Kendra seemed less perturbed than Adrian. When my dad had told her about his job, he had probably mentioned zombies, although he would have called them 'problem clients'.

The last thing I needed, on top of everything else, was a grisly wounded zombie strolling down my street. I dodged in front of Jerry and said, "Jerry, wait. You're pretty far from the field where you lost your dog. I'll drive you there and help you find your dog, alright?"

He smiled rather sweetly. "If you're not too busy, I would appreciate it."

"I'm not too busy," I said.

"Thank you." Jerry stood there waiting, as still as a statue.

"Uh, Elvis, is he really dead?" Adrian whispered.

I pulled a face. "He's dead, but I think he's going to have to come with us anyway."

"Come with us?" Adrian's eyes widened almost comically. "The guy that broke into my house?"

"He's just joined our team. Don't let him leave the room, I'll be right back." I ran up the stairs before anyone could protest. In my dad's bedroom, I pulled a big sweatshirt out of his drawer, then detoured into my room to grab my jean jacket. I was feeling chilled, inside and out, and put it on. I dashed back downstairs with the distinct feeling that I was losing the race to fix everything that needed to be fixed before it blew up in my face like a bomb.

Back in the kitchen, it didn't look like anyone had moved a muscle. I said, "Jerry, take your shirt off." Zombies respond best to simple and direct orders.

He pulled his shirt off over his head, getting it stuck in his gaping neck wound. I said, "Kendra, toss me the paper towels, and could you wet a couple. Jerry needs to clean up."

She wet a handful and tossed them over. I mopped off blood and helped Jerry get his shirt unstuck from his neck. Adrian turned away from the sight. I zipped Jerry into my dad's oversized black sweatshirt and he looked one hundred percent less gruesome.

"That feels better. Dryer," Jerry said. "Thank you."

"You're welcome." I raised the hood and made sure the zipper went right to the top, so his wound was completely hidden. "There, that will keep you nice and warm, Jerry. Now let's go find your dog."

"I miss my dog."

Death could be so sad. Because of evil's grip, my dad had been forced to kill a nice man. I hated to think about the torment he would suffer after the evil was out of him. It was not going to help him get his drinking under control.

I patted Jerry's cheek, blinked back tears, and said, "We'll take the van. We need to hurry."

We all filed out and I was not happy that the sun was up. I could only hope that it was early enough for most of the neighbours to still be tucked in their beds. I glanced at Adrian's kitchen and spotted his mom staring at us through the kitchen window. We certainly merited a second look. Two badly disheveled young people, a very big man concealed in a black hoodie, and Kendra, who looked like a prim middle-aged school teacher, except for the blood staining her blouse. We were not birds of a feather and wouldn't normally flock together, especially at this time of day.

"You're going to have some explaining to do when you get home," I said to Adrian.

"I saw her. We better get out of here." Adrian gave his mom a little wave before we piled into the van. I think Adrian was simply too uneasy to sit back there with the dead man, because he claimed the shotgun seat without offering it to Kendra. He was usually much more courteous than that. Kendra got in the back with Jerry.

I reversed out of the driveway and headed for the hospital. Adrian said, "Start talking, Elvis."

"Once I figure out where to start." I turned right automatically. No GPS was necessary to get us to the hospital.

"How about at the beginning."

I was glad Adrian hadn't lost his sense of humour. He was proving remarkably resilient in a crisis. He was proving to be someone I could count on, someone who had my back when the going got tough—as if I needed yet another reason to love him.

"Once upon a time there was a reaper," I said.

His brow lowered in confusion. "A what?"

"My dad's not really a private investigator. He's a grim reaper."

"Like in the movies? Or on Halloween? With a black robe and scythe?" He sounded incredulous, even after all that he had witnessed.

"No. Yes and no. Reapers don't dress like that anymore. They haven't for years, and they don't carry scythes. My dad carries a fanny pack, and he wears his black and gold jumpsuit." I turned left, cutting the corner a little too close and running a rear wheel over the curb.

"And he drives a black van with tinted windows," Adrian pointed out dryly.

"Right." I continued driving as if I hadn't dented a mailbox and the van's side panel. "A reaper, by definition, cuts and gathers crops at harvest when they're ripe, hence the symbolic scythe or sickle. But that's not the type of reaper that my dad is. He harvests souls, releasing them from the body when they're trapped in it by death. And I'm a reaper-in-training, following in his footsteps. It's kind of something you're born to do. It's why I'm not going to university or any school after high school," I added before the questions started coming.

"Because you're going to be a reaper. A grim reaper?"

"I am." I kept my eyes on the road, not wanting to hit anything else.

"It's true," Kendra said from the back. Jerry didn't add anything. He was mindlessly enjoying the scenery, or thinking about his dog.

The hospital appeared over a small rise. I pulled up near the emergency entrance. "Are you okay to go in alone?" I asked Kendra.

"I'll be fine. Phone me as soon as you have news about Adam." It sounded like she really did care, in spite of everything.

I promised her I would and watched her walk into the building. As soon as she was safely inside, I looped back onto the road. "James, I need to get back to the field where I reaped Carl Waring," I said to the GPS. As well as calming down Jerry, I hoped that seeing the place might revive his memories of that fateful night, before they were lost forever.

James the GPS told me to turn right, so I did.

"But what about finding your dad?" Adrian said.

"I think this detour might kill two birds with one stone." I probably should have phrased it differently.

"How can it help to find your father?"

In brief, I provided the back-story. I concluded with, "The evil possessing my dad originally escaped from Carl, and the field where we'll look for Jerry's dog is the location where Carl died, and Scott, the other reaper, died. Some of the evil possessed me the night I got hurt, that's why I bit you," I confessed.

"Oh. You remember that?"

"I do." I flashed him a grin. "It was the best part of my night. Anyway, my dad exorcised the evil that possessed me, except there was more. The rest of it has been possessing Jerry. And when he died, it transferred to my dad before he could trap it in the bones. Anyway, we might find some answers at the field.

It's as good a place as any to start looking for my dad." I didn't mention that the evil should never have been able to get out, since Jerry's soul was still in the body, anchoring it. Adrian had enough to absorb without me bringing up what was essentially a paradox.

James said, "Turn left at the next intersection." I did.

"I didn't understand most of what you just said," Adrian mentioned. "And how come you never told me any of this before?"

"I'm not supposed to talk about it. It's classified, but now that you've become involved, you deserve to know the truth. I'm sure you have questions." I raised an eyebrow in his direction.

"You think?"

I shrugged. "Go ahead, ask away."

He did. Adrian asked questions all the way to the field. And since I'd already made mincemeat of the confidentiality clause, I answered every last one, including the one about how Jerry could be both dead and animate. My use of the word 'zombie' did seem to alarm Adrian. I should have said 'problem client'. And then we arrived at the field, and what I hoped would be Jerry's final destination.

# 15. A Zombie's Best Friend

Under the morning light, the meadow was bright and pretty. Daisies and dandelions dotted it with colour. It certainly didn't look like the scene of a brutal, cannibalistic murder. Here and there, remnants of police tape fluttered in the breeze like party streamers.

"This is it." I got out and slid the side door opened so Jerry could disembark. He was looking a bit sleepy. I had high hopes that if he stopped being animate here, I could reap his soul and leave his body behind, far from my house. I didn't want my dad implicated in his murder in any way.

"It's a lovely day, isn't it? Let's hope it will be a good day, too," I said and stepped over the fallen boulders of the fieldstone wall that had tripped me up, and allowed the escaped evil to possess my body, starting the whole awful chain of events that I was still locked into.

Jerry had started to stiffen. He needed help to navigate the stones. I offered a hand. Adrian stayed a good six feet away. I don't think he was comfortable touching dead flesh, while I was simply used to it.

Our mismatched trio proceeded to where some stakes had been hammered into the ground around the crime scene to mark it. As soon as I stopped at the edge of the small patch of ground, Jerry stopped, too. "This is where I lost Jasper." He scanned the field, calling, "Jasper, Jasper."

"Jerry, do you remember what happened here?" I asked.

"Someone died."

"There was a second death that night. Do you remember? Did you see what happened?" I pressed.

"No. Jasper, Jasper!" He tried to whistle and his lips were far too dry. They had started to crack.

I did the whistling for him before I said, "Did you see anything unusual at all? Try to remember, Jerry Lavinsky." Sometimes, speaking the zombie's name helps them to focus.

"Only darkness. I fell down, everything got so heavy and dark. Smothering darkness outside and inside. Jasper, Jasper." His voice was weakening. His throat was probably getting too dry to talk, which is one of the reasons why zombies lose the power of speech, and start grunting and groaning like their counterparts in the movies. Horror movies do have that part right.

I heard something rustling toward us through the bushy vegetation. I spun around. I certainly didn't expect a dog to come hurtling out of the undergrowth, but one did. The golden lab made a beeline for Jerry, whimpering in a high pitch. Loyalty and love overcame the aura of death for the dog and it went right up to him.

Jerry sat down in the grass and hugged his dog close. They shared an emotional reunion and it seemed to exhaust Jerry. He reclined flat in the grass, the dog pressed against his side. The man closed his eyes and the dog began to whine softly. Jasper knew his best friend was gone. Dogs are smarter about death than most people give them credit for. Heck, dogs are smarter about death than your average human

Tears were running down my cheeks when I sat down beside Jerry and laid a hand over his heart. "What are you doing?" Adrian asked. I was surprised that I was still visible to him, then again, this was not your normal reap. Adrian had accompanied me to the scene with Jerry, and he now knew a lot more than he should about reapers.

"I'm going to release Jerry's soul. He's ready now that he's found Jasper."

"You're going to reap his soul? Here? Just like that?" Adrian's voice rose an octave.

"That's what I do. Maybe you should wait in the van." I wasn't used to being watched when I reaped, except by my dad.

"Okay, ya, I'll be in the van." His footsteps rustled through the grass away from me.

Jerry hadn't reacted to our conversation. He was truly relaxed now, and maybe asleep. I removed a capsule of *angelus spiritus* from the fanny pack and placed it between my teeth. His face wasn't messed up so I didn't bother with a protective mouth barrier. I plugged his nose, bent down and sealed our lips together. His were as dry and rough as sandpaper. I broke the capsule between my teeth and exhaled deeply into him. My kiss of death made his big chest rise as if he was taking his final breath, which he kind of was.

I sat back up and chanted the *Licentia Ex Obscurum* to draw his soul out of the black pit where it was hiding. I was hoping this part of the reap would work as normal since the renegade evil had left Jerry, and only his own evil should still be in there.

I only had to speak the incantation once to sense Jerry's soul, and I couldn't sense more than a trace of evil in him—little more than residue, if that. He did seem like a good and gentle man, but I should have been able to sense more evil than that.

My hand on his still heart, I spoke the *Flat Lux ad Astra* incantation. Jerry's soul was quick to abandon its flesh coffin. It rose, releasing an impressive amount of light as soon as it was clear of the body. As the wave of light passed through me, I was intimate with Jerry's essence and shared his soul's joy to be free. I wiped away tears and murmured, "Reach the stars, Jerry." And then he was gone.

There were two full vials of Devil's Ash in the fanny pack. I poured a generous amount into Jerry's opened mouth, just in case there was more evil than I could sense, hunkered down somewhere inside. Same for the natron salt. I spoke the *Corpus Delecti* incantation three times—I wasn't taking any chances—and the reap was complete.

I used a baby wipe from the fanny pack to clean my hands and dab away the tears that were still leaking from my eyes. I was also wondering what to do about the dog. I knew it was going to stay by Jerry's side, come hell or high water.

I patted Jasper and said, "Can I check your collar?" The dog allowed it. I was relieved to find a tag, complete with phone number. I keyed the number into my phone for the time being and said, "Someone will be here soon to take care of you." The dog licked my hand as if it understood. I swiped away more tears.

Adrian was waiting by the van, not inside it. "It's done." I said. "Jerry is at peace now."

"So, that's how you release a soul." His voice sounded odd, as if his vocal cords were too tight.

I met his gaze. "That's how a zombie soul is released."

"And the bright light?" He motioned upward.

"Jerry's soul. You could see the whole reap? I didn't turn invisible at all?" I asked.

"You can turn invisible?"

I leaned against the side of the van, feeling suddenly drained. "Not really, no. It's more like I can't be seen when I reap a soul. I already told you that."

"Ya, you did. You told me a lot of things, and most of them I didn't really get. But to actually see a soul being reaped - " He grimaced. "Well, what you did, it wasn't quite what I was expecting. I mean, the making out with a corpse bit kind of caught me by surprise. I don't think you ever mentioned that. In fact, I'm pretty sure you didn't. And it wasn't a little peck on the cheek, was it? And he's been dead awhile, hasn't he? Not to mention, he was a zombie a few minutes ago. He's got that big gaping neck wound and he's probably started to rot. You don't find that a turn on, do you?" He finally shut up and swallowed hard, twice.

"Are you going to be sick?" I asked.

"Of course not. I mean, you were just doing your job, right? Not something I could ever do, but ... but we all have our roles to play." He swallowed again, and I knew in my heart that he was never going to want to kiss me again. After seeing me sucking face with a zombie, he probably wouldn't kiss me if I was the hottest girl in the world, and I held a loaded gun to his head.

"Mouthwash kills germs." I got in the van and slammed the door, hard.

Adrian climbed in a couple of minutes later, after he made a trip into the trees. I started driving, not sure where I was going yet.

"I said the wrong thing, didn't I?" Adrian said, breaking the silence.

I shrugged with an irritated twitch. "You witnessed something miraculous and beautiful, something regular people never get to see. You saw a soul's light returning a lifetime of goodness to the world, yet you get all freaked out over a little kiss of death."

"It's your world, Elvis, not mine. You're used to it, I'm not. I just saw my first dead body, ever, and met my first zombie, and I didn't even know zombies existed, and then you started making out with it."

I wisely kept quiet about the fact that Jerry wasn't the first zombie he had met, or the first body he had seen. "You should be glad that's all I did. If this was a couple of hundred years ago, I would have been hacking Jerry's head off with an axe, or whatever other sharp object was handy. That's how reapers used to stop zombies and decapitating is much messier than one little kiss."

Adrian fixed his eyes straight ahead. "I'm allowed to freak out. Anybody in my shoes would be … majorly upset by all this."

It had been a trying, sad reap and I could have used a nice warm hug, but Adrian wasn't offering comfort. He was freaking out in his own controlled way … and I suddenly realized something. He was right to freak out, especially after last night. Any normal person would. I was the abnormal one.

"Yes, of course you're right, Adrian. It's just … this is my life so it's normal to me, and reaping Jerry was really sad, and his poor dog … it was just really sad. It isn't always the easiest job." I could feel a chasm opening up between us. I was starting to feel weepy again, and that wouldn't do, not when I had to save my dad.

"Anyway … I'm sorry, Adrian. I'm so sorry you got dragged into all this." I didn't know what else to say and kept my eyes on the road, driving without a destination, which was just stupid when there really was no time to waste. I cleared my throat and said to the GPS, "James, I need to find a payphone where I can make an anonymous call. I need a payphone without a surveillance camera anywhere in the vicinity."

James told me to take the next right turn. It was amazing the things James knew and he never let me down. Maybe I should date James the GPS.

I slammed on the brakes without intending to, when I had a huge eureka moment, and it wasn't dating James the GPS. Adrian would have hit the windshield if his seatbelt hadn't been on. Luckily, he never forgot to click it on, not when he was driving with me, at least.

"Why did you stop?" he said.

"I know how to find my dad, I think. Maybe. I have to check with James." I wasn't explaining things very well. "James, I need directions to my father. Where is he now?"

James said, "Adam Black is not at a fixed location. He is driving east on Carter Street and has just passed the intersection of Mapleridge Road."

"How can the GPS know that?" Adrian said.

"James is not your typical GPS. He's linked to my dad's cell phone in ... special ways. As long as my dad keeps his phone on him, we can track him." Now that I knew that, I felt hopeful that maybe, just maybe, I could put things right. But not until I had taken care of one very devoted dog and Jerry's earthly remains. I reminded James about the payphone and drove straight to it. It was beside a rundown convenience store. The area was completely camera-free.

I dug some change out of the ashtray and phoned the police to report a body. The second call I made was to the phone number on the dog's tag. No-one picked up and the voice mail was for Jerry and Jerry alone. Apparently he wasn't married or in a live-in relationship. I could foresee myself with a dog in the very near future, but that was okay. Maybe it would even fill a bit of the emptiness inside me, left by my mom's death.

Now that Jerry and Jasper were taken care of, it was time to capture my dad and perform my first exorcism, if I could. I returned to the van.

"Who did you call?" Adrian asked.

"The police tip line, it's anonymous. They'll find Jerry's body and take care of Jasper. I'm going in the store. Do you want anything?"

"I'll come with you." He got out of the van, moving gingerly. I'm sure his head was aching pretty badly, but he didn't complain.

We walked into the store without saying a word. Adrian had a preoccupied expression on his face. He seemed to be miles away, in mind if not in body. And I was simply brokenhearted, as usual, that he would never ever want to touch my lips with his again— a perfectly normal reaction after what he had witnessed.

Inside the store, I bought a small bottle of mouthwash, a bottle of water and some gum. Outside the store, I rinsed thoroughly with mouthwash and spat. Rinsed and repeated. I didn't worry about Adrian seeing me spitting out mouthwash, not after what he had already seen. Adrian had bought a bottle of water, too. And a bottle of aspirin. He held out a hand for the mouthwash, swigged some, rinsed and spat in the grass. He did it again before he swallowed more than the recommended dose of aspirin.

"You did puke, didn't you?" I said, to break the uncomfortable silence. After years of not talking to each other, I so did not want to go back to that.

He rolled his eyes. "Hey, it's been a gross morning, Elvis."

"Puking is much nastier than kissing a dead body," I pointed out, taking the bull by the horns. I grinned so he would know I was joking. Or attempting to.

He shook his head and winced in pain. "No, it's not."

"Oh yes it is. It is so much nastier. And you kissed Meghan. That's nastier than kissing a zombie."

He choked on the water he was sipping, then laughed, albeit weakly. The aspirin needed time to work. "I don't think most guys would agree with you," he said.

"Probably not," I allowed.

"But as a matter of fact, she's slobbery. It was kind of gross. You're a much better kisser. I'm sure Jerry would agree with me, if he wasn't dead."

I blinked. Had Adrian actually made a joke about me kissing a zombie? "I'm sure he would," I said. We were definitely making progress. Huge progress. Maybe he had just needed some time to adjust, get over the shock. Or maybe he had been jealous, too, of a zombie. Dream on, Elvis. And people kissed each other after they had seen each other puke. Well, not immediately after, but … regardless, the thought cheered me up no end. Maybe Adrian wouldn't be opposed to kissing me again someday. So I had kissed a body—he had puked, and that was worse, at least in my humble opinion.

Before I could open the van door, Adrian stepped close. "Come here, Elvis." He wrapped his arms around me and held on. I was surprised and delighted. I hugged him back, of course I did. He was warm and solid, and felt so wonderfully alive. I sighed deeply and rested my cheek against his. I wanted to stay like that forever.

"It's sad that Jerry is dead," Adrian murmured, his warm breath making my ear tingle. "And I could have handled the situation better. I should have been more supportive."

I had to smile. "You did have a whole lot of new and disturbing information to absorb. I think you handled it a lot better than most people would have." I stroked his back, loving the feel of his firm muscles.

"So we're good?" he said.

"We're good." We were more than good, we were great. Adrian was the world's best hugger. I truly did want to stay wrapped in his arms forever, but my dad was on an evil rampage, so I couldn't.

I sighed again and stepped out of his embrace, very reluctantly. "Now let's find my dad."

"Fun times," he said, and we got in the van. I had just pulled onto the road when Adrian said, "Hey, was that Stella woman a zombie?"

He had been doing some thinking, and I wasn't surprised he had figured it out. "As a matter of fact, she was a zombie," I said.

"And that's why you didn't want me to go with you, when you drove her home?"

I nodded. "Exactly."

"I thought you just didn't want to spend more time with me, that you needed a break from hanging out with me."

"Really?" Clearly, I had been hiding my crush a lot better than I had realized.

"Really. Did you kiss her, too?"

"I did. It's all part of the job." I glanced sideways. His eyebrows were raised high.

"That's quite a job you have," was all he said.

"It's never boring."

James interrupted us, to volunteer the information that my dad was heading north on Woodland Road. Adrian and I shared a grim look. "Do you think he's going back to your house?" Adrian said.

"It looks that way. But why?"

"I wish I knew, Elvis. I don't have a good feeling about this. My parents are there, and your dad is dangerous."

"It's the evil possessing him that's dangerous, not him." But that was simply semantics. "Fastest route home, James," I said, pressing the pedal to the metal.

As I raced for home like I was in the Grand Prix, James kept me updated on my dad's whereabouts, and any cops in the area. My dad was definitely heading for home. His purpose simply eluded me.

Adrian and I discussed how best to proceed with capturing my father, without him killing us or us killing him or any innocent bystanders getting slaughtered. We agreed that we shouldn't drive down our street and advertise our presence.

"Surprise is always a great advantage," Adrian said, "at least in the movies."

"Probably in real life, too," I agreed and when James confirmed that my dad had stopped at my house, I continued one street further and pulled into the graveyard's parking lot.

"Why here?" Adrian asked.

"I know a shortcut." I jumped out.

We took off running and most heads turned our way. People do not normally sprint through a graveyard, hurtling headstones. They usually walk placidly between the graves as if they have all the time in the world, which the gravestones prove they really don't. When I passed my mother's eight foot tall marble angel, I stopped and touched the cool rock. "I'll save him, Mom. I won't let the evil win. I promise," I whispered. I knew she wasn't there, but the words made me feel a little stronger inside.

I started moving again and glanced toward the thicket where Priscilla was planted. I caught just a glimpse of my white gauzy dress through the leaves. She was still there, luring the dying to lie down at her feet. There was probably quite a rotty pile surrounding her by now. It was simply a matter of time before someone noticed the smell.

When we neared the hedge behind my house, we slowed to a walk. After a bit of apparently sedate strolling between gravestones, I checked to make sure we were no longer being noticed. The few cemetery visitors in sight weren't paying us any attention.

"Here," I said and ducked into the hedge. I didn't cross through because I wanted to see what was happening first. Adrian crawled in after me and we huddled together, nice and close, spying.

"My mom's car is parked in your driveway, so he's probably in your house." Adrian leaned out of the hedge for a better view, pressing warmly against me. We could only see the kitchen window from an extreme angle, but I was pretty sure I spotted a flicker of movement inside the room. And I could sense the evil in my house.

"He's in there," I said. "He's not at your house."

"Are you sure?" he asked.

"Yes, I can sense the evil, even from this far away. Your parents are safe, Adrian."

He squeezed my hand in relief. We kept watching, like we were on a stakeout in a hedge. Elvis the Scaredeath looked creepy, staring blankly back at us. My legs began to cramp and I sat down, cross-legged. Adrian settled beside me. My house remained a little too quiet and that made me uneasy.

"My dad must be up to something. But what?" I said.

I felt Adrian's shrug. "Elvis, I think I should go to my house and try to explain to my parents what's happening. They can call the police. This situation has gotten really out of hand."

I turned to look at him in the shadowy mottled light. "If you do that, if the police are brought in, they're going to find blood evidence all over my house. And that cage. My dad will go to jail for killing Jerry. And he didn't kill Jerry, the evil did - "

"And the evil can't stand trial," Adrian finished for me.

"Only my dad can. He's all I have left, Adrian. I can't lose him, too. And he doesn't deserve to go to jail. He's never hurt anyone. In his way, he helps people." I brushed a leaf off my neck. "We have a really good chance to catch him since he's in the house. No-one is at risk right now, he's just in there alone and he doesn't know we're out here. "

Adrian put an arm around me, willingly. It was even his idea. "Okay, no police for now. Let's just hope things don't … escalate."

"If they do, we'll have no choice but to call the police," I said. I mean, I wasn't unreasonable.

After about ten minutes of inactivity, I said, "I'm going to take a peek in the window. Maybe I'll be able to see what's going on."

"Or you could stay here with me," Adrian said, tightening his arm around me.

I shook my head with more regret than he could ever know. "I have to go, but you stay here. You're my backup if anything goes wrong."

Adrian nodded. "Safer than both of us going, but be careful, Elvis. And make sure he doesn't see you. Just find out what he's up to and come right back here."

I nodded. We looked at each other, our faces almost touching. I was probably the most surprised girl in the world when he leaned closer and kissed me softly on the lips. He drew back and smiled. "Ya, I think I can get past the sight of you making out with a zombie."

"Good to know." I smiled back. Then and there, I vowed that I would never ever tell him about spending the night in my bed with a zombie. Sex or no sex, I would take that secret to my grave. "But I'm not sure I can get past you kissing Meghan," I added.

He shrugged. "We all make mistakes."

"So there was really no chemistry between you?"

"Zero. Not like with you." He leaned in again for a deeper longer hotter kiss. I let my hands wander, stroking his skin, and his hair. It was much softer than it looked. He moaned low in his throat and took a shuddering breath. "I wish we weren't in a hedge," he whispered.

"Too many pokey branches," I agreed.

He tucked my hair behind my ear and said, "I missed you after Optimus. I was really scared of you, but I still missed you. You didn't kill him, did you?"

"I honestly don't remember what happened, Adrian. Maybe I did, or maybe I was trying to practice reap him if he had died on his own. I don't know what happened. I missed you, too." And I had never stopped missing him.

He kissed me again, his lips so hot and sweet and velvety soft. His exploring tongue sent currents of pleasure shooting through my body like sizzling fireworks. He really was the most amazing kisser, and not just compared to zombies. I kissed him hungrily back, trying not to eat his face. I wanted to strip naked right there in the hedge and do so much more than kiss, except the cleared patch was smaller than the back seat of a car. And then there was Evil Dad to deal with.

I drew back. "I have to go."

"I know." He touched my cheek. "Be careful, Elvis. I can't wait to kiss you again, when we aren't in a hedge."

I didn't know what to say to that and, my heart racing like a hummingbird's, I ducked out of the shrubbery and squeezed through the wire fence. It was hard to focus on sneaking across the yard. All I could think about was kissing Adrian.

There was no window near the back corner of the house, so I aimed for that blind spot. Once there, I pressed against the house and traced the sidewall, all the way to the porch, with its door into the kitchen. I just hoped that Adrian's parents weren't peering out their kitchen window, watching me sneaking around my own house like a wannabe secret agent.

At the edge of the porch, I paused. I knew stepping up onto the porch in broad daylight to peek through the kitchen window was highly risky, but the other windows were too high off the ground for me to look through, and I couldn't march into the garage to get a ladder. The door was too noisy, and my dad had changed the code, so I couldn't get into the garage at all.

I strained my ears and everything was so quiet, I decided to risk the porch. I crept up the steps and ducked under the kitchen window. "Here goes nothing," I breathed and raised my head slowly, a few inches, until my eyes could see inside.

Evil dad was in the kitchen. His hair was wet, so it looked like he'd been in the shower. He had also changed out of the ripped jumpsuit and into some perfectly normal clothes. No blood was coming through the white T-shirt. He must have bandaged his chest wound. The evil was making itself right at home in my dad's body, and in my house. Through the wall, I could sense Carl's evil as clearly as if it was sandpapering my skin.

My dad opened the fridge and helped himself to a can of beer. I idly wondered if Carl's evil had a drinking problem, too. Can in hand, my dad turned around and headed for the door—the door to the porch where I was crouched.

"Oh shit," I gasped. There was no time to use the stairs. I crossed the porch in two strides, slid over the railing and dropped to the ground. I heard the door open and scanned desperately for somewhere to hide. A loose slat of board caught my eye. It was angled inward a little bit, as was the one beside it. I held my breath and pressed against the boards. They pushed inward with a barely audible creak. There was just enough of a gap for me to squeeze my body into the darkness beneath the porch. I eased the boards closed behind me, almost as if they were a door, and was completely hidden.

It was damp and cobwebby under the porch—the perfect insects' playground. Luckily, creepy crawlies don't bother me overly much. I was safe for the time being.

The porch boards creaked when my dad stepped on them. Chair legs dragged across wood and I knew he had sat down at the patio table. The beer fizzed when it opened.

A patch of faded cloth caught my eye, right against the wall of the house. Beside it, there was an angled trapdoor into the basement. It had been covered by the porch for long years. I had forgotten the old coal chute was there. I hadn't crawled around under the porch since I was little.

I squinted at the material while my eyes adjusted to the darkness and my dad slurped beer. The cloth was patterned with faded yellow flowers, familiar flowers that matched the curtains my mom had sewn for my room, the year I started grade one. With the scraps of leftover fabric, she had made some little pillows for my stuffed animals and a drawstring bag. I used to carry my toys around in it.

Silently, I crawled toward the dirty cloth. I stretched through a whole lot of spider webs to reach it, and a whole lot of spiders. More than one critter scuttled across my skin, tickling me. I picked up the cloth and it was heavier than I expected—and lumpier.

A ghost of a memory made me shiver. I moved the cloth into a beam of brighter light, and I could see what I held. It was the little bag my mom had sewed for me. I opened the drawstring top, reached a hand inside and groped around. The small canister I touched felt unnaturally cold, as if it had just come out of a freezer.

There were some lesser items inside the bag, but the canister was the focus of my attention. I removed it and held it up in the bar of light, knowing exactly what I would see. I wasn't disappointed, or maybe I was. The black spray can was a lot smaller than I had pictured, about the size of breath-freshening spray that would fit in your coat pocket. Regardless of the size, I knew I was holding the missing can of Dead Man's Breath. Evidence doesn't lie. I really had killed Optimus.

I shook the can gently. It felt almost full. A shout overhead made me jump. "Hello, Linda," my dad hailed in a friendly voice.

"There you are, Adam. Are you finished with my car? I would like to go to the grocery store," she called back. She spoke her words crisply, as if she was peeved. I really hoped my dad hadn't gotten bloodstains all over her upholstery.

I pressed my eye against a knothole in a wooden slat. Linda Lyon was standing at the white picket fence, her hand on the gate as if about to open it.

"No problem. The keys are inside the house. Have you seen Elvis and Adrian?" my dad asked, ever so casually.

"No. They went out for breakfast and I haven't seen them since. There were some odd characters with them. A tall young man and a woman in a bloody blouse. Do you know who those people are?" Mrs. Lyon opened the gate and stepped into enemy territory. My dad waited on the porch for her to come to him, as if it was a trap. Maybe he shook his head in answer to her question because she left it at that.

When she reached the bottom of the stairs, I had a close up view of her legs and sensible low-heeled beige shoes. "I don't know what to think about this sudden relationship they're having," she said. "And spending the night together, well, it's early days for that, and they're much too young. I just hope they took precautions, I'm not ready to be a grandmother."

"She thinks I'm a floozie," I mouthed.

Evil dad said, "Come on in. I'll get your keys, and we can discuss it."

I knew if Mrs. Lyon entered my house, she wasn't coming out again, except in a body bag. But if I revealed my presence, I would probably end up in a body bag, too. I hesitated, in a quandary about what to do. And then I spotted Adrian, striding across the lawn, and I couldn't stop him. By the time he reached the bottom of the stairs, Mrs. Lyon was at the top of them, about to enter the house.

"Mom, wait," he shouted.

The boards overhead creaked when she turned around. "Adrian, where did you come from?"

"Home. I just cut across the lawn. I need to talk to you right away."

"I'm just going to get my car keys, then we can talk," she said.

"No! I need to talk to you now. Right now. It's important." He sounded desperate.

Her feet didn't make a sound so I knew she wasn't moving. "I'll just be a minute, Adrian."

Evil Dad stepped closer to Adrian's mom. "Why don't you join us inside, Adrian? By the way, where is Elvis?"

Adrian didn't try to answer that question. He said, "I'll get the keys for you, Mom. I need to talk to Mr. Black anyway. In private."

"What a good idea," my dad drawled, but not like Elvis. "And I need to talk to Adrian, man-to-man, about what he's been up to with my daughter."

Mrs. Lyon didn't miss the dark undertones and took a step back from my dad. "I'm sure he has been a perfect gentleman." The fact that I hadn't behaved like a lady was implied.

"It's not about that," Adrian said. "I'll talk to you at home, Mom. Please go home, now."

His mother hesitated before she said, "Alright, Adrian, but we will talk at home. Don't forget my car keys." She started down the steps and I knew what was about to unfold. My dad would take Adrian into the house, lock all the doors, and torture him before he killed him. And what came after that was simply too sickening to imagine. I wasn't about to stay hidden under the porch and let that happen

Without conscious thought, I shoved the Dead Man's Breath into my jean jacket pocket. I was about to squeeze out between the boards when I remembered the trapdoor into the basement. The old coal chute was plenty big enough for me to use as a doorway into the house, if it wasn't sealed up on the other side. I really didn't know if it was, since I had never tried to use it.

I crawled across to the trapdoor and pulled quietly. Above, my dad said, "Go inside, Adrian, if you want your dear mother to stay alive, and I'm sure you do."

Adrian went and the door closed behind them. I yanked wildly on the trapdoor. The damp rotted wood gave with a soggy crack. A layer of Styrofoam insulation didn't even slow me down. I kicked it to pieces. As if I was lowering myself into a pool, I slid inside, feet first. My feet didn't find anything but air. I kept edging in and dropped to the floor in the pitch black.

I groped around. I was in a very tight space. A wall was right there, barring my way. I explored it by touch. It didn't feel very solid, more like a thin layer of wood paneling or veneer. I pushed on it and it bent. I shoved harder and I was able to detach it from the wooden framework it was nailed to. It left enough of a gap for me to squeeze through into the furnace room.

I had made it inside the house and no-one knew I was there. Things were definitely looking up. There were no lights on and no windows in that section of the basement. It was as dark as a crypt. At least I was familiar with the layout. I groped my way toward the door and ran my hand along the wall until I felt the light switch I knew was there. I clicked the light on.

Once I could see, I took a quick inventory. The furnace room was where my dad kept some old tools, so it was a good place to find a weapon. I certainly wasn't going to confront Evil Dad empty-handed. That would be suicide. I opted for a length of heavy rusty pipe that had probably once been part of the guts of the house. I swung it a few times and figured it would do to knock a man senseless without killing him, if I didn't swing it too hard.

With not a second to waste, I tiptoed up the steps clutching the pipe. I could hear the rhythmic beat of loud music as I moved upward. The door at the top of the staircase was closed, as always. I pressed my ear against it. It was vibrating from the base in the music, and the song wasn't one of Elvis's. It was hardcore heavy metal. To drown out the sound of Adrian's screams?

My heart cramped and I bit back a sob. I turned the knob slowly and pushed. My dad had never been big on maintaining the house. He wasn't inclined to oil hinges. They squeaked like irate mice, but not loudly enough to be heard over the cranked up music.

I moved down the hallway toward the kitchen, where the music seemed to be blasting from. At the doorway, I pressed against the wall and risked a quick peek into the room. It was empty, but the connecting door into the mudroom and garage was ajar. That's where the music was blaring from. No fresh puddles of blood stained the kitchen floor.

After a couple of fortifying breaths, I ducked into the kitchen and skirted around the table to reach the mudroom. It took every scrap of courage I had, and more, to simply look into the garage. I knew I might see Adrian mutilated and/or dead. But I had to look, so I did.

It took me a minute to figure out what I was seeing. It was not what I expected—Evil Dad looming over a bloody Adrian. Yes, Adrian was in the garage, locked in the cage again, but he was alive and all things considered, he looked healthy. No blood, no bites, no burns. I almost started sobbing when our eyes met. His widened and he shook his head emphatically, trying to communicate something to me. A shake of the head wasn't going to do it.

I couldn't see my dad and I scanned the garage everywhere. Unless he was crouched in or behind the Elvis-mobile, there really was nowhere for him to hide. And the convertible top was down so if he was in there, it wasn't a very good hiding spot. It didn't look like he was in the trunk, either, because that was closed tight. Evil was rampant in the air, yet I couldn't pinpoint its source of origin.

Pipe in a firm grip, I bypassed my dad's workbench, where his old stereo was pumping out music that was both loud and awful enough to make my ears bleed. I wanted to turn it off, but didn't dare. If my dad didn't know I was in the house yet, as I hoped, I wasn't going to blatantly announce the fact. On the downside, he could tap dance into the garage and I wouldn't hear him coming.

I ventured deeper, toward the car. Adrian shook his head again. I held up a finger signaling 'hang on' or 'hold your horses' or something along those lines.

One quick peek was all it took to confirm that my dad was not hiding in or around the Elvis-mobile. I verified that the trunk was locked and knew he wasn't in there either. So where was he? I noticed a whiff of the smell of death. I figured it was because Jerry had spent quite a bit of dead time in the garage, until the smell got a lot stronger.

A flash of movement caught my eye. Two strangers appeared, framed in the doorway into the house. Their eyes were cloudy and their movements jerky. Zombies. I wasn't expecting that. A third and fourth zombie appeared behind the first two. There might have been a fifth and sixth, or a seventh and eighth as well, except I couldn't see past the first four to know if a whole horde of zombies was closing in.

Each one was in possession of a long, sharp knife and each blade was pointed straight at me. I was trapped. I didn't know the code to open the only door to freedom, nor was I willing to abandon Adrian.

In all my years as a reaper-in-training, I had never heard of a reaper getting attacked by a gang of zombies. A scene like that was only supposed to happen in the movies, yet it was happening to me. I suppose there's a first time for everything, and maybe I was cursed.

# 16. It's All Fun and Games Until Somebody Loses a Head

Zombies One and Two lurched into the garage. Both were older, heavyset men. They were moving fast for zombies, no stiffened limbs on this pair. They looked kind of like gangsters, especially because each one had a single bullet hole in the middle of his forehead. They were brandishing their knives at me as if they knew how to use them.

Zombies Three and Four backed them up. Three was an elderly woman who looked as tough as steel-toed boots. No obvious cause of death on her. Four was an unkempt bearded man who had seen a lot of hard living, probably on the streets. At least that was all of them. No five and six, or seven and eight.

I was facing a barbershop quartet of zombies working together. It was atypical behaviour for the animate dead, who generally had nothing to do with each other.

"I guess my dad has given you simple and clear instructions to stab me. I bet he even showed you my picture," I shouted at them, although they probably couldn't hear me over the music.

Now I knew what Evil Dad had been doing, driving all over. He had been reading his reaper texts and collecting the dead, unreaped, ensuring they turned zombie. With his vast store of reaper knowledge, maybe he even had a few tricks up his sleeve to guarantee they did go zombie. He had created his own little army of zombies to sic on me. Mrs. Lyon's car would never be the same again. And neither would her son.

I darted a glance at Adrian to see how he was handling the zombie invasion. He was watching me, not them. Perhaps my dad had already introduced them.

"This is going to get messy. Don't look," I shouted loudly, hoping he could hear me, or read lips.

There was about to be a serious bloodbath. I so did not have the time to wait for the agitated zombies to fall asleep, so I could reap them. I was going to have to go old-school.

I scanned for a tool that I could use to lop off their heads. The chainsaw was close by. It would do the job, but did I have the stomach for something so grisly? The zombies were closing in fast. I didn't see another option.

"Chainsaw it is," I groaned, dropping my rusty pipe and grabbing the chainsaw. And to save Adrian, I could stomach decapitating a few zombies. It was just too bad that he was there to watch me do it. He would never want to kiss me again after he saw me sawing off human heads in the goriest possible way.

Our eyes met again. He already looked nauseous. I mouthed, "I'm sorry," and hoisted the chainsaw into position. It started with a press of the button and roared to life, whining as only chainsaws do. It backed up the heavy metal. I brandished it in a threatening manner, giving the zombies a chance to turn tail and flee, and really hoping they would.

They didn't, they kept coming. My dad must have told them some terrible lies about me to make them so focused on killing me. Maybe he had told them that I had murdered their nearest and dearest or something.

I backed up, delaying the gore-fest for as long as possible. When my shoulders pressed against the garage door, I was out of time and space. At least the zombies had spread out. One of the mafia types was a good yard ahead of the others. He staggered straight at me and slashed with his knife. His coordination left something to be desired and he tripped. As he fell, I swung the chainsaw toward his neck, gripping it as tightly as I could, braced for impact.

I really wanted to close my eyes, but I didn't dare. I couldn't afford to make mincemeat of my own leg or any other precious body part.

The blade bit through flesh and muscle. Red spray decorated the garage door and the floor, and a lot of me. The saw crunched through bone and the head fell, hitting the cement floor with a wet, hollow thud. The body slumped limply to the ground, no longer animate. One down, three to go.

From the corner of my eye, I spotted a second zombie lunging, knife raised high. I swung the chainsaw in an upward arc, aiming for the exposed neck of the tough old woman. Her knife-wielding arm got in the way. The chainsaw made short work of it and momentum carried the blade through her skinny neck, barely slowing down. Maybe she had osteoporosis, because her bones felt as insubstantial as bird bones. Her head fell toward me. It landed and kept rolling as if it was a bowling ball and I was a pin. I kicked it away and leapt back, skidding on the slippery wash of gore that now coated the floor. Her body was slower to fall. It teetered and tottered before it toppled like a chopped tree.

The remaining two zombies kept coming, undeterred by their fallen comrades. I gasped in a much needed breath and raised the chainsaw again, trying to decide which of the two was the greater threat—the bigger older man or the hard-living younger man. It was a tossup. Unfortunately, they were approaching as a united front. Two against one. Could I remove two heads with one swing of the chainsaw? Unlikely. I retreated and tripped over limp legs. I staggered to stay on my feet.

The two zombies lurched forward together, and suddenly they were right in my face. I swung the chainsaw at the bigger body and it bit in. When I saw the flash of a knife coming down toward my face, wielded by the other zombie, I raised my elbow to block it.

Instead of my face, the blade bit into my arm. It was vastly preferable to my eye or cheek. Regardless, the pain was excruciating. I almost dropped the chainsaw. Screaming in pain, I tightened my grip and leaned my weight on the weapon. It cut through a last bit of stubborn bone and another head bit the dust. This one rolled in Adrian's direction and came to rest against the side of his cage, which I'm sure he didn't appreciate.

"Last zombie standing," I said to the fourth and final attacker. There was so much sticky red blood everywhere, I couldn't tell how much was my own.

On the bright side, the last zombie had lost his grip on his knife when he stabbed me with it. He was standing still and looking around, perhaps for another knife he could pick up.

"Let's put us both out of our misery," I said. I dodged behind him. Even though he was dead, I preferred not to look him in the eye when I beheaded him. He didn't turn around, he kept searching for a knife. I bit my lip and swung the chainsaw one last time, removing his head. His body fell stiffly to the ground, landing on a couple of the other corpses.

Dazed, I watched blood trickle out of the stump of his neck and join the red wash on the garage floor. I could only hope a stream of it wasn't leaking outside and running down the driveway for the whole neighbourhood to see. I just kept standing there, staring at all the blood, holding the whining chainsaw and wishing someone would turn it off, until I realized I could. I did.

The sudden silence was a great relief until the significance of it hit me like a falling piano. The awful heavy metal music had been turned off at some point, while I was battling zombies.

I tightened my grip on the chainsaw and looked up. Evil Dad was standing beside his workbench, in front of the door to the house. I think I was in mild shock, because I simply stood there gaping at him. Unmoving. Unthinking. Rather like a zombie myself.

"Quite a show, Elvis," he said, clapping his hands together, applauding my performance.

"Why?" I managed to say. Blood meandered down my arm to hit the floor with a splat, splat, splat, like a dripping faucet. My blood.

"Because it was so bloody entertaining," he drawled in a snooty English accent, insane smile plastered on his face.

I wiped blood and sweat, and maybe even tears, from my eyes, trying to see more clearly. It didn't help much. My face was a mask of blood. I was dressed in a coat of blood. I was leaking blood. I was gorier than the star of the bloodiest slasher film ever made, because the gore was real. The bodies and bowling ball heads and flood of blood on the garage floor were all real. All my years as a reaper-in-training hadn't prepared me for this nightmare.

My eyes were drawn to Adrian, who was simply staring at me as if he was horrorstruck. I was pretty sure our burgeoning romance had just hit a brick wall, exploded and gone up in flames.

"Now it's time to get down to business." My dad moved toward me. I raised the chainsaw slowly, defensively, willing my finger to push the button and restart it. A chainsaw isn't much of a weapon if it's not turned on.

My finger balked. The thought of chain-sawing my dad, as I had just chain-sawed four zombies, was unthinkable. Impossible. I knew I had to press the button and start the chainsaw to save Adrian's life, and mine, but I couldn't. Hacking my dad to pieces with a chainsaw fell into the same category as flying to the moon by flapping my arms—I couldn't do it.

I tossed the chainsaw behind me and grabbed for my abandoned pipe. Maybe because of the mild shock or blood loss, I lacked coordination. I skidded in blood and dropped to one knee. When I reached for the pipe, my dad was quicker. He stomped on my hand and grabbed up my would-be weapon. I cried out in pain right before the rusty pipe clunked against the side of my head, then I didn't feel anything at all.

I woke up rolling around in the trunk of a car. I knew it was the Elvis-mobile because it has an uncommonly spacious trunk with plenty of room to roll around. The car was moving fast. Highway speeds. My hands were tied behind my back which meant I didn't even have usable arms to stop my body from bouncing off the perimeters like a ball in a pinball game. My stomped hand was throbbing and my burn blisters were bursting and my stabbed arm was still leaking blood. And then there was my pounding head and aching ribs. I really could have used a handful of painkillers, and a doctor or two.

The world kept fading in and out of focus as I endured the worst car ride I'd ever had in my life. At some point, the road got bumpy and rutted. My dad didn't even slow down. I started bouncing up and down as well as rolling. "Shake, rattle and roll until you die," I whimpered, defeated enough to give into despair.

The car finally stopped moving. The engine turned off. I was probably black and blue from head to toe, especially my hip. After that wild ride, it was throbbing as badly as my arm. The hard can of Dead Man's Breath was still in my pocket, and I had kept bouncing on it.

I expected the trunk to pop open, but it didn't. "Let me out! Let me out!" I shouted as loudly as I could.

The trunk didn't open and no-one shouted back. I could imagine Adrian's fate all too well and started to freak out. I screamed bloody murder. I kicked the lid, over and over. If I'd been wearing my Goth boots, I would have put about a hundred dents in the metal. I was only wearing sandals. I stopped kicking when my feet got sore.

After I had uselessly exhausted myself, I collapsed. Maybe my head had taken one too many whacks on the wild ride, or before the wild ride, because I passed out again. The opening lid roused me.

I blinked up at the night sky in a daze, trying to recall why I was in the trunk of the Elvis-mobile. The sky was filled with brilliant stars, so I knew I was outside the city, away from the city lights. The moon was full, beaming down brightly. I shifted and my abused body throbbed in pain. It all came rushing back. My dad was possessed. Evil Dad was about to kill me. And what had become of Adrian?

I crawled out of the trunk to find out. Or I tried to crawl out. No assistance was offered. Evil Dad stood out of range, watching and waiting. I ended up falling out. It was adding insult to injury.

As soon as I succeeded in standing upright, supported by the car fender, I could see where I had ended up. The car was parked in the middle of an abandoned playground at the edge of a lake. The headlights were on, illuminating a place I knew well.

My parents had taken me here for picnics, once upon a time. Adrian had even come with us on a few occasions. We had spent my eighth birthday here, paddling in the waves and building an elaborate sandcastle. The playground was a sorry sight now. The equipment was all broken down and decrepit. One lonely swing dangled by a single rusty chain. The metal slide was dented and bent inward, as if an elephant had tried to slide on it.

Only the carousel was still functional. It wasn't the fancy kind with horses, but a flat platform like a giant turntable. It spins and kids ride on it, hanging onto the metal railings for dear life. It was always my favourite ride because it was the wildest. My dad used to spin me so fast, I was sure I would fly right off the thing, like a bird.

Adrian was on it now, taped to one of the hand-railings. Evil Dad had given the carousel a spin. That's how I knew it still worked. It was making a horrible high-pitched creaking sound as it turned. The rusty metal sounded like it was being tortured.

Adrian was going round and round with his eyes closed. I'm not sure if it was the headlights, but he was looking as sickly green as a fish with the flu. At least he was still alive. I knew, because I couldn't sense his soul. I wasn't sure if he was blessedly unconscious. In a way, I hoped he was. He had suffered enough for one night.

"Why here?" I asked. It was a cruel choice. Evil Dad was replacing my happy childhood memories with a nightmare.

"Why not here? No-one around for miles to interrupt me. Let us see how Adrian is faring." He beckoned me closer and flashed his knife, in case I needed any convincing.

I didn't. I wanted to check on Adrian, too. I pushed off the fender and stumbled in the direction of the carousel. As soon as I reached it, I managed to stop it from spinning with my foot. The awful creaking was replaced by eerie silence.

Adrian opened his eyes. Their dullness brightened when he saw me. "Elvis, you're alive."

"Technically," I allowed.

"Are you going to take a ride with me?" His smile was a pathetic shadow of its former self.

"I don't know yet. How are you doing?" I whispered, my throat almost too tight to talk.

He simply shook his head, as if to acknowledge 'game over'.

Evil Dad said, "Hop on, love."

"Don't you dare call me that," I cried.

"Oh, I'll call you whatever the hell I want." He pressed the knife against my neck, until I felt the sting of its blade. "Do as I say and hop on, love."

I bit back my retort, because of the knife. I didn't think I could afford to lose more blood; my arm was still leaking, slowly but steadily.

I didn't hop on the carousel, I stepped carefully onto the wobbly platform. My dad pushed me over and removed the roll of duct tape he was wearing like a bracelet. My wrists were still bound together. He bent down and taped my ankles together, tightly.

"Duct tape should be outlawed," I snapped, filled with resentment.

He gave the carousel a hard spin. I almost slid off before I got a grip on a railing post at my back. My lower legs were pulled off the edge of the platform, due to centrifugal force. Since they were there, I dangled my feet over the lip. They dragged along the sand and slowed the spinning down significantly.

My dad grabbed a railing and jerked the ride to a stop, me right in front of him. He looked down and said, "Under the light of the full moon, evil blooms best. Who dies first? I'll let you choose." He gave the carousel another strong shove and it began spinning fast.

When I tried to slow it with my feet again, he kicked them. I had enough aches and pains to last a lifetime and jerked them back onto the platform, out of his reach. "How did Carl's evil get out of Jerry's body when his soul hadn't even been reaped?" I shouted at him. If I could have nothing else, I wanted answers.

"Carl's evil," he drawled. "Oh, you really don't have any idea what you are dealing with, little girl."

I glared at him resentfully. "Why don't you clue me in then, before I die?"

"Maybe I will, if you tell me who you've picked to die first."

That was easy. "Me. I pick me." I didn't plan to die, but playing along might buy some time.

Adrian yanked against his bonds, desperately trying to free his hands. "Elvis, no! Don't say that."

"I'm sorry, Adrian. I'm being selfish. I can't watch you die." I scowled at my dad. "Now tell me about Carl's evil. How can it be strong enough to make a good reaper eat the flesh of his client, and strong enough to make a father kill the daughter he loves?"

"I don't love you."

"Shut up!"

"I've never loved you. You are a cross I have to bear. And I never loved your mother, that's why I killed her. And Carl's evil is not Carl's evil," he hinted with enigmatic oiliness.

"Then whose evil is it?" I asked, trying to ignore his awful lies.

Instead of answering, he said, "I name it your evil since you birthed it into the world. You gave it life. That makes you its mommy."

"Stop trying to mess with my head," I screamed. "You're full of crap. I don't believe a stinking word that comes out of your mouth. My dad loves me and you aren't my dad."

He gave the carousel another energetic spin. I tried not to throw up. "How could so much evil be inside one man?" I shouted. It didn't make sense to me, unless that one man was some sort of devil. Maybe I was dealing with *the* honest-to-goodness Devil, if such a creature truly existed.

We kept spinning and the whole time, Adrian kept pulling against his bonds with quiet determination. After a few dozen unmerry-go-round circles, the carousel jerked to a stop. I skidded into a metal railing much too hard. My dad said, "The evil is my collection, collected over the years." The British accent was more apparent all of the sudden.

"What? Like stamps?"

The ride started spinning again. Adrian groaned sickly, but he didn't stop straining against the railing. I swallowed hard. Why had my dad brought us here? If it was to destroy my happy memories and torture me with nausea, he was doing a super-duper job.

The carousel jerked to a stop again. I lost my grip on the railing post. I slid into Adrian. My dad rotated the platform until we stopped in front of him. Adrian stilled. Evil Dad loomed over us and hissed, "Hundreds of men have contributed to my collection, and each of their vices have become my own. So many wonderful vices to indulge. A hundred lifetimes won't be enough to satisfy them all."

My head had a terrible time making sense of his words. "You're saying the accumulated evil of hundreds of men was amassed inside one man, or one body? Along with all their evil ways?" I thought that's what he was saying. But was such a thing possible?

"Aren't you clever." A more patronizing tone was hard to imagine.

"That's a lot of evil," I said.

"And when Adam Black dies, his evil will be added to my collection." Evil Dad licked his lips, as if salivating.

170

My head spun as if the carousel was whipping around again. "What do you mean, when Adam Black dies? You're Adam Black, sort of. You're squatting in his body, anyway."

"Evil can only be collected through death." He spoke the word so lovingly, it was like a feast in his mouth.

"So you can move from person to person …" My voice failed me, lost to terror.

"Gathering evil," Adrian finished for me.

My dad propped a hip against the railing. "In the beginning, I had to wait for the body I shared to die, but over the years, as I grew stronger, I was able to help death along, so I died at the most opportune time for me to move to the next suitably depraved host."

"Growing your evil with each body?" I gasped.

"Until - " He straightened, chuckled like a diabolical villain, and gave the carousel another spin.

"Until what?" I shouted.

"Oh, that is my little secret, one of many. One you won't learn before I revisit you, when Adam Black dies."

"And then I'll die." And then he would move into Adrian. And who would be next? Adrian's parents perhaps. If the evil wasn't stopped here and now, the chain of death would be without end. The writing was on the wall in big drippy blood red letters.

Evil Dad smiled maniacally. "Don't you go anywhere, I have to set the stage." He strode away, leaving us spinning.

Adrian began jerking against his tape again.

"Any ideas on how we can stop him," I asked, tears clouded my vision, "because I've got nothing."

"There's a jagged point of metal on this railing. It's cutting through my tape a bit at a time." Adrian rocked back and forth. "I think I'm about halfway through. Could you stop this thing from spinning? I don't want to puke."

I was close to losing the battle to control my own stomach. I wriggled closer to the edge and dragged my feet, stopping the rotation and awful shrieking of metal.

Adrian said, "That's so much better." He rocked harder, working at the tape.

Evil Dad was already heading back. "Stop," I whispered.

Adrian did. Evil Dad strolled up and dropped an armload of wood near the carousel. He gave it another spin.

"What's the wood for?" Adrian asked me quietly.

"You don't want to know." Wood meant a fire, which could be used for light and warmth, but I'm pretty sure that this fire would be used for something else entirely, like killing or torture, or cooking. Maybe all three.

My dad set off to gather more kindling. He was making a big fire. My blood ran colder and I began to shiver in the night air. Adrian resumed his rocking with greater urgency. I stopped the carousel from spinning with my feet again.

"Adrian, I need to tell you something," I said, to distract myself from dwelling on that woodpile. And confession was supposed to be good for the soul. I wanted my soul as pure as possible, just in case its light would be returning to the world in the immediate future.

"I only want to hear good news," he said.

"I did kill Optimus," I blurted out. "I don't think I knew what I was doing and I don't remember doing it, but I found the spray can under the porch today, when I was hiding from my dad. It's not really paint. It's one of my dad's tools of the trade."

"The reaper trade?"

I nodded. "It's called Dead Man's Breath. It's for unique cases when the soul has died but the body hasn't. When inhaled, it kills the body instantly, painlessly, so the soul can be reaped."

"Do you have it on you?" Adrian asked, as if it was important.

"In my pocket. Why?"

He cast me a resigned, sad sort of look and said, "Elvis." That's all, nothing more.

Maybe I was in denial, but I said, "What?"

"The spray, it could save us."

"Oh. Oh no. I can't, Adrian. I can't kill my dad."

"I know," he said after a pause so brief, it was no pause at all. And he didn't try to talk me into using the breath. He didn't point out that my dad was probably dead anyway. Adrian was too decent for that. And he would die for it. I could imagine how much light and goodness his soul would return to the earth. A lot more than mine.

"It's in my pocket," I said. At the same moment, he lurched forward. He had cut through the last of his tape. He was free. Without missing a beat, he leaned over and started unwinding the tape that restrained my arms behind my back. I gasped in pain when the tape removed burnt skin. At least he was quick about it, like yanking off a band-aid, and then I was free, too.

"I'm sorry," he said and rested his forehead warmly against mine for just a moment.

"It's okay, Adrian. You freed us." I kept both eyes on my dad, who was collecting wood near the shore of the lake. The dried driftwood always burned fast and hot. "The evil has to be stopped," I whispered. "I can't do it. I can't, but you can. Take the spray, he has to breathe it in." I bit my lip to stop myself from begging him not to. My brain knew it had to be done. My heart just couldn't handle it.

I pulled the little can out of my pocket. Adrian didn't reach for it. I pressed it into his palm, closing his fingers around it.

172

"I don't know if I can, Elvis," he said.

"He's dead anyway." It was all I could choke out. I began liberating my ankles. Adrian stuck the canister in his pocket and removed the tape from around his own ankles. My dad wasn't keeping much of an eye on us. Given his attitude of arrogant superiority, he must have thought we were well and truly trapped. Defeated.

"We can make a run for it instead," Adrian said.

It was what I wanted to do more than anything else in the world. Except I couldn't. If I ran away like a big chicken, Evil Dad would kill every innocent soul that crossed his path. The evil would keep growing stronger, and it would kill my dad anyway. The evil had to be stopped, here and now.

I looked at Adrian, the boy next door, and I had another eureka moment. I wasn't being at all fair to him. Asking him to kill my dad and save multiple lives, to foist that weighty responsibility onto Adrian's shoulders, it would change him forever. I didn't want him to change. I liked him just the way he was—loved him just the way he was.

Adrian hadn't been raised with death like I had. This wasn't his world or his mess. It was my mess, my world, and now that I fully understood the nature and scope of the evil I was dealing with, I knew it had to be stopped at all costs. It was my duty to stop the evil I had birthed into the world, no matter whose skin it wore. One way or another, I had to end it. Me, not Adrian.

"Adrian, you go. You can get away. I have to stay here," I whispered.

He frowned in confusion. "Why?"

"I can't let my dad escape. He'll go on a killing spree, or the evil will, and it's going to kill him anyway." I put my hand in his pocket and reclaimed the canister. "It wasn't fair to ask you to do my ... job."

"He's your dad, so rather me than you, Elvis. And I'm not going to leave you alone here. You must know that."

I did. Adrian was loyal to a fault, one more of his wonderful qualities, and that loyalty might well get him killed tonight. I noticed that my father was heading back through the darkness with an armload of wood.

"Pretend we're still tied up," I hissed, assuming the prisoner position, arms behind my back and one hand gripping the canister so tight, I could have crushed it. Adrian resumed his position, too. We were tense and silent as my dad approached. He even walked different now, with a vulgar strut, toes pointing slightly outward.

I jumped a little when he dropped the wood with a clatter and reached into his pocket. He pulled out a lighter. He lit some dry pine boughs and they flared bright, crackling and sparking. He stood back and sprayed lighter fluid on the flames. They grew wildly. He had come prepared.

He turned to us, firelight dancing across his face. "Time to wear a younger skin," he drawled, pulling his knife free from his belt. "But which one?" He pointed at us in turn, with the blade.

"Me, you have to kill me first. You let me pick," I reminded him, in case he'd forgotten.

"Do you honestly believe I give a fig what you think, young miss?" The snooty English accent was stronger than ever.

"No, I don't expect you do," I snapped back.

"Spot on." He pricked his thumb and licked it. "I've been dying to share one of my little secrets with you, Elvis Black. As a young reaper, you will find it fascinating."

"I doubt it."

"It's an ability I mastered just last week, after years of trying to accomplish it. Years! And you, my dear, were the catalyst to my achieving it." He inclined his head as if in respect.

I did my best to look unimpressed, not wanting to give the evil any satisfaction.

"Although, ability is such an understated word. Perhaps 'power' would be more apt. Or dare I say 'superpower'."

"Are you having delusions of grandeur? Do you think you're some kind of super-villain of evil?" I said with as much disdain as I could muster.

"Oh, I am and I am about to prove it to you, while you can still appreciate what I can do. You asked how I could depart Jerry's body while his soul still resided within." His eyes gleamed. "Watch closely."

Evil Dad stood there, as still as a statue for a moment, the gloating expression on his face. Oily blackness seemed to envelope him. It came oozing out of him, out of every pore. Like I was watching a train wreck, I couldn't look away.

"What's happening?" Adrian asked.

"I don't know. It's like the evil is coming out of him, except it shouldn't be able to, ever. A soul anchors evil, and my dad's not dead. He would have to be dead and his soul reaped for the evil to get out, and even then, someone has to be very near, or touching the body for it to … relocate." And none of those factors were applicable here. The evil was just coming out of my dad as if it was alive. An ugly mass of putrid blackness began to reform outside his body. The smell of sulfur filled the air. The mass floated toward me and Adrian, growing bigger and bigger, until it was as big as a man.

My dad's body stood poised for a moment, and then he slumped to the earth so limply, it was as if all the bones had been removed from within his skin.

"Dad, Dad!" I screamed. He didn't move. I was terrified that he was dead, but there was no time to check. "Run!" I gasped and staggered to my feet.

Adrian and I leapt off the carousel and raced for the trees. I risked a glance behind and didn't see the mass of evil. So where had it gone? I could sense it all around, I just couldn't see it.

"This way," Adrian said, veering toward the shore.

"Why?" I was already panting hard, as much from terror as hard running.

"Come on." He sprinted faster. I followed, hoping he had a great idea.

174

We reached the water's edge and he ran along it, splashing in and out of the shallows. I slowed down. "Adrian, where are you going? I have to check on my dad."

He stopped running and turned to face me. A chilling smile twisted his lips. I held treasured memories of every single one of his expressions. This was not one of them. Adrian had never smiled like a soulless monster, not once in his whole life. Adrian was no longer Adrian. He was the new face of evil.

# 17. Kiss of Death

Before I could flee for my life, Adrian grasped my wrists with unnatural strength. "Your father is dead," he snarled, forcing me backwards into the lapping water.

"No, you're lying! How did you … how can you … that's the little trick you were talking about?" I gasped, voice thick with suppressed tears.

"Not so little, is it?" He smirked, making Adrian's face ugly.

No, it wasn't little. It was huge. Earth-shattering. "But … how?"

"Is your itsy-bitsy brain hurting, trying to figure out the impossible?" He shoved me deeper into the water, until it was up to my knees. It was still early summer. The lake hadn't had time to warm up properly. It was icy cold, but not as cold as the chill that was spreading through me from evil's touch.

"What you just did is impossible. A soul anchors evil. Dead or not, my dad still has his soul," I cried. Even as a reaper-in-training, I knew that.

"What gives us life?" Adrian's grip tightened cruelly. He was intentionally squeezing my burnt wrists.

"A soul." I looked deep into his eyes, trying to find a trace of Adrian. All I could see was malice.

"How right you are. A soul!" he declared as if he was pulling a rabbit out of a hat. "One precious little soul makes all the difference in the world. Are you missing a soul by any chance?" he taunted and leaned forward as if to kiss me. He bit my lip instead, hard, and tugged.

I jerked back, tasting blood. "The missing soul? Scott's soul?" I guessed.

"Is all mine now."

"You're alive? Because you hijacked the reaper's soul?" The soul I couldn't reap.

"It is mine now. It gives me life." Adrian forced me further into the cold water, until it lapped at my crotch. "I can now move at will, collecting, growing stronger and stronger and stronger, forever and ever."

"Has sin ever had a soul before?" I asked, to keep him talking while I figured out what to do. Adrian lifted my burnt wrist to his mouth. He bit it so hard, I felt nauseous. "Has it?" I cried, trying not to swoon in pain, and I thought I might.

"Oh no, I am the first." He watched my arm as blood filled in the deep impressions of his teeth. Under the bright moonlight, the blood looked black rather than red.

"Where did your evil come from, originally? The first evil?"

"Originally? Oh, that was centuries ago. The man's true name would mean nothing to you, although some referred to him as Jack. Your nickname was spot on. That one man had enough sin inside him for it to slide into another at the time of his death, and the other was no better than him, and that is how it began. Chance, luck, and with each death, the evil grew until it was powerful enough to elude the reapers of old at will, while absorbing the evil of other men, growing ever stronger."

"So he was an evil-sucking killer parasite." It sounded like the tagline of a really cheesy movie. Adrian forced me deeper into the cold lake, up to my waist. "Are you going to drown me?" I asked.

"Killing you quickly would spoil all my fun." He leaned in and ground his mouth against mine, shoving his tongue so far down my throat, I gagged. It was the polar opposite of the kisses Adrian and I had already shared. It was a gross violation and I bit his tongue, hard. He jerked away and before I could haul in air, he shoved me under the water. He held me there, hands around my throat. Of all the awful scenarios I had envisioned, I had never imagined this one. My dad might well be dead and I was probably following in his footsteps. And Adrian would only live long enough for evil to find a new host, unless I could stop it—unless I could stop him.

I was almost out of air. My head was getting fuzzy. I didn't have a weapon on me, unless I courted the Dead Man's Breath. I tried to pull the canister out of my pocket while my hands were free. I couldn't get my hand in my wet pocket when I was half-drowned. And even if I could get my hand on the canister, how could I use it to save myself and stop the spread of evil?

There was no point in killing Adrian, as if I could have ever done that. The evil would simply move, probably into me. It could move at will now that it had captured a soul and was a living entity. Yet, if it was a living entity, surely it could be killed. Surely it could die.

Adrian released his stranglehold and I staggered to my feet, dragging in air. He caught both my wrists in one of his hands, and stroked water off my face in a parody of tenderness. The evil had made him unnaturally strong. He had no trouble keeping both my wrists imprisoned in his larger hand. He leaned in again and licked my cheek as if I was an ice cream cone or something.

"Don't," I sobbed.

"But Adrian wants to taste you. He has grown so hungry for you." He leaned close to my ear and whispered what Adrian was going to do to me, then he bit my earlobe with crushing force. I jerked back before he bit it right off. He snarled and without warning, clasped my bellybutton ring and ripped it out, tearing opened my skin.

I screamed in pain. He groaned as if sexually excited, before he pushed me under for a second time, and held me there. Again, my wrists were free while he used both hands to grip my neck and hold my head below the waves. I knew I was almost out of time. I had to do something—something drastic. I groped desperately for the canister and this time, managed to wrench it out of my pocket.

I had to use it in a creative way that he wouldn't see coming. I needed to get the evil out of Adrian, into the opened air, and hope the Dead Man's Breath could kill it now that it was, technically, a living entity. I didn't know for sure that it would absorb the substance, or that the substance would kill it, yet, it was all I had, except for my wits. They felt like they'd been shredded through a paper shredder, making it hard to think straight.

Step one was to drive the evil out of Adrian, and I could only think of one way to do that. It was not without risk. But I had breathed a ration of the Dead Man's Breath when I was little, and lived to tell about it, hadn't I?

Beneath the surface of the water, I raised the canister to my mouth. I sealed my lips around the business side of the little nozzle and sprayed one short burst of it into my mouth. I didn't inhale. The canister was back in my pocket before Adrian dragged me up out of the water. I was dying for air, but I couldn't inhale. I swayed toward him. He smirked before he squeezed my wet breasts and pinched my nipples so hard, I almost gasped in the mouthful of lethal breath.

I was standing stunned when he leaned in to kiss me, as I had hoped he would. Our lips sealed together. I exhaled, praying I wasn't giving him an overdose of death, but an underdose—one that he could survive, as I had survived the Dead Man's Breath as a little girl.

He inhaled and went very still. He stood motionless for several seconds before he staggered back, clutching his throat with one hand and his chest with the other. He gazed at me as if I was the monster. "You love me more than yourself. You would never murder me," he choked out before he splashed into the lake, face down.

It just about killed me to leave him there, bobbing in the water like a corpse. I counted my pounding heartbeats, wondering how long I could wait before Adrian would be beyond help. I was at twenty-three before the black evil began to seep out of Adrian. The seeping turned into spewing, as if it couldn't get out of the body fast enough. For a moment, it hovered just above the water, looking like an oil slick, then it rose higher. It amassed over his body, growing in size, before it shot toward me like it was being sprayed out of a hose.

My arm flew up, fully extended. I was already spraying the canister, hazing the air in front of me. I held my breath and just kept spraying. I did not lift my finger off the nozzle. The evil stream met the Dead Man's Breath head on, and the mist looked feeble and insubstantial when the blackness bulldozed through it. The evil didn't even falter. It surged into me, and there was so much more of it than the first time I had experienced such a possession.

My gamble hadn't paid off. The Dead Man's Breath hadn't stopped the living evil. Before it could take me over, I turned Adrian face up. His lips were blue. I felt for a pulse and couldn't find one. I plugged his nose and blew untainted air into his lungs, trying to revive him, trying to force the toxic air out. For the first time ever, I was administering a kiss of life, rather than death.

While I breathed into him, I towed him to shore. I managed to drag him partway out of the water. That's when I stopped trying to resuscitate him. I wasn't giving up. I was losing control of myself and losing track of myself. The evil inside was attempting to take me over, but it was behaving oddly. It felt like I had swallowed glowing coals that were burning up, crumbling to dust, and taking me with them.

My heartbeat faltered, the breath caught in my throat. I dropped to my knees on the sand and I knew—I knew I was dying along with the evil. It had taken the Dead Man's Breath into itself, and brought it into me, and I had sprayed a huge cloud of the deadly mist. I had completely overlooked this possibility, hadn't factored it in at all. Regardless, I would have done it anyway. The evil had to be stopped, and I had stopped it. I was simply collateral damage.

I rolled onto my back, arching until I thought my spine would snap, clutching at my heart which felt like it was shriveling up along with the dying evil, which was no longer hot. It had turned profoundly cold, making me so cold inside, my heart had to be turning to ice. A frozen heart can't beat.

Before I succumbed to death, I wanted to know if Adrian, at least, had survived. My dad was too far away for me to reach, but Adrian was close enough to touch.

It took a Herculean effort to turn my head in his direction. He looked pretty dead lying beside me, all still and pale. Tears blurred my failing vision. I tried to sense his soul. I couldn't, which gave me hope that he wasn't as dead as he looked. I tried to reach over, to touch him, to hold his hand. I couldn't move mine at all. And then his hand twitched and moved to grip my fingers. They couldn't grip his back. My hand was as limp as a dead fish. But Adrian was alive. I wished that I could smile at him. His head turned in my direction and I tried to focus on his beautiful face. I couldn't. Already, my vision was clouding over.

"Elvis," he whispered. "Stay with me."

I couldn't answer him.

When a large dark shape loomed over us, I thought it was the specter of dying evil departing my body until I heard music—my dad's phone playing *All Shook Up*. Was it telling him to reap my soul?

"Oh Elvis, what have you done." My dad's broken voice seemed to come from a universe away, and I knew that he, like Adrian, had survived.

I tried to say goodbye, to tell him I loved him, but I couldn't feel my face or move my mouth. All I could feel was numbing cold. Dying was taking a surprisingly long time. At least it didn't hurt as much as living.

My dad crouched beside me and checked for a pulse. Of course, he didn't find one. His trembling hand closed my eyes, which had been staring at Adrian.

"No! Is she …?" Adrian cried hoarsely. He still couldn't say the 'D' word.

My dad didn't answer. I don't think he could. I realized I was holding the can of Dead Man's Breath in the hand Adrian wasn't holding. I tried to show it to my dad so he would know why Adrian and I were in such a state. I was hoping that maybe, just maybe, he would have a miracle cure for Dead Man's Breath, once he knew that's what he was dealing with.

My hand still wouldn't move. It was as dead as me. My fingers unclenched of their own accord as my muscles relaxed, surrendering to death. The can rolled out onto the sand. My dad moved around me and I heard his foot kick it. He gasped, as though in great pain. A zipper unzipped, sounding overly loud. His fanny pack. He was preparing to reap me, get the ordeal over with, I suppose.

Adrian moved weakly. "Can't you do anything?"

"No, it's too … late." My dad's voice broke before he regained control.

Adrian tried to sit up. I don't think he could, because he groaned and went still. His hand relaxed, releasing mine.

"Oh Baby," my dad murmured softly, laying a hand on my still heart. I heard the familiar words of the *Flat lux ad astra* chant repeated three times and felt my soul fluttering up, not quite able to rise. My dad added the *Viribus Alas*, granting my soul the strength it needed. It rose higher and higher, and then I felt it leave, leaving me behind. Even through my closed eyelids, the world turned brilliantly bright for a lovely moment. My soul was a lot brighter than I would have expected. And it was odd, but I didn't feel any deader without my soul, and I certainly didn't feel at peace. My dad spoke the *Eradico malum*, and opened my mouth to sprinkle in the Devil's Ash and natron salt. It was a gritty combination and made me gag.

I coughed and choked with gusto. Maybe all the evil inside me hadn't died after all. Maybe some of it was still alive, trying to get out. My dad backed off, as if he didn't know what to do. I rolled onto my side, no longer paralyzed. I coughed some more and spat out the salty grit. I managed a few deep breaths, sat up and looked around. Belatedly, I noticed that my heart had started up again. It was beating like mad to make up for lost time.

My dad hung back, watching me as if I was a ghost, or a zombie, except he had reaped my soul, so I couldn't be a zombie.

"Dad, what's going on? I mean, I thought I was dead. I felt dead, really dead, but now I don't. And I'm moving, and breathing, and talking." And stating the obvious.

"Elvis, I reaped your soul," he said. "You can't be alive." He looked so shell-shocked, a stiff breeze would have knocked him over.

"I know. I felt my soul leave." I paused when I had a revelation. "Dad, the soul wasn't mine. I think you just reaped Scott's soul. The evil had captured it, giving itself life, and the evil was inside me when it died. I sprayed it with Dead

180

Man's Breath and that's what killed it. I knew it had a soul, so I knew it could die."

My dad nodded once, weakly.

"The Dead Man's Breath should have killed me, too, but I don't think I am dead." I checked that I had a pulse even though I could feel my heart pounding inside my chest. Perhaps I had lost a few too many brain cells, because I didn't sound or feel as sharp as usual. "Adrian!" I cried, turning to him. "Is he …?" Like a civilian, I couldn't say the 'D' word.

"He's alive. Unconscious again, but stable enough." My dad must have realized that I was indeed alive, not dead. He dropped down beside me on the sand and hugged me so long and hard, I almost died from asphyxiation, again. He even cried. We both cried. Against all odds, the three of us had survived. The living evil had been vanquished.

After our emotional reunion, we attended to Adrian. He was out cold, his lower half still in the water. We carried him to the car where my dad balked about putting the wet sandy young man into his precious Elvis-mobile.

Before he suggested the trunk, I said, "Dad, take a good look at your car. It's scratched, dented and bloody. You'll probably never get the stink of zombie out of it. And I would be surprised if it has any shocks left. Evil Dad did not handle your car with care," I stressed, not sure how much he remembered. "A little sand and water aren't going to matter. And Adrian needs a hospital."

"I know. I'd rather not think about … any of what happened. What's done is done and can't be undone." He opened the backdoor and we loaded Adrian in.

Hands free again, I hugged my dad tight. "Are you okay?" He shook his head. "Dad, none of what happened under evil's influence was your doing. You told me that, now I'm telling you that. You were just its vessel, and not responsible for killing Jerry."

He pressed his cheek against my hair. "I didn't kill Jerry, Baby. He slashed his own throat before I could stop him, releasing the evil before it could be contained. Carl must have done the same. The evil was strong enough to control them completely."

"Oh. That's so much better than you killing him," I mumbled against his shoulder.

"Much better than me doing it. I didn't kill anyone when the evil was inside me, but I did some terrible things."

"It wasn't you, Dad," I repeated, with emphasis.

"We'll talk later." He kissed my forehead and got behind the wheel. I got in the back, with Adrian's head on my lap. I was really worried about him, and ready to do mouth-to-mouth resuscitation again if necessary. My dad drove away from the park, avoiding the ruts and potholes as best he could. He drove straight to the hospital. He probably didn't want to face Adrian's parents any more than I did. And he still hadn't returned Mrs. Lyon's car keys.

We pulled up at the emergency entrance and sought help. Adrian was still deeply unconscious. His condition was alarming enough to make the staff step lively and fetch a stretcher. I lied and said that we'd been canoeing, had fallen into a cold lake and almost drowned. We were wet and sandy enough to be believed. My dad provided Adrian's name and address, and said he would notify Adrian's parents about the accident.

Adrian was wheeled out of sight, still looking more dead than alive. The staff wouldn't let me go with him. They took me off to get my arm stitched up, and my various other injuries attended to. I guess I didn't look so good under the bright hospital lights, either. My arm needed about twenty sutures. The doctor didn't sew nearly as well as my dad and I knew I was going to have a visible scar as a souvenir of the most awful night of my life. My torn bellybutton piercing needed a couple of stitches, too, and my burnt wrists were wrapped up.

The doctor asked about the unmistakable human bite mark on my injured arm. How could he not? I said vaguely, "I don't remember how it happened." I don't think he believed me, but he left it at that. A bite probably wasn't like a gunshot wound, which had to be reported to the police.

I returned to my dad. He wasn't alone. He had called Adrian's parents and they had been quick to arrive. He must have told them the same canoeing story, because they began to ask me questions about why and how Adrian and I had been canoeing in the middle of the night when we didn't even own a canoe.

By then, I was having a sort of delayed reaction, shaking with a chill that was so bone-deep, my teeth wouldn't stop chattering. They were chattering so hard, I couldn't talk, which was a good thing, since I didn't know what to say. And I wasn't in any condition to come up with believable lies.

My dad interjected and said that he was taking me home, that I needed to rest and recover. He rushed me out of the waiting room before they could protest.

At home, I had a hot shower and a hot chocolate and stayed far away from the door into the garage. I didn't even offer to help my dad clean up the zombies. I simply couldn't face the mess I had made.

Still inclined to shiver, I couldn't keep my eyes opened. I crawled into my bed under extra blankets. I woke up fourteen hours later, and then I felt like dirt for sleeping so long and not even checking on Adrian's condition. I stumbled downstairs to find out if my dad had any news.

He was in the kitchen frying bacon, and he wasn't even burning it. He hugged me for no reason, except maybe because I was alive. He handed me a crispy strip. Colin was there, too, sitting at the kitchen table drinking coffee. He was looking rather haggard. His thin brown hair was in disarray, not neatly combed over his bald spot as he usually wore it.

"Hi, Colin." I sat down across from him. "Has my dad been filling you in on our latest adventure?"

"I've seen your latest adventure with my own eyes," he said with a wan smile. "I helped clean up your latest adventure." I noticed several blood smears on his sweatshirt and jeans.

No wonder he was looking so ragged around the edges. "Oh. Sorry about the gore," I said with a grimace.

He raised his coffee cup as if in toast. "Four zombies. I can't believe you beheaded four zombies, I mean problem clients."

"I didn't really have a choice, it was them or me. Are you going to dispose of the remains?" I asked. Colin sometimes helped out that way, when a body could not be returned to the death site for some reason. In this case, the bodies could not go back because they were missing their heads.

"Already taken care of," Colin said.

"Already? Thank you, Colin, so much," I said, heartfelt.

He nodded, finished his coffee, gave my dad a back-slapping hug and departed. As soon as I was alone with my dad, I asked, "Have you called the Lyons?"

"I bit the bullet. Tried to mend some fences after the car debacle. Adrian is doing fine. He was in shock, unconscious, but he's doing well. He should be home tomorrow. Coffee?"

"Definitely. I might need a whole pot." I let him serve me, even though I had been sleeping and he had been cleaning up decapitated zombies, and probably reaping a backlog of souls, and chasing down a few more zombies. I simply had no strength to speak of. I guess being dead took quite a toll on the body.

After I ate every morsel of bacon and eggs on the plate he put before me, he refilled both our coffees. He sat down across from me with his reaper journal and a pen. I was about to be debriefed.

"ORB time," I said with resignation.

"Best to record it while the memories are fresh."

"I don't ever want to remember." The hand holding my cup trembled.

"I know, believe me. We can both do our best to forget, after the details have been recorded," he stressed. "And this is certainly one for the books."

I nodded, then didn't know where to start. My dad began asking questions. I answered them to the best of my ability. There was even mention of where I had found the missing Dead Man's Breath, and a tale about a dead hamster.

He scribbled lots of notes, which made the whole process take forever. In the end, by putting our heads together, we believed that we had made sense of most of what had happened, although we would probably never know all the details, and some of it was still guesswork.

We did know that a particularly bad man who was known as Jack, and I believed it was Jack the Ripper, had been so powerfully evil that upon his death, his evil had successfully eluded the reapers of old, cleverly collecting the evil of other bad men until this mass of evil was strong enough to influence its hosts, and then ultimately control them. The evil really had been like a devil.

My dad believed that once Scott became possessed, the evil had read the reaper's mind and tried to make him speak a phrase in 'the tongue of the gods', a phrase that would have caused some sort of destruction or disaster that the evil could have reveled in and taken advantage of. Except the evil couldn't force Scott to speak the forbidden language and by pushing too hard, it killed the reaper it had wanted to control.

At that point in his explanation, I asked my dad, "Why couldn't Scott or I speak the phrase? I mean, the evil could control everything I said and did, almost without effort, so why not that too?"

He lowered his brow thoughtfully. "It didn't even try to force me to speak this phrase. I think by then it knew it couldn't."

"But why not?"

"Some sort of inborn safeguard, I expect, so we can't speak words of destruction. We would die first, die trying. Reapers are different from other people in many ways."

"No kidding," I said. "So Scott dies and the evil is trapped in his body with no other host to transfer into." I snorted in disgust. "Not until I arrive on the scene. And it has finally grown strong enough to hijack a soul—Scott's soul— but it can't carry the precious soul out of its rightful body, until I gave it a helping hand with my chants." I had really screwed up there.

"You couldn't know, Elvis. And I think it was a setup from the beginning," my dad said.

"A setup?"

"Why else would Carl have stabbed himself all alone in the field? Evil would have been controlling his hand, and the evil had no host to move into, did it?"

I considered the matter and said, "No."

"I think the evil had grown strong enough to want to possess a reaper, someone with special abilities and superior knowledge of all things dead. Perhaps the evil even had some grand plan to get to my boss through a reaper," my dad said, which was a chilling thought indeed. "But instead it was trapped when Scott died."

I scowled. "And then I freed it."

"It wasn't your fault, Elvis. You couldn't know." He finally closed his journal. "I'll submit a report to my boss."

I still had some questions about what had happened by the lake. "Uh, Dad, I'm still not sure why I didn't die. I mean, I had a dead man's soul inside me and probably half a can of Dead Man's Breath. That's enough to kill a dozen men, isn't it?"

"A dozen times ten." He leaned back in his chair, his face tight. "I don't know, Elvis. I believed you were dead, well, I got a text."

"I never felt dead though, even though my heart had stopped beating. I think the text you got was so you could reap Scott's soul after the evil died, and his soul was inside me."

My dad considered that. "Maybe."

"You had the dead man's soul inside you, too, when you were possessed. You didn't sense it?"

"Nope, not a trace, not a whisper. I guess the evil was able to mask it. Like with a zombie's—problem client's soul, we couldn't sense it." He frowned. "But regardless … you weren't breathing, Baby, no pulse to speak of, so you were dead. You did die."

"But with all that Dead Man's Breath inside me, how did I come back?"

Some of the grimness left his face. "I think it was divine intervention." He reached over and squeezed my hand. We shared a smile, and perhaps he was right. Maybe The-Powers-That-Be had intervened. Maybe his boss hadn't wanted to take me from my dad so soon after taking my mom.

"We'll have to send my boss a thank-you card. I'll have to scrapbook a really special one," my dad added.

I smiled. "Yes, Dad. I think Adrian died for awhile too, in the water."

He shook his dead. "I didn't get a text about him."

"I know, but he wasn't breathing at all when I dragged him out of the lake."

Dad shrugged. "Well, he's breathing now. More divine intervention perhaps."

Or I had successfully resuscitated Adrian, but I didn't bother saying that. My dad really liked the possibility of divine intervention. It seemed to make him happy.

"And I'm not drinking anymore," he announced without preamble. I almost fell off my chair. After what he'd been through, I would have expected him to crawl inside a bottle and live there.

"What?" I said, in case I had misheard.

"The drinking is messing up your life, my life … our life. I'm lucky I haven't been fired. I almost lost you, Elvis, and I'm not going to risk that again, so I'm not going to drink anymore." He sounded in earnest, and he had never sworn off drinking before. I believed him.

I patted his hand. "That's great, Dad. I like you better when you're not drinking."

"Kendra prefers me sober, too," he said quietly.

"I like Kendra. She's great. You talked to her?"

"She called to see if I was still evil." He flashed me a rueful smile.

"So, she's willing to give you a second chance? After all she went through? And all she witnessed?" I asked, incredulously.

"She knows more about second chances than most," my dad said, a hint if ever I'd heard one.

"What does that mean?"

He sipped his coffee before he said, "Kendra had a heart transplant about four months ago."

He didn't need to say another word. My eyes filled with tears. Four months ago, my mom had died. Aside from the brain tumour, she had been young and healthy, and an organ donor.

"She has mom's heart," I said, which explained the scars on her chest.

"That's why I got to know her. Turned out, she has a good heart, in more ways than one." He squeezed my hand even tighter, as if he would never let go.

"Sounds like she's a keeper, Dad. I think Mom would approve." I got up and hugged him. I was so glad that I wasn't dead and that he wasn't alone, and that my mom's heart was still beating in the world, giving joy and life.

I went up to my room so I could have a good cry, but it wasn't a sad cry. After another hot shower to unclog my sinuses and sooth my puffy eyes, I went downstairs to phone the hospital. I couldn't wait to talk to Adrian.

My dad was still in the kitchen, cutting out the obituaries. "I'm going to visit Adrian in the hospital," I said, picking up the phone.

My dad put down his scissors. "That might not be such a good idea."

"Why not?"

He exhaled loudly. "The Lyons aren't feeling too friendly toward the Blacks at the moment."

"I don't imagine they are. What's the number for the hospital?" I asked.

"Elvis, they don't want you visiting him," he said, no more beating around the bush. "They made that very clear to me."

"It's not up to them. It's up to Adrian." I did not put down the phone.

He sighed. "They think you're a bad influence, and they think I'm a bit deranged after that business with Linda's car. There was a lot of blood and gore in it when she got it back."

I winced. "I bet the zombies made a hell of a mess."

"Ya. I tried to explain, said it had to do with a case I'm working on, a case that went south. I offered to pay to have it professionally cleaned, but that hasn't really done the trick." He sighed again. "I behaved badly when the evil was in charge, and they're not going to forget or understand that. And then Adrian almost died when he was with you, under very peculiar circumstances."

I shrugged. "I'm sure it will all blow over." I might have been in denial again, and not the river.

He looked at me, his grim look. "I don't think it will, Elvis."

"Well … I'm sure Adrian doesn't feel the same way as his parents."

My dad ran a hand through his hair. "If you go to the hospital, they're not going to let you in his room. Why don't you give them some time to settle down, before you go visiting Adrian?"

"But Dad, I want to make sure he's okay." I didn't say that I missed him so badly, it hurt.

"There's a reason reapers associate with other reapers. They have lots in common."

186

I scowled at him. "This is not the time to fix me up with another reaper's son."

"You might not want to hear this, Elvis, but Adrian would be better off if he dated a normal girl with a normal life," he said bluntly.

I gasped. "He would not!"

"Elvis, come on. Think about it."

I finally set down the phone I'd been clutching and I did think about what I already knew, deep down inside. Adrian had almost died multiple times because of me. And I was pretty sure he had died for a short time. He didn't like that I kissed zombies and got handsy with the dead. And his parents hated me now. Maybe they would even take out a restraining order against me. After our time together, Adrian would probably start having nightmares again, like when he was little. And he'd need therapy. If I truly cared about him, loved him, wouldn't I want him to be happy and safe? Shouldn't I put him first, ahead of what I wanted?

If I listened to my head and not my heart, I knew he would be better off with a normal girl. Not Meghan, but a nice normal girl. A girl who wasn't me. A girl who didn't have to dash off every time she got a text, a girl who didn't come home reeking of death. When it came right down to it, it would be selfish of me to insert myself into Adrian's life. And before evil banded us together, he had never shown any signs of wanting to date me. Quite the opposite. Maybe he still didn't want to date me in the true sense of the word. I mean, why would he? A few kisses in the heat of the moment did not a relationship make.

"Maybe I'll wait until Adrian gets home to talk to him," I said, and went back upstairs.

# 18. Would You Like Ketchup With That?

I moped in my room all day, resenting the chirping birds and sunny sky. The next day, I was sitting on the porch pretending to read a book when Mr. Lyon's car pulled into their driveway. Mr. and Mrs. Lyon got out and helped Adrian from the backseat. He looked like he'd been to hell and back. He was pale and shaky, and I could see bruises on his face that hadn't yet bloomed at the lake. Evil Dad had beaten him.

Adrian didn't appear to notice me and limped inside, flanked by his mom and dad. I wasn't nearly brave enough to cross the lawn and knock on his door. The other side of the white picket fence had never felt more like enemy territory. I might not see a coiled barbed wire fence and cannons pointed my way, but they were there in spirit.

I went upstairs and curled up in my bed. I had a very long nap. I slept until the next day, and I slept in. The only reason I got out of bed was because I had to pee. There wasn't any other reason to get out of bed that I could think of. I might have crawled right back into bed, except my dad called me. I thought I'd heard *All Shook Up* playing while I washed my hands.

Dressed in the first clothes that I picked up off the floor, I went downstairs. Clouds had rolled in overnight and the sky was heavy and gray, just like me.

"We've got to go to work," my dad said, already in his reaper black and gold.

"Do I have to go?" I asked.

"Yup. It's a double. And it'll do you good to get out of the house."

I didn't agree, especially since I would be getting out of the house to rub elbows with the freshly deceased, but I didn't argue. This was my job now, and my life. I poured coffee into a travel mug and followed him out to the van. Two hours and two souls later, we drove home again. It started pouring as we pulled into the driveway.

The day was so dismal, Adrian's bedroom light was on. Maybe he was still bedridden. Maybe nightmares about evil zombies were keeping him awake at night. Or worse, maybe nightmares about me were giving him insomnia. I started crying, just like the sky, and went up to my room. I fell asleep since it was better than being awake.

My dad woke me up at two a.m. to go reaping with him. It was a hospital job, we got a lot of those. While we were there, another call came in. Highway accident. Rain slick roads and poor visibility often resulted in death. It was a messy accident. A transport truck had flattened a couple of cars. By the time the last client was reaped, the risen sun was poking through the clouds.

We headed for home and stopped at a drive-thru for coffee and breakfast. As soon as my dad turned onto our street, his phone began playing *All Shook Up*. He slowed down and read the text.

"What is it?" I asked.

"A single. One of the victims from the car accident isn't hanging on any longer. You might as well go home, get out of those wet clothes. I'll take care of this one."

I yawned widely, in spite of the coffee. "Sounds good to me. Thanks, Dad."

He pulled me closer and kissed my cheek before he let me out of the car. He drove off. Half asleep, I dragged my butt up the porch steps to the kitchen door, sipping my coffee. Belatedly, I noticed that the front of my T-shirt wasn't only wet with water, it was also stained with blood. I knew better than to wear white to a reap. I guess I hadn't been thinking clearly at two in the morning. Another shirt would be going into the rag bag.

The kitchen door was locked. I dug in my pocket for my key. It wasn't there. I descended the porch stairs and looked under the biggest rock for the spare key we kept there. It wasn't there, either. I remembered using the key last month, and I didn't remember putting it back.

I headed for the garage and tried the code. It didn't work. I guess my dad had never gotten around to inputting the old code, and I had never gotten around to asking him for the new code. I tried the rarely-used front door on the off-chance that it had been left unlocked. It hadn't. Since our close call with living evil, I think my dad and I were both paranoid about making sure all the doors and windows were locked up tight before we bedded down for the night.

Evidently, I was locked out of my house until my dad came home, whenever that was. At least it wasn't raining anymore. It looked like the sun might drive away the clustering clouds.

I went into the backyard and lay down on the damp grass. I was simply too sleepy to sit up in a hard chair on the porch, waiting for my dad. The grass made a much softer bed than wood. Plus, I couldn't get any wetter. I kept an ear cocked for the van, until I must have drifted into a restless sleep.

Cold drops on my face roused me. Disoriented, I opened my eyes to gray skies and spitting rain. And Adrian. He was looking down at me from under a big black umbrella.

"You looked dead lying there," he said.

It seemed like an odd thing for him to say, or maybe I was dreaming his presence. He extended a hand and I took it. It was solid. He was really there. Adrian pulled me to my feet and held the umbrella over us.

"Are you okay?" he asked, eyes on my shirt as if the blood interested rather than disgusted him. Maybe he was used to blood and gore after spending time with me.

"It's not mine. I was ... on the job. I'm locked out of my house until my dad gets back." My eyes drank in the sight of his face. The bruises had faded a lot, but his skin was still paler than usual. The lines around his eyes tracked deeper, as if he had aged years in only a few days. "How are you?" I clenched my hands into fists to keep from reaching out to touch him.

"Okay. The headache is almost gone, and the dizziness."

Before I could make some inane comment, Adrian leaned in and kissed me long and hard, with lots of tongue. I half-expected his mother to run outside with a shotgun, and blast a hole through me. Perhaps that worry was what stopped me from feeling pleasure at his touch. I pulled away and darted a glance at his house. His mother wasn't at the window. All the windows were dark, even though it was a dreary day.

"I saw your dad drive away. Come with me." He took my hand and tugged me toward his house. Only then did I notice that both his parents' cars were parked in the driveway. It seemed odd. Why hadn't his dad gone to work? And didn't his mom volunteer at the hospital on this morning every week, regular as clockwork. "Your parents are home. Why didn't they go to work?" I asked.

"I guess they wanted a day off." He paused, then added, "But they won't interrupt us. Come on." He tugged me most insistently toward his house.

"Are you kidding? They won't even let me through the door. They hate me now."

Adrian didn't take me seriously. He gripped my hand tighter and kept tugging me along, all the way to his door. I wasn't keen on going in, but I wanted to be with him so badly, I stepped over the threshold. Inside, it seemed very quiet without the rain splashing down all around us. I toed off my wet shoes. I was soaked through. "I'm not sure this is such a good idea." I plucked at my shirt. "I'm too wet to sit down."

"I'll lend you a dry shirt and some shorts." He herded me upstairs as if he couldn't wait to get me in his bedroom. I would have been thrilled about that if I wasn't supposed to be keeping my distance, plus, his parents were home.

My ears were on high alert, yet I didn't hear a sound in the house. I would have thought it was empty if not for the two cars parked in the driveway. Without lights on anywhere, the house was shadowy and as dark as twilight.

"Where are your parents?" I whispered.

"They're rather tied up at the moment, so don't worry about it." He grinned and ducked into his room, taking me with him.

"I am worried about it. Your mom already thinks I'm ... easy." It was a gentler term than slut, a word I really didn't like.

Adrian pulled me against him and kissed me so hard, it hurt. Before I could protest, he shoved me down onto his bed and dropped on top of me. He jammed his knee between my legs to spread them. His touch didn't feel nice or right. In fact, the whole situation was growing more and more alarming.

I had to wrestle with him to get free, but I managed it. I stood up and took two steps back. "Where's that dry shirt?" I asked, to buy time.

"You won't need it yet. Just take that one off." His grin was predatory, wolfish—more of a leer than a smile, really. Some guys did smile like that at girls, but Adrian wasn't one of them. Had the evil that possessed him left a permanent taint on his soul? I hated to think that it was possible, but with the living evil, I suppose anything was possible.

"I'm chilly from being wet so long. I want to put on a dry shirt," I said, hugging myself protectively.

His eyes narrowed. "If it is a shirt you want, a shirt you shall have." He reached into his cupboard. The shirt he took out was yellowed with age and threadbare. There were very old bloodstains on it that would never wash out. It was a shirt I was all too familiar with, a shirt I had hated for a long time.

I fell back in shock. "Where did you get that?"

He feigned innocence. "From my closet."

"That shirt was locked up in my dad's safe." And only my dad knew the combination. My dad wouldn't have shared that secret with anyone. No, the only way Adrian could know about the shirt, and the combination, was if the living evil had shared that information with him, and the living evil would know all about the shirt after possessing my dad. Maybe my father had even taken the shirt out of the safe when the evil was ruling him. Maybe he had been planning to use it as a deadly weapon.

Regardless of how, Adrian now had the Dead Man's Shirt in his clutches. And he appeared to have had some sort of psychotic breakdown, perhaps because of all the trauma he had experienced. No, that was ludicrous. I *knew* Adrian, he was a sweet, caring guy. He was good. Could the evil have left some polluted dregs of itself behind in him when it shifted to me? As a safeguard in case things did not turn out as it had planned? Maybe it could even divide at will—another one of the tricks it had referred to. In my mind, that possibility seemed the most plausible.

I hadn't sensed any evil in Adrian, but if it was only a small amount, perhaps I wouldn't. He was certainly behaving in an evil manner, luring me up to his bedroom to do who knows what. Okay, he hadn't had to lure me, but that was neither here nor there.

He proved just how evil he was when he extended the morbid garment, saying, "Put it on."

I edged back. "No, I've already died enough lately."

"Then I'll put it on." Adrian yanked off his shirt and made a show of preparing to insert one arm into the sleeve.

I didn't want Adrian to die no matter how weird and awful he was acting. I grabbed the shirt away from him. "What the hell are you playing at?" I cried, bunching it up and sidling toward the door.

"Oh, I'm not playing. I am in earnest, deadly earnest," he alluded.

Through Adrian's window, I glimpsed my dad's van pulling into our driveway. Adrian had his back to the window and was quite unaware. Knowing my dad was nearby gave me courage. I darted for the door. Adrian lunged and caught me around the waist. I spun to face him before he could tighten his grip. My knee jerked up with as much force as I could generate. It made contact with his crotch and he dropped where he stood.

"Sorry," I gasped and ran. I needed to get to my dad and tell him about the flagrant change in Adrian's character. I needed to find out if he thought the evil might have contaminated Adrian in some fundamental way. Or if there could still be some inside him, possessing him. Adrian had never been exorcised, so I suppose it was a possibility.

I hurtled down the stairs. I was about to run out the front door when I heard a faint noise coming from the direction of the kitchen. I froze and listened hard. It came again—a sort of muffled, distressed sound. If I'd had antennae, they would have started wiggling in alarm. I couldn't abandon Adrian's parents if they were in trouble. He might slit their throats before I could get back with my dad. Slitting someone's throat took no time at all.

Some misdirection was called for.

I opened the front door and slammed it, to make it sound like I had left. Carrying my wet shoes, I tiptoed toward the kitchen. It was empty. I heard the noise again, coming from the mudroom. Silently, I eased open the mudroom door.

At that point, it wasn't even a surprise to discover Mr. and Mrs. Lyon, tied up with good old-fashioned rope. So, they really were tied up, as Adrian had said. It was a nice change from duct tape, but they were just as restrained, tied to chairs like in an old gangster movie. And they were gagged, nylons tied around their mouths.

For a moment, they stared at me. I stared back. Mrs. Lyon's eyes were red from crying and her face was splotchy. "Adrian tied you up?" I whispered. They both nodded.

I moved forward to untie them, and heard Adrian stumbling down the stairs. He had managed to find his feet faster than I would have expected. And now I was trapped.

Easing the mudroom door closed again, I whispered, "Don't let on that I'm here." I slipped into the coat closet, hunkered down behind a couple of long coats and held my breath, trying to figure out what the hell to do. I wished I was still asleep in the grass, having a bizarre nightmare, but I was pretty sure I was awake. Everything was simply too real, including the pinch I gave myself.

I realized I was still clutching the deadly shirt. I stuffed it into the corner of the cupboard behind the vacuum cleaner. I definitely didn't want Adrian to get his hands on it again, and I didn't want it anywhere near me. I had already used the Dead Man's Breath on Adrian, the shirt would be overkill. And it would kill him. There was no way to use only a ration of the shirt. It was all or nothing. Death or life.

If Adrian still had a portion of the evil squatting inside him, it would simply have to be nullified before he killed anyone. And that meant I had to catch him off guard. Tie him up. At least my dad was home to perform the exorcism.

Adrian's footsteps approached and the mudroom door opened. "Right where I left you," he said, sounding pissed. He was probably mad that I had gotten away, and kneed him in the rhinestones. "I am getting a bit peckish. A bite to eat wouldn't go amiss. I do believe we're about to have company, so I should start cooking." If I had needed further proof that Adrian was not himself, which I really didn't, his use of the words 'peckish' and 'amiss' would have done it. And was that the faintest trace of a British accent?

Chair legs scraped loudly across the tile floor. Adrian was dragging one of his parents into the kitchen, perhaps for a little slicing and dicing. When the chair was out of the room, I risked a peek. Mr. Lyon remained in the mudroom, trying to communicate something to me with his eyes. I'm pretty sure it was 'help'.

"It will be okay," I whispered.

I retreated back into the closet when Adrian returned for his father, saying, "I've turned the stove on. I'm going to fry up some meat. Would you like ketchup with that?" He laughed like a lunatic. I knew what meat he meant. I had to act quickly.

Adrian closed the mudroom door after he dragged his father away, which I really appreciated. It allowed me to sneak from the closet, unseen. I edged out of the closet, scanning for makeshift weapons. It was becoming something of a habit.

The golf clubs were still there, shiny clean as if they had been polished with TLC. A club had worked for me before. It had a nice long handle to keep me at a safe distance. And the big wooden one was hefty enough to do damage without killing a person.

With a sense of déjà vu, I slipped my chosen weapon up and out of the golf bag. Adrian's voice was a drone through the door. He had never been a chatty guy before, but it sounded like he was now. And then everything went quiet. Dead quiet. Alarmed, I strained my ears. Had he left the room? Or was he doing irreparable damage to his parents?

I opened the door a crack and couldn't see a damn thing. I widened the crack a fraction of an inch and could see the fridge and the stove, with a big frying pan on a red hot burner. Butter or oil was starting to sizzle and spit. But I still couldn't see Adrian or hear him.

I was standing there, unsure about how to proceed, when the door jerked opened and slammed back with force. Thrown off-balance, I couldn't react fast enough. The door whacked my forehead so hard, I saw stars and a few little tweety birds circling overhead. The impact also knocked me on my ass.

Before I could recover, Adrian was looming over me. I was in no position to hit him with the golf club, but I tried to swing it anyway. He grabbed the shaft and wrenched it out of my grasp, which was as weak as a baby bunny's at that point. He twirled it around over his head in a showy gesture before he pressed the head of the club under my chin. He applied pressure, cutting off my air supply. "Where is my shirt?" he bit out.

"It's not yours," I choked, my head spinning dizzily.

He shifted the golf club to the side of my head and struck an exaggerated golfer's pose. My head was where the ball would normally be and he took a few practice swings.

"Don't," I begged.

"Then tell me where I might find my shirt."

"Why do you want it?" I asked, delaying.

"It will come in very handy now that I must begin my collection from scratch." He scanned the mudroom and I tried to stand up. He swung the golf club and it clunked against the side of my head, but not nearly as hard as it could have. Clearly, he didn't want to kill me quite yet. Regardless, I went down again and lay there in a daze. He grabbed a pair of his mom's nylons off the top of the dryer and tied my ankles tight together, before I was recovered enough to put up a real fight.

"That's better," he said. He held my legs raised up so I was trapped on my back. "Now, where is my shirt?"

"I'm not going to tell you." The shirt in his hands would be disastrous.

He sighed with exaggerated weariness. "Oh, it shouldn't be too hard to locate in one small room." His eyes narrowed and he stepped toward the closet, dragging me by my ankles while I squirmed like a fish on a hook, to no avail. He rooted around in the closet with his free hand and found the shirt quickly enough. I should have hidden it in a far cleverer spot, but in my defense, I hadn't realized I needed to.

He grinned triumphantly and drawled, "There you are." He tossed the shirt over his shoulder and dragged me unceremoniously into the kitchen by my bound ankles, as if he was a caveman and I was his cavewoman, or his prey.

I was hauled all the way to the stove, kicking and screaming. A big knife appeared in Adrian's hand as if by magic, although he must have simply picked it up off the counter. The sizzling frying pan made my stomach clench and I swallowed hot bile.

"Stand up," Adrian said, releasing his bruising grip on my legs.

I managed the feat, but it wasn't easy with my ankles tied together. I stood there swaying, holding onto the counter for support, and he pressed the tip of the blade against my stomach, not cutting—much, but it hurt like hell. It was in the exact same spot as my still healing bellybutton wound.

"Don't move," he ordered and opened the cupboard beside the stove. My eyes widened when he took out salt and pepper shakers and set them on the counter. Next, he reached into the fridge for the ketchup, saying, "Looks so much like blood, doesn't it?" He flicked open the ketchup with his thumb and said, "Your hand, my dear."

"What?" I gasped, even though I had heard him.

"Hold out your hand," he snarled.

I hesitated too long and the knife pressed in a bit more. Pain shot through me. A spot of red appeared on my shirt, spreading out around the tip of the knife. I held out my hand.

Smiling like the madman he now was, Adrian squeezed the ketchup upside-down making a red spiral pattern that covered the palm of my hand. Sprinkles of salt and pepper were next, and Adrian didn't loosen his grip on the knife one iota. "Now put your hand in the frying pan," he said, almost panting with excitement.

His mom cried out through her gag, like a wounded animal.

"No, Adrian. Not that," I gasped, even though his words were no surprise, I mean, he had just seasoned my hand.

He didn't repeat himself. He didn't need to. We both knew I had two perfectly functioning ears, although the blood pounding in them sounded as thunderous as Niagara Falls.

"Do it." He licked his lips in anticipation.

"No, I won't. Who are you?" I cried. If he was like the evil I had already met, he would like to talk, or boast. Talking of any sort would delay the excruciating pain of my hand being cooked alive.

"I suppose you should know who I am." He rotated the knife back and forth, digging in, and that was pure agony. I swallowed down a scream of pain as he watched my face avidly. The little circle of blood spread like crimson watercolour paint on my wet, already blood-stained shirt.

"I am the first, the original, the founder." His lips twitched in delight. "I am the survivor."

"Jack?" I guessed.

He nodded graciously, as if I had bestowed a compliment "I began and ruled the collection, and now, alas, I must begin again. But it won't be as hard as the first time. I've learned so much and have forgotten nothing. In this room, I have the first three who will become part of me. And I have this handy little shirt, which will make it an easy task for me to amass all the evil I want, quickly and so mysteriously, no-one will be able to figure out why my victims are dying. In no time, I will capture and rule a soul again. In no time, I will be restored to my former glory." Adrian's face twisted sickly, like a mop in a wringer.

195

"Glory?" I choked out. "There's nothing glorious about you. You're nothing but lowlife scum."

He pressed the knife a fraction of an inch deeper into my skin and I almost fainted from the pain of the torture. I decided it would be wise to shut my mouth, so I did.

"And you, Elvis Black, will be the first, since you destroyed my collection. And you will not have the blessing of the shirt. Now put your hand in the frying pan."

"So this cannibal hunger thing is your vice?" I said, keeping my hand as far away from the spitting pan as I could.

"It is no vice. Once you try it, you'll understand."

I snorted defiantly. "I'm not going to try it."

"Yes, you will." He moved the knife so fast, I had no time to evade it. The razor sharp tip nicked my wrist and blood began to drip. Adrian tossed the knife on the counter, safely out of my reach. He clamped onto my fingers. He forced my hand over the pan so each drop of my blood landed on the redhot surface with a loud sizzle. Even six inches above that surface, the spattering grease stung my skin, as if I wasn't feeling more than enough pain already.

"You are going to sample your own flesh before you die. Now put your hand in the frying pan or I will cut it off and do it for you, or better yet, I'll cook your face." He snapped up the knife and a ragged sob of terror escaped me. It was actually a relief when Adrian returned the knife to my middle, rather than slashing my face. The relief was short-lived. He clamped onto the back of my head, his eyes burning with excitement every bit as hot as the frying pan. I jerked back and almost fell over. It's really hard to balance when your ankles are tied together.

Adrian tightened his grip, twisting his fingers into my hair. He forced my face closer and closer to the sizzling pan. Smoke made my eyes water and spattering grease stung my skin. I fought to keep my head up and the knife pressed in another fraction of an inch.

I screamed in pain and kept resisting. No way in hell was I going to get cooked. I dragged in a breath, to fortify myself for what I was about to do. I might get slashed a bit, but it was far better than the alternative. I groped for the handle of the frying pan, praying I wouldn't have to burn Adrian. It was hard to think of my attacker as Adrian, but it was his body that would pay the price if, no when, I retaliated. I had to do as little damage as possible.

My fingers wrapped around the handle. It was too hot to hold, but I held on anyway. Before I could raise the frying pan and lunge sideways in a desperate attempt to evade the knife, Adrian simply crumpled to the ground at my feet.

I released the frying pan and my dad materialized in front of me, holding a rolling pin in his hand. He wasn't wearing black and gold. He had on a pair of shorts and a T-shirt, and his fanny pack. He was wet from the rain.

"Dad!" I fell into his arms, shaking hard. "You ... you interfered. You broke the first reaper commandment."

"I couldn't let you die, Baby. Not again." His voice broke and he squeezed me tight and I felt safe. I felt safer still when he reached over, turned off the stove, and carefully slid the sizzling pan onto a cold back burner.

I just kept holding onto him. "You got a text, about me?"

"Death, ROV. Stabbing, I guess, or worse." He swallowed hard and stroked my hair. "Are you okay, Baby?"

"Mostly. Just a minor nick or two. No stitches necessary, or maybe just a few." I was talking and sobbing at the same time.

"No burns?" he asked.

"No. No real burns." A bit of scalding didn't count. I used his handy shoulder to soak up the tears that wouldn't stop flowing.

"Here, sit down." He moved me over to one of the kitchen chairs. He used the knife Adrian had dropped to cut through the nylon around my ankles. When Adrian began to stir, my dad was quick to take possession of the Dead Man's Shirt. He tossed it on the kitchen table and pulled a familiar bloodstained veil out of his pocket. He dropped it over Adrian like a mosquito net. "Brought it just in case," he said.

"There's still evil - " I began.

"I know, Baby. I saw enough to know. Can you untie the Lyons, while I do the reverse to Adrian?" Adrian's parents were both staring, as if they didn't believe what their eyes were seeing.

"Yes, yes. I can do that." I quickly rinsed the ketchup and blood off my hand and arm, wadded some paper towel over my still bleeding stomach, and got to work. I used the handy knife to cut Mrs. Lyon loose, although my hands were shaking so much, I was scared I would slice her instead of the ropes. She hugged me as soon as she was free, and pulled the gag off herself. I had forgotten about the gag.

"Elvis, what's wrong with Adrian?" she asked, her voice trembling as much as my hands. "And how did your father appear like that?"

"It's ... complicated. My dad can explain, and he can fix Adrian." I didn't say 'exorcise'. My dad could enlighten them if he felt it was necessary.

We turned to Mr. Lyon and started cutting through his ropes. Together, we freed him, and he had a lot more ropes on him than Mrs. Lyon. By the time we were finished, Adrian was the one tied to a chair, groggy and squirming. My dad had the veil draped over him, making him look like a dirty ghost.

"Is that necessary?" Mr. Lyon asked my dad.

"If you want your son back, it is very necessary." My dad started unpacking his fanny pack, putting his supplies on the table. There were some unexpected items in his kit, including a baggie of fine powder that looked premixed. He had probably been prepared to exorcise somebody for days. He just hadn't known who it would be.

"Uh, Dad? Is the confidentiality clause about to be waived?" I asked.

He raised one eyebrow in my direction. "Elvis, I've just broken the first commandment, and apparently materialized like magic, and now I'm about to perform an exorcism, so yes, the clause can be considered smashed to smithereens. Can you run home and get my book? You know the one." I did, all too well. "And my mortar and pestle, the black one. Oh, and the gravy baster, unless you have one, Linda."

She opened a drawer and handed one over without question. I ran.

By the time I got back with the supplies, I was soaked anew. It was still pouring and nature's shower had felt wonderfully refreshing on my sweaty skin.

I removed the aged tome from the grocery bag I had used to keep it dry. I handed it to my dad, who was talking gravely with the Lyons about what he did for a living. On a normal day, I think the Lyons would have judged my dad a nutcase, but since Adrian had tied them up and tried to cook me alive, they accepted his words as the truth, the whole truth, and nothing but the truth. Plus, he had materialized out of thin air, right before their eyes, like some sort of magical genie.

Everything was ready on the table. I set the mortar and pestle beside his supplies. Adrian was alert now, jerking wildly against his bonds, and while he wasn't foaming at the mouth, I knew he soon would be. He threatened us with all manner of archaic tortures and I tried to turn a deaf ear.

"Elvis, you can lend me a hand," my dad said.

"No." I backed away. "He'll hate me if I do."

"No, he won't. He'll thank you. He doesn't want that evil inside him. This is part of your training, Baby."

I bit my lip. "Can't I train on someone else?"

"I'm really hoping we won't encounter another case like this one, but if we do, you have to be prepared." My dad crooked a finger. "Familiarize yourself with the incantation while I grind the final ingredient into powder. That has to be ground fresh, immediately before use. Do you have a mixing bowl I could use, Linda?"

She got one out of the cupboard. I scanned the incantation while my dad ground up a small bone, then added it to the premixed powder in Mrs. Lyon's mixing bowl. "Read the incantation aloud while I burn this to ash," he instructed. He lit the mixture on fire and I read. When the flames died, he said, "That should do the trick." He picked up the gravy baster. "Get him in a headlock, Elvis."

Resigned, I wrapped my arm around Adrian's neck. "I'm so sorry about all this," I whispered in his ear. I jerked back when he tried to head-butt me.

After a certain amount of physical force, Adrian opened his mouth to drag in a breath. My dad raised the veil enough to insert the turkey baster and dose Adrian with the powder. It took two doses and a lot of chanting before the vile evil percolated high enough to be nullified. There wasn't nearly as much of the foul stuff as when I had been possessed, but the exorcism was every bit as horrible.

I closed my eyes through most of it, not wanting a visual memory of Adrian's suffering. The gagging, choking sounds were bad enough. If my dad hadn't needed my helping hands, I would have stuck my fingers in my ears.

When the deed was done and all the evil had been returned to the earth as harmless dirt, Adrian was almost insensible. My dad and Mr. Lyon walked him between them up the stairs and deposited him on his bed. He didn't move and his mom pulled his covers over him, tucking him in.

I knew he would recover in a few days, but I still felt like crap for all the suffering he had endured because he lived next door to me. This latest episode certainly proved how right my dad was about me staying far far away from Adrian. I should probably move to China. They needed reapers there as much as anywhere else, probably more so, because of the dense population.

My dad took my hand and led me downstairs. We all ended up sitting at the Lyon's kitchen table. They were silent and kind of shell-shocked. I don't think I was in any better shape. My dad made a pot of coffee and served everyone. I had to use two hands to hold my cup steady, so I was really glad I still had them both.

As soon as my dad sat down with his cup, Mr. Lyon cleared his throat. "So, you and Elvis are reapers for the souls of the dead?"

My dad wouldn't have had time to give Adrian's parents more than a barebones explanation, and clearly, they had questions.

"I'm only a reaper-in-training," I said, then shut up. That was neither here nor there. My dad simply nodded.

"And some sort of supernatural evil escaped from a dead body and possessed Adrian?" Mr. Lyon looked like he couldn't believe he was actually saying that.

My dad nodded again. "After it possessed a few other people, including me and Elvis, and the fellow who broke into your house. He's the tall young man that you saw leaving my house the other morning." He was wise enough to omit certain details, like that the tall young man had been quite dead at the time. He grimaced and added, "I was the one possessed by evil when I took your car, Linda. That's why it came back to you in such bad shape, and I can't apologize enough."

Mrs. Lyon offered a forgiving smile and reached over to grip my dad's hand. "A car is just a car, Adam, while a child is irreplaceable. Thank you for saving Adrian, and the rest of us. If not for you, I hate to think how things would have turned out."

"Not well at all, I dare say." My dad didn't mention that he had been summoned to reap three souls, but I strongly suspected that's exactly what his text had said.

"I guess we're going to have to fire up the scaredeath again," I said.

"And then some," my dad agreed. He looked at the Lyons in turn. "You're probably going to notice a number of dead critters around here for awhile."

"Like that camel?" Mrs. Lyon said.

"Like the camel."

"Why is that?" Mr. Lyon asked.

"By saving your lives, I cheated Death. The scales of life and death are going to be way out of whack until I can balance them, hence the scaredeath to scare away the dying that are drawn here."

"Imagine that," said Mr. Lyon. "I did wonder about that smoking Elvis scarecrow. Not what you would normally see in your neighbour's backyard."

Two cups of coffee later, the Lyons were remarkably well informed about my dad's job. There didn't seem to be any lingering hard feelings, because Mrs. Lyon even put out a plate of cookies. She had recovered her equilibrium faster than I would have expected. And I guess saving the life of her son had made my dad a true hero in her eyes.

Adrian kept sleeping. We were finishing the dregs of our coffee when my dad got a text. He read it and grinned. "Guess I haven't been fired. I've got to go."

"Do you want me to go with you?" I asked.

"No, Baby. You've been through enough today. You can pack up my supplies and take them home. And tend to your wounds."

"Okay." I could do with a few bandages. And reaper supplies should never be left unattended. They could be highly dangerous in the wrong hands, as the evil had proven in spades. The Dead Man's Shirt nestled amongst my dad's other supplies, the wrinkled cloth looking deceptively harmless.

While my dad said his farewells to the Lyons, I shoved the shirt into the grocery bag along with the veil, out of my sight, then packed in the rest of the supplies.

Before I headed home, I ventured upstairs to check on Adrian. I tiptoed into his room and he was still out of it. Sleep was the best antidote for what he had endured. I studied his face and it looked peaceful in repose. It looked like *his* face again. The most beautiful face in the world, at least to me.

In spite of the happy ending, I felt beaten and depressed. Adrian had suffered so much because of me. At least he wouldn't have to suffer anymore. I kissed him softly on the lips, wished him a silent and very final goodbye, and crept out of his room.

# 19. In the End

At home, I replaced my dad's supplies in his office. I wanted to lock the Dead Man's Shirt back in the safe, except I didn't know the combination. I held it in my hands and really looked at the stained cloth. It was handstitched and handwoven, from a time before electricity and automatic sewing machines. How many reapers had possessed the shirt? How many lives had it taken over the years? My mom's had been the last life, and the shirt had been locked in the safe since that awful day—until the evil claimed it.

I could now accept that the shirt had ended her agony. She was going to die anyway, so why should she have suffered longer? I had been selfish to want her to stay, living in pain, so I wouldn't be without her. I should never have hated the shirt. It had been a godsend, granting her a merciful death.

People did hard, brave things for the ones they loved, and that's what my mom had done. And my dad. I could imagine her begging him to put the shirt on her, to end all our suffering. And he had done it. He had been strong for her, strong enough to help her end her life painlessly before her appointment with death. And I could be strong, too, for Adrian. I could make sure he wasn't killed again, or hurt again—at least not by me or because of me.

I folded the shirt neatly into a little square and put it on my dad's desk, then went upstairs to bed. It was barely the afternoon, but I was exhausted.

Over the next couple of days, I told myself that I was not waiting for the doorbell to chime or the phone to ring, and I did my best to believe the lie. I went on a few jobs with my dad, but other than that, I hung around the house, not waiting for the doorbell to chime or the phone to ring. My cuts and bruises were healing nicely, although I would never be able to wear a bellybutton ring again. New tree growth had encroached on my view of Adrian's window. I left the leaves there, unpruned.

I didn't see Adrian, although his light went on and off at regular intervals. I did see the Lyons coming and going, business as usual. Life does go on, until death happens.

The Powers-That-Be emailed my dad instructions on how to balance the scales of life and death. It was a complex ritual, including a lengthy incantation, but it did not require any sacrifices, human or otherwise, only a recipe of ingredients, some that proved very tricky to acquire. We both learned how to balance the scales, just in case.

Five days after Adrian's exorcism, Mrs. Lyon brought my dad and me a coffeecake, and volunteered the information that Adrian was almost himself again. He would be starting his summer job the next week. I didn't know what his summer job was. I felt hurt and left out of his life. Already, the distance between us seemed as vast as the Atlantic Ocean. The cracks in my heart should have been healing, just like my injuries—instead, it felt like they were festering.

A whole week passed without a word from Adrian. It was proof enough that he had come to his senses and did not want me in his life. I had always known he was smart, and his actions proved it. He was getting on with his normal life. I needed to get on with my abnormal one.

After granting me a week to recover, my dad insisted I accompany him on most of his reaps, day and night, although he did say I could have one day off a week.

On my first day off, I went out with Carrie and Bianca to the movies and shopping. On my second day off, we went to the beach because it was hot and sunny. I think it was the first summer I didn't have a tan. In my bathing suit, I looked as white as if it was midwinter.

Yet another week limped by, feeling like a month to me. I kept my curtains closed. Catching glimpses of Adrian simply hurt too much. I felt lonelier than ever before. I didn't even have a dog. Jasper had been adopted by Jerry Lavinsky's sister. I had driven by her house, directed to the location by James the GPS, and spotted Jasper in the yard with two kids. They had all looked happy. Jasper's tail had been wagging a mile a minute.

My dad and Kendra saw each other whenever they could, and he hadn't had a drink since he'd sworn off alcohol. I was really proud of him, and hoped he could keep it up.

The whole world was moving on. I felt left behind, because I didn't seem able to do the same. Or maybe I wasn't giving it the old college try.

On Friday, facing another lonely, depressing weekend, I told my dad I would let him fix me up with a reaper boy. He smiled. "Good decision, Elvis. I hate to see you so sad."

"I'm not sad," I lied.

He patted me on the shoulder. "I'll see if Woody's son is free tomorrow night."

"So soon?"

"Saturday night is date night. I'll even give you the whole day and night off." He winked.

"Gee, thanks." My heart sank. True confession—I would have preferred hanging out with corpses over dating a guy who wasn't Adrian, but I had to try. I had to give the living a chance. And I should, in theory, have a whole lot in common with another reaper.

I went upstairs to look at my clothes. Most of them were littering the floor. I did laundry until the wee hours and the chore did not perk me up. In the end, all my clothes were hung up or in drawers, back where they belonged. I almost peeked through my curtains to see if Adrian's light was on, but I resisted temptation. It would only cause me pain. I went to bed instead.

On Saturday evening, my date showed up on time to the minute. I kind of expected that since he was a reaper. And I was ready—dressed and primped. I hadn't bothered with my appearance for weeks, not since I had pretend dated Adrian. I thought I looked pretty good after a uniform of slovenly sweatpants and comfortably aged T-shirts.

My dad introduced us. "Elvis, this is Reginald. Reginald, Elvis."

Reginald was a couple of inches taller than me, even in the heels I had opted to wear with flagrant disregard for my date's height. He had broad shoulders, a six-pack that showed through his shirt, hair as black as a raven's feathers, and a handsome if rather serious face. He looked every inch the reaper.

We greeted each other self-consciously and got the heck out of there. There's nothing like a hovering parent to kill conversation, even when that parent has the best of intentions. Reginald held the door of his car for me. It was an older sporty model that I couldn't identify. The black paint was as shiny as if it had been buffed.

"Nice car," I commented, since guys were usually into their cars.

"Thanks." He started the engine and reversed out of the driveway. I didn't mean to, but I lost control of my eyes. They glanced up to Adrian's window and there he was, watching me go on a date. It all felt so wrong, as wrong as drowning a bagful of baby squirrels. Reginald accelerated and I lost sight of Adrian. Regardless, I could still see him in my mind's eye, just standing there.

"So, Reginald the Reaper, how do you like the family business?" I said, trying to distract myself.

He glanced sideways. "You can call me Reggie or Reg."

"Not Reginald?"

"I prefer not."

"Okay." I smiled at him and he smiled back. He seemed really nice. "And you? Does anyone call you Ellie, or Elle?"

"Nope, just Elvis. I like my name," I said.

"I like it, too. It's original, especially for a girl."

"It is." There was no denying it.

"And to answer your question, I like the family business, well, as much as one can like it. We play an important role, and to know that our ancestors did the same, it gives me a feeling of continuity about life, even though I see more than enough death." He glanced sideways at me again. "As do you."

"Ya, as do I." I laughed a bit. It was more of a little snort.

"I hear you had a real exceptional case a few weeks back. Living evil that could possess the host and move at will, without death being a factor. The big boss sent all the reapers a copy of your dad's report, so they can be on the alert in case there are more such evil entities out there."

I shuddered. "I hope that was the only one."

"Did you really decapitate four zombies with a chainsaw?" he kind of blurted out.

I winced. "Not one of my finest moments, but necessary. They were attacking me."

"Wow. So it's really true?" Reggie looked impressed.

"It's the truth and nothing but the truth." I raised my hand as if I was being sworn into court. Since I hadn't read my dad's final report, I didn't know how detailed it was.

"I would love to hear all about it in your own words," he said.

Great, the last thing in the galaxy I wanted to talk about. "Sure, I'll tell you all about chain-sawing zombies' heads off over dinner." I grinned so he would know I was joking.

He chuckled. "No, I mean I would love to hear all about this living evil." He had a gorgeous smile, with dimples and white even teeth. He could have been a model instead of a reaper.

"Uh, where are we going for dinner?" I asked.

"Pizza place and then a movie. Standard first date stuff. How does that sound?" he asked.

"Fine, as long as the movie isn't a slasher flick."

He grinned again. "No zombies or chainsaws, I promise. I like comedies, or those quality animated kid's movies. How about you?"

We discussed movie choices all the way to the restaurant. Over pizza, I did relay the facts about the living evil my dad and I had vanquished. Reggie had read my dad's report, but he listened with interest anyway. And then we saw a second-rate comedy that didn't deserve all the hype it had received. The humour relied heavily on foul language and crudity, with the requisite amount of nudity thrown in. The popular Hollywood actors gave a superficial performance and probably rushed home to roll around in the millions of dollars they had been overpaid.

It was a humid summer night and we stretched our legs after the movie, walking along downtown streets, sipping iced coffee, and discussing the movie as if we were both movie critics. Reggie hadn't been any more impressed by it than I was.

He was a really good date—intelligent, polite, smoking hot body, and handsome, especially when he smiled. He seemed old beyond his years, but maybe that was normal for reapers, even the young ones, including me. As far as sparks went, there weren't any. We could have been two wet logs without a match between us.

After he drove me home, Reggie walked me to my door and we faced off. "Thanks for a lovely evening," I said, not inviting him in.

"I had a nice time, too." He leaned down and kissed me. I wasn't expecting it and had no chance to evade his lips. It was no polite peck, either. I was taken aback when his tongue snaked into my mouth to explore. Hadn't he noticed the lack of chemistry? Then again, he was a guy, so probably not. It didn't take much more than a warm body for a guy to imagine sparks flying in all directions. His breathing quickened and his arms tightened, pressing me against him. Yup, he was definitely feeling some sparks of his own, the evidence was pressed against my hip. He certainly knew what he was doing. If not for the ghost of Adrian haunting my heart, Reggie's lips and smoking hot body might have tempted me to get to know him a whole lot better.

I tried to ease away without an undignified struggle. His arms loosened immediately. "You're not feeling it, are you?" he said frankly.

"No, I'm sorry. You seem like a really nice guy, but ..." A person should never say 'but' unless they know where they're heading, especially if they're on a date.

"That's too bad, Elvis." He held out a hand. I shook it. "If you change your mind, make sure you call me. I would love to hear from you." Still holding my hand, he leaned forward to kiss my cheek quite sweetly.

"I will, Reggie."

"Stay safe, Elvis."

"You, too." I watched him descend the porch stairs and stride to his car, impressed by how maturely he had accepted my rejection. Was I a fool not to give him a chance? No, the heart wants what the heart wants, and my heart only wanted one guy. I just couldn't have him.

Reggie's taillights disappeared. I sat down on the porch steps, not ready to go in and face my dad, who would no doubt want to debrief me on my date. He would probably pull out his notebook and take notes. I was listening to the buzz of the heatbugs when a very familiar voice said, "How was your date?" Adrian materialized out of the darkness.

I stared at him as if he was a specter, until I convinced my tongue to move. "It was nice, fine, good." Faint praise indeed.

"Who was that guy?" Adrian tilted his head toward the road, where Reggie had driven off.

"A reaper's son. A reaper-in-training like me."

"He looked like a jerk." Adrian sounded sort of sad and mad at the same time.

"He wasn't. He was nice."

After a bit of awkward silence, Adrian said, "So, you're doing okay?" He stood at the bottom of the stairs, hands in the pockets of his shorts, his eyebrows lowered enough to blind him.

I stood up and walked down to his level, a moth drawn to flame. I was taller than him in my heels so I toed them off. "Okay is a bit of a stretch, but ... how are you? After everything that happened?" I studied his face, starved for the sight of it.

"Glad the nightmare is over. Glad it all worked out in our favour. I've been wanting to call you, to apologize." His eyes darkened with torment. "To say that I'm sorry, but I didn't think you'd want to hear from me. I shouldn't be here now, except I need to say how sorry I am."

I didn't understand. "Huh?" I sounded as clueless as Homer Simpson and should have said 'duh'.

His eyebrows lowered a hair more. "I'm sorry for … for what I did to you. For everything, and it's a pretty long and awful list."

I shook my head. "You didn't do anything to me. The living evil did, not you. You have nothing to be sorry about."

"Yes, I do." He rubbed his forehead as if his head had a cramp. "I tried to kill you, how many times? And took liberties." He sounded as old-fashioned as my dad. "And I tried to cook you." He swallowed hard as if he was feeling sick. "And I'm sorry for other stuff. I'm sorry I stopped being friends with you. I'm sorry your mother died … I'm sorry I hurt you." He took a step closer and gently touched my stomach. "I can't believe I used a knife on you, and ripped your piercing out, that was so cruel." His eyes squeezed closed, as if he couldn't bear the memory.

"It wasn't you, Adrian." I took his hand in mine and squeezed his fingers, trying to comfort. He shook his head as if he didn't believe me. "Hey, the evil made me try to kill my dad, and it made him try to kill me, and you, repeatedly. The evil turned that nice Jerry into a murderous stalker." I gripped his hands tighter, savouring the feel of them. "Why should you be any different? The evil was wearing your skin, you were its bitch. You couldn't stop what it made you do any more than the rest of us could. Let it go, Adrian. And if we're trading apologies, I apologize for killing you. I wasn't possessed by evil and I still killed you, just like I killed Optimus."

"I died?" Adrian said, the most incredulous look on his face.

"For a couple of minutes in the lake, you were dead. You didn't know?"

He shook his head. "I thought I was just unconscious."

It was true that we'd never had a chance to talk, so I hadn't debriefed him about that awful night. "No, you were dead. I had to use the Dead Man's Breath to kill you, to get the evil out of you. We both died that night."

"Shit. Wow. At least we both came back." He grimaced endearingly.

"So, can you forgive me for killing you?" I asked.

"You're forgiven. I think killing me saved my life." Our eyes met. "Can you forgive me for … everything?"

"I forgive you even though there's nothing to forgive, except …" I trailed off.

"Except what?"

206

"If you want to be sorry about something, you can be sorry about bringing Meghan on our date," I decided on the spot.

Adrian's eyebrow rose half an inch. "You really don't like her, do you?"

"She's not that bad, but you deserve better—much better."

"Do I? Do you have someone particular in mind?" It was a leading and loaded question.

"No," I said flatly. Adrian and I had been through so much together in such a short intense time. We had died together. And he now knew I was a reaper, so I didn't have to lie to him anymore, or hide major parts of my life. I felt bonded to him as well as in love with him, but facts were facts. He was far better off without me in his life. I had to be strong, for him.

I bent to pick up my shoes. "Who you date is up to you," I said with finality.

He didn't move. He just stood there, hands in his pockets, looking sad and rather lost. "Okay, I do understand."

I wasn't sure he did. I paused, my foot on the first porch step. "What do you understand?"

"What you felt for me ... died. You might forgive me, but you don't want me in your life after what I did. You don't want me to touch you again because I hurt you."

"Don't want you in my life?" I cried. Could he be that clueless? "Adrian, you shouldn't want me in your life. You've seen what I do. You died because you shared my life, you got beat up and hurt." I gestured at my top, which was white. "I don't often come home like this, clean. I come home smelling like death, or ... or ... sad ... or bloody. That's why reapers wear black, so you don't see the blood. And you could never count on me to be where I'm supposed to be. A reaper has to go when they're summoned, doesn't matter what they're doing. And you never wanted me in your life before." As soon as I said that, I realized it was the keystone that was giving me the strength to keep my vow to stay away from Adrian.

For some reason I couldn't fathom, he started to smile. "What's so funny about that?" I demanded.

"You do forgive me, don't you?" His smile got bigger.

"There's nothing to forgive. *You* didn't hurt me. The evil did that."

He stepped close, very close, but he didn't touch me. "I want to clear something else up. I was scared of you, because of what happened when we were little. The fear became ingrained, it never left. That's why I kept a safe distance. That's why I stayed away from you, even when I was attracted to you. But I understand now. And even though I died, I'm not scared anymore." Our eyes locked.

"You should be scared." My breathless voice was little more than a whisper.

He shrugged. "I'm not."

I felt hypnotized when he leaned closer and closer. I shut my eyes when our lips touched. His felt hot and soft and magical. I think lightning struck us at that moment and a minor earthquake shook the ground underfoot, while a twister spun us in circles. Or none of that happened, but it sure felt like it.

Our lips parted and Adrian cupped my face in both his warm hands. He leaned his forehead against mine. "I know the evil intended no good, but it shared something with me when it took me over."

"What?"

"It shared what was in your heart, all the love and vulnerability and bravery and hope, and the hurt and loneliness. It shared you, it shared what was in your soul." His voice was breathless, too.

"Why would it do that?" A blush was heating my face, to have my soul laid bare before Adrian.

"For all the wrong reasons. The fact that you cared so much gave it more power to hurt you, and it thrives on pain and suffering. The more a person loves, the more they can be hurt, and the evil wanted to hurt you." Adrian sounded a whole lot older and wiser than he had a month ago. He even sounded a bit like a reaper, and I realized that Adrian wasn't the same boy anymore. His experiences with the living evil had changed him, but not necessarily in a bad way.

"Well, there goes the mystery in our relationship," I said, embarrassed that he knew how much I loved him.

"Oh, I think there are still plenty of mysteries we need to explore." He leaned in and kissed me again, finding the perfect balance between tender and fierce. Even his kiss had new depths to it, just like him.

I slid my hand under his T-shirt and pressed my palm against his smooth chest to feel his heartbeat. It was beating as fast as mine. I knew I had lost the battle to keep Adrian at a distance, although it felt more like I had won the war.

When our lips parted, I said, "I hope you know what you're getting yourself into, Adrian." I should have felt regret that I wasn't strong enough to let him lead a normal life, yet all I could feel was joy.

He grinned. "Does it get any worse than an evil monster possessing everybody and trying to take over the world?"

"No, I don't think so." I certainly hoped not anyway.

"Then I know what I'm getting myself into. And I love you, too." He wrapped me tight in his arms and kissed me again, hotly and hungrily, and I thought I could sense his heart and soul in that kiss. Maybe I could. I did have ESSP, after all.

# The End

Join the author's mailing list to win monthly give-aways
And receive author/artist updates –
**SrigleyArts.com**

www.ingramcontent.com/pod-product-compliance
Lightning Source LLC
Chambersburg PA
CBHW031332170626
46807CB00002B/669